BEN HUR

A Classic Story of
Revenge and Redemption

BEN HUR

A Classic Story of Revenge and Redemption

LEW WALLACE

EDITED AND ABRIDGED FOR TODAY'S READER
BY JAMES S. BELL, JR.

MOODY PRESS
CHICAGO

Lew Wallace (1827–1905) was an American soldier and novel writer. He was the U.S. Minister to Turkey from 1881–1885. He wrote *Ben Hur* in 1880.

James S. Bell, Jr. (B.A., College of the Holy Cross; M.A., University College, Dublin) is editorial director at Moody Press. He is the former director of religious publishing at Doubleday and the former executive director of Bridge Publishing. He, his wife, and four children live in West Chicago, Illinois.

ISBN: 0-8024-7101-3

1 3 5 7 9 10 8 6 4 2

Printed in the United States of America

To my son Brendan,
the warrior from the fiery hill.
Put on the full armor of God,
and, remember,
the battle is not yours,
but the Lord's.

Cast of Characters
(in order of appearance)

The Three Wise Men
> Balthasar, an Egyptian prince and priest
> Melchior, a Hindu Brahman
> Gaspar, son of Cleanthes the Athenian

Joseph, Mary, and the Christ child, of the line of David

Herod the Great, ruler of the Jews

Hillel, head of the college of rabbis

Judah Ben Hur, son of Ithamar, a wealthy Jewish merchant of the house of Hur

Messala, a young Roman noble whose father was a close friend of the emperor

Amrah, maidservant to Ben Hur's family

The mother of Ben Hur

Tirzah, sister of Ben Hur

Valerius Gratus, procurator of Judea

Quintus Arrius, Roman tribune and sea captain

Simonides, steward of the father of Ben Hur

Esther, daughter of Simonides

Malluck, servant of Simonides

Sheik Ilderim, Arabian patriarch, owner of herds of camels and horses

Flavius, Drusus, and Cecilius, comrades of Messala

Gesius, keeper of the Tower of Antonia

Tribune at the Tower of Antonia

The Galileans, a group of zealots seeking to overthrow Roman rule

Judas Iscariot, betrayer of Jesus

Introduction

For some of us, *Ben Hur* conjures up the image of the bloodied warrior played by Charlton Heston in the Hollywood film epic. Yet there is more to this richly textured novel than exciting action. Author Lew Wallace explores the wide range of human experience in extraordinary circumstances—revenge, romance, cruelty, adoration, despair, and ambition. His approach, nevertheless, is the reserved, painstaking, and thoughtful process of an earlier classic style.

The friendships of childhood often transcend the barriers of class or national origin. Yet the cold realities of adult life can fracture these relationships and can even turn former friends into enemies. Two childhood friends in this novel, one a noble Roman, the other a prominent Jew, are, through their natural abilities, destined for greatness.

The Roman Messala has a lust for power and a greed for fortune. The Jew Judah Ben Hur seeks the liberation of Israel through a messianic kingdom that will surpass that of Rome. Judah, son of Ithamar, of the line tracing directly back to Hur, the associate of Aaron, is a God-fearing Jew of a wealthy merchant family. The dramatic chariot race against his enemy Messala in the Circus at Antioch is only one element of the story.

The apparent betrayal and frustration of worthy ideals seem to stalk Ben Hur. His merchant father has passed away, and Ben Hur is about to inherit his vast shipping business in the prime of youth. He will amply provide for his mother, his sister Tirzah, and servant-maid Amrah. Because of his great physical strength and prowess, he aspires to obtain skill in arms and pursues his quest in Rome.

Yet afterward, as he watches a triumphal Roman procession from the roof of his Jewish villa, a single loose tile falls, causing an accident that transforms his and his family's destiny. His family banished at the hands of his enemy, Ben Hur seeks to survive the cruel life of a galley-slave on the high seas. Yet another twist of fate gives him a new opportunity both to seek revenge upon his personal enemy and to discover if his family is still alive. Ultimately, he seeks to destroy the system his enemy represents and restore to Israel her lost glory.

With first-hand testimony of the Messiah's presence in the land, Ben Hur's integrity and noble goals of conquest gain him allies among these witnesses. Then Ben Hur confronts the Christ, following Him to Golgotha to begin the rebellion.

Like *Quo Vadis*, the story of Ben Hur encompasses exotic settings and lavish lifestyles—in this case, of the Eastern world rather than of Rome. We meet majestic sheiks on stately camels, coursing through burning sands toward the Orchard of Palms. We travel with pilgrims of the love-deities in the sensuous Grove of Daphne. There is hand-to-hand combat between Romans and pirates on the high seas. Macabre leper colonies and dungeon cells contrast with the opulence of the Palace of Ildernee.

As well as his quest for revenge, Ben Hur contends with the allures and mysteries of love. The ravishing daughter of Balthasar, one of the three wise men, is leading him on—but where? Esther, quiet daughter of the honorable Jew Simonides, his father's old steward, appreciates his finer qualities. How will both women influence his purposes?

Most of all, *Ben Hur* is really "a tale of the Christ," as Wallace subtitled it. Three wise and learned Gentiles, separately seeking after the one God, are sovereignly called to view the numinous star of Bethlehem and are bathed in the light of its divine and angelic glory. One of them will live to see and understand its full meaning.

Yet of all the scenes depicted none is so compelling and riveting as the crucifixion. The fondest hopes and dreams of Ben Hur and his other wise and holy colleagues—Jew and Gentile alike—are put through a fiery furnace. Their faith is stretched beyond the bounds of their old religious systems.

Indeed, testing the limits of the human heart and spirit is the theme of *Ben Hur*. This is seen as he faces the seductions of romantic love, the trials of unjust suffering, and the temptation to use wealth and influence for vengeful purposes.

A brawny crusader who fought against overwhelming odds, Ben Hur could get only so far to "redeem" his family and country. Yet the Divine can do that which he cannot and provides surprises at various twists and turns, subtle though they may be. Enjoy *Ben Hur* and discover the two wills at work together.

JAMES S. BELL, JR.
Editor

1

Into the Desert

A traveler journeyed along the bed of the Jabbok River, heading toward the desert. Judged by his appearance, he was at least forty-five years old. His beard, once of the deepest black, flowing over his breast, was streaked with white. His face was brown as a parched coffee berry and so hidden by a red kerchief as to be only partly visible. Now and then he raised his large and dark eyes. He was clad in the flowing garments so common in the East. He sat under a miniature tent atop a great white dromedary camel.

Westerners may never overcome the impression made upon them by the first view of a camel equipped and loaded for the desert. As is the kindness of the sea to a ship, so is that of the desert to its creature. It clothes him with all its mysteries, creating a sense of wonder. The animal that now came out of the ravine might well have claimed the customary homage. Its color and height; its body overlaid with muscle; its long, slender neck of swanlike curvature; the head, wide between the eyes and tapering to a muzzle that a lady's bracelet might have almost clasped; its serene motion—all certified its Syrian blood, old as the days of Cyrus, and absolutely priceless.

There was the usual bridle, covering the forehead with scarlet fringe and the throat with bronze chains, each ending with a tinkling silver bell. The furniture perched on its back consisted of two wooden boxes, barely four feet in length, balanced so that one hung at each side. The inner space, softly lined and carpeted, was arranged to allow the master to sit or lie half-reclined. Over it all was stretched a green awning. In this way the ingenious sons of Cush had tried to lessen the sunburnt ways of the wilderness.

When the dromedary lifted itself out of the last ravine, the traveler had passed the boundary of El Belka, home of the ancient Ammonites. It was morning, and before him was the sun, half-curtained in fleecy mist, and the desert—not the realm of drifting sands, which was farther on, but the region where the shrubs began to dwarf and the surface is strewn with boulders of granite, dotted with acacias and tufts of camel-grass.

They now reached the end of the path. The camel quickened its pace, its head pointed straight toward the horizon. Through the wide nostrils it drank the wind in great draughts. The litter swayed and rose and fell like a boat in the waves. A perfume similar to absinthe sweetened the air. White partridges ran whistling and clucking out of the way. Occasionally a fox or a hyena quickened his gallop, to study the intruders at a safe distance.

Off to the right rose the hills of the Jebel, the pearl-gray veil resting upon them and changing momentarily into purple. Over their highest peaks a vulture sailed on broad wings into widening circles. But the occupant under the green tent saw nothing, or, at least, made no sign of recognition. His eyes were fixed and dreamy.

For two hours the camel swung forward, trotting steadily due east. At full speed he can overtake the ordinary winds. The rapid advance caused the face of the landscape to change. The Jebel River stretched along the western horizon, like a pale-blue ribbon. Now and then basaltic stones lifted their round crowns, outposts of the mountain against the forces of the plain. All else, however, was sand, sometimes smooth as the beaten beach, then heaped in rolling ridges and chopped waves. The risen sun had drunk its fill of dew and mist and warmed the breeze that kissed the wanderer under the awning, tinting the earth with faint milk-whiteness.

Two hours more passed without rest or deviation from the course. Vegetation entirely ceased. The sand became so crusted on the surface that it broke into rattling flakes at every step. The Jebel was out of view, and there was no landmark visible.

No one seeks the desert for a pleasure-ground. Life and business cross it by paths along which the bones of dead objects are scattered. The heart of the most veteran sheik beats quicker when he finds himself alone in these pathless tracts. So the man on the camel could not have been in search of pleasure, nor was he a fugitive. When men are lonely, a dog often becomes a comrade, a horse becomes a friend, but the camel received no notice—not a touch, not a word.

Exactly at noon the dromedary of its own will stopped and uttered a cry, protesting the overload, craving attention and rest. The master woke from his reverie. He threw up the curtains, identified the location, and said, "At last, at last!" A moment later, he bowed his head and prayed silently. He then prepared to dismount and shouted the command heard by the favorite camels of Job—"*Ikh! Ikh!*"—the signal to kneel. Slowly the animal obeyed, grunting all the while. The rider then put his foot upon the slender neck and stepped upon the sand.

2

Meeting of the Wise Men

The man was of admirable proportions, not so tall as power-ful. Loosening the silken rope that held the kerchief on his head, he brushed the fringed folds back until his face was bare—a strong face, brown in color. Yet the low, broad forehead, aquiline nose, the outer corners of the eyes turned slightly upward. His hair was long, straight, and of metallic luster, falling to the shoulder in many plaits. The Pharaohs looked like this, as did Mizraim, father of the Egyptian race.

He wore a white cotton shirt, tight-sleeved, open in front, extending to the ankles and embroidered down the collar and breast, over which was thrown a brown woolen cloak, an outer garment with a long skirt and short sleeves, lined inside with mixed cotton and silk, edged all around with a fringe of clouded yellow. His feet were protected by sandals, attached by thongs of soft leather. A sash held the skirt to his waist. Considering that he was alone and that the desert was the haunt of leopards, lions, and wild men, he carried no arms, not even the crooked stick used for guiding camels. He was either uncommonly brave or under extraordinary protection.

The traveler's limbs were numb, for the ride had been long and wearisome, so he rubbed his hands and stamped his feet and walked round the faithful servant, whose lustrous eyes were closing in calm content with the grass he had already found to eat. He was expecting company, though not by an appointment.

Though presently disappointed, there could be little doubt of the stranger's confidence in the coming of this expected company. He produced a sponge and a small bottle of water, with which he washed the face and nostrils of the camel. From the same box he drew a circular cloth, red-and-white striped, a bundle of rods, and a stout cane. The latter, after some work, formed a center pole higher than his head. When the pole was planted and the rods set around it, he spread the cloth over them and was literally at home—a home much smaller than that of the sheik, yet similar in all other respects. From the litter again he brought a square rug and covered the floor of the tent on the side from the sun.

Except for a distant jackal galloping across the plain and an eagle flying toward the Gulf of Akaba, the waste below, like the blue above it, was lifeless.

He turned to the camel, and in a tongue strange to the desert said, "We are far from home, O racer with the swiftest winds—we are far from home, but God is with us. Let us be patient!"

Then he took some beans from a pocket in the saddle and put them in a bag made to hang below the animal's nose. When he saw the relish with which the good servant took to the food, he turned and again scanned the world of sand, dim with the glow of the vertical sun.

"They will come," he said calmly. "He that led me is leading them. I will be ready."

From the pouches that lined the interior of the cot, and from a willow basket, which was part of its furniture, he produced materials for a meal—wine in small skins; mutton dried and smoked; stoneless shami, or Syrian pomegranates; dates of El Shelebi; cheese like David's "slices of milk"; and leavened bread from the city bakery. As the final preparation, he laid three pieces of silk cloth about the provisions used among refined people of the East to cover the knees of guests while at table—reflecting the number of people he awaited.

All was now ready. He stepped out, and there in the east was a dark speck on the face of the desert. He stood as if rooted by something supernatural. The speck grew, became large as a hand, and then assumed defined proportions. A little later, another dromedary, tall and white, and bearing the traveling litter of India. Then the Egyptian looked to heaven.

"God only is great!" he exclaimed, his eyes full of tears, his soul in awe.

The stranger viewed the kneeling camel, the tent, and the man standing prayerfully at the door. He crossed his hands, bent his head, and prayed silently. Then he stepped from his camel's neck to the sand and advanced toward the Egyptian. They looked at each other, then they embraced—that is, each threw his right arm over the other's shoulder, and the left round the side, placing his chin first upon the left, then upon the right breast.

"Peace be with you, O servant of the true God!" the stranger said.

"And to you, O brother of the true faith! Peace and welcome," the Egyptian replied with fervor.

The newcomer was tall and gaunt, with lean face, sunken eyes, white hair and beard, and a complexion between the hues of cinnamon and bronze. He, too, was unarmed. His costume was Hindu. Over the skull cap a shawl was wound in great folds, forming a turban. His garments were in the style of the Egyptian's, except that the cloak was shorter, exposing wide, flowing breeches gathered at the ankles. In place of sandals, his feet were clad in half slippers of red leather, pointed at the toes. Except the slippers, the costume from head to foot was of white linen. The air of the man was high, stately, severe. He had the wisdom of Brahma—Devotion Incarnate. Only in his eyes was there proof of humanity; when he lifted his face from the Egyptian's breast they were glistening with tears.

"God only is great!" he exclaimed, when the embrace was finished.

"And blessed are they that serve him!" the Egyptian answered. "But let us wait," he added, "for see, the other comes from there!"

They looked to the north, where, already plain to view, a third camel appeared. They waited until the newcomer arrived, dismounted, and advanced toward them.

"Peace to you, O my brother!" he said, while embracing the Hindu.

And the Hindu answered, "God's will be done!"

The last traveler was unlike his friends. His frame was slighter, his complexion white, a mass of waving light hair forming a perfect crown for his small but handsome head. The warmth of his dark-blue eyes certified a delicate mind and a cordial, brave nature. Under the folds of the Tyrian blanket that he wore with unconscious grace appeared a tunic, short-sleeved and low-necked, gathered to the waist by a band and reaching nearly to the knee, leaving the neck, arms, and legs bare. Sandals guarded his feet. Fifty years had spent themselves upon him, with no other effect than to tinge his demeanor with gravity and temper his words with forethought.

The Egyptian said with a trembling voice, "The Spirit brought me first. I am a servant of my brethren. The tent is set, and the bread is ready for the breaking. Let me perform my office."

Taking each by the hand, he led them within and removed their sandals and washed their feet, and he poured water upon their hands and dried them with napkins.

Then, when he had washed his own hands, he said, "Let us eat, and we will each learn who the others are and where they come from and their names."

He took them to the meal and seated them. Together they prayed, "Father of all—God! What we have here is of Thee. Take our thanks and bless us, that we may continue to do Thy will."

With the last word they raised their eyes and looked at each other in wonder. Each had spoken in a language never before heard by the others. Yet each understood perfectly what was said. Their souls were overcome with emotion, for by this miracle they recognized the Divine Presence.

3

The Athenian Speaks—Faith

The meeting just described took place in the year 4 B.C. The month was December, and winter reigned over all the regions east of the Mediterranean. Those who travel the desert in this season do not go far without a keen appetite. The company under the little tent were not exceptions to the rule. They were hungry and ate heartily, and, after the wine, they talked.

"To a wayfarer in a strange land nothing is so sweet as to hear his name on the tongue of a friend," said the Egyptian. "Before us lie many days of companionship. It is time we knew each other. So, if it be agreeable, he who came last shall be first to speak."

Then, slowly at first, like one careful of his words, the Greek began. "What I have to tell, my brethren, is so strange that I hardly know where to begin or what I may properly reveal. I do not yet understand myself. The most I am sure of is that I am doing a Master's will and that the service is a constant ecstasy. When I think of the purposes I am sent to fulfill, there is in me a joy so inexpressible that I know the will is God's."

The good man paused, unable to proceed, while the others, in sympathy with his feelings, dropped their gaze.

"Far to the west of here," he began again, "there is a land that may never be forgotten, if only because the world is too much its debtor. The indebtedness is for things of the arts, nothing of philosophy, of eloquence, of poetry, of war. O my brethren, hers is the glory that must shine forever, by which him we go to find and proclaim will be made known to all the earth. The land I speak of is Greece. I am Gaspar, son of Cleanthes the Athenian."

"My people," he continued, "were given wholly to study, and from them I received the same passion. It happens that two of our philosophers, the very greatest of the many, teach the doctrine of a soul in every man and its immortality, and the doctrine of one

God, infinitely just. From the many subjects about which the schools were disputing, I separated them as alone worth the effort of finding a solution, for I thought there was a relation between God and the soul as yet unknown. On this theme the mind can reason only to a point, and then all that remains is to stand and cry aloud for help. So I did. But no voice came to me over the divide. In despair, I left the cities and the schools."

At these words a grave smile of approval lighted the gaunt face of the Hindu.

"In the northern part of my country—in Thessaly," the Greek proceeded to say, "there is a mountain famous as the home of the gods, where Theus, whom my countrymen believe supreme, has his abode. Olympus is its name. I went there and found a cave in a hill. There I dwelt, giving myself up to meditation—for revelation. Believing in God, invisible yet supreme, I also believed it possible so to yearn for him with all my soul that he would have compassion and give me an answer."

"And he did—he did!" exclaimed the Hindu, lifting his hands from the silken cloth upon his lap.

"Hear me, brethren," said the Greek. "The door of my hermitage looks over an arm of the sea, over the Themaic Gulf. One day I saw a man flung overboard from a ship sailing by. He swam ashore. I received and took care of him. He was a Jew, learned in the history and laws of his people, and from him I came to know that the God of my prayers did indeed exist and had been for ages their lawmaker, ruler, and king. What was that but the revelation I dreamed of? My faith had not been fruitless. God answered me!"

"As he does all who cry to him with such faith," said the Hindu.

"But, alas!" the Egyptian added, "how few are there wise enough to know when he answers them!"

"That was not all," the Greek continued. "The man so sent to me told me more. He said the prophets who, in the ages that followed the first revelation walked and talked with God, declared he would come again. He gave me the names of the prophets, and from the sacred books quoted their very language. He told me, further, that the second coming was at hand—was looked for momentarily in Jerusalem."

19

The Greek paused, and the brightness of his countenance faded.

"It is true," he said after a while. "The man told me that as God and the revelation of which he spoke had been for the Jews alone, so it would be the same again. He that was to come should be King of the Jews.

"'Has he nothing for the rest of the world?' I asked. 'No,' was the answer, given in a proud voice—'No, we are his chosen people.' The answer did not crush my hope. Why should such a God limit his love and care to one land and to one family? I set my heart upon knowing. At last I broke through the man's pride and found that his fathers had been merely chosen servants to keep the truth alive, that the world might at last know it and be saved.

"When the Jew was gone, and I was alone again, I chastened my soul with a new prayer—that I might be permitted to see the King when he came and worship him. One night I sat by the door of my cave trying to get nearer the mysteries of my existence and to know God. Suddenly, on the sea below me, or rather in the darkness that covered its face, I saw a star begin to burn. Slowly it arose and drew near and stood over the hill and above my door, so that its light shone fully on me.

"I fell down and slept, and in my dream I heard a voice say, 'O Gaspar! Your faith has conquered! Blessed are you! With two others, coming from the uttermost parts of the earth, you shall see him that is promised and be a witness for him and testify on his behalf. In the morning arise and go meet them and keep trust in the Spirit that shall guide you.'

"And in the morning I awoke with the Spirit as a light within me surpassing that of the sun. I removed my hermit's garb and dressed myself as of old. From a hiding place I took the treasure that I had brought from the city. A ship went sailing past. I hailed it, was taken aboard, and landed at Antioch. There I bought the camel and his accessories. Through the gardens and orchards that adorn the banks of the Orontes, I journeyed to Emesa, Damascus, Bostra, and Philadelphia, and now here. And so, brethren, you have my story. Let me now listen to you."

4

Speech of the Hindu—Love

The Egyptian and the Hindu looked at each other. The former waved his hand; the latter bowed and began. "Our brother has spoken well. May my words be as wise."

He broke off, reflected a moment, then resumed. "You may know me, brethren, by the name of Melchior. I speak to you in a language that, if not the oldest in the world, was at least the first to be reduced to letters—I mean Sanscrit of India. I am a Hindu by birth. My people were the first to walk in the fields of knowledge. The four Vedas are the primal fountains of religion and useful intelligence. The Upa-Vedas, delivered by Brahma, were derived from them and teach medicine, archery, architecture, music, and the sixty-four mechanical arts. The Ved-Angas, revealed by inspired saints, are devoted to astronomy, grammar, prosody, pronunciation, charms and incantations, religious rites and ceremonies. The Angas, written by the sage Vyasa, teaches cosmogony, chronology, and geography.

"Such, O brethren, are some of the Great Shastras, or book of sacred ordinances. They are dead to me now; yet through all time they will serve to illustrate the budding genius of my race. They were promises of quick perfection. Why have the promises failed? The books themselves closed all the gates of progress. Saying they cared for all creatures, their authors imposed the fatal principle that a man must not seek discovery or invention, as heaven had provided him with all things needful. When that condition became a sacred law, the lamp of Hindu genius was let down a well, where ever since it has lighted narrow walls and bitter waters.

"These motives, brethren, are not from pride, as you will understand when I tell you that the Shastras teach a Supreme God called Brahm. Also, they tell us of virtue and good works and of the soul. So if my brother will permit the saying"—the speaker

21

bowed deferentially to the Greek—"ages before his people were known, the two great ideas, God and the soul, had absorbed all the forces of the Hindu mind.

"I was born a Brahman of the highest caste. My life was ordered down to its least act, its last hour. My first nourishment; taking me out the first time to see the sun; investing me with the triple thread by which I became one of the twice-born; my induction into the first order—were all celebrated with sacred texts and rigid ceremonies. I might not walk, eat, drink, or sleep without danger of violating a rule.

"And the penalty, O brethren, the penalty was to my soul! According to the degrees of omission, my soul went to one of the heavens—or it was driven back to become the life of a worm, a fly, a fish. The reward for perfect observance was Beatitude, or absorption into the being of Brahm, which was not existence as much as absolute rest."

The Hindu gave himself a moment's thought. Proceeding, he said, "The part of a Brahman's life called the first order is his student life. When I was ready to enter the second order—that is to say, when I was ready to marry and become a householder—I questioned everything, even Brahm. I was a heretic. From the depths of the well I had discovered a light above and yearned to go up and see what all it shone upon. At last—ah, with years of toil!—I stood in the perfect day and beheld the principle of life, the prime element of religion, the link between the soul and God—love!"

The shrunken face of the good man kindled visibly, and he clapped his hands forcefully. A silence ensued, during which the Hindu looked at them through tears. At length he resumed.

"The happiness of love is in action. Its test is what one is willing to do for others. I could not rest. Brahm had filled the world with so much wretchedness. I went to the island of Ganga Lagor. There lies the sacred waters of the Ganges, which disappear into the Indian Ocean. In the shade of the temple built there to the sage Kapila, in a union of prayers with his disciples, I thought to find rest. But pilgrimages came twice every year—Hindus seeking the purification of the waters. Their misery strengthened my love. I clenched my jaws, for one word against Brahm or the Shastras would doom me. One act of kindness to the outcast Brahmans who now and then dragged themselves to die on the burning sands—a blessing said, a cup of water given—and I became one of them, lost to family, country, privileges, caste. But my love conquered!

"I spoke to the disciples in the temple; they drove me out. I spoke to the pilgrims; they stoned me from the island. On the highways I attempted to preach; my hearers fled from me or sought my life. In all India, finally, there was not a place in which I could find peace or safety—not even among the outcasts. For though fallen, they were still believers in Brahm. In my pain, I looked for a solitude in which to hide from all but God. I followed the Ganges, where the river in unstained purity leaps to its courses through the muddy lowlands.

"I prayed for my race and thought myself lost to them forever. Through gorges, over cliffs, across glaciers, by peaks that seemed star-high, I made my way to the Lang Tso, a lake of marvelous beauty, asleep at the feet of the mountains, giants that flaunt their crowns of snow everlastingly in the face of the sun. There, in the center of the earth, where the Indus, Ganges, and Brahmaputra rise to run their different courses, where mankind first settled. There I went to abide alone with God, praying, fasting, waiting for death."

Again the voice fell, and the bony hands met in a fervent clasp. "One night I walked by the shores of the lake and spoke to the listening silence, 'When will God come and claim his own? Is there to be no redemption?' Suddenly a light began to glow—shimmering out on the water. Soon a star arose and moved toward me and stood overhead. The brightness stunned me. While I lay upon the ground, I heard a voice of infinite sweetness say, 'Your love has conquered. Blessed are you, O son of India! The redemption is at hand. With two others, from far quarters of the earth, you shall see the Redeemer and be a witness that he has come. In the morning arise and go meet them and put all your trust in the Spirit who shall guide you.'

"And from that time the light has stayed with me. So I knew it was the visible presence of the Spirit. In the morning I went back into the world by the way I had come. In a cleft of the mountain I found a stone of vast worth, which I sold in Hurdwar. I bought the camel in Isfahan and then was led to Baghdad. I traveled alone, fearless, for the Spirit was with me and is with me yet. What glory is ours, O brethren! We are to see the Redeemer—to speak to him—to worship him! I am finished!"

5

The Egyptian's Story—Good Works

The lively Greek burst forth in expressions of joy and congratulations. After this the Egyptian said, with characteristic gravity, "I salute you, my brother. You have suffered much, and I rejoice in your triumph. If you are both pleased to hear me, I will now tell you who I am. Wait for me a moment."

He went out and tended the camels. Coming back, he resumed his seat. "Your words, brethren, were of the Spirit," he said, "and the Spirit helps me to understand them. You each spoke of your countries, and there was a great reason for that, which I will explain. But to make the interpretation complete, let me first speak of myself and my people. I am Balthasar the Egyptian." The last words were spoken quietly but with so much dignity that both listeners bowed to the speaker.

"There are many distinctions I might claim for my race," he continued, "but I will content myself with one. History began with us. We were the first to explain events by records kept. So we have no traditions, and instead of poetry we offer you certainty. On the facades of palaces and temples, on the inner walls of tombs, we wrote the names of our kings and what they did. And to the delicate papyri we entrusted the wisdom of our philosophers and the secrets of our religion—all the secrets but one, whereof I will presently speak.

"Older than the Vedas of Para-Brahm, O Melchior; older than the songs of Homer or the metaphysics of Plato, O my Gaspar; older than the sacred books or kings of the people of China; older than the Genesis of Moses the Hebrew—oldest of human records are the writings of Menes, our first king." Pausing an instant, he fixed his large eyes kindly upon the Greek, saying, "In the youth of Hellas, who, O Gaspar, were the teachers of her teachers?"

The Greek bowed, smiling.

"By those records," Balthasar continued, "we know that when the fathers came from the Far East, from the region of the birth of the three sacred rivers, from the center of the earth—of which you spoke, O Melchior—came bringing with them the history of the world before the Flood, and of the Flood itself, as given to the Aryans by the sons of Noah, they taught God the Creator and the Beginning, and the soul, deathless as God. When the duty that calls us now is happily done, if you choose to go with me, I will show you the sacred library of our priesthood—among others, the Book of the Dead, in which is the ritual to be observed by the soul after Death has sent it on its journey to judgment.

"The ideas—God and the immortal soul—were given to Mizraim on the banks of the Nile. They were then in their purity, easy to understand, so was the first worship of God—a simple song and prayer coming naturally to a joyous soul, which was hopeful and in love with its Maker."

Here the Greek threw up his hands, exclaiming, "Oh! The light deepens within me!"

"And in me!" said the Hindu with equal fervor.

The Egyptian regarded them benignly, then went on, saying, "Religion is merely the law that binds man to his Creator. In its purity it has but these elements—God, the soul, and their mutual recognition, out of which, when put in practice, spring worship, love, and reward. Such, my brothers, was the religion of the first family. Such was the religion of our father Mizraim. Perfection is God; simplicity is perfection. The curse of curses is that men will not let truths like these alone."

He stopped, as if considering in what manner to continue. "Many nations have loved the sweet waters of the Nile," he said next. "The Hebrew, the Assyrian, the Persian, the Macedonian, the Roman—of whom all, except the Hebrew, have at one time or another been its masters. So much coming and going of peoples corrupted the old Mizraimic faith. The Supreme One was divided into eight, each personating a creative principle in nature, with Ammon-Re at the head. Then Isis and Osiris and their circle, representing water, fire, air, and other forces, were invented."

"In all which there was the old folly!" cried the Greek impulsively. "Only the things out of reach remain as they came to us."

The Egyptian bowed and proceeded. "Later rose the mighty monuments that dot the riverbank and the desert—obelisk, labyrinth, pyramid, and tomb of king and the tomb of the crocodile. Into such miserable depths, O brethren, the sons of the Aryan fell!"

Here, for the first time, the calmness of the Egyptian left him. Though his expression remained passive, his voice broke. "Do not despise my countrymen too much. They did not all forget God. I said awhile ago that to papyri we entrusted all the secrets of our religion except one. Of that I will now tell you.

"We had as king once a certain pharaoh, who wanted many changes. To establish the new system, he strove to drive the old entirely out of mind. The Hebrews then dwelt with us as slaves. They clung to their God, and when the persecution became intolerable, they were delivered in a manner never to be forgotten. I speak from the records now. Moses, himself a Hebrew, came into the palace and demanded permission for the slaves, then millions in number, to leave the country. The demand was in the name of the Lord God of Israel. Pharaoh refused. Hear what followed.

"First, all the water in the lakes and rivers, like that in the wells and vessels, turned to blood. Yet the monarch refused. Then frogs came up and covered all the land. Still he was firm. Then Moses threw ashes into the air, and plague attacked the Egyptians. Next, all the cattle except those of the Hebrews were struck dead. Locusts devoured the green things of the valley. At noon the day was turned into a darkness so thick that lamps would not burn. Finally, in the night all the firstborn of the Egyptians died; not even Pharaoh's escaped. Then he yielded.

"But when the Hebrews were gone he followed them with his army. At the last moment the sea was divided, so that the fugitives passed through it on dry ground. When the pursuers drove in after them, the waves rushed back and drowned horse, footmen, charioteers, and king. You spoke of revelation, my Gaspar—"

The blue eyes of the Greek sparkled. "I had the story from the Jew," he cried. "You confirm it, O Balthasar!"

"Yes, but through me Egypt speaks, not Moses. The priests of that time wrote in their way what they witnessed, and the revelation has lived. So I come to the one unrecorded secret. In my country, brethren, we have, from the day of the unfortunate pharaoh, always had two religions—one private, the other public—one of many gods, practiced by the people; the other of one God, cherished only by the priesthood. Rejoice with me, O brothers! All the trampling of many nations, all the inventions of enemies, all the changes of time, have been in vain. Like a seed under the mountains waiting its hour, the glorious truth has lived. And this—this is its day!"

The wasted frame of the Hindu trembled with delight, and the Greek cried aloud, "It seems to me the very desert is singing."

From a flask of water nearby the Egyptian took a draught and proceeded. "I was born at Alexandria, a prince and a priest, and had the education usual to my class. But very early I became discontented. Part of the faith taught that after death, upon the destruction of my body, the soul at once began its former progression from the lowest level up to humanity, the highest and last existence, and without any reference to conduct in the mortal life. If, as my teacher taught, God was just, why was there no distinction between the good and the bad?

"Finally it became clear to me that death was only a point of separation at which the wicked are left or lost, and the faithful rise to a higher life—not the heaven of Buddha, or the negative rest of Brahma, O Melchior; nor the better condition in hell, which is all of heaven allowed by the Olympic faith, O Gaspar; but life—joyous, everlasting—*life with God!* Why should the truth be longer kept a secret for the selfish comfort of the priesthood?

"One day in the most splendid and crowded quarter of Alexandria, I arose and preached. The East and West contributed to my audience. Students going to the Library, priests from the Serapeion, idlers from the Museum, patrons of the racecourse—a multitude—stopped to hear me. I preached God, the soul, right and wrong, and heaven, the reward of a virtuous life. You, O Melchior, were stoned; my listeners first wondered, then laughed. I tried again; they pelted me with epigrams, covered my God with ridicule, and darkened my heaven with mockery. Not to linger needlessly, I fell before them."

The Hindu here drew a long sigh, as he said, "The enemy of man is man, my brother."

Balthasar lapsed into silence. "Up the river, a day's journey from the city, there is a village of herdsmen and gardeners. I took a boat and went there. In the evening I called the people together, men and women, the poorest of the poor. I preached to them exactly as I had preached in Alexandria. They did not laugh. Next evening I spoke again, and they believed and rejoiced and carried the news abroad. At the third meeting a society was formed for prayer. I returned to the city then. Drifting down the river, under the stars, I evolved this lesson: to begin a reform, do not go into the places of the great and rich. Go rather to those whose cups of happiness are empty—to the poor and humble.

"And then I devoted my life to this. As a first step, I secured my vast property, so that the income would be certain and always at call for the relief of the suffering. From that day, O brethren, I have traveled up and down the Nile in the villages and to all the tribes, preaching one God, a righteous life, and reward in heaven. I have done good—it does not become me to say how much. I also know that part of the world to be ripe for the reception of him we go to find.

"Brethren, the world is now in the condition that, to restore the old Mizraimic faith, the reformer must have a more than human authority. He must not merely come in God's name. He must have the evidence subject to his word. He must demonstrate all he says, even God himself. So preoccupied are we with myths and systems, so much do false deities crowd every place—earth, air, sky, so they have become a part of everything—that a return to the first religion can only be along bloody paths, through fields of persecution. That is to say, the converts must be willing to die rather than deny it. And who in this age can carry the faith of men to such a point but God himself? To redeem the race—I do not mean destroy it—to redeem the race, He must make himself completely known. *He must come in person.*"

The three were filled with wonder and joy. "Are we not going to find him?" exclaimed the Greek.

"You understand why I failed in the attempt to organize," said the Egyptian, when the spell was passed. "I had not the authority. To know that my work must be lost made me intolerably wretched. I believed in prayer, and to make my appeals pure and strong, like you, my brethren, I went out of the beaten ways—I went where men had not been, where only God was. Above the fifth cataract, above the meeting of rivers in Sennar, up the Bahr el Abiad, into the far unknown of Africa I went. There, in the morning a mountain blue as the sky flings a cooling shadow wide over the western desert and, with its cascades of melted snow, feeds a broad lake nestling at its base on the east. The lake is the mother of the great river. For a year and more the mountain gave me a home. "One night I walked in the orchard close by the little sea. 'The world is dying. When will You come? Why may I not see the redemption, O God?' So I prayed. The glassy water was sparkling with stars. One of them seemed to leave its place and rise to the surface, where it became a brilliancy burning to the eyes. Then it moved toward me and stood over my head, apparently in hand's reach. I fell down and hid my face.

"A voice, not of the earth, said, 'Your good works have conquered. Blessed are you, O son of Mizraim! The redemption comes. With two others, from the remote parts of the world, you shall see the Savior and testify for him. In the morning arise and go meet them. And when you have all come to the holy city of Jerusalem, ask the people, Where is he that is born King of the Jews? For we have seen his star in the East and are sent to worship him. Put all your trust in the Spirit that will guide thee.'

"And the light became an inward illumination not to be doubted and has stayed with me. It led me down the river to Memphis, where I prepared for the desert. I bought my camel and came here without rest, by way of Suez and Kufileh and up through the lands of Moab and Ammon. God is with us, O my brethren!"

He paused, and they all arose and looked at each other.

"I said there was a purpose with which we described our peoples and their histories," said the Egyptian. "Here we go to find him who was called 'King of the Jews.' By that name we are bidden to ask for him. But now that we have met and heard from each other, we may know him to be the Redeemer, not of the Jews alone but of all the nations of the earth. The patriarch who survived the Flood had with him three sons and their families, by whom the world was repopulated. From the old Aryana-Vaejo, the well-remembered Region of Delight in the heart of Asia, they parted. India and the Far East received the children of the first. The descendants of the youngest, through the North, streamed into Europe. Those of the second overflowed the deserts about the Red Sea, passing into Africa. And though most of the latter are still dwellers in shifting tents, some of them became builders along the Nile."

The three joined hands.

"Could anything be more divinely ordered?" Balthasar continued. "When we have found the Lord, the brothers and all the generations that have succeeded them will kneel to him in homage with us. And when we part to go our separate ways, the world will have learned a new lesson—that heaven may be won, not by the sword, not by human wisdom, but by faith, love, and good works."

There was silence, broken by sighs and sanctified with tears, for the joy that filled them overflowed. It was the unspeakable joy of souls on the shores of the River of Life, resting with the redeemed in God's presence.

Then their hands parted, and together they went out of the tent. The desert was as still as the sky. The sun was sinking fast. The camels slept.

A little while after, the tent was closed and, with the remains of the meal, restored to the cot. Then the friends mounted and set out single file, led by the Egyptian. Their course was due west, into the chilly night. The camels swung forward in a steady trot, keeping the line so exact that those following seemed to tread in the tracks of the leader. The riders did not speak once.

By and by the moon came up. And as the three tall, white figures sped, with soundless tread, through the opalescent light, they appeared like specters flying from hateful shadows. Suddenly, in the air before them, not farther up than a low hilltop, a flame appeared. As they looked at it, the apparition contracted into a focus of dazzling luster. Their hearts beat fast; their souls thrilled; and they shouted as with one voice, "The star! The star! God is with us!"

6

The Joppa Gate

The market at the Joppa Gate during the first hour of the day was in full session and very lively. The massive walls had been wide open since dawn. Business, always bustling, had pushed through the arched entrance into a narrow lane and court, which, passing by the walls of the great tower, went on into the city. As Jerusalem is in the hill country, the morning air on this occasion was not quite crisp. The rays of the sun, with their promise of warmth, lingered on the battlements and turrets of the great buildings where the crooning of pigeons was heard, and the whir of the flocks of goats and sheep coming and going.

At the corner where the lane opens out into the court, some women sat with their backs against the gray stones of the wall. Their dress was that common to the humbler class of the country—a full length linen frock loosely gathered at the waist, and a veil broad enough, after covering the head, to wrap the shoulders. Their merchandise was contained in a number of earthen jars, still used in the East for bringing water from the wells, and some leather bottles. Among the jars and bottles played half a dozen half-naked children, rolling upon the stony floor, regardless of the crowd and cold, often in danger but never hurt, with brown bodies, jetty eyes, and thick black hair. Sometimes the mothers looked up and hawked their trade: in the bottles "honey of grapes," in the jars "strong drink."

"Their entreaties were generally lost in the general uproar, and they did poorly against the many competitors: brawny fellows with bare legs, dirty tunics, and long beards, going about with bottles lashed to their backs and shouting, "Honey of wine! Grapes of En-Gedi!" When a customer halted one of them, the bottle came around, and into the ready cup gushed the deep-red blood of the luscious berry.

Scarcely less blatant were the dealers in birds—doves, ducks, and frequently the singing bulbul, or nightingale, most frequently pigeons. And buyers, receiving them from the nets, seldom failed to think of the dangerous life of the catchers, bold climbers of the cliffs, hanging with hand and foot to the face of the cliff, then swinging in a basket far down the mountain fissure.

Along with peddlers of jewelry, sharp men were cloaked in scarlet and blue, top-heavy under oversized white turbans. They knew the power there was in the luster of a ribbon and the incisive gleam of gold, whether in a bracelet or necklace, or in rings for the finger or the nose. There were peddlers of household utensils, dealers in wearing apparel, retailers of perfumes, and hucksters of all articles, screaming and coaxing, vendors of animals—donkeys, horses, calves, sheep, bleating kids, and awkward camels; animals of every kind except the outlawed swine.

7

Typical Characters at the Joppa Gate

Let us take our stand by the gate, just out of the edge of the currents—one flowing in, the other out—and use our eyes and ears awhile.

"Gods! How cold it is!" says a powerful figure in armor with a brazen helmet on his head and on his body a shining breastplate. "How cold it is! Do you remember, my Caius, that vault in the Comitium at home, which the flamens say is the entrance to the lower world? By Pluto, I would stand there this morning long enough at least to get warm again!"

The other man drops the hood of his military cloak and replies with an ironic smile. "The helmets of the legions that conquered Marc Antony were full of Gallic snow. But you—ah, my poor friend!—you have just come from Egypt, bringing its summer in your blood."

Then they disappear through the entrance. Though they had been silent, the armor and sturdy step would have given them away as Roman soldiers.

A Jew comes next through the crowd, slim, round-shouldered, and wearing a coarse brown robe. Over his eyes and face and down his back hangs a mat of long, uncombed hair. He is alone. Those who meet him laugh, if they do not do worse, for he is a Nazarite and appears strange.

Suddenly there is a commotion in the crowd. The cause is a Hebrew man in features and dress. The mantle of snow-white linen, held to his head by cords of yellow silk, flows free over his shoulders. His robe is richly embroidered. A red sash with fringes of gold wraps his waist several times. A leper? No; he is only a Samaritan. The shrinking crowd, if asked, would say he is a mongrel—an Assyrian—the touch of whose robe is pollution; from whom, consequently, an Israelite, though dying, might not accept life.

34

In fact, this is not a blood feud. When David set his throne here on Mount Zion, with only Judah to support him, the ten tribes went to Shechem, a city much older and at that time infinitely richer in sacred memories. The final union of the tribes did not settle the dispute. The Samaritans clung to their tabernacle on Gerizim, and, while maintaining its superior sanctity, laughed at the angry priests and leaders in Jerusalem. Time brought no lessening of hate. Under Herod, conversion to the faith was open to all the world except the Samaritans. They alone were absolutely and forever shut out from communion with Jews.

Then appear men of unusual stature and physique. Their eyes are blue, and they have fair complexions. Their hair is light and short. Their heads, small and round, rest squarely upon necks like tree trunks. They are gladiators—wrestlers, runners, boxers, swordsmen—professionals unknown in Judea before the coming of the Romans. Herod, more a Greek than a Jew and with a Roman's love of games and bloody spectacles, has built vast theaters and now keeps schools of fighting men, drawn from the Gallic provinces and the Slavic tribes on the Danube.

"By Bacchus!" says one of them, drawing his clenched hand to his shoulder, "their skulls are not thicker than eggshells!"

Opposite is a fruit stand. The proprietor has a bald head, a long face, and a nose like the beak of a hawk. The wall at his back is filled with boxes of almonds, grapes, figs, and pomegranates.

A handsome Greek approaches him. Below his scarlet tunic is a girdle of buff leather, which is clasped in front by a beautiful device of shining gold. His skirt drops to the knee in folds heavy with embroidery of the same royal metal. A woolen scarf of mixed white and yellow crosses his throat and falls trailing at his back.

The dealer bends forward.

"What have you, this morning, O son of Paphos?" says the young Greek, looking at the boxes. "I am hungry. What do you have for breakfast?"

"Fruits from the Pedius—genuine—such as the singers of Antioch take on mornings to restore their voices," the dealer answers.

"A fig, but not one of your best, for the singers of Antioch!" says the Greek. "Do you see this girdle? A gift of the mighty Salome—"

"The king's sister!" exclaims the older man.

"And of royal taste and divine judgment. And why not? She is more Greek than the king. But—my breakfast! Here is your money—red coppers of Cyprus. Give me grapes and—"

"Will you not take the dates also?"

"No, I am not an Arab."

"Nor figs?"

"That would make me a Jew. No, nothing but the grapes. No waters mix so sweetly as the blood of the Greek and the blood of the grape."

A singer comes up the road slowly, his face toward the ground. At times he stops, crosses his hands upon his breast, and turns his eyes toward heaven, as if about to break into prayer. Nowhere, except in Jerusalem, can such a character be found. On his forehead, attached to the band that keeps the mantle in place, is a square leather case. Another similar case is tied by a thong to the left arm. The borders of his robe are decorated with deep fringe. These signs—the phylacteries, the enlarged borders of his garment, and the display of intense holiness make him a Pharisee, one of those whose bigotry and power will shortly bring the world to grief.

And so, toward noon, the steady currents of business habitually flow in and out of the Joppa Gate, carrying with them every variety of character, including representatives of all the tribes of Israel, all the religious and social divisions, all the adventurous rabble who revel in Herod's generosity, and all peoples of the world under the caesars and their predecessors, especially those dwelling within the Mediterranean area.

Jerusalem, rich in sacred history and prophecies—the Jerusalem of Solomon, in which silver was as stones and cedars as the sycamores of the valley—had come to be but a copy of Rome, a center of unholy practices, a seat of pagan power. A Jewish king one day put on priestly garments and went into the Holy of Holies of the first Temple to offer incense, and he came out a leper. But this time Pompey entered the Holy of Holies of Herod's Temple and came out without harm, finding but an empty chamber and no sign of God.

8

Joseph and Mary Going to Bethlehem

It was now the third hour of the day at the Joppa Gate, and many of the people had left. Some of the newcomers consisted of a man, a woman, and a donkey. The man stood by the animal's head, holding a strap and leaning upon a stick that seemed to have been chosen for the double purpose of goad and staff. The mantle from his head and the robe from neck to heel were probably the garments he was accustomed to wear to the synagogue on Sabbath days. His features were exposed, and they told of fifty years of life, confirmed by the gray that streaked his otherwise black beard. He looked around him with the half-curious, half-vacant stare of a stranger and a country person.

The donkey ate leisurely from an armful of green grass, of which there was an abundance in the market. Nor was it mindful of the woman sitting upon its back on a cushion. An outer robe of dull wool completely covered her, while a white veil covered her head and neck. Once in a while, in curiosity to see or hear something passing, she drew it aside, but so slightly that the face remained invisible.

"Are you not Joseph of Nazareth?" asked a rabbi. The speaker was standing close by.

"I am," answered Joseph, turning gravely around. "And you—ah, peace be unto you, my friend, Rabbi Samuel!"

"The same I give back to you." The rabbi paused, looking at the woman, then added, "To you and to your house and all your helpers, be peace."

The woman had by this time withdrawn the veil enough to show the face of a very young woman, almost a girl.

"There is so little dust upon your garments," the rabbi said familiarly, "that I believe you passed the night in this city of our fathers."

"No," Joseph replied, "we could only make Bethany before the night came. We stayed there and took to the road again at daybreak."

"The journey before is long, then—not to Joppa, I hope."

"Only to Bethlehem."

The face of the Rabbi, up till now open and friendly, became disapproving. "Yes, yes—I see," he said. "You were born in Bethlehem and go there now with your daughter, to be counted for taxation, as ordered by Caesar. The children of Jacob are as the tribes in Egypt were—only they have neither a Moses nor a Joshua. How the mighty have fallen!"

Joseph answered, without delay or discomfort, "The woman is not my daughter."

But the rabbi clung to the safer explanation, and he went on, without noticing. "What are the Zealots doing down in Galilee?"

"I am a carpenter, and Nazareth is a village," said Joseph, cautiously. "The street on which my bench stands is not a road leading to any city. Hewing wood and sawing plank leave me no time to take part in the disputes of parties."

"But you are a Jew," said the rabbi earnestly. "You are a Jew, and of the line of David. It is not possible you can find pleasure in the payment of any tax except the shekel given by ancient custom to Jehovah."

Joseph held his peace.

"I do not complain," his friend continued, "of the amount of the tax—a denarius is a trifle. Oh, no! The tax itself is an offense. And, besides, paying it is submission to tyranny! Tell me, is it true that Judas claims to be the Messiah? You live in the midst of his followers."

"I have heard his followers say he was the Messiah," Joseph replied.

At this point the veil was drawn aside, and for an instant the whole face of the woman was exposed. The eyes of the rabbi surveyed her, and he had time to see a countenance of rare beauty, kindled by a look of intense interest. Then a blush overspread her cheeks and brow, and the veil was returned to its place.

"Your daughter is comely," he said, speaking lower.

"She is not by daughter," Joseph repeated.

The curiosity of the rabbi was aroused, and seeing this, the Nazarene hastened to say further, "She is the child of Joachim and Anna of Bethlehem, of whom you have at least heard, for they were of great repute—"

"Yes," remarked the rabbi reverently, "I know them. They were directly descended from David. I knew them well."

"Well, they are dead now," the Nazarene added. "They died in Nazareth. Joachim was not rich, yet he left a house and garden to be divided between his daughters Marian and Mary. This is one of them, and to save her portion of the property, the law required her to marry her next of kin. She is now my wife."

"And you were—"

"Her uncle."

"Yes, yes! And as you were both born in Bethlehem, the Roman compels you to take her there with you to be also counted."

The rabbi clasped his hands and looked indignantly to heaven, exclaiming, "The God of Israel still lives! The vengeance is his!"

With that he turned and abruptly departed. A stranger near by, observing Joseph's amazement, said quietly, "Rabbi Samuel is a Zealot. He is more dedicated than Judas himself."

Joseph, not wishing to talk with the man, appeared not to hear and busied himself gathering grass that the donkey had tossed around. Then he leaned upon his staff again and waited.

In another hour the party went through the gate and, turning to the left, took the road to Bethlehem. The descent into the Valley of Hinnom was difficult, filled here and there with straggling wild olive trees. Carefully and tenderly, the Nazarene walked by the woman's side, leading-strap in hand. On their left, reaching to the south and east round Mount Zion, rose the city wall, and on their right the steep prominence that formed the western boundary of the valley.

Slowly they passed the Lower Pool of Gihon, keeping parallel with the aqueduct from the Pools of Solomon, until near the site of the country house on what is now called the Hill of Evil Counsel, they began to ascend to the plain of Rephaim. The sun streamed over the stony face of this famous area, and under its influence Mary the daughter of Joachim dropped the veil entirely and bared her head. Joseph told the story of the Philistines surprised in their camp there by David.

She was not more than fifteen, in the period of transition from girlhood. Her face gave the appearance of warmth, tenderness, and trust. The eyes were blue and large, and she possessed a flood of golden hair falling unconfined down her back to the cushion on which she sat. To these charms of her features and character were added an air of purity that only the soul can impart. Now and then Joseph turned to look at her and, catching the expression kindling her face as with light, bowed his head, wondering, and plodded on.

So they traveled the great plain and finally reached the elevation of Mount Elias, from which, across a valley, they viewed Bethlehem, known as the House of Bread, its white walls crowning a ridge and shining above the town surrounded by leafless orchards. They paused there and rested, while Joseph pointed out the places of sacred renown.

Then they went down into the valley to the well, which was the scene of one of the marvelous exploits of David's strong men. The narrow space was crowded with people and animals. Joseph became concerned, because the town was so crowded that there might not be room for his gentle Mary. Without delay, he hurried on, past the pillar of stone, marking the tomb of Rachel, up the gardened slope, greeting no one until he stopped before the portal that stood outside the village gates near a junction of roads.

9

The Cave at Bethlehem

Eastern inns were different from the inns of the Western world. They were fenced enclosures, without house or shed, often without gate or entrance. Their sites were chosen according to the amount of shade and protection, or the availability of water. These inns sheltered Jacob when he went to seek a wife in Padan-Aram.

Yet some of them, especially on the roads between great cities, such as Jerusalem and Alexandria, were princely establishments, monuments to the piety and ingenuity of the kings who built them. Normally they were no more than the headquarters of a sheik, from which he ruled his tribe. Lodging the traveler was the least of their uses. They were markets, factories, or forts—places of assembly and residence for merchants and artisans quite as well as places of shelter for wayfarers. Within their walls the town's transactions occurred.

There was no host, clerk, cook, or kitchen—only a steward at the gate officiated. The strangers who arrived stayed at will without paying a bill. Yet whoever came had to bring his food with him or buy it from dealers in the inn. The same rule held for his bed and bedding and food for his animals. The peace of nearby synagogues was sometimes broken by brawling patrons, but never in the hostels. The houses and all that was inside were sacred, as much as any well for drinking.

The inn at Bethlehem where Joseph and his wife stopped was a good specimen of its class, being neither very primitive nor very princely. The building was purely oriental, a square block of rough stones, one story high, flat-roofed, without windows and only one principal entrance—a gateway in front. The road ran so near the door that the chalk dust half-covered the lintel. A fence of flat rocks extended many yards down the slope to a limestone bluff, providing what was essential to a respectable inn—a safe enclosure for animals.

In a village such as Bethlehem, as there was only one sheik, or ruler, there could not be more than one inn. Though born in the place, the Nazarene, having left long ago, had no claim to hospitality in the town. Also, the reason for which he was coming might take weeks or months. Roman deputies in the provinces were proverbially slow, and to impose himself and wife for an uncertain period upon acquaintances or relations was out of the question.

So as he drew near the great house, he feared that he might not find accommodations in the inn, and this became a painful anxiety. He found the road thronged with men and boys who were taking their cattle, horses, and camels to and from the valley, some to water, some to the neighboring caves. And when he was close by he discovered a crowd entering the door of the establishment, while the square next door, large as it was, seemed already full.

"We cannot reach the door," Joseph said, in his deliberate way. "Let us stop here and find out what has happened."

His wife, without answering, quietly drew her veil aside. The look of fatigue upon her face changed to one of interest. She found herself at the edge of an assembly that was common enough at the inns on any of the highways that the great caravans crossed. Men on foot ran and shouted in all the tongues of Syria; men on horseback screamed to men on camels; men struggled with frightened cows and sheep; men peddled bread and wine. Everything seemed to be in motion at the same time.

The fair spectator was too weary to be long attracted by the scene. She sighed and settled down on the cushion, as if in search of peace and rest, and looked off to the tall cliffs of the Mount of Paradise, then faintly reddening under the setting sun.

A man pushed his way out of the crowd and, stopping close by the donkey, faced them with an angry scowl.

The Nazarene spoke to him.

"As I am what I take you to be, good friend—a son of Judah—may I ask the reason for this large gathering?"

The stranger turned fiercely, but, seeing the solemn expression of Joseph, in keeping with his deep, slow voice and speech, he raised his hand in half-greeting and replied, "Peace be to you,

42

rabbi! I am a son of Judah and will answer you. I dwell in Beth-Dagon, which, you know, is in what used to be the land of the tribe of Dan."

"On the road to Joppa from Modin," said Joseph.

"Ah, you have been in Beth-Dagon," the man said, his face softening yet more. "What wanderers we of Judah are! I have been away from the ridge—old Ephrath, as our father Jacob called it—for many years. When the proclamation went out requiring all Hebrews to be numbered at the cities of their birth . . . I arrived here, rabbi."

Joseph's face appeared as a mask, while he remarked, "I have come for that also—I and my wife."

The stranger glanced at Mary and kept silence. She was looking up at the bald top of Gedor. The sun touched her upturned face and filled the violet depths of her eyes. Upon her parted lips trembled a whisper that could not have been spoken to a mortal. For the moment, all the humanity of her beauty seemed transformed. She was as those who sit close by the gate in the transfiguring light of heaven. The Beth-Dagonite saw the original of what, centuries after, came as a vision of genius to many artists and left them famous.

"What was I speaking about? Ah! I remember. I was about to say that when I heard of the order to come here, I was angry. Then I thought of the old hill and the town and the valley falling away into the depths of Cedron; of the vines and orchards and fields of grain, unfailing since the days of Boaz and Ruth; of the familiar mountains—Gedor, Gibeah, Mount Elias—which, when I was a boy, were the walls of the world to me. And I forgave the tyrants and came—I and Rachel, my wife, and Deborah and Michal, our roses of Sharon."

The man paused again, looking abruptly at Mary. Then he said, "Rabbi, will your wife go to mine? You may see her over there with the children, under the leaning olive tree at the bend of the road. I tell you"—he turned to Joseph and spoke assuredly—"I tell you the inn is full. It is useless to ask at the gate."

Joseph hesitated but finally replied, "The offer is kind. Whether there be room for us or not in the house, we will go see your people. Let me speak to the gatekeeper myself. I will return quickly."

And, putting the lead-strap in the stranger's hand, he pushed into the stirring crowd.

The keeper sat on a great cedar block outside the gate. A javelin leaned against the wall behind him. A dog squatted on the block by his side.

"The peace of Jehovah be with you," said Joseph, at last confronting the keeper.

"What you give, may you find again, and, when found, be it multiplied many times to you and yours," returned the watchman, gravely, though without moving.

"I am a Bethlehemite," said Joseph in his most deliberate way. "Is there not room for—"

"There is not."

"You may have heard of me—Joseph of Nazareth. This is the house of my fathers. I am of the line of David."

If these words failed him, further appeal was useless, even offering many shekels. To be a son of Judah was important—indeed, a great thing—but for a Hebrew to be of the house of David, there could be no higher boast. A thousand years and more had passed since the boy shepherd became the successor of Saul and founded a royal family. Wars, calamities, other kings, and the process of time had, in terms of fortune, lowered his descendants to the common Jewish level. The bread they ate came to them of humble toil, yet they had the benefit of a history sacredly kept. And wherever they went in Israel, they found respect close to reverence.

If this were so in Jerusalem and elsewhere, certainly one of the sacred line of David might reasonably count upon it to provide entrance at the door of the inn in Bethlehem. To say, as Joseph said, "This is the house of my fathers," was literally true, for it was the very house Ruth ruled as the wife of Boaz—the very house in which Jesse and his sons, David the youngest, were born; where Samuel came seeking a king and found him; the very house in which Jeremiah, by prayer, rescued the remnant of his race fleeing before the Babylonians.

The appeal had an impact. The keeper of the gate slid down from the cedar block and, laying his hand upon his beard, said, respectfully, "Rabbi, I cannot tell you when this door first opened in welcome to the traveler, but it was more than a thousand years ago. And in all that time there is no known instance of a good man turned away, except when there was no room to rest him in. I cannot say no to one of the line of David. I will show you that there is not a lodging place left in the house, neither in the chambers nor in the court—not even on the roof. May I ask when you came?"

"This moment."

The keeper smiled. "'The stranger that dwells with you shall be as one born among you, and you shall love him as yourself.' Is that not the law, rabbi?"

Joseph was silent.

"If it be the law, how can I say to one coming a long distance, 'Go your way; another is here to take your place'?"

Yet Joseph held his peace.

"And, if I said so, to whom would the place belong? See the many that have been waiting, some of them since noon."

"Who are all these people?" asked Joseph, turning to the crowd. "And why are they here at this time?"

"That which doubtless brought you, rabbi—the decree of the Caesar brought most of those who have lodging in the house. And yesterday the caravan passing from Damascus to Arabia and Lower Egypt arrived. These you see here belong to it—men and camels."

Still Joseph persisted. "The court is large," he said.

"Yes, but it is heaped with cargos—with bales of silk and pockets of spices and goods of every kind."

Joseph said, "I do not care for myself, but I have my wife with me, and the night is cold—colder on these heights than in Nazareth. She cannot live in the open air. Is there not room in the town?"

"These people"—the keeper waved his hand to the throng before the door—"have all sought in the town, and they report its accommodations are full."

Again Joseph studied the ground, saying, half to himself, "She is so young! If I make her bed on the hill, the frosts will kill her!"

Then he spoke to the keeper again. "It may be you knew her

parents, Joachim and Anna, once of Bethlehem and, like myself, of the line of David."

"Yes, I knew them. They were good people. That was in my youth."

Suddenly the keeper raised his head. "If I cannot make room for you," he said, "I cannot turn you away. Rabbi, I will do the best I can for you. How many are of your party?"

Joseph reflected, then replied, "My wife and a friend with his family, from Beth-Dagon, a little town over by Joppa. Six of us in all."

"Very well. You shall not lie out on the ridge. Bring your people and hasten. For, when the sun goes down behind the mountain, you know the night comes quickly, and it is nearly there now."

"I give you the blessing of the houseless traveler; that of the sojourner will follow."

Saying this, the Nazarene went back joyfully to Mary and the Beth-Dagonite. In a little while the latter brought up his family, the women mounted on donkeys. The wife was matronly, the daughters were images of what she must have been in youth, and as they drew near to the door, the keeper knew them to be of the humble class.

"This is she of whom I spoke," said the Nazarene. "And these are our friends."

Mary's veil was raised.

"Blue eyes and hair of gold," muttered the steward to himself, seeing only Mary. "David looked like this when he went to sing before Saul."

Then he took the leading-strap from Joseph and said to Mary, "Peace to you, O daughter of David!" Then to the others, "Peace to you all!" Then to Joseph, "Rabbi, follow me!"

The party was conducted into a wide passage paved with stone, from which they entered the court of the inn. By a crowded lane reserved for the storage of cargos and then by a passage similar to the one at the entrance, they emerged into the enclosure adjoining the house and came upon camels, horses, and donkeys, tethered and dozing in close groups. Among them were the keepers, men of many lands, and they too slept or kept silent

46

watch. They went down the slope of the crowded yard slowly, for the carriers of the women had wills of their own. At length they turned into a path running toward the gray limestone bluff overlooking the inn on the west.

"We are going to the cave," said Joseph sadly.

The guide lingered till Mary came to his side. "The cave to which we are going," he said to her, "must have been a refuge of your ancestor David. From the field below us and from the well down in the valley, he used to drive his flock to it for safety. And afterwards, when he was king, he came back to the old house here for rest and health, bringing great trains of animals. The mangers yet remain as they were in his day. Better a bed upon the floor where he has slept than one in the courtyard or out by the roadside. Ah, here is the house before the cave!"

To the Jew of that period, staying in caverns was a normal practice, made so by everyday necessities and due to Sabbath regulations. For Jews of Bethlehem this practice was especially commonplace, for in their locality were caves great and small. Some had been dwelling places from the time of the Horites. There was no offense in the fact that the cavern to which they were being taken had been, or was, a stable. They were the descendants of a race of herdsmen, whose flocks regularly shared both their living quarters and wanderings. In keeping with a custom derived from Abraham, the tent of the Bedouin still shelters his horses and his children alike.

So they obeyed the keeper cheerfully and gazed at the dwelling. Everything associated with the history of David was interesting to them.

The building was low and narrow, projecting only a little from the rock to which it was joined at the rear, and there were no windows. In its blank front there was a door, swung on enormous hinges and thickly daubed with clay. While the wooden bolt of the lock was being pushed back, the women were assisted from their cushions.

The keeper called out, "Come in!"

The guests entered and stared about them. It became apparent immediately that the house was but a covering for the mouth of a natural cave, or grotto, probably forty feet long, nine or ten high, and twelve or fifteen in width. The light streamed through the doorway, over an uneven floor, falling upon piles of grain and fodder, and earthenware and household property, occupying the center of the chamber. Along the sides were mangers, low enough for sheep and built of stones laid in cement. There were no stalls of any kind. Dust and chaff yellowed the floor, filled all the crevices and hollows, and thickened the spider webs, which dropped from the ceiling like bits of dirty linen. Otherwise the place was clean and as comfortable as the inn itself.

"Come in!" said the guide. "These piles upon the floor are for travelers like yourselves. Take what you need."

Then he spoke to Mary. "Can you rest here?"

"The place is sanctified," she answered.

"I leave you then. Peace be with you all!"

When he was gone, they busied themselves making the cave habitable.

10

The Light in the Sky

At a certain hour in the evening the shouting and stir of the people in and around the inn ceased. At the same time, every Israelite, if not already upon his feet, arose, looked solemnly toward Jerusalem, crossed his hands over his chest, and prayed, for it was the sacred ninth hour, when sacrifices were offered in the Temple on Mount Moriah, and God was present there. When the hands of the worshipers fell, the commotion broke out again. Everybody hastened to eat his bread or to make up his pallet for sleep. A little later the lights were put out, and there was silence, and then sleep.

About midnight someone on the roof cried, "What light is that in the sky? Awake, brethren, awake and see!"

The people, half-asleep, sat up and looked, then became wide-awake and struck with wonder. The stir spread to the court below, and in the surrounding area soon all the tenants of house and court and enclosure were out gazing at the sky.

They saw a ray of light, beginning at a height well beyond the nearest stars and dropping all the way to the earth. At its top was a vanishing point, wide at its base, its core a rosy electrical splendor. The apparition seemed to rest on the nearest mountain southeast of the town, making a pale crown along the line of the summit. The inn was bathed in light, so that those upon the roof saw each other's awestruck faces.

Steadily the ray lingered, and then the wonder changed to fear. The timid trembled. The boldest spoke in whispers.

"Have you ever seen anything like this?" asked one.

"It seems just over the mountain there. I cannot tell what it is, nor did I ever see anything like it," was the answer.

"Can it be that a star has burst and fallen?" asked another, his speech wavering.

"When a star falls, its light goes out."

"I have it!" cried one, confidently. "The shepherds have seen a lion and made fires to keep him from the flocks."

The men next to the speaker drew a breath of relief and said, "Yes, that is it! The flocks were grazing in the valley over there today."

A bystander dispelled the comfort. "No, no! Though all the wood in all the valleys of Judah was brought together in one pile and burned, the blaze would not throw a light so strong and high."

After that there was silence on the housetop, broken only once while the mystery continued.

"Brethren!" exclaimed a Jew of venerable reputation, "what we see is the ladder our father Jacob saw in his dream. Blessed be the Lord God of our fathers!"

11

Christ Is Born

At the side farthest from the town, under a bluff, there was an extensive sheep hut, ages old. In some long-forgotten skirmish the building had been unroofed and almost demolished. The enclosure attached to it remained intact, however, and that was of more importance to the shepherds who drove their herds than the house itself. The stone wall around the lot was the height of a man, yet not so high but that sometimes a panther or a lion, hungering from the wilderness, leaped boldly in.

On this particular day, a number of shepherds, seeking fresh grazing for their flocks, led them up to this plain. From early morning the groves resounded the blows of axes, the bleating of sheep and goats, the tinkling of bells, the lowing of cattle, and the barking of dogs. When the sun went down, they led the way to this sheep pen, and by nightfall they had everything secured in the field. Then they kindled a fire down by the gate, partook of their humble supper, and sat down to rest and talk, leaving one shepherd on watch.

There were six of these men, omitting the watchman, and after a while they assembled in a group near the fire. Their beards covered their throats and fell in mats down their chests. Lambskin mantles wrapped them from neck to knee, leaving the arms exposed. Broad belts girded the rude garments at their waists. They had coarse sandals. From their right shoulders hung slings for food and selected stones as weapons. On the ground near each one lay his crook, a symbol of his calling and also a weapon of offense.

These were the shepherds of Judea. They appeared as rough and savage as the gaunt dogs sitting with them around the blaze, and simple-minded and tender-hearted, perhaps due in part to the pastoral life they led, but more because of their constant care for lovable and helpless creatures.

51

They rested and talked about their flocks—a dull subject to the world, yet a theme that was the entire world to them. They named and trained the lambs; these were their companions, their constant objects of interest, to enliven and share in their wanderings. In their defense the shepherd might be called on to face a lion or robber—and possibly to die.

Great events were trifles to them, if they ever heard of them. They occasionally heard what Herod was doing in a certain city, and they were sometimes startled by the blare of trumpets, and, peering out, they would see a cohort, sometimes a Roman legion, marching. When the glittering crests were gone and the exciting incident over, they struggled to understand the meaning of the eagle and gilded globes of the solders and the glamour of a life so opposite their own.

Yet these shepherds had a knowledge and a wisdom of their own. On Sabbaths they were accustomed to purify themselves and go up into the synagogues and sit on the benches farthest from the Ark. When the priests took the Torah around, they kissed it with greatest zest. When the text was read, they listened to the interpreter with absolute faith, and they remembered the elder's sermon and thought of it more afterwards. In one verse they found all the learning and all the law applied to their simple lives—that their Lord was one God and that they must love him with all their souls. And they loved him, and this was their wisdom, which surpassed that of kings.

Before the first watch was over, one by one the shepherds went to sleep.

The night, like most nights of the winter in the hill country, was clear, crisp, and sparkling with stars. There was no wind. The atmosphere never seemed so pure, and the stillness was more than silence—it was a holy hush, a warning that heaven was stooping low to whisper something good to the listening earth.

By the gate, hugging his mantle close, the watchman walked. At times he stopped, attracted by a stir among the sleeping herds or by a jackal's cry off on the mountainside. The midnight was slow in coming, but finally it came. His task was done.

He moved toward the fire, then paused. A light was shining around him, soft and white, like the moon's. He waited breathlessly. The light deepened; the whole field became visible. A chill of fear sharper than that of the frost air struck him. He looked up, and the stars were gone. The light was piercing down as from a window in the sky. It became magnificent, then in terror he cried, "Awake! Awake!"

The dogs sprang up and, howling, ran away. The bewildered herds rushed together.

The men clambered to their feet, weapons in hand. "What is it?" they asked in one voice.

"See!" cried the watchman. "The sky is on fire!"

Suddenly the light became intolerably bright, and they covered their eyes and dropped upon their knees. Then, as their souls shrank with fear, they fell upon their faces blind and fainting and would have died had not a voice said to them, "Fear not!"

And they listened.

"Fear not: for behold, I bring you good tidings of great joy, which shall be to all people."

The voice was sweet and soothing and supernatural, and it penetrated all their being and filled them with assurance. They rose upon their knees and, worshiping, beheld in the center of this great glory the appearance of a man, clad in an intensely white robe. Above his shoulders, with shining and folded wings, a star glowed with steady luster, brilliant as Hesperus. His hands were stretched toward them in blessing; his face was serene and divinely beautiful.

They had often heard and in their simple way talked of angels, and they did not doubt now, but said to themselves, "The glory of God is about us, and this is he who of old came to the prophet by the river of Ulai."

The angel continued. "For unto you is born this day, in the city of David, a Savior who is Christ the Lord!"

The angel paused while the words sank into their minds. "And this shall be a sign to to you," the angel said next. "You shall find the babe wrapped in swaddling clothes, lying in a manger."

The herald did not speak again, yet he stayed awhile. Suddenly the light where he was at the center turned a deeper rosy color and began to quiver. Then up, far as the men could see, there was a flashing of white wings and the coming and going of radiant forms and voices chanting in unison, repeating the anthem of glory to God.

Then the herald's wings stirred, spreading slowly and majestically. He rose lightly without effort, floating out of view and taking the light up with him. Long after the angel was gone the heavenly refrain, "Glory to God in the highest, and on earth peace, goodwill toward men!" was heard.

When the shepherds came fully to their senses, they stared at each other until one of them said, "It was Gabriel, the Lord's messenger to men."

No one replied.

"Christ the Lord is born. Did he not say so?"

Then another, recovering from shock, replied, "That is what he said."

The first shepherd gazed into the fire thoughtfully and finally said with resolve, "There is only one place in Bethlehem where there is a manger—just one, and that is in the cave near the old inn. Brethren, let us go see this thing that had come to pass. The priests and doctors of our religion have been looking for a long time for the Christ. Now he is born, and the Lord has given us a sign in order to know him. Let us go and worship him."

"But who will tend the flocks!" exclaimed the other.

"The Lord will take care of them. Let us make haste."

Then they all arose and left the field.

They passed around the mountain and through the town and came to the gate of the inn, where there was a guard on watch.

"What is your business?" he asked.

"We have seen and heard great things tonight," they replied.

"Well, we, too, have seen great things but heard nothing. What did you hear?"

"Let us go down to the cave next to the sheep pen so that we may be sure; then we will tell you all. Come with us and see for yourself."

"It is a fool's errand."

"No, the Christ is born."

"The Christ! How do you know?"

"Let us go and see first."

The man laughed scornfully. "The Christ indeed! How are you to know it is him?"

"He was born tonight and is now lying in a manger, so we were told. And there is only one place in Bethlehem with mangers."

"The cave?"

"Yes. Come with us."

They went through the courtyard without being noticed, although some people were awake even then talking about the wonderful light. The door of the cavern was open. A lantern was burning within, and they entered without ceremony.

"I give you peace," the watchman said to Joseph and his friend from Beth-Dagon. "Here are people looking for a child born tonight. They will know him by finding him in swaddling clothes and lying in a manger."

For a moment the face of the unemotional Nazarene was moved. Turning away, he said, "The child is here."

They were led to one of the mangers, where the child was resting. The lantern was brought nearby, and the shepherds stood by in silence. The little child gave no recognition, similar to newborns.

"Where is the mother?" asked the watchman.

One of the women took the baby and went to Mary lying nearby and put it in her arms. Then the bystanders gathered around the two.

"It is the Christ!" said a shepherd at last.

"The Christ!" they all repeated, falling upon their knees in worship. One of them repeated a number of times, "It is the Lord, and his glory is above the earth and heaven."

And the common men, never doubting, kissed the hem of the mother's robe and departed with joyful faces. They told their story to all the people aroused and crowding about them in the inn. Through the town and all the way back to their fields, they chanted the refrain of the angels: "Glory to God in the highest, and on earth peace and goodwill toward men!"

The story was spread throughout the land, confirmed by the light so many had seen. The next day, and for days after that, the cave was visited by curious crowds, and some believed, though the greater part laughed and mocked.

12

The Wise Men Arrive at Jerusalem

On the eleventh day after the birth of the child in the cave, about mid-afternoon, the three wise men approached Jerusalem by the road from Shechem. After crossing the Cedron Brook, they passed many people who did not fail to stop and look after them curiously.

Judea was, because of its location, an international trade route. It formed a narrow ridge, raised by the desert on the east and the sea on the west. Over the ridge had stretched the line of trade between the east and the south, and this was where her wealth was found. The riches of Jerusalem resulted from the tolls she levied on passing commerce. Nowhere else, except in Rome, was there such a constant assembly of so many people from so many different nations. In no other city was a stranger less strange to the residents than within her walls. And yet these three men excited the wonder of all whom they met on the way to the gates.

A child belonging to some women sitting by the roadside opposite the Tombs of the Kings saw the party coming. Immediately he clapped his hands and cried, "Look, look! What pretty bells! What big camels!"

The bells were silver; the camels were of unusual size and whiteness and moved with stateliness; the owners sat under the little canopies exactly as they appeared at the previous rendezvous. Yet it was not the bells or the camels or their trappings or the manner of the riders that were so wonderful. It was the question put by the man who rode foremost among the three.

"Good people," said Balthasar, stroking his plaited beard and bending from his camel, "is not Jerusalem close by?"

"Yes," answered the woman in whose arms the child had rested. "If the trees were a little lower, you could see the towers in the marketplace."

Balthasar gave the Greek and the Hindu a look, then asked, "Where is he that is born King of the Jews?"

56

The women gazed at each other without reply.

"You have not heard of him?"

"No."

"Well, tell everybody that we have seen his star in the east and have come to worship him."

Then the friends rode on. They asked the same question of others, with a similar result. A large company whom they met going to the Grotto of Jeremiah were so astonished by the inquiry and the appearance of the travelers that they turned around and followed them into the city.

The three were consumed with the idea of their mission, and they did not consider the view that presently rose before them in the utmost magnificence: Bezetha, Mizpah, and Olivet, over on their left; the wall of strength, partly to gratify the critical taste of the kingly builder; Zion, tallest of the hills, crowned with marble palaces, and never so beautiful; the glittering terraces of the Temple on Moriah, admittedly one of the wonders of the earth; and the regal mountains rimming the sacred city round about until it seemed to be in the hollow of a mighty bowl.

They came at last to a tower of great height and strength, overlooking the gate that at that time was called the Damascus Gate and marked the meeting place of the three roads from Shechem, Jericho, and Gibeon. A Roman guard protected the passageway. By this time the people following the camels formed a line sufficient to draw the idlers hanging around the portal. When Balthasar stopped to speak to the sentinel, the three instantly became the center of a close circle eager to hear all that had occurred.

"I give you peace," the Egyptian said, in a clear voice.

The sentinel made no reply.

"We have come great distances in search of one who is born King of the Jews. Can you tell us where he is?"

The soldier raised the visor of his helmet and called loudly. From an apartment at the right of the passage an officer appeared.

"Give way," he cried to the crowd, which had pressed closer in. And as they seemed slow to obey, he advanced, twirling his javelin to gain room.

"What do you want?" he asked of Balthasar, speaking in the dialect of the city.

And Balthasar answered the same way. "Where is he that is born King of the Jews?"

"Herod?" asked the officer, confused.

"Herod's kingship is from Caesar. Not Herod."

"There is no other King of the Jews."

"But we have seen the star of him we seek and come to worship him."

The Roman was perplexed. "Go farther," he said, at last. "I am not a Jew. Carry the question to the doctors in the Temple, or to Annas the priest, or better still to Herod himself. If there be another King of the Jews, he will find him."

Then he made way for the strangers, and they passed the gate. But before entering the narrow street, Balthasar lingered to say to his friends, "We have told our story. By midnight the whole city will have heard of us and of our mission. Let us go to the inn now."

13

The Witnesses Before Herod

That evening, before sunset, some women were washing clothes on the upper step of the flight that led down into the basin of the Pool of Siloam. They each knelt before a large earthenware bowl. A girl at the foot of the steps kept them supplied with water and sang while she filled the jar. The song was cheerful and no doubt lightened their labor. Occasionally they would sit and look up the slope of Ophel and around to the summit of what is now the Mount of Offense, then faintly glorified by the dying sun.

While they kept busy with their hands, rubbing and wringing the clothes in the bowls, two other women came to them, each with an empty jar upon her shoulder.

"Peace to you," one of the newcomers said.

The laborers paused, sat up, wrung the water from their hands, and returned the greeting.

"It is nearly night—time to quit."

"There is no end to work," was the reply.

"But there is a time to rest and—"

"To hear what may be passing," interjected another.

"What news have you?"

"Then you have not heard?"

"No."

"They say the Christ is born," said the news gatherer, plunging into her story.

It was curious to see the faces of the laborers brighten with interest. On the other side the jars came down, which, in a moment, were turned into seats for their owners.

"The Christ!" the listeners cried.

"So they say."

"Who?"

"Everybody. It is common talk."

"Does anybody believe it?"

"This afternoon three men came across Brook Cedron on the road from Shechem," the speaker replied, intending to smother doubt. "Each one of them rode a spotless white camel and larger than any ever before seen in Jerusalem."

The eyes and mouths of the listeners opened wide.

"To prove how great and rich the men were," the narrator continued, "they sat under awnings of silk. The buckles of their saddles were of gold, as was the fringe of their bridles. The bells were of silver and made real music. Nobody knew them—they looked as if they had come from the ends of the world. Only one of them spoke, and of everybody on the road, even the women and children, he asked this question—'Where is he that is born King of the Jews?'

"No one gave them an answer—no one understood what they meant—so they passed on, leaving behind this message: 'For we have seen his star in the east and have come to worship him.' They put the question to the Roman at the gate, and he, no wiser than the simple people on the road, sent them up to Herod."

"Where are they now?"

"At the inn. Hundreds have been to look at them already, and hundreds more are going."

"Who are they?"

"Nobody knows. They are said to be Persians—wise men who communicate with the stars—prophets, they may be, like Elijah and Jeremiah."

"What do they mean by King of the Jews?"

"The Christ, and that he is just born."

One of the women laughed and resumed her work, saying, "Well, when I see him I will believe."

Another followed her thinking. "And I—well, when I see him raise the dead, I will believe."

A third said quietly, "He has been a long time promised. It will be enough for me to see him heal one leper."

And the group sat talking until the night came and, with the help of the frosty air, drove them home.

Later in the evening, about the beginning of the first watch, there was a crowd of scholars in the palace on Mount Zion, proba-

60

bly fifty persons, who never came together except by order of Herod and then only when he had demanded to know the deeper mysteries of the Jewish law and history. It was a meeting of the teachers and the chief priests and the doctors most noted in the city for learning—princes of the Sadducees, Pharisaic debaters, stoical philosophers of the Essene sect.

The chamber in which the session was held belonged to one of the interior courtyards of the palace and was quite large and Romanesque. The floor was covered with marble blocks. The walls, unbroken by a window, were frescoes in panels of saffron yellow. A couch occupied the center of the room, covered with cushions of bright yellow cloth. There was also an immense bronze tripod, curiously inlaid with gold and silver, over which a chandelier dropped from the ceiling, having seven arms, each holding a lighted lamp.

The company sat upon the couch in the style of orientals. They were mostly men advanced in years. Immense beards covered their faces. To their large noses were added large black eyes deeply shaded by strong brows. Their demeanor was grave and dignified. This was the session of the Sanhedrin.

He who sat before the tripod at the head of the couch, with all the rest of his associates on his right and left, would have instantly absorbed the attention of any spectator. He had been quite large but was now shrunken and stooped to ghastliness.

His white robe dropped from his shoulders in folds that gave no hint of any muscle but only an angular skeleton. His hands, half concealed by white-and-crimson-striped sleeves of silk, were clasped upon his knees. His head was a splendid dome. A few hairs whiter than fine-drawn silver fringed the base. His skin was drawn close over a broad, full-sphered skull that shone in the light with distinct brilliance. His temples were like deep hollows, from which the forehead protruded like a wrinkled crag. His eyes were pale and dim; his nose was pinched. And his lower face was muffled in a flowing beard as venerable as Aaron's. His name was Hillel the Babylonian. The line of prophets, long extinct in Israel, was now succeeded by a line of scholars. He was the first in learning—a prophet in all but divine inspiration. At the age of one hundred six he was still the head of the great college.

On the table before him lay a roll of parchment inscribed with Hebrew characters. Behind him, in waiting, stood a richly clothed page.

There had been discussion, but at this moment the group had reached a conclusion. Each one now waited, and the venerable Hillel, without moving, called the page.

"Young man!" The youth advanced respectfully.

"Go tell the king we are ready to give him an answer." The boy hurried away.

Later two officers entered and stopped on each side of the door. Slowly following after them was a most striking person— an old man clad in a purple robe bordered with scarlet and girded to his waist by a band of gold so finely linked that it was pliable as leather. The buckles of his shoes sparkled with precious stones. A narrow crown shone outside a veil of softest plush crimson, which, encasing his head, fell down the neck and shoulders, leaving the throat and neck exposed. Instead of a seal, a dagger dangled from his belt. He walked slowly, leaning heavily upon his staff. When he reached the couch he paused and looked up from the floor. Then, as for the first time conscious of the company, he looked haughtily around like one startled and searching for an enemy—with a dark, suspicious, and threatening glance. This was Herod the Great—his body broken by diseases, his conscience seared with crimes, his mind magnificently capable, his soul fit for brotherhood with the caesars. He was now sixty-seven years old but guarding his throne with a jealousy never so vigilant, a power never so despotic, and a cruelty never so furious.

There was a general movement on the part of the assembly— bending forward in a bow by the more aged, a standing by the more courtly, followed by low genuflections, with hands upon beard or breast.

Herod looked around and moved on until he arrived at the tripod opposite the venerable Hillel, who met his cold glance with a slight nod.

"The answer!" said the king, with simplicity, addressing Hillel and planting his staff before him with both hands. "The answer!"

The eyes of the patriarch glowed mildly. Raising his head and looking the inquisitor full in the face, he answered, "With you, O king, be the peace of God, of Abraham, Isaac, and Jacob!"

His manner was that of a blessing. Changing it, he resumed. "You have demanded of us where the Christ should be born."

The king bowed, though the evil eyes remained fixed upon the sage's face. "That is the question."

"Then, O king, speaking for myself and all my brethren here, not one dissenting, I say, in Bethlehem of Judea."

Hillel glanced at the parchment on the tripod, and pointing with his finger he continued. "In Bethlehem of Judea, for so it is written by the prophet, 'And thou, Bethlehem, in the land of Judea, art not the least among the princes of Judah; for out of thee shall come a governor that shall rule my people Israel.'"

Herod's face was troubled, and he looked at the parchment while he thought. Those watching him scarcely breathed. They did not speak, nor did he. Finally he turned about and left the chamber.

"Brethren," said Hillel, "we are dismissed." The company then arose and departed in groups.

"Simeon," said Hillel again.

A man at least fifty years old, but in the hearty prime of life, answered and came to him.

"Take up the sacred parchment, my son. Roll it tenderly."

The order was obeyed.

"Now lend me your arm.I will go to the litter."

The strong man stooped, and with his withered hands the old one took the offered support and, rising, moved feebly to the door.

So departed the famous teacher and Simeon, his son, who was to be his successor in wisdom, learning, and office.

Yet later in the evening the wise men were lying awake in the inn. The stones that served them as pillows raised their heads so they could look out of the open arch into the depths of the sky. And as they watched the twinkling of the stars, they thought of the next manifestation of God. How would it come? What would it be? They were in Jerusalem at last. They had asked at the gate for him. They had born witness of his birth. It remained only to find him, and for that they placed all trust in the Spirit. Men listening for the voice of God, or waiting for a sign from heaven, cannot sleep.

Then a man stepped in under the arch, darkening the interior. "Awake!" he said to them. "I bring you a message that will not wait."

They all sat up. "From whom?" asked the Egyptian.

"Herod the king." Each one felt his spirit surge.

"Are you not the steward of the inn?" Balthasar asked next.

"I am."

"What would the king want with us?"

"His messenger is outside. Let him answer."

"You were right, O my brother!" said the Greek, when the steward was gone. "The question put to the people on the road and to the guard at the gate has given us immediate recognition. I am impatient; let us go quickly."

They arose, put on their sandals, put their mantles about them, and went out.

"I salute you and give you peace and pray your pardon, but my master, the king, has sent me to invite you to the palace, where he would speak with you privately."

A lamp hung in the entrance, and by its light they looked at each other and knew the Spirit was upon them. Then the Egyptian approached the steward and said, so as not to be heard by the others, "You know where our goods are stored in the court and where our camels are resting. While we are gone, make all things ready for our departure, if we should need it."

"Go your way assured. Trust me," the steward replied.

"The king's will is our will," said Balthasar to the messenger. "We will follow you."

Following their guide, the brethren proceeded without a word. Through the dim starlight, made dimmer by the walls on both sides and almost lost under bridges connecting the housetops, they climbed a hill. At last they came to a portal. In the light of fires blazing before it in two great braziers, they caught a glimpse of some guards leaning motionlessly. They passed into the building unchallenged.

Then by passages and arched halls, through courts and under colonnades not always lighted, up long flights of stairs, past innumerable cloisters and chambers, they were conducted into a tower of great height.

Herod-yellow

Suddenly the guide halted and, pointing through an open door, said to them, "Enter. The king is there."

The air of the chamber was heavy with the perfume of sandalwood. Upon the floor, covering the central space, a tufted rug was spread, and a throne was set upon that. The visitors had but time, however, to catch a general idea of the place—of carved and gilt ottomans and couches, of fans and jars and musical instruments, of golden candlesticks glittering in their own lights, of walls painted in the style of the gorgeous Grecian school, at which one look would make a Pharisee hide his head with holy horror. Herod sat upon the throne to receive them.

They advanced uninvited to the edge of the rug and prostrated themselves. The king rang a bell, and an attendant came in and placed three stools before the throne.

"Seat yourselves," said the monarch graciously.

"From the North Gate," he continued, when the three settled down, "I received this afternoon a report of the arrival of three strangers, curiously mounted on camels and appearing as if they were from far countries. Are you the men?"

The Egyptian took the sign from the Greek and the Hindu and answered, with the most profound bow, "Were we other than we are, the mighty Herod, whose fame is as incense to the whole world, would not have sent for us. We do not doubt that we are the strangers."

Herod acknowledged the speech with a wave of his hand. "Who are you? Where do you come from?" he asked, adding significantly, "Let each speak for himself."

In turn they spoke to him, referring simply to the cities and lands of their birth and the routes by which they came to Jerusalem. Somewhat disappointed, Herod probed them more directly.

"What was the question you put to the officer at the gate?"

"We asked him, Where is he that is born King of the Jews?"

"I see now why the people were so curious. You excite me no less. Is there another King of the Jews?"

The Egyptian did not hesitate. "There is one newly born."

An expression of pain knit the dark face of the monarch, as if his mind were swept by a harrowing recollection.

"Not to me, not to me?" he exclaimed.

Possibly the accusing images of his murdered children flitted before him. Recovering from the emotion, whatever it was, he asked, steadily, "Where is the new King?"

"That, O king, is what we ask."

"You bring me a wonder—a riddle surpassing any of Solomon's," the inquisitor said next. "As you see, I am in the time of life when curiosity is as strong as it was in childhood, when to trifle with it is cruelty. Tell me further, and I will honor you as kings honor each other. Give me all you know about the newly born, and I will join you in the search for him. And when we have found him, I will do what you wish. I will bring him to Jerusalem and train him in kingcraft. I will use my grace with Caesar for his promotion and glory. Jealousy shall not come between us, I swear. But tell me first how, so widely separated by seas and deserts, you all came to hear of him."

"I will tell you truly, O king."

"Speak on," said Herod.

Balthasar raised himself erect and said solemnly, "There is an almighty God."

Herod was visibly startled.

"He told us to come here, promising that we should find the Redeemer of the world—that we should see and worship him and bear witness that he was to come, and, as a sign, we were each given sight of a star. His Spirit stayed with us. O king, his Spirit is with us now!"

An overpowering feeling seized the three. With difficulty the Greek restrained an outcry. Herod's gaze darted quickly from one to the other. He was more suspicious and dissatisfied than before.

"You are mocking me," he said. "If not, tell me more. What is to follow the coming of the new king?"

"The salvation of men."

"From what?"

"Their wickedness."

"How?"

"By the divine agencies—faith, love, and good works."

"Then"—Herod paused, and from his look no man could have known his true feelings—"you are the heralds of the Christ. Is that all?"

Balthasar bowed low. "We are your servants, O king."

The monarch touched a bell, and the attendant appeared. "Bring the gifts," the master said.

The attendant went out, but in a little while returned and, kneeling before the guests, gave to each one an outer robe or mantle of scarlet and blue and a girdle of gold. They acknowledged the honors with low Eastern bows.

"A word further," said Herod, when the ceremony was ended. "To the officer of the gate and now to me you spoke of seeing a star in the east."

"Yes," said Balthasar. "His star, the star of the newly born."

"What time did it appear?"

"When we were bidden to come here."

Herod arose, signifying the meeting was over. Stepping from the throne toward them, he said, with all graciousness, "If, as I believe, O illustrious men, you are indeed the heralds of the Christ just born, know that I have this night consulted those wisest in Jewish matters, and they say with one voice he should be born in Bethlehem of Judea. I say to you, go there. Go and bring me word again, that I may come and worship him. There shall be no hindrance to your going. Peace be with you!"

And folding his robe about him, he left the chamber.

Then the guide came and led them back to the street and then to the inn, at the portal where the Greek said, impulsively, "Let us go to Bethlehem, O brethren, as the king has advised."

"Yes," cried the Hindu. "The Spirit burns within me."

"Be it so," said Balthasar, with equal warmth. "The camels are ready."

They gave gifts to the steward, mounted their saddles, received directions to the Joppa Gate and departed. At their approach the great gates were unbarred, and they passed into the open country, taking the road so lately traveled by Joseph and Mary.

As they came out of Hinnom, on the plain of Rephaim, a light appeared, at first widespread and faint. Their pulses fluttered fast. The light intensified rapidly. They closed their eyes against its burning brilliance. When they dared look again, there was the star, perfect as any in the heavens, but low and moving slowly before them. And they shouted and rejoiced with exceeding great joy.

"God is with us! God is with us!" they repeated in frequent chants, all the way, until the star, rising out of the valley beyond Mount Elias, stood still over a house on the slope of the hill near the town.

14

The Wise Men Find the Child

It was now the beginning of the third watch, and at Bethlehem the morning was breaking over the mountains in the east, but so feebly that it was yet night in the valley. The watchman on the roof of the old inn, shivering in the chilly air, was listening for the first familiar sounds of life greeting the dawn, when a light came moving up the hill toward the house. He thought it was a torch in someone's hand. The brilliance grew, however, until it proved to be a star. Very afraid, he cried out and brought everybody within the walls to the roof. As it continued to approach, the rocks, trees, and roadway under it shone as if in a glare of lightning and became blinding. The more timid of the observers fell upon their knees and prayed, with their faces hidden. The boldest covered their eyes and crouched. The inn and everything about it lay under an intolerable radiance. The star stood still directly over the house in front of the cave where the child had been born.

In the midst of this scene the wise men came up and dismounted at the gate, shouting for admission. When the steward mastered his terror to give them heed, he drew the bars and opened to them. The camels looked spectral in the unnatural light, and besides their outlandishness there were on the faces and manner of the three visitors an eagerness and exaltation that still further alarmed the gatekeeper. He fell back and for a time could not answer the question they put to him.

"Is not this Bethlehem of Judea?"

But others came, and their presence gave him assurance.

"No, this is but the inn. The town lies further on."

"Is there a newborn child?"

The bystanders turned to each other marveling, though some of them answered, "Yes."

"Show us the way to him!" said the Greek impatiently.

Balthasar said with gravity, "We have seen his star, even that which you behold over the house, and have come to worship him."

The Hindu clasped his hands, exclaiming, "God indeed lives! Make haste! The Savior is found. Blessed are we above men!"

The people from the roof came down and followed the strangers as they were taken through the court and out into the enclosure, though some who were afraid turned back. As the strangers neared the house, the orb arose. When they were at the door, it was high up overhead and began to vanish. When they entered, it went out, lost to everyone's sight. There was a conviction that a divine relationship existed between the star and the strangers, which extended to even some of the occupants of the cave. When the door was opened, they crowded in.

The place was lighted by a lantern enough to enable the strangers to find the mother and the child awake in her lap.

"Is the child yours?" asked Balthasar of Mary.

And she, who had kept all these things affecting the little one and pondered them in her heart, held it up in the light, saying, "He is my son!"

And they fell down and worshiped him.

They saw the child was as other children. He made no sound. If he heard their expressions of joy, their invocations, their prayers, he made no sign whatever but, babylike, looked longer at the flame in the lantern than at them. In a little while they arose and, returning to the camels, brought gifts of gold, frankincense, and myrrh and laid them before the child, continuing with their worshipful speeches. This was the Savior they had come so far to find! And they worshiped without any doubts.

Their faith rested upon the signs sent them by him we know as the Father. And they were of the type of men to whom his promises were so all-sufficient that they asked nothing about his ways. There were few who had seen the signs and heard the promises— the mother and Joseph, the shepherds, and the three—yet they all believed the same message. In this period of the plan of salvation, God was all, and the child was yet to be revealed.

15

Jerusalem Under the Romans

It was now twenty-one years later, at the beginning of the administration of Valerius Gratus, the fourth imperial governor of Judea—a period full of political rebellion in Jerusalem, when the opening of the final quarrel between the Jews and the Romans unfolded.

Herod the Great died within one year after the birth of the child. Caesar deposed Archelaus, his son, and reduced Judea to a Roman province. So, instead of a king's ruling royally from the palace left by Herod on Mount Zion, the city fell into the hands of a second-grade officer. The procurator was not even permitted to establish himself in Jerusalem. Caesarea was his seat of government. Most humiliating, however, Samaria was joined to Judea as a part of the same province. What misery the bigoted Pharisees endured at finding themselves elbowed and laughed at in the procurator's presence in Caesarea by the Samaritans!

The high priest still occupied the Herodian palace in the marketplace and kept a kind of court there without real authority. Judgment of life and death remained with the procurator. The mere presence of the high priest in the palace kept the Jews reminded of the covenants and the promises of the prophets and the ages when Jehovah governed the tribes through the sons of Aaron. So their hopes lived and helped them grimly wait for the Son of Judah who was to rule Israel.

16

Ben Hur and Messala

It was one noonday in the middle of July, when the heat of summer was at its highest.

By the palace on Mount Zion was a garden with verandas shading the doors and windows of the lower story, while retreating galleries, guarded by strong balustrades, adorned and protected the upper. Here and there appeared low colonnades allowing other parts of the house to be seen, revealing its magnitude and beauty. The arrangement of the ground was equally pleasant to the eye. There were walks and patches of grass and shrubbery and a few large trees, rare palms, grouped with carob, apricot, and walnut trees. Below there was a reservoir, or deep marble basin, broken in places by little gates that, when raised, emptied the water into channels bordering the walks.

Not far from the fountain was a small pool of clear water nourishing a clump of cane and oleander, like those growing near the Jordan and down by the Dead Sea. Between the clump and the pool, unmindful of the sun shining full upon them in the breathless air, two boys, one about nineteen, the other seventeen, sat engaged in earnest conversation.

They were both handsome and, at first glance, would have been taken for brothers. Both had black hair and eyes; their faces were deeply tanned; and, sitting, they seemed to be the proper size according to the difference in their ages.

The elder was bareheaded. A loose tunic, dropping to the knees, was his complete attire, except sandals and a light blue mantle spread under him on the seat. The garb left his arms and legs exposed, and they were brown as his face. Nevertheless, a certain grace of manner and refinement of features clearly showed his rank. The gray-tinted tunic, bordered with red at the neck, sleeves, and edge of the skirt and bound with a tasseled silken cord, certified he was a Roman.

Ben Hur-yellow Messala-pink

In the terrible wars between the first caesar and his great enemies, Messala had been the friend of Brutus. After Philippi, without sacrifice of his honor, he and the conqueror became
reconciled. Yet later, when Octavius disputed for the empire, Messala supported him. Octavius, as the Emperor Augustus, remembered the service and showered this family with honors. Among
other things, Judea was reduced to a province, and he sent the
son of his old client to Jerusalem charged with management of
the taxes levied in that region. And in that service the son had
remained, sharing the palace with the high priest.

The young man just described was his son, who remembered
well the relation between his grandfather and the great Romans of
his day.

The associate of Messala was smaller, and his garments were
of fine white linen of the prevalent style in Jerusalem. A cloth covered his head, held by a yellow cord and arranged to fall from the
forehead over the back of his neck. An observer skilled in studying his features more than his garments would have soon discovered him to be of Jewish descent.

The forehead of the Roman was high and narrow, his nose
sharp and aquiline, while his lips were thin and straight and his
eyes cold and close under the brows. The face of the Israelite, on
the other hand, was low and broad. His nose was long, which, in
connection with the round chin, full eyes, and oval cheeks reddened with a winelike glow, gave his face the softness, strength,
and beauty peculiar to his race.

"Did you not say the new procurator is to arrive tomorrow?"

The question came from the younger of the friends and was
spoken in Greek, at the time the language everywhere prevalent in
Judea, having passed from the palace into the camp and college,
and then, nobody knew exactly when or how, into the Temple
itself.

"Yes, tomorrow," Messala answered.

"Who told you?"

"I heard Ishmael, the new governor in the palace—you call
him high priest—tell my father so last night. The news had been
more credible, I grant you, coming from an Egyptian, who is from
a race that has forgotten what truth is, or even from an Idumaean,

73

whose people never knew what truth was. But to be quite certain, I saw a centurion from the Tower this morning, and he told me preparations were going on for the reception—that the armorers were taking care of the helmets and shields and regilding the eagles and globes. And that apartments long unused were being cleansed and aired as if for an addition to the garrison—the bodyguard, probably, of the great man."

Reverence as a quality of the Roman mind was fast breaking down, or rather it was becoming unfashionable. The old religion had nearly ceased to be a faith. At most it was a mere habit of thought and expression, cherished principally by the priests who found service in the temple profitable and the poets who, in the writing of their verses, could not dispense with the familiar deities. As philosophy was taking the place of religion, satire was fast substituting for reverence. In Latin opinion it was to every conversation like the aroma to wine.

The young Messala, educated in Rome but lately returned, had adopted this habit and manner, his speech affected as the best way to convey the idea of general indifference, but more particularly because of the opportunities it afforded for certain pauses thought to be of prime importance to enable the listener to receive the stinging epigram. This occurred in the answer just given, at the end of the allusion to the Egyptian and Idumaean.

The color in the young Jewish man's cheeks deepened, and he may not have heard the rest of the speech, for he remained silent, looking absently into the depths of the pool.

"Our farewell took place in this garden. 'The peace of the Lord go with you!'—your last words. 'The gods keep you!' I said. Do you remember? How many years have passed since then?"

"Five," answered the Jew, gazing into the water.

"Well, you have reason to be thankful to—whom shall I say? The gods? No matter. You have grown handsome—the Greeks would call you beautiful—happy achievement of the years! If Jupiter would stay content with one Ganymede, what a cupbearer you would make for the emperor! Tell me, my Judah, why is the coming of the procurator of such interest to you?"

Judah bent his large eyes upon the questioner. His gaze was grave and thoughtful as he replied, "Yes, five years. I remember the parting. You went to Rome. I saw you go and cried, for I loved you. The years are gone, and you have come back to me accomplished and princely—I do not jest—and yet—yet—I wish you were the Messala you were when you went away."

The satirist stirred, and he put on a longer drawl as he said, "No, no—not a Ganymede. An oracle, my Judah. A few lessons from my teacher of rhetoric by the Forum—I will give you a letter to him when you become wise enough to accept a suggestion that I am reminded to make to you—a little practice of the art of mystery, and Delphi will receive you as Apollo himself. At the sound of your solemn voice, the Pythia will come down to you with her crown. Seriously, O my friend, in what am I not the Messala I was? I once heard the greatest logician in the world. His subject was disputation. One saying I remember—'Understand your antagonist before you answer him.' Let me understand you."

The boy reddened under the cynical look to which he was subjected. Yet he replied firmly, "You have made the most of your opportunities. From your teachers you have brought away much knowledge. You talk with the ease of a master. Yet your speech carries a sting. My Messala, when he went away, had no poison in his nature. Not for the world would he have hurt the feelings of a friend."

The Roman smiled as if complimented and raised his patrician head a little higher.

"O my solemn Judah, be plain. How have I hurt you?"

The other drew a long breath and said, "In the last five years, I too have learned somewhat. Hillel may not be the equal of the logician you heard, and Simeon and Shammai are, no doubt, inferior to your master by the Forum. Their learning does not go out into forbidden paths. Those who sit at their feet arise enriched simply with knowledge of God, the law, and Israel. And the result is love and reverence for everything that pertains to them. Attendance at the Great College and study of what I heard there have taught me that Judea is not what it used to be. I resent the degradation of my country. Ishmael is not lawfully high priest, and he cannot be while the noble Annas lives. Yet he is a Levite, one of the devoted who for thousands of years have acceptably served the Lord God of our faith and worship. His—"

Messala broke in upon him with a biting laugh. "Oh, I understand you now. Ishmael, you say, is a usurper, yet to believe an Idumaean sooner than Ishmael is to sting like an adder. By the drunken sons of Semele, what it is to be a Jew! All men and things, even heaven and earth, change. But Jews—never. To him there is no backward or forward. He is what his ancestor was in the beginning. In this sand I draw you a circle—there! Now tell me what more a Jew's life is? Round and round, Abraham here, Isaac and Jacob there, God in the middle. And the circle—by the master of all thunders! The circle is too large. I draw it again—." He stopped, put his thumb upon the ground, and swept his fingers round it. "See, the thumb-spot is the Temple, the finger-lines Judea. Outside the little space is there nothing of value? The arts! Herod was a builder; therefore he is accursed. Painting, sculpture! To look upon them is sin. Poetry you make fast to your altars. Except in the synagogue, who of you attempts eloquence? In war all you conquer in the six days you lose on the seventh. Such is your life. Who shall object if I laugh at you? Satisfied with the worship of such a people, what is your God to our Roman Jove, who lends us his eagles that we may circle the universe with our arms? Hillel, Simeon, Shammai—what are they to the masters who teach that everything is worth knowing that can be known?"

The Jew arose, his face flushed. "No, no, keep your place, my Judah, keep your place," Messala cried, extending his hand.

"You mock me."

"Listen a little further. Soon"—the Roman smiled derisively—"soon Jupiter and his whole family, Greek and Latin, will come to me and make an end of serious speech. I am mindful of your goodness in walking from the old house of your fathers to welcome me back and renew the love of our childhood—if we can. 'Go,' said my teacher, in his last lecture—'go, and, to make your lives great, remember Mars reigns and Eros has found his eyes.' He meant love is nothing, war everything. It is this way in Rome. Marriage is the first step to divorce. Virtue is a tradesman's jewel. Cleopatra, dying, gave her arts and is avenged. She has a successor in every Roman's house. The world is going the same way. So, as to our future, down Eros, up Mars! I am to be a soldier; and you, O my Judah, I pity you. What can you be?

"Yes, I pity you, my fine Judah. From the college to the synagogue. Then to the Temple. Then—oh, a crowning glory!—the seat in the Sanhedrin. A life without opportunities. The gods help you. But I—"

Judah looked at him in time to see the flush of pride that kindled in his haughty face as he went on.

"But I—ah, the world is not all conquered. The sea has islands unseen. In the north there are nations yet unvisited. The glory of completing Alexander's march to the Far East remains for someone. See what possibilities lie before a Roman."

In the next instant he resumed his drawl.

"A campaign into Africa, another into Scytha, then—a legion! Most careers end there, but not mine. I will give up my legion for a prefecture. Think of life in Rome with money—money, wine, women, games—poets at the banquet, intrigues in the court, dice all year round. Such a rounding of life may be—a fat prefecture, and it is mine. O my Judah, here is Syria! Judea is rich, Antioch a capital for the gods. I will succeed Cyrenius, and you shall share my fortune."

The philosophers and orators who thronged the public resorts of Rome, almost monopolizing the business of teaching her patrician youth, might have approved of these sayings of Messala for they agreed with the popular thinking. To the young Jew, however, they were new and unlike the solemn conversation to which he was accustomed. He belonged to a race whose laws, modes, and habits of thought forbade satire and humor. Very naturally, therefore, he listened to his friend with varying feelings, one moment indignant, then uncertain how to take him. The superior airs assumed had been offensive to him in the beginning, but soon they became irritating.

To the Jew of the Herodian period patriotism was a savage passion scarcely hidden under his common humor and so related to his history, religion, and God that it responded instantly to a challenge to them. Thus Messala's progress down to the last pause was exquisite torture to Judah.

At that point Judah said, with a forced smile, "There are a few, I have heard, who can afford to make a jest of their future. You convince me, O my Messala, that I am not one of them."

The Roman studied him, then replied, "Why not the truth in a jest as well as a parable? The great Fulvia went fishing the other day. She caught more than all the company besides. They said it was because the barb of her hook was covered with gold."

"Then you are not merely jesting?"

"My Judah, I see I did not offer you enough," the Roman answered, his eyes sparkling. "When I am a prefect, with Judea to enrich me, I will make you high priest."

The Jew turned away angrily. "Do not leave me," said Messala.

The other stopped, undecided.

"Gods, Judah, how hot the sun shines!" cried the patrician, observing his perplexity. "Let us seek shade."

Judah answered, coldly, "We had better part. I wish I had not come. I sought a friend and find a—"

"Roman," said Messala quickly.

The hands of the Jew clenched, but controlling himself again he started off. Messala arose and, taking the mantle from the bench, flung it over his shoulder and followed. When he reached Judah's side, he put his hand upon his shoulder and walked with him.

"This is the way—my hand like this—that we used to walk when we were children. Let us keep it as far as the gate."

Apparently Messala was trying to be serious and kind, though he could not remove the habitual sarcastic expression. Judah permitted this familiarity.

"You are a boy. I am a man—let me talk like one. My Judah, why did you get angry when I spoke of succeeding old Cyrenius? You thought I meant to enrich myself plundering your Judea. Suppose so—it is what some Roman will do. Why not I?"

Judah shortened his step. "There have been strangers in mastery of Judea before the Roman," he said, with lifted hand. "Where are they, Messala? Judea has outlived them all. What has been will be again. My faith rests on the rock that was the foundation of the faith of my fathers back further than Abraham; on the covenants of the Lord God of Israel."

"Too much passion, my Judah. How my master would have been shocked had I been guilty of so much heat in his presence! There were other things I had to tell you, but I fear to now."

When they had gone a few yards the Roman spoke again. "I think you can hear me now, especially as what I have to say concerns yourself. I would serve you, O handsome as Ganymede. I would serve you with real goodwill. I am dedicated to you. I told you I meant to be a soldier. Why not you also? Why not step out of the narrow circle that is all of noble life your laws and customs allow?"

Judah made no reply.

"Who are the wise men of our day?" Messala continued. "Not they who exhaust their years quarreling about dead things—about Baals, Joves, and Jehovahs, about philosophies and religions. Give me one great name, O Judah. I do not care where you go to find it—to Rome, Egypt, the East, or here in Jerusalem—Pluto take me if it does not belong to a man who made his fame out of the material furnished to him by the present circumstances— holding nothing sacred that did not contribute to the end, scorning nothing that did! How did Herod do it? How with the Maccabees? Imitate them. Now. Rome is as ready to help you as she was the Idumaean Antipater, Herod himself."

The Jewish boy trembled with rage, and, as the garden gate was close by, he quickened his steps, eager to escape.

"O Rome, Rome!" he muttered.

"Be wise," continued Messala. "Give up the follies of Moses and the traditions. See the situation as it is. Dare look our gods in the face, and they will tell you Rome is the world. Ask them of Judea, and they will answer, 'She will be what Rome wills.'"

They were now at the gate. Judah stopped and took the hand gently from his shoulder and confronted Messala, tears trembling in his eyes.

"I understand you, because you are a Roman. You cannot understand me—I am an Israelite. You have caused me suffering today by convincing me that we can never be the friends we have been—never! Here we part. The peace of the God of my fathers abide with you!"

Messala offered him his hand. The Jew walked on through the gateway. When he was gone, the Roman was silent a while. Then he, too, passed through, saying to himself, "Be it so. Eros is dead, Mars rules! Love is dead, war reigns!"

79

17

A Judean Home

Not long after the young Jew parted from the Roman at the palace up on the marketplace, he stopped before the western gate of a house and knocked. The wicket was opened to admit him. He stepped in hastily and failed to acknowledge the low bow of the porter.

The passage into which he was admitted appeared not unlike a narrow tunnel with paneled walls and pitted ceiling. There were benches of stone on both sides, stained and polished by long use. Twelve or fifteen steps carried him into a courtyard. The lower floor was divided into apartments, while the upper was terraced and defended by strong battlements. Servants came and went along the terraces. There was the noise of millstones grinding.

Clearing the second passage, the young man entered a second court, spacious, square, and set with shrubbery and vines, kept fresh and beautiful by water from a basin erected near a porch on the north side. A flight of steps on the south ascended to the terraces of the upper story, over which great awnings were stretched as a defense against the sun. In this quarter also there was observable everywhere a scrupulous neatness, which, allowing no dust in the angles, not even a yellow leaf upon a shrub, contributed to the delightful general effect. A visitor breathing the sweet air knew immediately the refinement of the family he was about to call on.

A few steps within the second court, the young man turned to the right and ascended to the terrace—a broad pavement of white and much worn brown flagstones. Making his way under the awning to a doorway on the north side, he entered an apartment. He proceeded in darkness, moving over a tile floor to a couch. He flung himself on it, face downwards, and lay at rest.

About nightfall a woman came to the door and called. He answered, and she went in.

"Supper is over, and it is night. Is not my son hungry?" she asked.

"No."

"Are you sick?"

"I am sleepy."

"Your mother has asked for you."

"Where is she?"

"In the summerhouse on the roof."

He stirred himself and sat up. "Very well. Bring me something to eat."

"What do you want?"

"What you please, Amrah. I am not sick but indifferent. Life does not seem as pleasant as it did this morning. A new ailment, O my Amrah. And you who know me so well and never failed me, you may think of the things now that are used for food and medicine. Bring me what you choose."

Amrah's questions and the sympathetic voice in which she put them proved an endearing relation between the two. She laid her hand upon his forehead, then—satisfied—went out, saying, "I will see."

After a while she returned, bearing on a wooden platter a bowl of milk, some thin cakes of broken white bread, a delicate paste of brayed wheat, a broiled bird, and honey and salt. On one end of the platter there was a silver goblet full of wine, on the other a brazen lighted lamp.

The room's walls were smoothly plastered. The ceiling was broken by great oaken rafters, brown with rainstains and time. The floor was of small diamond-shaped white and blue tiles. There were a few stools with legs carved in imitation of the legs of lions; a couch raised a little above the floor, trimmed with blue cloth and partially covered by an immense striped woolen blanket or shawl—in brief, a Hebrew bedroom.

Drawing a stool to the couch, she placed the platter upon it, then knelt close by, ready to serve him. Her face was that of a woman of fifty, dark-skinned, dark-eyed, and at the moment softened by a look of almost maternal tenderness. A white turban covered her head, leaving the lobes of her ears exposed and the sign that showed her condition—an opening bored by a thick awl. She was a slave of Egyptian origin, to whom not even the sacred fiftieth year could have brought freedom. Nor would she have accepted it, for the boy she was attending was her life. She had nursed him through babyhood, tended him as a child, and could not cease this service. To her, he could never become a man.

He spoke but once during the meal. "You remember, O my Amrah, the Messala who used to visit me here days at a time."

"I remember him."

"He went to Rome some years ago and is now back. I called upon him today." A shudder of disgust filled him.

"I knew something had happened," she said, deeply interested. "I never liked the Messala. Tell me all."

But he reflected and to her repeated inquiries only said, "He is much changed, and I will have nothing more to do with him."

When Amrah took the platter away he also went out and up from the terrace to the roof.

The roof was raised above the level of the shimmering plain enough for cool air and sufficiently above the trees to allure the stars into shining brighter. So the roof became a playground, sleeping chamber, rendezvous for the family, a place of music, dance, and prayer.

The motive that prompts the decoration, at whatever cost, of interiors in colder climates influenced the Oriental in embellishing his housetop. The parapet ordered by Moses became a potter's triumph. Still later, kings and princes crowned their roofs with summerhouses of marble and gold. When the Babylonians hung gardens in the air, extravagance could go no further.

Judah walked slowly across the housetop to a tower built over the northwest corner of the palace. He entered, passing under a half-raised curtain. The interior was all darkness, except that on four sides there were arched openings like doorways through which the sky, lighted with stars, was visible. In one of the openings, reclining against a cushion, he saw the figure of a woman, indistinct even in white floating drapery. At the sound of his steps upon the floor, the fan in her hand stopped, glistening where the starlight struck the jewels with which it was sprinkled, and she sat up and called his name.

"Judah, my son!"

"It is I, Mother," he answered, hurrying.

Going to her, he knelt. She put her arms around him and with kisses pressed him to her bosom.

18

The Strange Things Ben Hur Wants to Know

The mother resumed her seat against the cushion, while the son took his place on the couch, his head in her lap. Both of them, looking out of the opening, could see a line of lower house-tops in the vicinity, a shroud of blue-blackness over in the west that they knew to be mountains and the sky, its shadowy depths brilliant with stars. The city was still. Only the winds stirred.

"Amrah tells me something has happened to you," she said, caressing his cheek. "When my Judah was a child, I allowed small things to trouble him, but he is now a man. He must not forget"—her voice became very soft—"that one day he is to be my hero."

She spoke in the language almost lost in the land, but that a few—and they were always as rich in blood as in possessions—cherished in its purity, that they might be separate from Gentile peoples—the language in which the beloved Rebekah and Rachel sang to Benjamin.

The words appeared to set him thinking again. He caught the hand with which she fanned him and said, "Today, my mother, I have been thinking of many things that never had entered my mind before. Tell me, first, what am I to be?"

"Have I not told you? You are to be my hero."

"You are very kind, my mother. No one will ever love me as you do. I think I understand why you would have me forget the question," he continued. "Thus far my life has belonged to you. How gentle your control has been! I wish it could last forever. But that may not be. It is the Lord's will that I will one day become owner of myself—a day of separation and therefore a dreadful day to you.

"Let us be brave and serious. I will be your hero, but you must allow me my way. You know the law—every son of Israel must have some occupation. I am not exempt and ask now, shall I

84

tend herds? Or till the soil? Or drive the saw? Or be a clerk or lawyer? What shall I be? Dear, good mother, help me to answer."

"Gamaliel has been lecturing today," she said, thoughtfully.

"If so, I did not hear him."

"Then you have been walking with Simeon, who, they tell me, inherits the genius of his family."

"No, I have not seen him. I have been up on the marketplace, not to the Temple. I visited the young Messala."

A certain change in his voice attracted the mother's attention. An intuition quickened the beating of her heart. The fan became motionless again.

"The Messala!" she said. "What could he say to so trouble you?"

"He is very much changed."

"You mean he has come back a Roman."

"Yes."

"Roman!" she continued, half to herself. "To all the world the word means master. How long has he been away?"

"Five years."

She raised her head and looked off into the night. "The airs of the Via Sacra are good enough in the streets of Egypt and Babylon, but in Jerusalem—our Jerusalem—the covenant abides." And full of this thought, she settled back into her reclining position.

"What Messala said, my mother, was sharp enough in itself. But, taken with the manner, some of the sayings were intolerable."

"I think I understand you. Rome, her poets, orators, senators, courtiers, are mad with affectation of what they call satire."

"I suppose all great peoples are proud," he went on, scarcely noticing the interruption. "But the pride of that people is unlike all others. In these latter days it has so increased that the gods barely escape it."

"The gods escape!" said the mother, quickly. "More than one Roman has accepted worship as his divine right."

"Well, Messala always had his share of that disagreeable quality. When he was a child I have seen him mock strangers whom even Herod condescended to receive with honors. Yet he always spared Judea. For the first time, in conversation with me

85

today, he trifled with our customs and God. As you would have wished me to do, finally I parted with him.

"And now, my dear mother, I would know with more certainty if there is just ground for the Roman's contempt. In what am I his inferior? Is ours a lower order of people? Why should I, even in Caesar's presence, feel like shrinking as a slave? Tell me especially why, if I have the soul and so choose, I may not hunt the honors of the world in all its fields? Why may I not take a sword and indulge the passion of war? As a poet, why may not I sing of all themes? I can be a worker in metals, a keeper of flocks, a merchant, why not an artist like the Greek? Tell me, Mother—and this is all that troubles me—why may not a son of Israel do all a Roman may?"

The mother, listening with all her faculties awake, understood what would have been lost upon one less interested in him. She sat up and in a voice quick and sharp as his own, replied, "I see, I see! From association Messala, in boyhood, was almost a Jew. Had he remained here he might have become a proselyte or convert, so much do we all borrow from the influences that shape our lives. But the years in Rome have been too much for him. I do not wonder at the change. Yet"—her voice fell—"he might have dealt tenderly at least with you. It is a hard, cruel nature that in youth can forget its first loves."

Her hand dropped lightly upon his forehead, and the fingers caught in his hair and lingered there lovingly, while her eyes sought the highest stars in view. Her pride responded to his, not merely in echo, but in the unison of perfect sympathy. She would answer him. At the same time, not for the world would she have allowed the answer to be less than complete. An admission of inferiority might weaken his spirit for life. She faltered with misgivings of her own powers.

"What you propose, my Judah, is not a subject for treatment by a woman. Let me put its consideration off till tomorrow, and I will have the wise Simeon—"

"Do not send me to the teacher," he said abruptly.

"I will have him come to us."

"No, I seek more than information. While he might give me that better than you, my mother, you can do better by giving me what he cannot—the resolution that is the soul of a man's soul."

86

She swept the heavens with a rapid glance, trying to compass all the meaning of his questions. "While craving justice for ourselves, it is never wise to be unjust to others. To deny valor in the enemy we have conquered is to underrate our victory. And if the enemy be strong enough to hold us at bay, much more to conquer us"—she hesitated—"self-respect calls us to seek some other explanation of our misfortunes than accusing him of qualities inferior to our own."

Speaking to herself rather than to him, she began. "Take heart, my son. The Messala is nobly descended. His family has been illustrious through many generations. In the days of Republican Rome—how far back I cannot tell—they were famous, some as soldiers, some as civilians. I can recall only one consul of that name. Their rank was senatorial and their patronage always sought because they were always rich. Yet if today your friend boasted of his ancestry, you might have shamed him by citing yours. If he referred to the ages through which his line is traceable, or to deeds, rank, or wealth—such facts, except when great occasion demands them, are tokens of small minds—if he mentioned them in proof of his superiority, then without dread and standing on each point, you might have challenged him to a comparison of records."

Taking a moment's thought, she proceeded: "One of the ideas of taking hold now is that time has much to do with the nobility of races and families. A Roman boasting of his superiority on that account over a son of Israel will always fail when put to the test. The founding of Rome was his beginning. The very best of them cannot trace their descent beyond that period. Few of them pretend to do so, and of such as do, I say not one could make good his claim except by resort to tradition. Messala certainly could not. Let us look now to ourselves. Could we do better?"

A little more light would have enabled him to see the pride that diffused itself over her face.

"Let us imagine the Roman putting us to the challenge. I would answer him, neither doubting nor boastful."

Her voice faltered. A tender thought changed the direction of the argument.

"Your father, my Judah, is at rest with his fathers. Yet I remember, as though it were this evening, the day he and I, with many rejoicing friends, went up into the Temple to present you to the Lord. We sacrificed the doves, and I gave your name to the priest, which he wrote in my presence—'Judah, son of Ithamar, of the House of Hur.' The name was then carried away and written in a book of the division of records devoted to this devout family.

"I cannot tell you when the custom of registration in this mode began. We know it prevailed before the flight from Egypt. I have heard Hillel say Abraham caused the record to be first opened with his own name and the names of his sons, moved by the promises of the Lord that separated him and them from all other races and made them the highest and noblest, the very chosen of the earth. The covenant with Jacob was similar. 'In thy seed shall all the nations of the earth be blessed'—so said the angel to Abraham in the place of Jehovah-jireh. 'And the land whereon thou liest, to thee will I give it, and to thy seed'—so the Lord himself said to Jacob asleep at Bethel on the way to Haran.

"Afterwards the wise men looked forward to a just division of the land of promise. And, that it might be known in the day of partition who were entitled to portions, the Book of Generations was begun. But not for that alone. The promise of a blessing to all the earth through the patriarch reached far into the future. One name was mentioned in connection with the blessing—the benefactor might be the humblest of the chosen family, for the Lord our God knows no distinction of rank or riches. So to make the performance clear to men of the generations who were to witness it and that they might give the glory to whom it belonged, the record was required to be kept with absolute certainty. Has it been kept this way?"

Her fan moved back and forth until, becoming impatient, he repeated the question. "Is the record absolutely true?"

"Hillel said it was, and of all who have lived no one was so well-informed upon the subject. Our people have at times been heedless of some parts of the law, but never of this part. The good teacher himself has followed the Books of Generations through three periods—from the promises to the opening of the Temple, thence to the Captivity, thence, again, to the present. Only once

were the records disturbed, and that was at the end of the second
period. But when the nation returned from the long exile, as a first
duty to God Zerubbabel restored the Books, enabling us once
more to carry the lines of Jewish descent back unbroken fully two
thousand years. And now—"

She paused as if to allow the hearer to measure the generations that had passed in the scope of this statement.

"And now," she continued, "what becomes of the Roman
boast of blood enriched by ages? By that test the sons of Israel
watching the herds on old Rephaim yonder are nobler than the
noblest of the Marcii."

"And I, mother—by the Books, who am I?"

"What I have said thus far, my son, was in reference to your
question. I will answer you. If Messala were here he might say, as
others have said, that the exact trace of your lineage stopped
when the Assyrians took Jerusalem and razed the Temple with all
its precious stones. But you might remind him of the pious action
of Zerubbabel and respond that all verity in Roman genealogy
ended when the barbarians from the West took Rome and en-
camped six months upon her desolate site. Did the government
keep family histories? If so, what became of them in those dreadful days?

"No, no. There is verity in our Books of Generations, and following them back to the Captivity, back to the foundation of the
first Temple, back to the march from Egypt, we have absolute assurance that you are lineally sprung from Hur, the associate of
Joshua. In the matter of descent sanctified by time, is not the hon-
or perfect? Do you care to pursue this any further? If so, take the
Torah and search the book of Numbers and of the seventy-two generations after Adam. You can find the very ancestor of your house."

There was silence for a time in the chamber on the roof. "I
thank you, Mother," Judah next said, clasping both her hands in
his. "I thank you with all my heart. I was right in not having the
good teacher called in. He could not have satisfied me more than
you have. Yet to make a family truly noble, is time alone sufficient?"

"Ah, you forget. Our claim rests not merely upon time. The
Lord's preference is our special glory."

"You are speaking of the race, and I, Mother, of the family—our family. In the years since Father Abraham, what have they achieved? What have they done? What great things to lift them above the level of their fellows?"

She hesitated, thinking she might all this time have mistaken his purpose. The information he sought might have been for more than satisfaction of wounded vanity. Youth is but the painted shell within which, continually growing, lives that wondrous thing, the spirit of a man, biding its moment of appearance, earlier in some than in others.

She trembled under a perception that this might be the supreme moment for him—that as crying children at birth reach out their untried hands grasping for shadows, so his spirit might, in temporary blindness, be struggling to take hold of its unknowable future. They to whom a boy comes asking, Who am I, and what am I to be? have need to be careful. Each word in their answer may prove to the life after what each finger-touch of the artist is to the clay he is modeling.

"I have a feeling, my Judah," she said, patting his cheek with the hand he had been caressing. "I have the feeling that all I have said has been in battle with an antagonist more real than imaginary. If Messala is the enemy, do not leave me to fight him in the dark. Tell me all he said."

19

Rome and Israel—A Comparison

The young Israelite told her of Messala's speeches in contempt of the Jews and their customs. She listened, understanding the situation plainly. Judah had gone to the palace on the marketplace, allured by friendship of a playmate whom he thought to find exactly as he had been at their parting years before. This man met him, and, in place of laughter and references to the sports of the past, the man had spoken of the future and talked of glory to be won and of riches and power. Unconscious of the effect, the visitor had come away with his pride hurt, yet feeling his own natural ambition. But she, the jealous mother, saw it and, not knowing the direction his hopes might take, became fearful.

What if it lured him away from the faith of his fathers? In her view that consequence was more dreadful than any or all others. She could discover only one way to avoid it, and she began the task. Her energy was reinforced by love, and her speech took a man's strength and a poet's fervor.

"There never has been a people," she began, "who did not think themselves at least equal to any other—never a great nation, my son, that did not believe itself superior. When the Roman looks down upon Israel and laughs, he merely repeats the folly of the Egyptian, the Assyrian, and the Macedonian. And as the laugh is against God, the result will be the same."

Her voice became firmer.

"There is no law to determine the superiority of nations. So it is vain and idle to dispute about it. A people rise, run their race, and die either by themselves or at the hands of someone else, who, succeeding to take their place, take possession and upon their monuments write new names. This is merely history.

"If I were called upon to symbolize God and man in the simplest form, I would draw a straight line and a circle. About the line

91

I would say, 'This is God, for he alone moves forever straightforward,' and of the circle, 'This is man—this is his progress.' I do not mean that there is no difference between the history of nations—no two are alike. The difference, however, is not, as some say, in the extent of the circle they describe or the amount of space on earth they cover but in the sphere of their movement, the highest being nearest to God.

"Let us compare the Hebrews and the Romans. The simplest of all the signs is the daily life of the people. Of this I will only say, Israel has at times forgotten God, while the Roman never knew him. So comparison is not possible.

"Your friend—or your former friend—charged, if I understand you correctly, that we have had no poets, artists, or warriors. He meant, I suppose, to deny that we have had great men, the next most certain of the signs. A just consideration of this charge requires a definition.

"A great man, my boy, is one whose life proves him to have been recognized, if not called, by God. A Persian was used to punish our rebellious fathers, and he carried them into captivity. Another Persian was selected to restore their children to the Holy Land. Greater than either of them, however, was the Macedonian through whom the desolation of Judea and the Temple was avenged. The special distinction of the men was that they were chosen by the Lord, each for a divine purpose, and that they were Gentiles does not lessen their glory. Do not lose sight of this while I continue.

"There is an idea that war is the most noble occupation of men and that the most exalted greatness is the growth of battlefields. Because the world has adopted the idea, do not be deceived. That we must worship something is self-evident. The prayer of the barbarian is a wail of fear addressed to Strength, the only divine quality he can clearly understand. So his faith in heroes. What is Jove but a Roman hero? The Greeks have their great glory because they were the first to set Mind above Strength. In Athens the orator and philosopher were more revered than the warrior. The charioteer and the swiftest runner are still idols of the arena, yet the immortals are reserved for the sweetest singer. But was the Greek the first to deny the old barbaric faith?

"No, my son, that glory is ours. Against heathenism, our fathers erected God. In our worship, the wail of fear gave place to the hosanna and the psalm. Both Hebrew and Greek wish to carry humanity forward and upward. But the government of the world presumes war as an eternal condition. Over Mind and above God, the Roman has enthroned his caesar, the summation of all attainable power, not allowing for any other greatness.

"The rule of the Greek was a flowering time for genius. In return for the liberty it then enjoyed, what a company of thinkers the study of the mind produced. There was a glory for every excellence and a perfection so absolute that in everything but war even the Romans imitate them. A Greek is now the model of the orators in the Forum. Listen, and in every Roman song you will hear the rhythm of the Greek. If a Roman opens his mouth speaking wisely of morality or of the mysteries of nature, he is either an imitator or the disciple of some school that had a Greek for its founder.

"In nothing but war, I say again, has Rome a claim to originality. Her games and spectacles are Greek inventions, covered with blood to gratify the lust of her rabble. Her religion, if it may be called this, is made up of contributions from the faiths of all other peoples. Her most venerated gods are from Olympus—even Mars and, for that matter, the Jove she magnifies. So it happens, my son, that of the whole world Israel alone can dispute the superiority of the Greeks and debate with them who was the original genius.

"The egotism of a Roman is a blindfold to the excellencies of other peoples, as thick as his breastplate. Oh, the ruthless robbers! The earth trembles under their trampling like a floor beaten with whips. Along with other nations, we are fallen—I have to say it to you, my son! They own our highest places and the holiest, and no man can tell the end. But this I know—they may smash Judea as an almond broken with hammers and devour Jerusalem, which is the oil and sweetness of it, yet the glory of the men of Israel will remain a light in the heavens overhead.

"Their history is the history of God, who wrote with their hands, spoke with their tongues, and was himself involved in all the good they did, even among the least of them. There was a lawgiver on Sinai, a guide in the wilderness, a captain in war, a king in government, who showed the people the way to happiness and how they should live and made them promises binding the strength of his almightiness with everlasting covenants.

"My son, could it be that they with whom Jehovah lived did not gain anything from him? That in their lives and deeds the common human qualities should not in some degree have been mixed and colored with the divine? That their genius should not have, even after the passing of ages, some small bit of heaven?"

For a time the rustling of the fan was all that was heard in the chamber.

"In the limitation of art to sculpture and painting, it is true," she next said, "Israel has had no artists."

The admission was made regretfully, for it must be remembered she was a Sadducee, whose faith, unlike that of the Pharisee, permitted a love of the beautiful in every form, without reference to its origin.

"Still, he who wishes to do justice," she continued, "will not forget that the skill of our hands was bound by the prohibition 'Thou shalt not make unto thee any graven image, or any likeness of anything,' which was wickedly extended beyond its purpose and time.

"Nor should it be forgotten that long before Daedalus appeared in Attica and with his wooden statues so transformed sculpture as to make possible the schools of Corinth and their ultimate triumphs, two Israelites—Bezaleel and Aholiab, the master builders of the Tabernacle, said to have been skilled 'in all manner or workmanship'—forged the cherubim of the mercy seat above the Ark. They were beaten of gold, not chiseled, and they were statues in both human and divine form. 'And they shall stretch forth their wings on high . . . and their faces shall look one to another.' Who will say they were not beautiful?"

"Oh, I see now why the Greeks outstripped us," said Judah, intensely interested. "And the Ark—accursed be the Babylonians who destroyed it."

"No, Judah, be of faith. It was not destroyed, only lost, hidden away, too, safely in some cavern of the mountains. One day—Hillel and Shammai both say so—one day, in the Lord's good time, it will be found and brought out, and Israel will dance before it, singing as of old. And they who look upon the faces of the cherubim then, though they have seen the face of the ivory Minerva, will be ready to kiss the hand of the Jew because of love for his genius, asleep through thousands of years."

"You are so good, my Mother," he said, in a grateful way. "And I will always say so. Shammai could not have talked better, nor Hillel. I am a true son of Israel again."

"Flatterer!" she said. "You do not know that I am only repeating what I heard Hillel say in an argument he had one day in my presence with a Sophist from Rome."

"Well, the hearty words are yours."

"I always think of great men marching down the centuries in groups, separated according to nationalities—here the Indian, there the Egyptian and the Assyrian; above them the music of trumpets and the beauty of banners; and on their right hand and left, as reverent spectators, numberless generations from the beginning. As they go, I think of the Greek saying, 'Lo! The Hellene leads the way.' Then the Roman replies, 'Silence! What was your place is ours now. We have left you behind like dust trampled on.' And all the time, from the very back of the line, as well as forward into the farthest future, streams a light of which these people know nothing, except that it is forever leading them on—the Light of Revelation! Who are they that carry it? Ah, the old Judean blood! How it leaps at the thought! By the light we know them. Three times blessed, our fathers, servants of God, keepers of the covenants! You are the leaders of men, the living and the dead. The front is yours, and though every Roman were a caesar, you shall not lose it!"

Judah was deeply stirred.

"Do not stop, I pray," he cried. "I am hearing the sound of timbrels. I wait for Miriam and the women who went after her dancing and singing."

She saw his interest and, with ready wit, wove it into her speech.

"Very well, my son. If you can hear the timbrel of the prophetess, you can do what I was about to ask you—you can use your fancy and stand with me, as if by the wayside, while the chosen of Israel pass us at the head of the procession.

"Here they come—the patriarchs first and next the fathers of the tribes. I almost hear the bells of their camels and the lowing of their herds. Who is he that walks alone between the crowds? An old man, yet his eye is not dim, nor his natural force spent. Moses knew the Lord face to face! Warrior, poet, orator, lawgiver, prophet, his greatness is as the sun at morning, its flood of splendor quenching all other lights, even that of the first and noblest of the caesars. After him the judges. And then the kings—David the son of Jesse, a hero in war and a singer of songs eternal as that of the sea. And his son Solomon, who, surpassing all other kings in riches and wisdom, while making the desert habitable, in its waste places planting cities, forgot not Jerusalem, which the Lord had chosen for his throne on earth.

"Bend lower, my son! These that come next are the first of their kind, and the last. Their faces are raised as if they heard a voice in the sky and are listening. Their lives were full of sorrows. Their garments smell of tombs and caverns. Hearken to a woman among them! 'Sing to the Lord, for he has triumphed gloriously!' Put your forehead in the dust before them! They were tongues of God, his servants, who looked through heaven and, seeing the future, wrote what they saw and left the writing to be proven by time.

"Kings turned pale as they approached them, and nations trembled at the sound of their voices. The very winds waited upon them. In their lands they carried every bounty and every plague. See Elijah the Tishbite and his servant Elisha! See the sad son of Hilkiah, Ezekiel, the seer of visions, by the river of Chebar! And the three children of Judah who refused the image of the Babylonian! And Daniel, that one who, in the feast for the thousand lords, so confounded the astrologers.

"And beyond—O my son, kiss the dust again!—yonder the gentle son of Amoz, from whom the world has its promise of the Messiah to come!" Her voice sank low. "You are tired."

"No," he replied, "I was listening to a new song of Israel."

The mother was still intent upon her purpose and passed the pleasant speech. "In such light as I could, my Judah, I have set our great men before you—patriarchs, legislators, warriors, singers, prophets. Now let us turn to the best of Rome. Against

Moses place Caesar, and Tarquin against David; Sylla against either of the Maccabees; the best of the consuls against the judges; Augustus against Solomon, and you have your answer. Comparison ends there. But think then of the prophets—greatest of the great."

She laughed scornfully. "Pardon me. I was thinking of the soothsayer who warned Julius Caesar against the Ides of March and fancied him looking for the omens of evil that his master despised in the entrails of a chicken. From that picture turn to Elijah sitting on the hilltop on the way to Samaria, amid the smoking bodies of the captains and their fifties, warning the son of Ahab of the wrath of our God. Finally, Judah—if such speech be reverent—how shall we judge Jehovah and Jupiter unless it is by what their servants have done in their names? And as for what you shall do . . ."

She spoke these words slowly and hesitantly. "As for what you shall do, my boy—serve the Lord, the Lord God of Israel, not Rome. For a child of Abraham there is no glory except in the Lord's ways, and in them there is much glory."

"I may be a soldier then?" Judah asked.

"Why not? Did not Moses call God a man of war?" After a silence she said, "You have my permission, if only you serve the Lord instead of Caesar."

He was content with this answer and finally fell asleep. She arose, put the cushion under his head and, throwing a shawl over him, kissed him tenderly and went away.

97

20

The Accident to Gratus

When Judah awoke, the sun was up over the mountains. The pigeons were flying in flocks, filling the air with the gleams of their white wings, and off to the southeast he viewed the Temple, a vision of gold in the blue sky.

Herod's favors had left many friends with vast estates. Where this fortune was connected to lineal descent from some famous son of one of the tribes, especially Judah, that individual was considered a prince of Jerusalem—a distinction that brought him the homage of his less favored countrymen and the respect, if nothing else, of the Gentiles he did business with in the marketplace.

None had won in private or public life a higher regard than the father of young Judah. He had been true to the king and served him faithfully at home and abroad. Business had taken him to Rome, where his conduct attracted the notice of Augustus, who made him his friend. In his house were many presents, which had gratified the vanity of kings—purple togas and ivory chairs—chiefly valuable because of the imperial hand that had honorably given them. This man could not fail to be rich. Yet his wealth was not altogether the result of royal patrons.

Many herdsmen reported to him as their employer. In the cities by the sea he carried on business. His ships brought him silver from Spain, whose mines were then the richest known, while his caravans came twice a year from the East, laden with silks and spices.

His faith was that of a Hebrew, observing the law and all its rites. He took his place in the synagogue and Temple. He was thoroughly learned in the Scriptures. He delighted in the society of the teachers of the law and carried his reverence for Hillel almost to the point of worship. Yet he was in no sense a Separatist. His hospitality took in strangers from every land. The complaining Pharisees even accused him of having more than once entertained Samaritans at his table. Had he been a Gentile and lived, the world might have heard of him as the rival of Herodes Atticus. Unfortunately, he perished at sea some ten years before these events, in the prime of life, and was mourned everywhere in Judea. Besides his widow and son, the only other child was a daughter.

Tirzah was her name, and as she and Judah looked at each other, their resemblance was plain. Her features were of the same Jewish type. They had also the charm of a childish innocency of expression. She wore a silken cap, Tyrian-dyed, and over that a striped scarf of the same material, beautifully embroidered and wound about in thin folds topped by a tassel dropping from the crown point of her cap. She had rings in her ears and on her fingers, gold anklets and bracelets, and around her neck was a collar of gold, curiously garnished with a network of delicate chains. Her hair fell in two long plaits down her back. A curled lock rested upon each cheek in front of the ear. It would be impossible to deny her grace, refinement, and beauty.

"Very pretty, my Tirzah, very pretty!" Judah said, with animation.

"The song?" she asked.

"Yes—and the singer too. It has the sound of a Greek. Where did you get it?"

"You remember the Greek who sang in the theater last month? They said he used to be a singer at the court for Herod and his sister Salome. He came out just after an exhibition of wrestlers, when the house was very noisy. At his first note everything became so quiet that I heard every word. I got the song from him."

"But he sang in Greek."

"And I in Hebrew."

"Ah, yes. I am proud of my little sister. Is anyone as good?"

"Very many. But let them go now. Amrah sent me to tell you she will bring you your breakfast and that you need not come down. She should be here by this time. She thinks you are sick—that a dreadful accident happened to you yesterday. What was it? Tell me, and I will help Amrah doctor you. She knows the cures of the Egyptians, who were always an important group. But I have a great many recipes of the Arabs who—"

"Are even more ignorant than the Egyptians," he said, shaking his head.

"Do you think so? Very well then. We will have nothing to do with any of them. I have something better—the amulet that was given to some of our people—I cannot tell when, it was so far back—by a Persian magician. See, the inscription is almost worn out."

She offered him the earring, which he took, looked at, and handed back, laughing. "If I were dying, Tirzah, I could not use the charm. It is a relic of idolatry, forbidden to every believing son and daughter of Abraham. Take it, but do not wear it anymore."

"Forbidden! Not so," she said. "Our father's mother wore it many Sabbaths of her life. It has cured many people—more than three anyhow. It is approved—look, here is the mark of the rabbis."

"I have no faith in amulets."

She raised her eyes to his in astonishment. "What would Amrah say?"

"Amrah's father and mother tended a garden on the Nile."

"But Gamaliel!"

"He says they are godless inventions of unbelievers and Shechemites."

Tirzah looked at the ring doubtfully. "What should I do with it?"

"Wear it, my little sister. It suits you—it helps make you beautiful, though I think you are that without help from jewelry."

Satisfied, she returned the amulet to her ear just as Amrah entered the summer chamber, bearing a platter with a washbowl, water, and napkins.

Not being a Pharisee, the washing was short and simple with Judah. The servant then went out, leaving Tirzah to fix his hair.

"I am going away. What do you think, Tirzah?"

She dropped her hands with amazement. "Going away! When? Where? For what?"

He laughed. "You know the law requires me to follow some occupation. Our good father set me an example. Even you would despise me if I spent in idleness the results of his industry and knowledge. I am going to Rome."

"Oh, I will go with you."

"You must stay with mother. If both of us leave her, she will die."

The brightness faded from her face.

"Ah, yes! But—must you go? Here in Jerusalem you can learn all that is needed to be a merchant—if that is what you are thinking of."

"But that is not what I am thinking of. The law does not require the son to be what the father was."

"What else can you be?"

"A soldier," he replied, with a certain pride in his voice.

Tears came into her eyes. "You will be killed."

"If God's will, let it be so. But, Tirzah, soldiers are not all killed."

She threw her arms around his neck, as if to hold him back. "We are so happy! Stay at home, my brother."

"Home cannot always be what it is. You yourself will be going away before long."

"Never!"

He smiled at her earnestness. "A prince of Judah, or some other one of the tribes, will come soon and claim my Tirzah and ride away with her to be the light of another house. What will then become of me?"

She answered with sobs.

"War is a trade," he continued, more soberly. "To learn it thoroughly, one must go to school, and there is no school like a Roman camp."

"You would not fight for Rome?" she asked, holding her breath.

"And you—even you hate her. The whole world hates her. In that, Tirzah, find the reason of the answer I give you—yes, I will fight for her, if in return she will teach me how one day to fight against her."

"When will you go?"

Amrah's steps were then heard returning. "Shhh!" he said. "Do not let her know of what I am thinking."

The faithful slave came in with breakfast and held it upon a stool before them. She remained to serve them. They dipped their

101

fingers in a bowl of water and were rinsing them when a noise caught their attention. They heard military music in the street on the north side of the house.

"Soldiers from the Praetorium! I must see them!" he cried, springing from the divan and running out.

Soon he was leaning over the parapet of tiles that guarded the roof at the extreme northeast corner, so absorbed that he did not notice Tirzah by his side, resting one hand upon his shoulder.

Their position—the roof being the highest one in the locality—commanded the housetops eastward as far as the huge irregular Tower of Antonia. The people heard, when they emerged, an uproar of trumpets and the shrill call so delightful to the soldiers.

The parade came into view at the house of the Hurs. First, a vanguard of the lightly armed men—mostly slingers and bowmen—marching in their ranks and files, next a body of heavily armed infantry bearing large shields, then the musicians and an officer riding alone, then a column of infantry also heavily armed, which, moving in close order, crowded the street and appeared to be endless.

The brawny limbs of the men; the sparkle of buckles and breastplates and helms, all perfectly burnished; the plumes nodding above the tall crests; the sway of ensigns and iron-shod spears; the bold, confident step, exactly timed and measured—the machinelike unity of the whole moving mass made an impression upon Judah, but as something deeply felt rather than merely seen.

Two objects caught his attention—the eagle of the legion first, perched on a tall shaft, with wings outspread until they met above its head. He knew that, when brought from its chamber in the Tower, it had been received with divine honors.

The officer riding alone in the midst of the column was the other attraction to Judah. His head was bare. Otherwise he was in full armor. At his left hip he wore a short sword. In his hand, however, he carried a club, which looked like a roll of white paper. He sat upon a purple cloth instead of a saddle and held a bridle of gold and reins of yellow silk broadly fringed at the lower edge.

Judah observed that his presence was sufficient to stir up the people looking at him into angry excitement. They would lean over the parapets or stand out boldly and shake their fists at him. They followed him with loud cries and spit at him as he passed under the bridges. The women even flung their sandals. When he was nearer, the yells became distinguishable—"Robber, tyrant, dog of a Roman! Away with Ishmael! Give us back our Annas!"

Judah could see that the man's face was dark and sullen and that he cast looks at his persecutors that were full of menace. The very timid shrank from them.

Now the young man had heard of the custom, borrowed from a habit of the first caesar, of the chief commanders, to indicate their rank, appearing in public with only a laurel vine upon their heads. By that sign he knew this officer—it was Valerius Gratus, the new Procurator of Judea.

The Roman had the young Jew's sympathy. So, when he reached the corner of the house, Judah leaned yet farther over the parapet to see him go by and rested a hand upon a tile that had been cracked and gone unnoticed. As the tile slipped and began to fall, a thrill of horror shot through Judah. He reached out to catch it, which made it look as though he was throwing it. The effort failed, and he shouted with all his might. The soldiers of the guard looked up. So did the great man, and at that moment the missile struck him, and he fell from his seat as if he were dead.

The cohort halted. The guards leaped from their horses and hastened to cover the chief with their shields. On the other hand, the people who witnessed the affair, never doubting that the blow had been purposely dealt, cheered the young man as he yet stooped in full view over the parapet, transfixed by what he saw and by anticipation of the consequences.

A rebellious spirit flew with incredible speed from roof to roof along the line of march. They laid hands upon the parapets and tore up the tiling and the sunburnt mud and with blind fury began to fling them upon the legionnaires halted below. A battle then ensued. Discipline, of course, prevailed.

Judah arose from the parapet, his face very pale. "O Tirzah! What will become of us?"

She had not seen the occurrence below but was listening to the shouting and watching the mad activity of the people in view on the houses. Something terrible was going on, she knew, but what it was, or the cause, or that she or any of those dear to her were in danger, she did not know.

"What has happened? What does it all mean?" she asked in sudden alarm.

"I have killed the Roman governor. The tile fell upon him."

Her face grew white instantly. She put her arm around him. His fears had passed to her, and the sight of them gave him strength.

"I did not do it purposely, Tirzah—it was an accident," he said more calmly.

"What will they do?" she asked.

He looked over the tumult momentarily deepening in the street and on the roofs and thought of the menacing face of Gratus. If he were not dead, where would his vengeance stop? And if he were dead, to what height of fury would the violence of the people lash the legionnaires? He peered over the parapet again, just as the guards were assisting the Roman to remount his horse.

"He lives, Tirzah! Blessed be the Lord God of our fathers! "Do not be afraid, Tirzah. I will explain how it happened, and they will remember our father and his services and not hurt us."

He was leading her to the summerhouse, when the roof jarred under their feet and a crash of strong timbers, followed by a cry of surprise and agony, arose apparently from the courtyard below. He stopped and listened. The cry was repeated. Then came voices lifted in rage blened with voices in prayer and the screams of women in mortal terror. The soldiers had beaten in the north gate and were in possession of the house. His first impulse was to flee—but where?

Tirzah, her eyes wild with fear, caught his arm. "O Judah, what does it mean?"

He thought the servants were being butchered—and his mother! Was not one of the voices he heard hers? With all the will left in him, he said, "Stay here and wait for me, Tirzah. I will go down and see what is the matter and come back to you."

His mother's cry was shrill. He hesitated no longer. "Come, then, let us go."

The terrace at the foot of the steps was crowded with soldiers. At one place a number of women on their knees clung to each other or prayed for mercy. One with torn garments and long hair streaming over her face struggled to tear lose from a man. Her cries were shrillest of all, rising to the roof.

Judah sprang to her—his steps were long and swift, almost a winged flight. "Mother, Mother!" he shouted. She stretched her hands toward him. But as he almost touched them he was seized and forced aside. Then he heard someone say, speaking loudly, "There he is!" Judah looked—and saw Messala.

"What, the assassin—that?" said a tall man, in legionary armor. "Why, he is but a boy."

"Gods!" replied Messala. "A new philosophy! What would Seneca say to the proposition that a man must be old before he can hate enough to kill? You have him, and that is his mother. There is his sister. You have the whole family."

For love of them, Judah forgot his quarrel. "Help them, O my Messala! Remember our childhood and help them. I—Judah—pray you."

Messala pretended not to hear. "I cannot be of further use to you," he said to the officer. "There is richer entertainment in the street. Down Eros, up Mars!"

With the last words he disappeared. Judah understood him and, in the bitterness of his soul, prayed. "In the hour of Your vengeance, O Lord," he said, "be mine the hand to put it upon him!"

By great exertion he drew nearer the officer.

"Sir, the woman is my mother. Spare her, spare my sister. God is just—he will give you mercy for mercy."

The man appeared to be moved. "To the tower with the women!" he shouted. "But do them no harm. I will demand this of you." Then to those holding Judah, he said, "Get cords and bind his hands and take him to the street. His punishment is reserved."

The mother was carried away. Little Tirzah was frozen with fear and went passively with her captors. Judah gave each of them a last look. He may have shed tears, though no one saw them.

The circumstances through which he had come did not bring out the harsher elements of his nature, if such he had. At times he had felt the stir and impulses of ambition, but they had been like the formless dreams of a child walking by the sea and gazing at the coming and going of stately ships. But now it was like an idol, dashed suddenly from its altar. Yet there was no sign that the young Ben Hur had undergone a change, except that when he raised his head and held his arms out to be bound the bend of Cupid's bow had vanished from his lips. In that instant he had put off childhood and become a man.

A trumpet sounded in the courtyard. The gallery was cleared of the soldiers, many of whom, as they dared not appear in the ranks with visible plunder in their hands, flung what they had upon the floor. When Judah descended, the officer waited to see his last order executed.

The mother, daughter, and entire household were led out of the north gate, where ruins cluttered the passageway and the cries of the servants were heard. When the horses and other animals were driven past him, Judah began to comprehend the scope of the procurator's vengeance. Concerning the order of execution, nothing living was to be left within its walls. If in Judea there were others desperate enough to think of assassinating a Roman governor, the story of what befell the princely family of Hur would be a warning to them, while the ruin of the home would keep the story alive.

The officer waited outside while a detail of men temporarily restored the gate. In the street the fighting had almost ceased. Clouds of dust told where the struggle was yet continuing. The cohort was, for the most part, standing at rest, its splendor and its ranks no less diminished. Past the point of caring for himself, Judah was only concerned for the prisoners, and he looked in vain for his mother and Tirzah.

Suddenly a woman arose and ran swiftly back to the gate. Some of the guards reached out to seize her. She ran to Judah and, dropping down, clasped his knees, her coarse, black hair powdered with dust veiling her eyes.

"O Amrah, good Amrah," he said to her. "God help you; I cannot."

She could not speak. He bent down and whispered, "Live, Amrah, for Tirzah and my mother. They will come back and—"

A soldier drew her away. Then she sprang up and rushed through the gateway and passage into the vacant courtyard.

"Let her go," the officer shouted. "We will seal the house, and she will starve."

The men resumed their work and, when it was finished there, passed around to the west side. That gate was also secured, and the palace of the Hurs ceased to function.

The cohort marched back to the Tower, where the procurator stayed to recover from his hurts and dispose of his prisoners. Ten days later he visited the marketplace.

21

A Galley Slave

The next day a detachment of legionnaires went to the deserted palace of the Hurs and, closing the gates permanently, plastered the corners with wax and at the sides nailed a notice in Latin:

THIS IS THE PROPERTY
OF THE EMPEROR

The day after that, about noon, a decurion with his command of ten horsemen approached Nazareth from the south—from the direction of Jerusalem. The place was then a straggling village perched on a hillside and so insignificant that its one street was little more than a path well beaten by the coming and going of flocks and herds. The great plain of Esdraelon crept close to it on the south, and from the height on the west a view could be seen of the shores of the Mediterranean, the region beyond the Jordan, and Hermon. The valley below and the country on every side contained gardens, vineyards, orchards, pastures, and groves of palm trees. The houses were of the humbler class—square, one-story, flat-roofed, and covered with bright green vines. The drought that had burned the hills of Judea to a crisp stopped at the boundary line of Galilee.

A trumpet sounded when the cavalcade drew nearer the village and aroused the inhabitants. Out of the gates and front doors poured forth groups eager to be the first to catch the meaning of this unusual visitation.

A prisoner whom the horsemen were guarding was the object of curiosity. He was on foot, bareheaded, half naked, his hands bound behind him. A thong fixed to his wrists was looped over the neck of a horse. The dust clung to the party, wrapping him in yellow fog and sometimes in a dense cloud. He drooped forward, footsore and faint. The villagers could see he was young.

The decurion halted at the well and, with most of the men, dismounted. The prisoner sank down in the dust of the road, numb, saying nothing, apparently in the last stage of exhaustion. Seeing, when they came near, that he was but a boy, the villagers would have helped him had they dared.

In the midst of their perplexity and while the pitchers were passing among the soldiers, a man was seen coming down the road from Sepphoris. At sight of him a woman cried out, "Look! Here comes the carpenter. Now we will hear something."

He was quite venerable in appearance. Thin, white locks fell below the edge of his full turban, and a mass of still whiter beard flowed down the front of his coarse gray gown. He came slowly, for, in addition to his age, he carried some tools—an axe, a saw, and a drawing knife, all very rude and heavy—and had evidently traveled some distance without rest.

He stopped close by to survey the crowd. "Oh, Rabbi, good Rabbi Joseph!" cried a woman, running to him. "Here is a prisoner. Come, ask the soldiers about him so that we may know who he is and what he has done and what they are going to do with him."

The rabbi's face remained fixed. He glanced at the prisoner, however, and then went to the officer.

"The peace of the Lord be with you!" he said, with gravity.

"And that of the gods with you," the decurion replied.

"Are you from Jerusalem?"

"Yes."

"Your prisoner is young."

"In years, yes."

"May I ask what he has done?"

"He is an assassin."

The people repeated the word in astonishment, but Rabbi Joseph pursued his line of questioning.

"Is he a son of Israel?"

"He is a Jew," said the Roman dryly.

The wavering pity of the bystanders returned.

"I know nothing of your tribes but can speak of his family," the soldier continued. "You may have heard of a prince of Jerusalem named Hur—Ben Hur, they call him. He lived in Herod's day."

"I have seen him," Joseph said.

"Well, this is his son."

There were exclamations throughout the crowd, and the decurion hastened to stop them.

"In the streets of Jerusalem, day before yesterday, he nearly killed the noble Gratus by flinging a tile upon his head from the roof of a palace—his father's, I believe."

There was a pause in the conversation, during which the Nazarenes gazed at the young Ben Hur as at a wild beast.

"Did he kill him?" asked the rabbi.

"No."

"He is under sentence?"

"Yes—the galleys for life."

"The Lord help him!" said Joseph.

Then a youth who came up with Joseph, but had stood behind him unobserved, laid down an ax he had been carrying and, going to the great stone standing by the well, took from it a pitcher of water. The action was so quiet that before the guards could interfere, had they wished to do so, he was stooping over the prisoner and offering him a drink.

The hand laid kindly upon his shoulder awoke the unfortunate Judah, and looking up he saw a face he never forgot—the face of a boy about his own age, shaded by locks of yellowish bright chestnut hair; a face lighted by dark blue eyes, at the time so soft, so appealing, so full of love and holy purpose, that they had all the power of command and will. The spirit of the Jew, hardened though he was by days and nights of suffering and so embittered by wrong that his dreams of revenge took in all the world, melted under the stranger's look and became as a child's. He put his lips to the pitcher and drank long and deep. Not a word was said to him, nor did he say a word.

When the draught was finished, the hand that had been resting upon the sufferer's shoulder was placed upon his head and stayed there in the dusty locks long enough to say a blessing. The stranger then returned the pitcher to its place on a stone and, taking his ax again, went back to Rabbi Joseph. All eyes followed him, the decurion's as well as those of the villagers.

When the men and horses had drunk, the march was resumed. But the mood of the decurion was changed. He himself

raised the prisoner from the dust and helped him on a horse behind a soldier. The Nazarenes went to their houses—among them
Rabbi Joseph and his apprentice.

And so, for the first time, Judah and the son of Mary met and
parted.

22

Quintus Arrius Goes to Sea

The city of Misenum gave the name to the promontory that it crowned, a few miles southwest of Naples. An account of ruins is all that remains of it in the Year of our Lord 24. The place was one of the most important on the western coast of Italy. The Roman government had two harbors in which great fleets were constantly kept—Ravenna and Misenum.

A traveler coming to the promontory to observe the view would have mounted a wall and looked over the bay of Neapolis and seen the matchless shore and the sky and waves so deeply blue—Ischia on one end and Capri at the other. Through the purple air, his gaze would have found half the reserve navy of Rome astir or at anchor below him. Misenum was a very proper place for three masters to meet and at leisure parcel the world among them.

The watchman on the wall above the gateway was disturbed, one cool September morning, by a party coming down the street in noisy conversation. He gave one look, then settled into his reverie again.

There were twenty or thirty persons in the party, the greater number slaves with torches that flamed and smoked, leaving the smell of Indian nard. The masters walked in advance, arm in arm. One of them, around fifty years old, slightly bald and wearing a crown of laurel over his scant locks, seemed, from the attention paid to him, the central object of some affectionate ceremony. They all sported ample togas of white wool broadly bordered with purple. At a glance the watchman knew. He knew, without question, they were of high rank and escorted a friend to a ship after a night of festivity.

"No, my Quintus," said one, speaking to him with the crown. "It is ill of Fortune to take you from us so soon. Only yesterday you returned from the seas beyond the Pillars. Why, you have not even got back your land legs."

"By Castor! If a man may swear a woman's oath," said another, somewhat affected by wine, "let us not be sorry. Our Quintus is but going to find what he lost last night. Dice on a rolling ship is not dice on shore—eh, Quintus?"

"Abuse not Fortune!" exclaimed a third. "She is not blind or fickle. At Antium, where our Arrius questions her, she answers him with nods, and at sea she stays with him, holding the rudder. She takes him from us but does she not always give him back with a new victory?"

"The Greeks are taking him away," another broke in. "Let us abuse them, not the gods. In learning to trade, they forgot how to fight."

The group passed the gateway and came upon the mole, with the beautiful bay before them in the morning light. To the veteran sailor the splash of the waves was like a greeting. He drew a long breath, as if the perfume of the water were sweeter than that of the nard, and held his hand up.

"My gifts were at Praeneste, not Antium—and see! Wind from the west. Thanks, Fortune, my mother!" he said, earnestly.

The friends all repeated this, and the slaves waved their torches.

"She comes—yonder!" he continued, pointing to a galley. "What need has a sailor for another mistress? Is your Lucrece more grateful, my Caius?"

He gazed at the coming ship and confirmed his pride. A white sail was bent low to the mast, and the oars dipped and rose in perfect time.

"Yes, spare the gods," he said, soberly, his eyes on the vessel. "They send us opportunities. It is our fault if we fail. And as for the Greeks, you forget, O my Lentulus, the pirates I am going to punish are Greeks. One victory over them is more important than a hundred over the Africans."

"Then your voyage is to the Aegean?"

The sailor's thoughts were on his ship. "What grace, what freedom! A bird has not less care for the waves. See!" he said, but almost immediately added, "Your pardon, my Lentulus. I am going to the Aegean. And since my departure is so near, I will tell you the occasion. When next you meet him, I would not that you abuse the duumvir.* He is my friend. The trade between Greece and Alexandria, as you may have heard, is hardly inferior to Alexandria and Rome. At all events, the trade is so grown that it will allow for interruption for a day. You may also have heard of the Chersonesana pirates, nested up in the Euxine—none bolder, by the Bacchae! Yesterday word came to Rome that, with a fleet, they had rowed down the Bosphorus, sunk the galleys of Byzantium and Chalsedon, and, still unsatisfied, burst through into the Aegean. The corn merchants who have ships in the East Mediterranean are frightened. They spoke with the emperor himself, and from Ravenna a hundred galleys leave today, and from Misenum"—he paused, as if to arouse the curiosity of his friends and ended with an emphatic—"one."

"Happy Quintus! We congratulate you!"

"The privilege means eventual promotion. We salute you, duumvir—nothing less."

"Quintus Arrius, the duumvir, has a better sound than Quintus Arrius, the tribune."

They showered him with congratulations.

"Thanks, many thanks!" Arrius replied, speaking to them all. "Perpol! I will go further and show what master readers of the future you are!"

From the folds of his toga he took out a roll of paper and passed it to them, saying, "I received this while eating last night—from Sejanus."

The name was already a great one in the Roman world—great and not so infamous as it afterwards became.

"Sejanus!" they exclaimed, with one voice, closing in to read what the minister had written.

Sejanus to C. Caesulius Rufus, Duumvir.

Rome, XIX. Kal. Sept.

Caesar has given good report concerning Quintus Arrius, the tribune. In particular he has heard of his valor, demonstrated in the western seas. It is his will that Quintus be transferred instantly to the East.

* One of two officers or magistrates constituting an executive board in the Roman Republic, appointed for a specific function.

It is our Caesar's will, further, that you cause a hundred ships of the first class and fully appointed to be despatched without delay against the pirates who appeared in the Aegean and that Quintus be sent to command the fleet.

Details are yours, my Caecilius.

The necessity is urgent, as you will be advised by the reports enclosed for your perusal and the information of Quintus.

Sejanus

Arrius paid little attention to the reading. As the ship drew more plainly into view, he became more and more interested in her. Finally he tossed the loosened folds of his toga in the air. In reply to the signal, over the fan-like fixture at the stern of the vessel, a scarlet flag was displayed, while several sailors appeared upon the bulwarks and swung themselves hand over hand up the ropes to the antenna, or yard, and furled the sail. The bow was put round, and the speed of the oars increased one-half so that at racing speed she bore down directly toward him and his friends. His eyes brightened as he observed the maneuvering. Her instant response to the rudder and the steadiness with which she kept her course were especially noticeable as virtues to be relied upon in battle.

"By the Nymphae!" said one of the friends, giving back the roll containing the letter. "We may no longer say our friend will be great. He is already great. Our love will now have famous things to feed upon. What more do you have for us?"

"Nothing more," Arrius replied. "What you know of the affair is by this time old news in Rome, especially between the palace and the Forum. The duumvir is discreet. What I am to do, where to go to find my fleet, he will let me know on the ship, where a sealed package is waiting me. If, however, you have offerings for any of the altars today, pray to the gods for a friend using oar and sail somewhere in the direction of Sicily. But she is here and will come this way," he said, reverting to the vessel. "I have an interest in her masters. They will sail and fight with me. It is not an easy thing to be on the shipside of the shore like this. So let us judge their training and skill."

"Is the ship new to you?"

"I never saw her before, and I do know not if she will bring me one person I know."

115

"Is that well?"

"It matters only a little. We of the sea come to know each other quickly. Our loves, like our hates, come from sudden dangers."

The vessel was long, narrow, low in the water, and modeled for speed and quick maneuvering. The bow was beautiful. A jet of water spun from its foot as she came on, sprinkling all the prow, which rose in graceful curves twice a man's stature above the floor of the deck. In the front were figures of Triton blowing shells.

Except for the sailors who had reefed the sail and lingered on the yard, only one man was to be seen by the party on the mole, and he stood by the prow helmeted and with a shield. The hundred and twenty oaken blades rose and fell as if operated by the same hand and drove the galley forward with a speed rivaling that of a later steamer.

So rapidly did she come forward that the landsmen of the tribune's party were alarmed. Suddenly the man by the prow raised his hand with a peculiar gesture. All the oars flew up, poised a moment in air, then fell straight down. The water boiled and bubbled around them. The galley shook in every timber. With another gesture of the hand the ship swung around to the right, then caught by the wind she settled gently broadside to the mole.

The movement brought the stern to view, with all its ornaments—Tritons like those at the bow; the name in large raised letters; the rudder at the side; the elevated platform upon which the helmsman sat, a stately figure in full armor, his hand upon the rudder rope.

In the midst of the turning, a trumpet was blown brief and shrill, and out poured the marines from the hatchways, all in superb equipment, brazen helms, burnished shields, and javelins. While the fighting men went to quarters ready for action, the sailors themselves climbed the shrouds and perched themselves along the yard. The officers and musicians took their posts. When the oars touched the mole, a bridge was sent out from the helmsman's deck.

The tribune turned to his party and said with a seriousness he had not before shown: "Duty now, my friends."

He took the wreath from his head and gave it to the dice player. "You take the myrtle!" he said. "If I return, I will seek my money again. If I am not victor, I will not return. Hang the crown in your hallway."

He opened his arms to the company, and they came one by one and received his parting embrace.

"The gods go with you, O Quintus!" they said.

"Farewell," he replied.

To the slaves waving their torches he waved his hand. Then he turned to the waiting ship, beautiful with its ordered ranks and crested helms and shields and javelins. As he stepped upon the bridge the trumpets sounded, and the flag of the commander of the fleet rose over them.

23

At the Oar

The tribune, standing upon the helmsman's deck with the order of the duumvir open in his hand, spoke to the chief of the rowers.

"What force do you have?"

"Two hundred and fifty-two oarsmen, ten supernumeraries."

"Making reliefs of—"

"Eighty-four."

"And your habit?"

"It has been to take off and put on every two hours."

The tribune thought a moment. "The division is hard, and I will revise it, but not now. The oars may not rest day or night." Then to the sailing master he said, "The wind is fair. Let the sail help the oars."

When the two addressed were gone, he turned to the chief pilot. "What service have you had?"

"Thirty-two years."

"In what seas chiefly?"

"Between our Rome and the East."

"You are the man I would have chosen."

The tribune looked at his orders again.

"Past the Camponellan cape, the course will be to Messina. Beyond that, follow the bend of the Calabrian shore till Melito is on your left, then—do you know the stars that govern in the Ionian Sea?"

"I know them well."

"Then from Melito course eastward for Cythera. The gods willing, I will not anchor until in the Bay of Antemona. The duty is urgent. I rely on you."

Arrius was a prudent man and of the class that, while enriching the altars at Praeneste and Antium was of the opinion, nevertheless, that the favor of the blind goddess depended more upon the devotee's care and judgment than upon his gifts and vows. All night, as master of the feast, he had sat at the table drinking and playing. Yet the odor of the sea returned him to the mood of the sailor, and he would not rest until he knew his ship.

Knowledge leaves no room for chances. Having begun with the chief of the rowers, the sailing master, and the pilot, in company with the other officers—the commander of the marines, the keeper of the stores, the master of the machines, the overseer of the kitchen—he passed through the several quarters.

Nothing escaped his attention. When he went through, of all the community crowded within the narrow walls he alone knew perfectly all there was of material preparation for the voyage and its possible dangers. And, finding the preparation complete, there was left only one thing further—thorough knowledge of the staff at his command. As this was the most delicate and difficult part of his task, requiring much time, he went about it in his own way.

At noon that day the galley was skimming the sea off Paestum. The wind was still coming from the west, filling the sail to the master's content. The watches had been established. On the foredeck the altar had been set and sprinkled with salt and barley, and before it the tribune had offered solemn prayers to Jove and to Neptune and all the Oceanidae and, with vows, poured the wine and burned the incense. And now, to better study his men, he was seated in the great cabin, appearing to be a very martial figure.

The cabin was the central compartment of the galley, lighted by three broad hatchways. A row of stanchions ran from end to end, supporting the roof, and near the center the mast was visible, all bristling with axes and spears and javelins. This was the heart of the ship, the home of the eating-room, sleeping-chamber, field of exercise, lounging-place off duty—uses made possible by the laws that reduced life there to minute details and a routine relentless as death.

Upon the platform above the chief of the rowers sat. In front of him was a sounding table, and with a gavel he beat time for the oarsmen. At his right was a water-clock to measure the reliefs and watches. Above him, on a higher platform, well guarded by gilded railing, the tribune had his quarters, overlooking everything and furnished with a couch, a table, and a cushioned chair—articles that the imperial dispensation permitted to be of the utmost elegance.

At ease, lounging in the great chair, swaying with the motion of the vessel, with the military cloak half draping his tunic and his sword in his belt, Arrius kept watchful eye over his command and was as closely watched by them. He critically saw everything in view but looked longest upon the rowers.

As to the rowers, those upon the first and second benches sat, while those upon the third, having longer oars to work, were forced to stand. The oars were loaded with lead in the handles and near the point of balance hung to pliable thongs, making possible the delicate touch called feathering, but at the same time increasing the need of skill, since a large wave might at any moment catch a heedless rower and hurl him from his seat.

Each oarhole was a vent through which the laborer at the other end had plenty of cool air. Light streamed down upon him from the grating that formed the floor of the passage between the deck and the bulwark over his head. In some respects, therefore, the condition of the men might have been much worse. Still, it must not be imagined that there was any pleasantness in their lives.

Communication between them was not allowed. Day after day they filled their places without speech. In hours of labor they could not see each other's faces. Their short respites were given to sleep and the snatching of food. They never laughed. No one ever heard one of them sing. What is the use of tongues when a sigh or a groan will tell what all men feel while, by force, they think in silence? Existence for the poor wretches was like a stream underground sweeping slowly, laboriously on to its outlet, wherever that might chance to be.

In those days, for captives there was drudgery on the walls, in the streets and mines, and the galleys both of war and commerce were neverending. When Druilus won the first sea fight for his country, Romans manned the oars, and the glory went to the rower not less than the marine. These benches testified to the change that comes with conquest and illustrated both the policy and the prowess of Rome.

Nearly all nations had sons there, mostly prisoners of war, chosen for their brawn and endurance: in one place a Briton; before him a Libyan; behind him a Crimean; elsewhere a Scythian and a Gaul. Roman convicts were cast down to consort with Goths, Jews, Ethiopians, and barbarians from the shores of Maeotis. Here an Athenian, there a red-haired savage from Hibernia or blue-eyed giant of the Cimbri.

In the labor of the rowers there was not enough art to occupy their minds, rude and simple as they were. Even the care forced upon them by the sea outside grew in time to be an instinctive thing. So, as the result of long service, the poor wretches became spiritless, obedient—creatures of vast muscle and exhausted intellects, who lived upon generally few but dear recollections.

From right to left, hour after hour, the tribune, swaying in his easy chair, thought of everything other than the wretchedness of the slaves upon the benches. Their motions became monotonous after a while. Then he amused himself by singling out individuals. With his stylus he made notes of objections, thinking, if all went well, he would find better men for the places among the pirates.

There was no need for keeping the proper names of the slaves brought to the galleys as to their graves. So for convenience they were usually identified by the numerals painted upon the benches to which they were assigned. As the sharp eyes of the great man moved from seat to seat on either hand, they numbered sixty.

The bench of the man known as number sixty was slightly above the level of the platform and but a few feet away. The light glinting through the grating over his head brought the rower into the tribune's view—erect and, like all his fellows, naked, except a covering about the loins. There were, however, some points in his favor. He was very young, not more than twenty. Furthermore, Arrius was not merely given to dice; he was a connoisseur of men physically and when ashore indulged a habit of visiting the gymnasium to see and admire the most famous athletes. Doubtless from someone he had discovered the idea that strength was as much of the quality as the quantity of muscle, while superiority in performance required a certain mind as well as strength. Having adopted this belief, like most men with a hobby he was always looking for illustrations to support it.

The particular movement of the oars certainly proved the rower's art and put the critic in the great armchair in search of the combination of strength and cleverness that was his way of judging performance.

In the course of his observations, Arrius noticed the youth of one especially competent rower. He also recognized that he was of good height and that his limbs, both upper and lower, were each perfect. The arms were, perhaps, too long but that was well hidden under a mass of muscle swelling and knotting like kinking cords. Every rib in his round body was noticeable. In this rower's action there was a certain harmony that confirmed the tribune's theory and stimulated both his curiosity and general interest.

He waited to catch a view of the man's face in full. The head was shapely and balanced upon a broad neck, yet of exceeding grace. The features in profile were of an Eastern outline and contained a delicacy of expression that has always been thought a sign of a sensitive spirit. With these observations, the tribune's interest in the subject deepened.

"By the gods," he said to himself, "the fellow impresses me! He promises to do well. I want to know more of him."

Immediately the tribune caught the view he wished—the rower turned and looked at him.

"A Jew! And a boy!"

Under the gaze fixed steadily on him, the large eyes of the slave grew larger—the blood surged to his very brows—the blade lingered in his hands. But instantly, with an angry crash, the gavel of the foreman fell. The rower was startled, turned away from the inquisitor and, as if personally rebuked, dropped the half-feathered oar. When he glanced again at the tribune, he was quite astonished—he was met with a kindly smile.

Meantime the galley entered the Straits of Messina and skimming past the city turned eastward, leaving the cloud in the sky over Aetna on the stern side.

As often as Arrius returned to his platform in the cabin he returned to study the rower, and he kept saying to himself, "The fellow has a spirit. A Jew is not a barbarian. I wish to know more of him."

122

24

Arrius and Ben Hur on Deck

The fourth day out, the *Astraea*—as the galley was named—sped through the Ionian Sea. The sky was clear, and the wind blew as if bearing the goodwill of all the gods.

Since it was possible to overtake the fleet before reaching the bay east of the island of Cythera, Arrius became impatient and spent a lot of time on deck. He took note diligently of matters pertaining to his ship and, as a rule, was well pleased. In the cabin, revolving in the great chair, he thought continually of the rower on number sixty.

"Do you know the man who just came from that bench?" he at length asked the foreman. A break was going on at that moment.

"From number sixty?" returned the chief.

"Yes."

The chief looked sharply at the rower, walking forward.

"As you know," he replied, "the ship is only a month old, and the men are as new to me as the ship."

"He is a Jew," Arrius remarked thoughtfully.

"The noble Quintus is shrewd."

"He is very young," Arrius continued.

"But our best rower," said the other. "I have seen his oar bend almost to the breaking point."

"How is his attitude?"

"He is obedient. I don't know more. Once he made a request of me."

"For what?"

"He wishes me to change him alternately from the right to the left of the ship."

"Did he give a reason?"

"He had observed that the men who are confined to one side become misshapen. He also said that some day when there is a storm or battle there might be a sudden need to change him, and he might then be unusable."

"Perpol! The idea is new. What else have you observed of him?"

"He is cleanly above his companions."

"In that he is Roman," said Arrius approvingly. "Have you nothing of his history?"

"Not a word."

The tribune reflected a while and turned to go to his own seat. "If I should be on deck when his time is up," he paused to say, "send him to me. Let him come alone."

About two hours later Arrius stood under the galley with the attitude of one who, seeing himself carried swiftly toward an event of great importance, has nothing to do but wait—with the utmost calm, ready for anything. The pilot sat with a hand upon the rope by which the rudder paddles, one on each side of the vessel. In the shade of the sail some sailors lay asleep, and up on the yard there was a lookout.

Lifting his eyes from the solarium set for reference in keeping the course, Arrius saw the rower approaching.

"The chief called you the noble Arrius and said it was your will that I should seek you here. I have come."

Arrius surveyed the figure, tall, sinewy, glistening in the sun and tinted by the rich red blood within—surveyed him admiringly and with a thought of the gladiator in the arena. Yet his manner was not without effect: there was in his voice a suggestion of life at least partly spent under refining influences. The eyes were clear and more curious than defiant. To the shrewd, demanding, masterful glance bent upon it, the face gave back nothing to mar its youthful, handsome qualities—nothing of accusation or sullenness or menace, only the signs that a great long-borne sorrow imprints, as time mellows the surface of pictures. In tacit acknowledgment of this impression, the Roman spoke as an older man to a younger, not as a master to a slave.

"The foreman tells me you are his best rower."

"The foreman is very kind," the rower answered.

"Have you seen much service?"

"About three years."

"At the oars?"

"I cannot recall a day of rest from them."

"The labor is hard. Few men bear it even a year without breaking, and you are but a boy."

"The noble Arrius forgets that the spirit has much to do with endurance. By its help the weak sometimes thrive, when the strong perish."

"From your speech, you are a Jew."

"My ancestors further back than the first Roman were Hebrews."

"The stubborn pride of your race is not lost in you," said Arrius, observing a flush upon the rower's face.

"Pride is never so loud as when in chains."

"What cause do you have for pride?"

"That I am a Jew."

Arrius smiled. "I have not been to Jerusalem," he said, "but I have heard of its princes. I knew one of them. He was a merchant and sailed the seas. He was fit to have been a king. Of what class are you?"

"I must answer you from the bench of a galley. I am of the class of slaves. My father was a prince of Jerusalem, and as a merchant he sailed the seas. He was known and honored in the guest chamber of the great Augustus."

"His name?"

"Ithanar, of the house of Hur."

The tribune raised his hand in astonishment. "A son of Hur—you?"

After a silence, he asked, "What brought you here?"

Judah lowered his head, and his breath labored hard. When his feelings were sufficiently mastered, he looked the tribune in the face and answered, "I was accused of attempting to assassinate Valerius Gratus, the procurator."

"You!" cried Arrius, yet more amazed and retreating a step. "You were that assassin! All Rome rang with the story. It came to my ship in the river by Lodinum."

The two regarded each other silently. "I thought the family of Hur was blotted from the earth," said Arrius, speaking first.

A flood of tender recollections carried the young man's pride away, and tears shone upon his cheeks. "Mother—Mother! And my little Tirzah! Where are they? O tribune, noble tribune, if you know anything of them"—he clasped his hands in appeal—"tell me all you know. Tell me if they are living—if living, where are they? And in what condition? Oh, I pray you, tell me!" He drew nearer Arrius, so near that his hands touched the cloak where it dropped from the latter's folded arms.

"The horrible day is three years gone," he continued. "Three years, O tribune, and every hour a whole lifetime of misery—a lifetime in a bottomless pit with death and no relief but in labor—and in all that time not a word from anyone, not a whisper. Oh, if, in being forgotten, we could only forget! If only I could hide from that scene—my sister torn away from me, my mother's last look! I have felt the plague's breath and the shock of ships in battle. I have heard the tempest lashing the sea and laughed, though others prayed. Death would have been a relief. Bend the oar—yes, in the strain of mighty effort trying to escape the haunting of what that day occurred.

"Tell me they are dead, if no more, for they cannot be happy while I am lost. I have heard them call me in the night. I have seen them walking on the water. Oh, there was never anything so true as my mother's love! And Tirzah—her breath was as the breath of white lilies. She was the youngest branch of the palm—so fresh, so tender, so graceful, so beautiful! She made my day all morning. She came and went in music. And mine was the hand that laid them low! I—"

"Do you admit your guilt?" asked Arrius sternly.

The change that came upon Ben Hur was wonderful to see, it was so instant and extreme. His voice sharpened. His hands arose tight clenched. Every fiber thrilled. His eyes flamed.

"You have heard of the God of my fathers," he said. "Of the infinite Jehovah. By his truth and almightiness and by the love with which he has followed Israel from the beginning, I swear I am innocent!"

The tribune was much moved.

"O noble Roman!" continued Ben Hur. "Give me a little faith, and into my darkness, deeper darkening every day, send a light!"

Arrius turned away and walked the deck. "Did you have a trial?" he asked, stopping suddenly.

126

"No."

The Roman raised his head, surprised.

"No trial—no witnesses? Who passed judgment on you?" Romans were at no time such lovers of the law and its forms as in the ages of their decay.

"They bound me with cords and dragged me to a vault in the Tower. I saw no one. No one spoke to me. The next day soldiers took me to the seaside. I have been a galley slave ever since."

"What could you have proven?"

"I was a boy, too young to be a conspirator. Gratus was a stranger to me. If I had meant to kill him, that was not the time or the place. He was riding in the midst of a legion, and it was broad daylight. I could not have escaped. I was of a class most friendly to Rome. My father had been distinguished for his services to the emperor. We had a great estate to lose. Ruin was certain to myself, my mother, my sister. I had no cause for malice, while every consideration—property, family, life, conscience, the law—to a son of Israel as the breath of his nostrils—would have kept my hand from doing wrong, even if the foul intent had been ever so strong. I was not mad. Death was preferable to shame. And believe me, I pray it is so yet."

"Who was with you when the blow was struck?"

"I was on the housetop—my father's house. Tirzah was with me—at my side—the soul of gentleness. Together we leaned over the parapet to see the legion pass. A tile gave way under my hand and fell upon Gratus. I thought I had killed him. Ah, what horror I felt!"

"Where was your mother?"

"In her chamber below."

"What became of her?"

Ben Hur clenched his hands and drew a breath like a gasp. "I do not know. I saw them drag her away—that's all I know. Out of the house they drove every living thing, even the dumb cattle, and they sealed the gates. The purpose was that she should not return. I too ask for her. Oh, for one word! She, at least, was innocent. I can forgive—but I pray your pardon, noble tribune! A slave like me should not talk of forgiveness or of revenge. I am bound to an oar for life."

127

Arrius listened intently. He brought all his experience with slaves to his aid. If the feeling shown in this instance were assumed, the acting was perfect. On the other hand, if it were real, the Jew's innocence might not be doubted. And if he were innocent, with what blind fury the power had been exercised! A whole family blotted out to atone for one accident! The thought shocked him.

Our occupations, however rude or bloody, do not always wear us out morally. Such qualities as justice and mercy, if they really possess us, continue to live on under them, like flowers under the snow. The tribune could be stern or else he would not be fit for the roles of his occupation. He could also be just, and to arouse his sense of wrong was to allow him to right the wrong. The crews of the ships in which he served came after a time to speak of him as the good tribune.

In this instance there were many circumstances certainly in the young man's favor and some to be supposed. Possibly Arrius knew Valerius Gratus without approving of him. Possibly he had known the elder Hur. In the course of his appeal Judah had asked him that, and he had made no reply.

For once the tribune was at loss and hesitated. His power was ample. He was monarch of the ship. His inclinations all moved him to mercy. His belief was won. Yet, he said to himself, there was no haste—or, rather, there was haste to get to Cythera. The best rower could not then be spared. He would wait. He would learn more. He would at least be sure this was the prince Ben Hur and that he was of a proper character. Ordinarily slaves were liars.

"It is enough," he said. "Go back to your place."

Ben Hur bowed, looked once more into the master's face, but saw nothing for hope. He turned away slowly, looked back, and said, "If you do think of me again, O tribune, let it not be forgotten that I asked you only for word of my people—mother, sister." He moved on.

Arrius followed him with admiring eyes. "Perpol!" he pondered. "With teaching, what a man for the arena! What a runner! Ye gods! What an arm for the sword or the mace! Stay!" he said aloud.

Ben Hur stopped, and the tribune went to him. "If you were free, what would you do?"

"The noble Arrius mocks me!" Judah said, with trembling lips.

"No. By the gods, no!"

"Then I will answer gladly. I would give myself to duty first. I would know no other. I would know no rest until my mother and Tirzah were restored to home. I would give every day and hour to their happiness. I would wait upon them. A slave never more faithful. They have lost much, but, by the God of my fathers, I would give them more!"

The answer was unexpected by the Roman. For a moment he forgot his purpose.

"I spoke of your ambition," he said, recovering. "If your mother and sister were dead, or not to be found, what would you do?"

A distinct paleness overspread Ben Hur's face, and he looked over the sea. There was a struggle with some strong feeling. When it was conquered, he turned to the tribune. "What pursuit would I follow?" he asked.

"Yes."

"Tribune, I will tell you truly. Only the night before the dreadful day of which I have spoken, I obtained permission to be a soldier. I am of the same mind yet. And, as in all the earth there is but one school of war, there I would go."

"The Palaestra!" exclaimed Arrius.

"No. A Roman camp."

"But you must first acquaint yourself with the use of arms."

Now a master may never safely advise a slave. Arrius saw his indiscretion and, in a breath, restrained his voice and manner. "Go now," he said, "and do not expect anything from what has passed between us. Perhaps I only play with you. Or"—he looked away musingly—"if you do think of it with any hope, choose between the renown of a gladiator and the service of a soldier. The former may come with more favor from the emperor. There is no reward for you in the latter. You are not a Roman. Go!"

A short while after Ben Hur was upon his bench again. A man's task is always light if his heart is light. Handling the oar did not seem so toilsome to Judah. A hope had come to him, like a singing bird. He could hardly see the visitor or hear its song. That it was there, though, he knew. His feelings told him so. The caution of the tribune—"Perhaps I only play with you"—was dismissed as often as it recurred to his mind. That he had been called by the great man and asked his story was the bread upon which he fed his hungry spirit. Surely something good would come of it.

The light about his bench was clear and bright with promises, and he prayed, "O God! I am a true son of the Israel You have so loved! Help me, I pray You!"

25

Number 60

In the Bay of Antemona, east of Cythera the island, the hundred galleys assembled. There the tribune one day inspected them. He sailed then to Naxos, the largest of the Cyclades, midway between the coasts of Greece and Asia, like a great stone planted in the center of a highway, from which he could challenge everything that passed. At the same time he would be in position to go after the pirates instantly, whether they were in the Aegean or out on the Mediterranean.

As the fleet, in order, rowed in toward the mountain shores of the island, a galley was spotted coming from the north. Arrius went to meet it. She proved to be a transport just from Byzantium, and from her commander he learned the particulars of which he needed most.

The pirates were from the farther shores of the Euxine. Their preparations had been done with the greatest secrecy. Their first appearance was off the entrance to the Thracian Bosphorus, followed by the destruction of the fleet there. Everything afloat had fallen their prey at the outlet of the Hellespont. There were sixty galleys in the squadron, all well manned and supplied. A Greek was in command, and the pilots, said to be familiar with all the Eastern seas, were Greek. The plunder had been incalculable. The panic, consequently, was not on the sea alone. Cities, with closed gates, sent their people nightly to the walls. Traffic had almost ceased.

Where were the pirates now? To this question Arrius received an answer. After sacking Hephaestia, on the island of Lemnos, the enemy had sailed across to the Thessalian group and, by last account, disappeared in the gulfs between Euboea and Hellas.

Then the people of the island, drawn to the hilltops by the rare spectacle of a hundred ships sailing in united squadron, saw the advance division suddenly turn to the north and the others follow, wheeling upon the same point like cavalry in a column.

News of the pirates' descent had reached them, and now, watching the white sails until they faded from sight between Rhene and Syros, the perceptive among them took comfort and were grateful. What Rome seized with a strong hand she always defended. In return for their taxes, she gave them safety.

The tribune was more than pleased with the enemy's movements. He was doubly thankful to Fortune. She had brought swift and sure intelligence and had lured his foes into the waters where, of all other seas, destruction was most assured. He knew the havoc one galley could play in a broad sea like the Mediterranean and the difficulty of finding and overhauling her. He knew, also, how those very circumstances would enhance the service and glory, if at one blow he could put a finish to the entire army of the pirates.

The towns along the Pelasgic and Meliac gulfs were rich and had seductive plunder. All things considered, therefore, Arrius judged that the robbers might be found somewhere below Thermopylae. Welcoming the chance, he resolved to enclose them from the north and south, and not an hour could be lost. Even the fruits and wines and women of Naxos must be left behind. So he sailed away without stopping until, a little before nightfall, Mount Ocha was seen upreared against the sky, and the pilot reported the Euboean coast.

At a signal the fleet rested its oars. When the movement was resumed, Arrius led a division of fifty of the galleys, intending to take them up the channel, while another division, equally strong, turned their prows to the outer or seaward side of the island, with orders to make all haste to the upper inlet and sweep the waters.

To be sure, neither division was equal in number to the pirates. But each had advantages to compensate for this, among them a discipline impossible to be found among a lawless horde, however brave. Besides, it was a shrewd count on the tribune's side—if one should be defeated, the other would find the enemy shattered by his victory and in a condition to be easily overwhelmed.

Meanwhile Ben Hur kept his bench, relieved every six hours. The rest in the Bay of Antemona had freshened him, so that the oar was not troublesome, and the chief on the platform found no fault with him.

The sensation of being lost is distressful. Still worse is the feeling of driving blindly into unknown places. But the feeling had dulled with Ben Hur. Pulling away, sometimes days and nights together, the longing to know where he was and where he was going, was always present with him.

But now it seemed stronger because of the hope that had come to life in his heart since the interview with the tribune. He seemed to hear every sound of the ship in labor and listened to each one as if it were a voice come to tell him something. He looked to the grating overhead, and through it into his small portion of light, expecting, he knew not what. And many times he caught himself yielding to the impulse to speak to the chief on the platform. No circumstance of battle would have astonished the dignitary more.

In his long service, by watching the shifting of the meager sunbeams upon the cabin floor when the ship was under way, he had come to know, generally, the quarter into which she was sailing. This, of course, was only on clear days like those good fortune was sending the tribune. Thinking they were heading toward the old Judean country, he was sensitive to every variation northward.

It must be remembered that, in common with his fellow slaves, he knew nothing of the voyage and had no interest in it. His place was at the oar, and he was held there irresistibly, whether at anchor or under sail. Once only in three years, in his interview with Arrius, had be been permitted an outlook from the deck. He had no idea that following the vessel he was helping drive was a great squadron close at hand and in beautiful order. Nor did he know the object of which it was in pursuit.

When the sun, going down, withdrew its last ray from the cabin, the galley still went northward. Night fell—yet Ben Hur could discern no change. About that time the smell of incense floated down the gangways from the deck.

The tribune is at the altar, he thought. *Can it be we are going into battle?* He became observant.

Now he had been in many battles without having seen one. From his bench he had heard them above and about him, until he was familiar with all their notes, almost as a singer with a song. He had become acquainted with many of the preliminary rituals of an engagement, of which, with a Roman as well as a Greek, the most invariable was the sacrifice to the gods. The rites were the same as those performed at the beginning of a voyage, and to him, when noticed, they were always a preparation.

A battle, it should be observed, was for him and his fellow slaves of the oar an interest unlike that of the sailor and marine. It appeared, not because of the danger encountered, but of the fact that defeat, if survived, might bring an alteration of condition— possibly freedom—at least a change of masters, which might be for the better.

In good time the lanterns were lit and hung by the stairs, and the tribune came down from the deck. At his word the marines put on their armor. At his word again, the machines were gotten ready, and spears, javelins, and arrows in great sheaves were brought and laid upon the floor, together with jars of inflammable oil and baskets of cotton balls wound loose like the wicks of candles. Then, finally, Ben Hur saw the tribune mount his platform and don his armor and get his helmet and shield out. The meaning of the preparations might not be any longer doubted.

To every bench, as a fixture, there was a chain with heavy anklets. These the foreman began to lock upon the oarsmen, leaving no choice but to obey and, in event of disaster, no possibility of escape.

In the cabin a silence fell, broken only by the sound of the oars turning in the leather cases. Every man upon the benches felt shame, Ben Hur more keenly than his companions. He would have gotten rid of it at any price. Soon the clanking of the fetters notified him of the progress the chief was making in his round. He would come to him in turn. But would the tribune interpose for him?

Perhaps vanity or selfishness at that moment took possession of Ben Hur. He believed the Roman would interpose on his behalf. Anyhow, the circumstances would test his feelings. If, intent upon the battle, he would but think of him, it would be proof of his opinion—proof that he had been tacitly promoted above his associates in misery—such proof as would justify his hope.

Ben Hur waited anxiously. The time seemed like an age. At every turn of the oar he looked toward the tribune, who, his preparations made, lay down upon the couch and rested. Whereupon number sixty scolded himself, laughed grimly, and resolved not to look that way again.

The foreman approached. Now he was at number one—the rattle of the iron links sounded horribly. At last number sixty. Calm from despair, Ben Hur held his oar and gave his foot to the officer. Then the tribune stirred, sat up, and beckoned to the chief.

A strong revulsion seized the Jew. From the foreman the great man glanced at him. And when he dropped his oar the entire section of the ship on his side seemed to glow. He heard nothing of what was said. The notes of the gavel were never so like music. He pushed the oar with all his might—pushed until the shaft bent as if about to break.

The chief went to the tribune and, smiling, pointed to number sixty. "What strength!" he said.

"And what spirit!" the tribune answered. "Perpol! He is better without the irons. Put them on him no more."

The ship sailed on hour after hour under the oars in water scarcely rippled by the wind. And the people not on duty slept.

Ben Hur was relieved, but he could not sleep. Three years of night and through the darkness a sunbeam at last! At sea adrift and lost, and now land! Dead so long, and the thrill and stir of resurrection. Sleep was not for such an hour. Sorrows relieved; his home and the fortunes of his house restored; mother and sister in his arms once more—these were the most important hopes that made him happier that moment than he had ever been. That he was rushing, as on wings, into horrible battle had, for the time, nothing to do with his thoughts. His joy was so full, so perfect, that there was no room in his heart for revenge. Messala, Gratus, Rome, and all the bitter, passionate memories connected with them, were as dead plagues—swamps of the earth above which he floated, far and safe, listening to singing stars.

The deeper darkness before the dawn was upon the waters, when a man, descending from the deck, walked swiftly to the platform where the tribune slept and awoke him. Arrius arose, put on his helmet, sword, and shield, and went to the commander of the marines.

"The pirates are close by. Up and ready!" he said and went to the stairs, calm and confident.

26

The Sea Fight

Every soul aboard awoke. Officers went to their quarters. The marines took arms and were led out, looking in all respects like legionnaires. Sheaves of arrows and armfuls of javelins were carried on deck. The oil tanks and fireballs by the central stairs were set ready for use. Additional lanterns were lighted. Buckets were filled with water. The rowers in relief assembled under guard in front of the chief.

As providence would have it, Ben Hur was one of the latter. Overhead he heard the muffled voices for the final preparations—of the sailors furling sail, spreading the nettings, unslinging the machines, and hanging the armor of bullhide over the sides.

A sound like the rowing of galleys astern attracted Ben Hur, and the *Astraea* rocked as if in the midst of countering waves. The idea of a fleet at hand occurred to him—a fleet in maneuver—forming probably for attack. His blood surged with this realization.

Another signal came down from the deck. The oars dipped, and the galley started imperceptibly. There was no sound from without and none from within, yet each man in the cabin seemed instinctively poised himself for a shock. The very ship seemed to catch this sense and hold its breath and go forward tigerlike.

In such a situation, time stands still. Ben Hur could form no judgment of the distance gone. At last there was a sound of trumpets on deck, full and clear. The chief beat the sounding board until it rang. The rowers reached forward full length and, deepening the dip of their oars, pulled suddenly with all their united efforts. The galley, shaking in every timber, answered with a leap. Other trumpets joined in the clamor—all from the rear—from the latter quarter there was only a rising sound of voices.

There was a mighty blow. The rowers in front of the chief's platform reeled, and some of them fell. The ship bounded back, recovered, and rushed on more irresistibly than before. The shrieks of men in terror, shrill and high, rose over the blare of trumpets and the grind and crash of the collision. Then under his feet, under the keel, pounding, rumbling, breaking to pieces, Ben Hur felt something happen. The men about him looked at each other. A shout of triumph from the deck—the beak of the Roman had won! But who were they whom the sea had drunk? Of what tongue, from what land were they?

The *Astraea* rushed forward, and as it went some sailors ran down and, plunging cotton balls into the oil tanks, tossed them dripping to comrades at the head of the stairs where fire was to be added.

Directly the galley heeled over so far that the oarsmen on the uppermost side kept their benches with difficulty. Again the hearty Roman cheer, and with it despairing shrieks. An opposing vessel, caught by the grappling hooks of the great crane swinging from the prow, was being lifted into the air so that it might be dropped and sunk.

The shouting increased on both sides. Occasionally there was a crash, followed by sudden peals of fright, telling of other ships conquered and their crews drowned in the deeps.

Nor was the fight all on one side. Now and then a Roman in armor was carried down the hatchway and laid bleeding, sometimes dying, on the floor.

Sometimes, also, puffs of smoke blended with steam and, foul with the scent of roasting human flesh, poured into the cabin, turning the dimming light into yellow murk. Gasping for breath, Ben Hur knew they were passing through the cloud of a ship on fire and burning up with the rowers chained to the benches.

Suddenly the *Astraea* stopped. The forward oars were dashed from the hands of the rowers, and the rowers from their benches. On deck, there was a furious trampling and on the sides a grinding of ships into each other. Men sank on the floor in fear or looked about seeking a hiding place.

In the midst of the panic a body plunged or was pitched headlong down the hatchway, falling near Ben Hur. He beheld the half-naked carcass, a mass of hair blackening the face, and under it a shield of bullhide and wickerwork—a barbarian from the white-skinned nations of the North whom death had robbed of plunder and revenge.

How did he come here? An iron hand had snatched him from the opposing deck—no, the *Astraea* had been boarded! The Romans were fighting on their own deck? A chill smote the young Jew. Arrius was hard-pressed—he might be defending his own life. If he should be slain! *God of Abraham, intervene!* The hopes and dreams that had so lately come, were they only hopes and dreams? Mother and sister—house—home—Holy Land—was he not to see them after all?

The tumult thundered above him. He looked around. In the cabin all was confusion—the rowers on the benches paralyzed; men running blindly here and there; only the foreman sat on his seat immovable, vainly beating the sounding board and waiting the orders of the tribune—in the red murk illustrating the matchless discipline that had conquered the world.

The example had a good effect upon Ben Hur. He controlled himself enough to think. Honor and duty bound the Roman to the platform. But what had he to do with such motives then? The bench was a thing to run from. If he were to die a slave, who would be the better for the sacrifice? With him living was duty, if not honor. His life belonged to his people. They arose before him ever so real: he saw them, their arms outstretched. He heard them imploring him. And he would go to them. He started —stopped. A Roman judgment held him in doom. While it endured, escape would be profitless. In the whole earth there was no place in which he would be safe from the imperial demand— upon land or sea. He required freedom according to the forms of law, so he could only abide in Judea and fulfill the purpose for his family to which he would devote himself. In other lands he would not live.

Dear God! How he had waited and watched and prayed for such a release! And how it had been delayed! But at last he had seen it in the promise of the tribune. What else could the great man's meaning be? And what if the recent benefactor should now be slain! The dead do not come back to redeem the pledges of the living. It should not be—Arrius should not die. At least, better perish with him than survive a galley slave.

Once more Ben Hur looked around. Upon the roof of the cabin the battle yet raged. Against the sides the hostile vessels yet crushed. On the benches the slaves struggled to tear loose from their chains and, finding their effort in vain, howled like madmen. The guards had gone upstairs. Discipline was out, and panic took over. No, the foreman kept his chair, unchanged, calm as ever. Except for the gavel, he was weaponless. Ben Hur gave him a last look, then broke away—not in flight, but to seek the tribune.

A very short space lay between him and the stairs of the hatchway. He took it with a leap and was half-way up the steps—up far enough to catch a glimpse of the sky blood-red with fire and the ships alongside, the sea covered with ships and wrecks.

The fight closed in about the pilot's quarter, when suddenly his foothold was knocked away, and he pitched backward. The floor, when he reached it, seemed to be lifting itself and breaking to pieces. Then, in a twinkling, the whole afterpart of the hull broke asunder, as if it had all the time been lying in wait. The sea, hissing and foaming, leaped in, and all became darkness and surging water.

It cannot be said that the young Jew helped himself in this stress. Besides his usual strength, he had the indefinite extra force that nature keeps in reserve for just such perils to life. Yet the darkness and the whirl and roar of water numbed him.

The influx of the flood tossed him forward like a log into the cabin, where he might have drowned. As it was, fathoms under the surface the hollow mass vomited him forth, and he arose along with the loosened debris. In the act of rising he clutched something and held to it. The time he was under seemed like an age. At last he gained the top. With a great gasp he filled his lungs and, tossing the water from his hair and eyes, climbed higher on the plank he held and looked around him.

Death had pursued him closely under the waves. He found it waiting for him when he was risen also. Smoke lay upon the sea like a semitransparent fog, with pockets of intense brilliance. He realized that they were ships on fire. The battle was still going on. None could say who was victor. Within the radius of his vision now and then ships passed, shooting their shadows. Farther on he caught the crash of other ships colliding.

The danger, however, was closer at hand. When the *Astraea* went down, her deck held her own crew and the crews of the two galleys that had attacked her at the same time—all were engulfed. Many of them came to the surface together, and on the same plank or support of whatever kind, continued the combat. Writhing and twisting in deadly embrace, sometimes striking with sword or javelin, they kept the sea tossing around them.

He had nothing to do with their struggles. They were all his enemies. All of them would kill him for the plank upon which he floated. He hurried to get away.

About that time he saw a galley coming down upon him. The tall prow seemed doubly tall, and the red light playing upon its carving gave it an appearance of snaky life. Under its foot the water churned to flying foam.

He reached out, pushing the plank, which was very broad and unmanageable. Seconds were precious—half a second might save or lose him. In the crisis of the effort, up from the sea, within arms reach, a helmet shot like a gleam of gold. Next came two hands with fingers extended. Their hold once fixed might not be loosed.

Ben Hur swerved from them and was appalled. Up rose the helmet and the head it encased—then two arms, which began to beat the water wildly—the head turned back and gave its face to the light. The mouth gaping wide; the eyes open, but sightless; the bloodless pallor of a drowning man—never was anything more ghastly! Yet he gave a cry of joy at the sight, and as the face was going under again, he caught the sufferer by the chain that passed from the helmet beneath the chin and drew him to the plank.

The man was Arrius, the tribune.

For a while the water foamed violently about Ben Hur, taxing all his strength to hold to the support and at the same time keep the Roman's head above the surface. The galley had passed, leaving the two barely outside the stroke of its oars. Right through the floating men she drove, in her wake nothing but the sea sparkled with fire. A muffled crash, succeeded by a great outcry, made the rescuer look again from his charge. A certain savage pleasure touched his heart—the *Astraea* was avenged.

After that the battle moved on. Resistance turned to flight. But who were the victors? Ben Hur was aware how much his freedom and the life of the tribune depended upon that event. He pushed the plank under the latter until it was floating under him, hoping only to keep him there. The dawn came slowly. He watched its growing hopefully, yet sometimes afraid. Would it bring the Romans or the pirates? If the pirates, his hope was lost.

At last morning broke in full. The air was still. Off to the left he saw land, too far away to think of attempting to make it. Here and there men were adrift like himself. In spots the sea was blackened by charred and sometimes smoking fragments. A galley up a long way was lying with a torn sail hanging from the tilted yard, and the oars were idle. Still farther away he could discern moving specks that he thought might be ships in flight or pursuit, or they might be white birds calling.

An hour passed, and his anxiety increased. If relief did not come speedily, Arrius would die. Sometimes he seemed already dead, he lay so still. He took the helmet off and then his breastplate. He found the heart fluttering. He took hope at the sign and held on. There was nothing to do but wait and, after the way of his people, pray.

27

Arrius Adopts Ben Hur

Arrius agonized through recovery from drowning and, to Ben Hur's delight, reached the point of speech. Gradually, he asked about the battle. The doubt of victory stimulated his faculties to full return, a result aided by a long rest—such as could be had on their frail support. After a while he became talkative. "Our rescue, I see, depends on the result of the fight. I see also what you have done for me. To speak fairly, you have saved my life at the risk of your own. I make the acknowledgment graciously, and, whatever comes, you have my thanks. More than that, if fortune does serve me kindly, and we survive this peril, I will do you such a favor as suits a Roman who has power and opportunity to prove his gratitude. Yet, it is still to be seen if, with your good intent, you have really done me a kindness or, rather, seeking your own good-will—" he hesitated "—I would demand of you a promise to keep for me, in any event, the greatest favor one man can do for another—and of that let me have your pledge now."

"If the thing is not forbidden, I will do it," Ben Hur replied.

Arrius rested again.

"Are you, indeed, a son of Hur, the Jew?" he next asked.

"It is as I have said."

"I knew your father—"

Judah drew himself nearer, for the tribune's voice was weak—he drew nearer and listened eagerly—at last he thought to hear of home.

"I knew him and loved him," Arrius continued. There was another pause, during which something diverted the speaker's thought.

"It cannot be," he proceeded, "that you, a son of his, have not heard of Cato and Brutus. They were very great men and never as great as in death. In their dying, they left this law—'A Roman may not survive his good fortune.' Are you listening?"

142

"I hear."

"It is a custom of gentlemen in Rome to wear a ring. There is one on my hand. Take it now." He held the hand to Judah, who did as he asked.

"Now put it on your own hand." Ben Hur did so.

"The trinket has its uses," said Arrius next. "I have property and money. I am seen as rich even in Rome. I have no family. Show the ring to my freedman who has control in my absence. You will find him in a villa near Misenum. Tell him how it came to you and ask anything, or all he may have. He will not refuse the demand. If I live, I will do even better for you. I will make you free and restore you to your home and people. Or you may give yourself to the pursuit that pleases you most. Do you hear?"

"I could not choose but hear."

"Then pledge me. By the gods—"

"No, good tribune. I am a Jew."

"By your God, then, or in the form most sacred to those of your faith—pledge me to do what I tell you now and as I tell you. I am waiting. Let me have your promise."

"Noble Arrius, I am warned by your manner to expect something of gravest concern. Tell me your wish first."

"Will you promise then?"

"That were to give the pledge and—blessed be the God of my fathers! Here comes a ship!"

"In what direction?"

"From the north."

"Can you tell her nationality by outward signs?"

"No. My service has been at the oars."

"Has she a flag?"

"I cannot see one."

Arrius remained quiet for some time, apparently in deep reflection.

"Now she has a sail set and comes swiftly—that is all I can say of her."

"A Roman in triumph would have many flags out. She must be an enemy. Hear, now," said Arrius, becoming grave again, "hear, while yet I may speak. If the galley belongs to a pirate, your life is safe. They may not give you freedom—they may put you to

143

the oar again, but they will not kill you. On the other hand, I . . ." The tribune faltered.

"Perpol!" he continued resolutely. "I am too old to submit to dishonor. In Rome let them tell how Quintus Arrius, as became a Roman tribune, went down with his ship in the midst of the foe. This is what I would have you do. If the galley proves to be a pirate ship, push me from the plank and drown me. Do you hear? Swear you will do it."

"I will not swear," said Ben Hur, firmly. "Neither will I do the deed. The law, which is to me most binding, tribune, would make me answerable for your life. Take back the ring"—he took the seal from his finger—"take it back and all your promises of favor in the event of delivery from this peril. The judgment that sent me to the oar for life made me a slave, yet I am not a slave. No more am I your freedman. I am a son of Israel and this moment, at least, my own master. Take back the ring."

Arrius remained passive.

"You will not?" Judah continued. "Not in anger, then, nor in any despite, but to free myself from a hateful obligation, I will give your gift to the sea. See, O tribune!"

He tossed the ring away. Arrius heard the splash where it struck and sank, though he did not look.

"You have done a foolish thing," he said, "foolish for one placed as you are. I am not dependent on you for death. Life is a thread I can break without your help. And if I do, what will become of you? Men determined on death prefer it at the hands of others, for the reason that the soul that Plato gives us is rebellious at the thought of self-destruction; that is all.

"If the ship be a pirate, I will escape from the world. My mind is fixed. I am a Roman. Success and honor are all in all. Yet I would have served you. You would not. The ring was the only witness of my will available in this situation. We are both lost. I will die regretting the victory and glory wrested from me. You will live to die a little later, mourning the pious duties undone because of this folly. I pity you."

Ben Hur saw the consequences of his act more distinctly than before, yet he did not falter. "In the three years of my servitude, O tribune, you were the first to look upon me kindly. No, no!

There was another." His voice dropped, and he saw plainly, as if it were then before him, the face of the boy who helped him to a drink by the old well at Nazareth. "At least," he proceeded, "you were the first to ask me who I was. And if, when I reached out and caught you, blind and sinking the last time, I too had thought of the many ways in which you could be useful to me in my wretchedness, still the act was not all selfish. This I ask you to believe. Also, seeing as God allows me now, the ends I dream of are to be completed by fair means alone. As a matter of conscience I would rather die than be your slayer. My mind is firmly set as yours. Though you were to offer me all Rome, O tribune, and it was within your power to make the gift possible, I would not kill you. Your Cato and Brutus were as little children compared to the Hebrew whose law a Jew must obey."

"But my request. Have—"

"Your command would be of more weight, and that would not move me. I have said."

Both became silent, waiting.

Ben Hur looked often at the coming ship. Arrius rested with closed eyes, indifferent.

"Are you sure she is an enemy?" Ben Hur asked.

"I think so," was the reply.

"She stops and puts a boat over the side."

"Do you see her flag?"

"Is there no other sign by which she may be known if Roman?"

"If Roman, she has a helmet over the mast's top."

"Then be of cheer. I see the helmet."

Still Arrius was not assured.

"The men in the small boat are taking in the people afloat. Pirates are not humane."

"They may need rowers," Arrius replied, remembering, possibly, times when he had made rescues for that purpose.

Ben Hur was watchful of the actions of the strangers. "The ship moves off," he said.

"Where?"

"Over on our right there is a galley that I take to be deserted. The newcomer heads toward it. Now she is alongside. Now she is sending men aboard."

145

Then Arrius opened his eyes and was finally assured. "Thank your God," he said to Ben Hur, after a look at the galleys. "Thank your God, as I do my many gods. A pirate would sink, not save, that ship. By the act and the helmet on the mast, I know a Roman. The victory is mine. Fortune has not deserted me. We are saved. Wave your hand—call to them—bring them quickly. I will be duumvir, and you—I knew your father and loved him. He was a prince indeed. He taught me a Jew was not a barbarian. I will take you with me. I will make you my son. Give your God thanks, and call the sailors. Haste! The pursuit must be kept. Not a robber shall escape. Hasten them!"

Judah raised himself upon the plank and waved his hand and called with all his might. At last he drew the attention of the sailors in the small boat, and they were speedily taken up.

Arrius was received on the galley with all the honors due a hero who was the favorite of Fortune. Upon a couch on the deck he heard the particulars of the conclusion of the fight. When the survivors afloat upon the water were all saved and the prize secured, he spread his captain's flag anew and hurried northward to rejoin the fleet and perfect the victory. In due time the fifty vessels coming down the channel closed in upon the fugitive pirates and crushed them utterly. Not one escaped. To swell the tribune's glory, twenty galleys of the enemy were captured.

Upon his return from the cruise, Arrius had a warm welcome at Misenum. The young man attending him attracted the attention of his friends there. As to their questions as to who he was, the tribune proceeded in the most affectionate manner to tell the story of his rescue and introduce the stranger, omitting carefully all that pertained to the latter's history.

At the end of the narrative, he called Ben Hur to him and said, with a hand resting affectionately upon his shoulder, "Good friends, this is my son and heir, who, as he is to take my property—if it be the will of the gods that I leave any—shall be known to you by my name. I encourage you all to love him as you love me."

Speedily as opportunity permitted, the adoption was formally perfected. And in such manner the brave Roman kept his promise to Ben Hur, giving him a strong introduction into the imperial world. The month succeeding Arrius's return there were celebrations with great significance in the theater at Scaurus. One side of the structure was taken up with military trophies. Among which by far the most conspicuous and most admired were twenty prows cut bodily from as many galleys. And over them, so as to be legible to the eighty thousand spectators in the seats, was this inscription:

TAKEN FROM THE PIRATES IN THE GULF OF EURIPUS
BY QUINTUS ARRIUS, DUUMVIR

28

Ben Hur Returns East

It was now July, the Year of our Lord 23, in Antioch, Queen of the East, and next to Rome the strongest, if not the most populated, city in the world. There is an opinion that the extravagance and dissoluteness of the age had their origin in Rome and spread from there throughout the empire—that the great cities but reflected the manners of their mistress on the Tiber. That is doubtful. The effects of the conquest would seem to have been upon the morals of the conqueror. Rome found a spring of corruption in Greece and also in Egypt. The flow of the demoralizing river was from the East westwardly, and the city of Antioch, one of the oldest seats of Assyrian power and splendor, was a principal source of the deadly stream.

A transport galley entered the mouth of the river Orontes from the blue waters of the sea. It was noon, and the heat was great, yet all on board who could avail themselves of the privilege were on deck—Ben Hur among others.

The five years had brought the young Jew to perfect manhood. Though the robe of white linen in which he was attired somewhat masked his form, his appearance was unusually attractive.

For an hour and more he had occupied a seat in the shade of the sail, and in that time several fellow passengers of his own nationality had tried to engage him in conversation, but without avail. His replies to their questions had been brief, though gravely courteous and in the Latin tongue. The purity of his speech and his cultivated manners served to stimulate their curiosity all the more. Those who observed him closely were struck by the difference between his manner, which had the ease and grace of a patrician, and certain points of his personality.

The galley, in coming, had stopped at one of the ports of Cyprus and picked up a Hebrew of a most respectable appearance, quiet and reserved. Ben Hur ventured to ask him some questions. The replies won his confidence and resulted finally in an extended conversation.

It chanced also that as the galley from Cyprus entered the receiving bay of the Orontes River, two other vessels that had been sighted out in the sea met it and passed into the river at the same time. And as they did so both the strangers threw out small flags of the brightest yellow. There was much conjecture as to the meaning of the signals. Then a passenger addressed the respectable Hebrew for information about this.

"Yes, I know the meaning of the flags," he replied. "They do not signify nationality—they are merely marks of ownership."

"Has the owner many ships?"

"He has."

"You know him?"

"I have dealt with him."

The passengers looked at the speaker as if wishing him to go on. Ben Hur listened with interest.

"He lives in Antioch," the Hebrew continued, in his quiet way. "That he is vastly rich has brought him some notice, and the talk about him is not always kind. There used to be in Jerusalem a prince of a very ancient family named Hur."

Judah strove to be composed, yet his heart beat quicker. "The prince was a merchant with a genius for business. He created many enterprises, some reaching far East, others West. In the great cities he had branch houses. The one in Antioch was in charge of a man said by some to have been a family servant called Simonides, Greek in name, yet an Israelite. The master was drowned at sea. His business, however, went on and was scarcely less prosperous.

"After a while misfortune overtook the family. The prince's only son, nearly grown, tried to kill the Procurator Gratus in one of the streets of Jerusalem. He failed by a narrow chance and has not since been heard of. In fact, the Roman's rage destroyed the whole house—not one of his name was left alive. Their palace was sealed up and is now a rookery for pigeons. The estate was confiscated. Everything that could be traced to the ownership of the Hurs was confiscated. The procurator cured his hurt with a golden salve."

The passengers laughed. "You mean he kept the property," said one of them.

"They say so," the Hebrew replied. "I am only telling a story as I received it. And, to go on, Simonides, who had been the prince's agent here in Antioch, opened trade in a short time on his own account and in an incredibly brief space became the master merchant of the city. In imitation of his master, he sent caravans to India. And on the sea at present he has enough galleys to make a royal fleet. They say nothing goes amiss with him. His camels do not die, except of old age. His ships never founder. If he throws a chip into the river, it will come back to him gold."

"How long has he been going on this way?"

"Not ten years."

"He must have had a good start."

"Yes, they say the procurator took only the prince's property ready at hand—his horses, cattle, houses, land, vessels, goods. The money could not be found, though there must have been vast sums of it. What became of it has been an unsolved mystery."

"Not to me," said a passenger, with a sneer.

"I understand you," the Hebrew answered. "Others have had your idea. That it furnished old Simonides his start is a common belief. The procurator is of that opinion—or he has been—for twice in five years he has caught the merchant and tortured him."

Judah gripped the rope he was holding with crushing force.

"It is said," the narrator continued, "that there is not a sound bone in the man's body. The last time I saw him he sat in a chair, a shapeless cripple, propped against cushions."

"So tortured!" exclaimed several listeners in a breath.

"Disease could not have produced such a deformity. Still the suffering made no impression upon him. All he had was his lawfully, and he was making lawful use of it—that was the most they wrung from him. Now, however, he is past persecution. He has a license to trade signed by Tiberius himself."

"He paid roundly for it, I warrant."

"These ships are his," the Hebrew continued, passing the remark. "It is a custom among his sailors to salute each other upon meeting by throwing out yellow flags, the sight of which is as much as to say, 'We have had a fortunate voyage.'"

150

The story ended there.

When the transport was in the channel of the river, Judah spoke to the Hebrew.

"What was the name of the merchant's master?"

"Ben Hur, prince of Jerusalem."

"What became of the prince's family?"

"The boy was sent to the galleys. I may say he is dead. One year is the ordinary limit of life under that sentence. The widow and daughter have not been heard of. Those who know what became of them will not speak. They died, doubtless, in the cells of one of the castles that dot the waysides of Judea." Judah walked to the pilot's quarter. So absorbed was he in thought that he scarcely noticed the shores of the river, which from sea to city were surpassingly beautiful with orchards of all the Syrian fruits and vines, clustered about villas rich as those of Neapolis. No more did he observe the vessels passing in an endless fleet, nor hear the singing and shouting of the sailors, some in labor, some in merriment. The sky was full of sunlight, lying in hazy warmth upon the land and the water. Only over his life was there a shadow.

Only once he awoke to a momentary interest, and that was when someone pointed out the Grove of Daphne, discernible from a bend in the river.

29

On the Orontes

When the city came into view, the passengers were on deck, eager that nothing of the scene might escape them. The respected Jew said, "The river here runs to the west. Now the whole river-front is taken up with wharves and docks. Yonder—" the speaker pointed southward "—are the Mountains of Orontes, looking across to its brother Amnus in the north. And between them lies the Plain of Antioch. Farther on are the Black Mountains, where the Ducts of the Kings bring the purest water to wash the thirsty streets and people. Yet they are a wilderness, dense and full of birds and beasts."

"Where is the lake?" one asked.

"Over north there. You can take a horse, if you wish to see it—or, better, a boat, for a tributary connects it with the river."

"The Grove of Daphne!" he said to a third inquirer. "Nobody can describe it. Only beware! It was begun by Apollo and completed by him. He prefers it to Olympus. People go there for one look—just one—and never come back. They have a saying that tells it all—'Better be a worm and feed on the mulberries of Daphne than a king's guest.'"

"Then you advise me to stay away from it?"

"Not I! Go if you wish. Everybody goes. So sure am I of what you will do that I assume to advise. Do not take quarters in the city—that will be loss of time—but go at once to the village in the edge of the grove. The way is through a garden, under the spray of fountains. The lovers of the god and his Penaean maid built the town, and in its porticos and paths and thousand retreats you will find what is elsewhere impossible. But the wall of the city! There it is, the masterpiece of Xeraeus, the master of mural architecture.

"On the top there are four hundred towers, each a reservoir of water," the Hebrew continued. "Look now! Over the wall, tall as it is, see in the distance two hills. The structure on the farthest one is the citadel, garrisoned all the year round by a Roman legion. Opposite it this way rises the temple of Jupiter and under that the front of the legate's residence—a palace full of offices and yet a fortress against which a mob would dash harmlessly as a south wind."

At this point the sailors began taking in the sail, then the Hebrew exclaimed, heartily, "See! You who hate the sea and you who have vows, get ready your curses and your prayers. The bridge yonder, over which the road to Seleucia is carried, marks the limit of navigation. What the ship unloads for further transit, the camel takes up there. Above the bridge begins the island upon which Calinicus built his new city, connecting it with five great viaducts so solid time has made no impression upon them, nor floods nor earthquakes. Of the main town, my friends, I have only to say you will be happier all your lives for having seen it."

As he concluded, the ship turned and headed slowly for her wharf under the wall, bringing even more fairly to view the life with which the river at that point was filled. Finally, the lines were thrown, the oars shipped, and the voyage was done. Then Ben Hur sought the respectable Hebrew.

"Let me trouble you for a moment before saying farewell."

The man bowed assent.

"Your story of the merchant has made me curious to see him. You called him Simonides?"

"Yes. He is a Jew with a Greek name."

"Where is he to be found?"

The acquaintance gave a sharp look before he answered—

"I may save you humiliation. He is not a moneylender."

"Nor am I a money borrower," said Ben Hur, smiling at the other's shrewdness.

The man raised his head and considered an instant.

"One would think," he then replied, "that the richest merchant in Antioch would have a house for business corresponding to his wealth. But if you would find him in the day, follow the river to that bridge, under which he quarters in a building that looks like a buttress of the wall. Before the door there is an immense landing, always covered with cargoes coming and going. The fleet that lies moored there is his. You cannot fail to find him."

"I give you thanks."

"The peace of our fathers go with you."

"And with you." With that they separated.

Two street porters, loaded with his baggage, received Ben Hur's orders upon the wharf. "To the citadel," he said, a direction that implied an official military connection.

On the right and left there were palaces, and between them indefinitely extended double colonnades of marble, leaving separate ways for footmen, beasts, and chariots, all under shade and cooled by fountains flowing incessantly.

Ben Hur was not in the mood to enjoy the spectacle. The story of Simonides haunted him. Arriving at the Omphalus—a monument of four arches wide as the streets, superbly illustrated and erected to himself by Epiphanes, the eighth of the Seleucidae—he suddenly changed his mind.

"I will not go to the citadel tonight," he said to the porters. "Take me to the inn nearest the bridge on the road to Seleucia."

The party turned around, and in good time he entered an inn of primitive but ample construction, within a stone's throw of the bridge under which old Simonides had his quarters. He lay upon the housetop through the night. In his inner mind a thought continued. *Now—now I will hear of home—and Mother—and the dear little Tirzah. If they are on earth, I will find them.*

30

The Demand on Simonides

Next day early, neglecting the city, Ben Hur sought the house of Simonides. Through a narrow gateway he passed to a string of wharves, then up the river to the Seleucian Bridge, under which he paused to take in the scene. There, directly under the bridge, was the merchant's house, a mass of unhewn gray stone, of no style, looking, as the voyager had described it, like a buttress of the wall against which it leaned.

Two immense doors in front opened to the wharf. Some heavily barred holes near the top served as windows. Weeds waved from the crevices, and in places black moss splotched the otherwise bald stones. The doors were open. Through one of them clients went in, and groups of slaves, stripped to the waist, were laboring.

Below the bridge lay a fleet of galleys, some loading, others unloading. A yellow flag blew out from each masthead. From fleet and wharf and from ship to ship the directors of traffic passed in noisy countercurrents.

Above the bridge, across the river, a wall rose from the water's edge, over which towered the fanciful cornices and turrets of an imperial palace, covering every foot of the island spoken of in the Hebrew's description.

But, with all its beautiful sights, Ben Hur scarcely noticed it. Now, at last, he thought to hear of his people—certainly if Simonides had indeed been his father's slave. But would the man acknowledge the relation? That would be to give up his riches and the sovereignty of trade so royally witnessed on the wharf and river. And what was of still greater consequence to the merchant would be to forgo his career in the midst of amazing success and give himself up voluntarily once more to become a slave. That thought seemed to be a monstrous audacity. Stripped of all the polite language, it was as if to say, "You are my slave; give me all you have and—yourself."

Yet Ben Hur drew strength for the meeting from faith in his rights and the great hope in his heart. If the story he heard were true, Simonides belonged to him, with all he had. For the wealth, be it said on his behalf, he did not care for at all. When he started for the door, determined in his mind, it was with a promise to himself—"Let him tell me of mother and Tirzah, and I will give him his freedom without delay."

He went boldly into the house. The interior was that of a vast depot where, in ordered spaces and under careful arrangement goods of every kind were heaped. Though the light was murky and the air stifling, men moved about briskly, and in places he saw workmen with saws and hammers making packages for shipments. He walked slowly down a path between the piles, wondering if the man of whose genius was evident could have been his father's slave? If so, to what class had he belonged? If a Jew, was he the son of a servant? Or was he a debtor or a debtor's son? Or had he been sentenced and sold for theft? These thoughts, as they occurred, in no way disturbed the growing respect for the merchant.

Finally a man approached and spoke to him. "What do you want?"

"I would see Simonides, the merchant."

"Will you come this way?"

By a number of paths left in the storage, they finally came to a flight of steps, and ascending he found himself on the roof of the depot and in front of a structure that cannot be better described than as a smaller stone house built upon another, invisible from the landing below and out west of the bridge under the open sky. The roof, hemmed in by a low wall, seemed like a terrace, which was brilliant with flowers. In the rich surroundings, the house sat squat—a plain square block, unbroken except by a doorway in front. A dustless path led to the door, through a bordering of shrubs of Persian roses in perfect bloom. Breathing a sweet perfume, he followed the guide.

At the end of a darkened passage within, they stopped before a half-parted curtain. The man called out, "A stranger to see the master."

A clear voice replied, "In God's name, let him enter."

A Roman might have called the apartment into which the visitor was ushered his atrium. The walls were paneled. Each panel was divided like a modern office desk and each compartment crowded with labeled folios all soiled with age and use. Between the panels, and above and below them, were borders of wood once white, now tinted like cream, and carved with marvelous intricacy of design. Above a cornice of gilded balls, the ceiling rose in pavilion style until it broke into a shallow dome set with hundreds of panes of violet glass, permitting a flood of light that was refreshing. The floor was carpeted with gray rugs so thick that a foot would fall half buried and soundless.

In the middle of the room were two persons—a man resting in a high-backed chair and lined with soft cushions. And at his left, leaning against the back of the chair, was a girl well into womanhood. At the sight of them Ben Hur felt the blood redden his cheeks. Bowing, as much to recover himself as in respect, he shivered when they caught sight of him—an emotion that quickly passed. When he raised his eyes the two were in the same position, except the girl's hand had fallen and was resting lightly upon the elder's shoulder. Both of them were regarding him closely.

"If you are Simonides, the merchant and Jew"—Ben Hur stopped an instant—"then the peace of the God of our father Abraham upon you and—yours." The last word was addressed to the girl.

"I am the Simonides of whom you speak, by birthright a Jew," the man answered, in a voice singularly clear. "I am Simonides and a Jew. And I return you your salutation, with prayer to know who calls upon me."

Ben Hur looked as he listened, and where the figure of the man would have been in healthful roundness, there was only a formless heap sunk in the depths of the cushions and covered by a quilted robe of somber silk. Over the heap shone a royally proportioned head—the ideal head of a statesman and conqueror—a broad-based head, domelike in front, such as Angelo would have modeled for Caesar. White hair dropped in thin locks over the white brows, deepening the blackness of the eyes shining through them like sullen lights. The face was bloodless and much puffed with folds, especially under the chin. In other words, the head and face were those of a man who might move the world more readily than the world could move him—a man twelve times tortured into the shapeless cripple he was, without a groan, much less a confession—a man to yield his life but never a purpose or a point; a man born in armor and assailable only through his loves.

To him Ben Hur stretched his hands, open and palm up, as he would offer peace at the same time he asked it.

"I am Judah, son of Ithamar, late head of the House of Hur and a prince of Jerusalem."

The merchant's right hand lay outside the robe—a long, thin hand, deformed with suffering. It closed tightly. Otherwise there was not the slightest expression of feeling of any kind on his part, nothing to warrant an inference of surprise or interest, nothing but this calm answer: "The princes of Jerusalem, of the pure blood, are always welcome in my house. You are welcome. Give the young man a seat, Esther."

The girl took an ottoman nearby and carried it to Ben Hur. As she arose from placing the seat, their eyes met. "The peace of our Lord be with you," she said modestly. "Be seated and at rest."

When she resumed her place by the chair, she had not understood his purpose. The powers of woman do not go this far: if the matter is of finer feeling, such as pity, mercy, sympathy, that she detects. And there is a difference between her and a man that will endure as long as she remains by nature alive to such feelings. She was simply sure he brought some wound of life for healing.

Ben Hur did not take the offered seat but said, deferentially, "I pray that the good master Simonides will not hold me an intruder. Coming up the river yesterday, I heard he knew my father."

"I knew the Prince Hur. We were associated in some enterprises lawful to merchants who find profit in lands beyond the sea and the desert. But sit, I pray you—and, Esther, some wine for the young man. Nehemiah speaks of a son of Hur who once ruled the half of Jerusalem—an old house, by the faith! In the days of Moses and Joshua even some of them found favor in the sight of the Lord and divided honors with those princes among men. It can hardly be that their descendant, lineally come to us, will refuse a cup of wine-fat of the genuine vine of Sorek, grown on the south hillsides of Hebron."

By the conclusion of this speech, Esther was standing before Ben Hur with a silver cup filled from a vase upon a table near the chair. She offered the drink shyly. He touched her hand gently to put it away. Again their eyes met.

He noticed that she was small, not nearly to his shoulder in height, but very graceful, and had a fair and sweet face, with black and inexpressibly soft eyes. *She is kind and pretty, he thought, and looks as Tirzah would were she living. Poor Tirzah!* Then he said aloud, "No, your father—if he is your father—" He paused.

"I am Esther, the daughter of Simonides," she said with dignity.

"Then, fair Esther, your father, when he has heard my further speech, will not think worse of me if yet I am slow to take his wine of famous extract. No less I hope not to lose grace in your sight. Stand here with me a moment!"

Both of them turned to the merchant. "Simonides!" he said, firmly, "my father, at his death, had a trusted servant of your name, and it has been told to me that you are the man!"

There was a sudden start of the wrenched limbs under the robe, and the thin hand clenched. "Esther, Esther!" the man called sternly. "Here, not there, as you are your mother's child and mine—here, not there, I say!"

The girl looked once from father to visitor. Then she replaced the cup upon the table and went dutifully to the chair. Her face expressed her wonder and alarm.

Simonides lifted his left hand and put it into hers, lying lovingly upon his shoulder, and said without emotion, "I have grown old in dealing with men—old before my time. If he who told you that was a friend acquainted with my history and did not speak of it harshly, he must have persuaded you that I could be nothing more than a distrustful man. The God of Israel help him who, at the end of life, is constrained to acknowledge so much! My loves are few, but they are there. One of them is a soul that"—he carried the hand holding his to his lips, in an unmistakable manner—"a soul that to this time has been unselfishly mine and such sweet comfort that, were it taken from me, I would die."

Esther's head drooped until her cheek touched his.

"The other love is but a memory, of which I will say further that it has a compass to contain a whole family, if only"—his voice lowered and trembled—"if only I knew where they were."

Ben Hur's face flushed, and, advancing a step, he cried impulsively, "My mother and sister! Oh, it is of them you speak!"

Esther, as if spoken to, raised her head, but Simonides returned to his calm and answered coldly, "Hear me to the end. Because I am what I am and because of the loves of which I have spoken, before I answer your demand touching my relation to the Prince Hur, and as something that of right should come first, do you show me proofs of who you are? Is your witness in writing? Or does it come in person?"

The demand was plain, and the right of it was indisputable. Ben Hur blushed, clasped his hands, stammered, and turned away at a loss. Simonides pressed him. "The proofs, the proofs, I say! Set them before me—lay them in my hands!"

Yet Ben Hur did not have an answer. He had not anticipated the requirement, and now that it was made, as never before there came to him the awful fact that the three years in the galley had carried away all proofs of his identity. His mother and sister were gone, and his identity was not well known to anyone. Many were acquainted with him, but that was all. Had Quintus Arrius been present, he could have only said that he found him and that he believed the pretender to be the son of Hur. But it turned out that the brave Roman sailor was dead. Judah had felt loneliness before, but now to the core of his being. Simonides respected his suffering and waited in silence.

"Master Simonides," he said finally, "I can only tell my story, and I will not do that unless you withhold judgment for a while and listen with goodwill."

"Speak," said Simonides, who was now master of the situation, "speak, and I will listen more willingly because I have not yet denied that you are the very person you claim to be."

Ben Hur proceeded then and told his life story hurriedly, yet with strong emotion. "My benefactor was loved and trusted by the emperor, who heaped upon him honorable rewards. The merchants of the East contributed magnificent presents, and he became doubly rich among the rich of Rome. May a Jew forget his religion? Or his birthplace, if it were the Holy Land of our fathers? The good man adopted me as his son by formal rites of law, and I attempted to repay him in every way. No child was ever more dutiful to his father than I to him. He wished me to be a scholar—in art, philosophy, and rhetoric—and he would have provided me with the most renowned teacher. I declined though he insisted, because I was a Jew and could not forget the Lord God or the glory of the prophets or the city set on the hills by David and Solomon.

"You ask why I accepted any of the provisions of this Roman? I loved him. Also I thought I could, with his help, secure influences that would enable me one day to unseal the mystery that held the fate of my mother and sister. And there was yet another motive of which I shall not speak except to say it controlled me so much that I devoted myself to becoming a soldier and the acquisition of everything that seemed essential to a thorough knowledge of the art of war.

"In the palaces and arenas and camps of the city I toiled, and in all of them I have a name but not that of my fathers. The crowns I won—and on the walls of the villa by Misenum there are many of them—they all came to me as the son of Arrius, the duumvir. Only in that relation am I known among Romans.

"In steadfast pursuit of my secret aim, I left Rome for Antioch, intending to accompany the Consul Maxentius in the campaign he is organizing against the Parthians. Master of various skills in all arms, I seek now the higher knowledge pertaining to the conduct of men in the field. The consul has introduced me to one member of his military family. But yesterday, as our ship entered the Orontes, two other ships sailed in with us flying yellow flags. A fellow passenger and countryman from Cyprus explained that the vessels belonged to Simonides, the master-merchant of Antioch. He told us, also, who the merchant was—his marvelous success in commerce; of his fleets and caravans and their coming and going; and, not knowing I had interest in this story beyond my fellow listeners, he said Simonides was a Jew, once the servant of the Prince Hur. Nor did he conceal the cruelties of Gratus or their purpose."

At this allusion Simonides bowed his head, and, as if to help him conceal his feelings and her own deep sympathy, the daughter hid her face in his neck. Immediately he raised his eyes and said in a clear voice, "I am listening."

"O good Simonides!" Ben Hur then said, advancing a step, his whole soul seeking expression, "I see you are not convinced and that I yet stand in the shadow of your distrust."

The merchant held his features fixed as marble and his tongue as still.

"I see the difficulties of my position clearly," Ben Hur continued. "I can prove all my Roman connections. I have only to call upon the consul, now the guest of the governor of the city. But I cannot prove the particulars of your demand upon me. I cannot prove I am my father's son. They who could serve me in that are dead or lost."

He covered his face with his hands. Then Esther arose and, taking the rejected cup to him, said, "The wine is of the country we all so love. Drink, I pray you!"

The voice was sweet as that of Rebekah offering a drink at the well near Nahor. He saw there were tears in her eyes, and he drank, saying, "Daughter of Simonides, your heart is full of goodness, and you are merciful to let a stranger share it with your father. Be blessed of our God! I thank you."

Then he spoke to the merchant again. "As I have no proof that I am my father's son, I will withdraw what I have demanded of you, Simonides, and trouble you no more. Only let me say I did not seek your return to servitude nor an account of your fortune. In any event, I would have said, as I say now, that all which is the product of your labor and genius is yours. I welcome you to keep it. I have no need of any part of it. When the good Quintus, my second father, sailed on the voyage that was his last, he left me his heir, rich as a prince. If you do think of me again, remember this question that, as I swear by the prophets and Jehovah, your God and mine, was the chief purpose of my coming here: What do you know—what can you tell me—of my mother and Tirzah, my sister—she who should be in both beauty and grace equal to Esther, the sweetness of your life, if not your very life? What can you tell me of them?"

The tears ran down Esther's cheeks, but the man was self-controlled and in a clear voice replied, "I have said I knew the Prince Ben Hur. I remember hearing of the misfortune that overtook his family. I remember the bitterness with which I heard it. He who created such misery to the widow of my friend is the one who, in the same spirit, has since affected me. I will go further and say to you, I have made a diligent quest concerning this family, but I have nothing to tell you of them. They are lost."

Ben Hur uttered a loud groan. "Then another hope is broken!" he said, struggling with his feelings. "I am used to disappointments. I pray that you pardon my intrusion. And if I have annoyed you forgive it because of my sorrow. I have nothing now to live for but vengeance. Farewell."

At the curtain he turned and said, simply, "I thank you both."

"Peace go with you," the merchant said.

Esther could not speak because of her sobbing, and so he departed.

31

Simonides and Esther

Scarcely was Ben Hur gone, when Simonides seemed to wake as from sleep. His face was flushed. The sullen light of his eyes brightened, and he said cheerily, "Esther, ring—quick!"

She went to the table and rang a service bell. One of the panels in the wall swung back, exposing a doorway that admitted a man who passed around the merchant and saluted him with a half salaam.

"Malluch, here—nearer—to the chair," the master said. "I have a mission that shall not fail though the sun should. Listen! A young man is now descending to the storeroom. He is tall, handsome, and in the garb of Israel. Follow him and be his faithful shadow. Every night send me a report of where he is, what he does, and the company he keeps. If, without discovery, you overhear his conversations, report them word for word, together with whatever will help to expose him and his habits and motives.

"Do you understand? Go quickly! Malluch! If he leaves the city, go after him—and, mark you, Malluch, be as a friend. If he speaks to you, tell him what you think most suited to the occasion, except, of course, that you are in my service. Of that, not a word. Haste—make haste!"

The man saluted as before and was gone.

Then Simonides rubbed his pale hands together and laughed. "What is the day, daughter?" he said in the midst of this new mood. "What is the day? I wish to remember it for happiness has come. See, and look for it laughing, and laughing tell me, Esther."

The merriment seemed unnatural to her, and, as if to understand it, she answered sorrowfully, "Woe's me, father, that I should ever forget this day!"

"True, most true, my daughter!" he said, without looking up. "This is the twentieth day of the fourth month. Today five years ago, my Rachel, your mother, fell down and died. They brought

164

me home broken as you see, and we found her dead of grief. Oh, to me she was a cluster of camphor in the vineyards of En-gedi! I have gathered my myrrh with my spice. I have eaten my honeycomb with my honey. We laid her away in a lonely place—in a tomb cut in the mountain. No one near her.

"Yet in the darkness she left me a little light, which the years have increased to the brightness of morning." He raised his hand and rested it upon his daughter's head. "Dear Lord, I thank You that now in my Esther my lost Rachel lives again!"

Then he lifted his head and said suddenly, "Is it not a clear day outside?"

"It was, when the young man came in."

"Then let Abimelech come and take me to the garden, where I can see the river and the ships, and I will tell you, dear Esther, why but only now my mouth was filled with laughter and my tongue with singing, and my spirit was like a roe or a young hart upon the mountains of spices."

In answer to the bell a servant came and at her bidding pushed the chair, set on little wheels for the purpose, out of the room to the roses and by beds of other flowers, all triumphs of careful attendance, but now unnoticed. He was rolled to a position from which he could view the palace tops on the island, the bridge as a backdrop to the farther shore, and the river below the bridge crowded with vessels, all swimming amidst the dancing splendors of the early sun upon the rippling water. There the servant left him with Esther.

The shouting and pounding of laborers did not disturb him any more than the trampling of people on the bridge floor almost overhead. These were as familiar to his ear as the view before him was to his eyes. They served only as the promise of profits.

Esther sat on the arm of the chair nursing his hand and waiting for his reply.

"When the young man was speaking, Esther, I observed you and thought you were won by him."

Her eyes fell as she replied, "Do you speak of faith, father? I believed him."

"In your eyes, then, he is the lost son of the Prince Hur?"

"If he is not—" She hesitated.

"And if he is not, Esther?"

"I have been your handmaiden, Father, since my mother answered the call of the Lord God. By your side I have heard and seen you deal in wise ways with all types of men seeking profit, holy and unholy. And now I say, if indeed the young man is not the prince he claims to be, then before me falsehood never played so well the part of righteous truth."

"By the glory of Solomon, daughter, you speak earnestly. Do you believe your father is his father's servant?"

"I understood him to say that was something he had only heard."

For a time Simonides' gaze swam among his swimming ships, though they had no place in his mind. "Well, you are a good child, Esther, of genuine Jewish cleverness and old enough to hear a sorrowful tale. So give me an ear, and I will tell you of myself and of your mother and of many things pertaining to the past that are not in your knowledge or your dreams—things withheld from the persecuting Romans and from you that your nature should grow toward the Lord straight as the reed to the sun.

"I was born in a tomb in the valley of Hinnom, on the south side of Zion. My father and mother were Hebrew bond-servants, tenders of the fig and olive trees growing, with many vines, in the King's Garden close to Siloam. And in my boyhood I helped them. They were of the class that were bound to serve forever. They sold me to the Prince Hur, then, next to Herod the King the richest man in Jerusalem. From the garden he transferred me to his storehouse in Alexandria of Egypt, where I came of age. I served him six years, and in the seventh by the law of Moses I went free."

Esther clapped her hands lightly. "Oh, then, you are not his father's servant?"

"No, daughter, hear. Now, in those days there were lawyers in the cloisters of the Temple who disputed vehemently, saying the children of servants bound forever remained in the condition of their parents. But the Prince Hur was a man righteous in all things and an interpreter of the law like the strictest sect, though not of them. He said I was a Hebrew servant bought, in the true meaning of the great lawgiver, and by sealed writings which I yet have he set me free."

"And my mother?" Esther asked.

"You will hear all, Esther. Be patient. Before I am through you will see it was easier for me to forget myself than your mother. At the end of my service I came up to Jerusalem to the Passover. My master entertained me. I loved him greatly already, and I sought to continue in his service. He consented, and I served him yet another seven years, but as a hired son of Israel. In his behalf I had charge of business on the sea in ships and of commerce on land by caravans eastward to Susa and Persepolis and the lands of silk beyond them. They were perilous passages, my daughter, but the Lord blessed all I undertook. I brought home vast gains for the prince and richer knowledge for myself, without which I could not have mastered the business since given to me.

"One day I was a guest in his house at Jerusalem. A servant entered with some sliced bread on a platter. She came to me first. It was then I saw your mother and loved her and hid her in my innermost heart. After a while a time came when I asked the prince to make her my wife. He told me she was a bond-servant forever, but if she wished he would set her free that I might be gratified. She gave me love for love, but was happy where she was and refused her freedom.

"I prayed and sought the Lord, seeking him over a period of time. She would be my wife, she continued to say, if I would become her companion in servitude. Our father Jacob served a second seven years for his Rachel. Could I not do as much for her? But your mother said I must become as she, to serve forever. I came away, but went back. Look, Esther, look here."

He pulled out the lobe of his left ear. "Do you see the scar of the awl?"

"I see it," she said, "and I see how you loved my mother!"

"Loved her, Esther! She was to me more than the Shulamite to the singing king, fairer, more spotless—a fountain of gardens, a well of living waters, and streams from Lebanon. The master, even as I required him, took me to the judges and back to his door and thrust the awl through my ear into the door, and I was his servant forever. So I won my Rachel. And was there ever a love like mine?" Esther stooped and kissed him, and they were silent, thinking of the dead wife and mother.

167

"My master was drowned at sea, the first sorrow that ever fell upon me," the merchant continued. "There was mourning in his house, and in mine here in Antioch, my home at the time. Now, Esther, mark you! When the good prince was lost, I had risen to be his chief steward, with all of his property belonging to him under my management and control. You judge how much he loved and trusted me! I hastened to Jerusalem to render an account to his widow. She continued my role as his steward. I applied myself with even greater diligence. The business prospered and grew year by year.

"Ten years passed. Then came the blow that you heard the young man just here tell about—the accident, as he called it, related to the Procurator Gratus. The Romans interpreted it as an attempt to assassinate him. Under that pretext, with permission from Rome, he confiscated to his own use the immense fortune of the widow and children. Nor did he stop there. So that there might be no reversal of this judgment, he removed all the parties that were involved.

"From that dreadful day to this the family of Hur has been lost. The son, whom I had seen as a child, was sentenced to the galleys. The widow and daughter are supposed to have been buried in some of the many dungeons of Judea, which, once closed upon the doomed, are like sepulchers sealed and locked. They passed from the knowledge of men as utterly as if the sea had swallowed them unseen. We could not hear how they died—no, not even if they were dead."

Esther's eyes filled with tears.

"Your heart is good, Esther, good as your mother's was, and I hope that it does not have the same fate of most good hearts—to be trampled upon by the unmerciful and blind. But listen further. I went up to Jerusalem to give help to my master's wife and was seized at the gate of the city and carried to the sunken cells of the Tower of Antonia. I did not know until Gratus himself came and demanded from me the wealth from the House of Hur, which he knew, after our Jewish custom of exchange, were subject to my drafts at money exchanges in the different markets of the world. He required me to sign his order. I refused.

"He had the houses, lands, goods, ships, and movable prop-

168

erty of those I served, but he had not their money. I saw that if I kept favor in the sight of the Lord I could rebuild their broken fortunes. I refused the tyrant's demands. He put me to torture, but my will remained strong, and he set me free, nothing gained.

"I came home and began again, in the name of Simonides of Antioch, instead of the Prince Hur of Jerusalem. You know, Esther, how I have prospered—that the increase of the prince's millions in my hands was miraculous. You know how, at the end of three years, while going up to Caesarea, I was taken and a second time tortured by Gratus to compel a confession that my goods and money were subject to his order of confiscation. You know he failed as before. Broken in body, I came home and found my Rachel dead of fear and grief for me.

"The Lord our God reigned, however, and I lived. I bought from the emperor himself immunity and license to trade throughout the world. Today—praised be he who makes the clouds his chariot and walks upon the winds!—today, Esther, that given to me for stewardship is multiplied into talents sufficient to enrich a caesar."

He lifted his head proudly. Their eyes met; each read the other's thought. "What shall I do with the treasure, Esther?" he asked, without lowering his gaze.

"My father," she answered in a low voice, "did not the rightful owner call for it just now?"

Still his steady gaze did not fail. "And you, my child, shall I leave you a beggar?"

"No, father. I am, because I am your child, his bond-servant too. It is written, 'Strength and honor are her clothing, and she shall rejoice in time to come.'"

A gleam of inexplicable love lighted his face as he said, "The Lord has been good to me in many ways, but you, Esther, are the sovereign excellence of his favor." He drew her to his heart and kissed her.

"Hear me now," he said. "Hear now why I laughed this morning. The young man who faced me was the image of his father in his handsome youth. My spirit arose to greet him. I felt my old days of trial were over and my labors ended. I hardly could keep from crying out. I longed to take him by the hand and show the profits I had earned and say, 'Look, it is all yours! And I am your servant, ready now to be removed away.' And I would have done this, Esther, but at that moment three thoughts restrained me. I must be sure he is my master's son, was the first thought. If he is my master's son, I will learn somewhat of his nature. Many of those born to riches, Esther, are producing curses for themselves."

He paused with his hands clutched, and his voice was filled with passion. "Esther, consider the pains I endured at the Roman's hands. Not Gratus's alone—the merciless wretches who did his bidding during those times of torture were Romans, and they all laughed to hear me scream. Consider my broken body and the years I have been shorn of my stature. Consider your mother in her lonely tomb, crushed of soul as I am of body. Consider the sorrows of my master's family if they are living and the cruelty of their punishment if they are dead. And with heaven's love about you, tell me, daughter, shall not a hair fall or a red drop run in payment for this? Do not tell me, as the preachers sometimes do, that vengeance is the Lord's. Does he not work his will with wrath as well as in love? Does he not have his men of war, which are more numerous than his prophets? Is not the law "Eye for eye, hand for hand, foot for foot"? In all these years I have dreamed of vengeance, and prayed and provided for it, and gathered patience from storing up this desire, thinking and promising, as the Lord lives, one day I will see the punishment of the wrongdoers. And when, speaking of his practice with weapons, the young man said it was for a nameless purpose, I named the purpose even as he spoke—vengeance! And that, Esther, was the third thought that held me captivated while his pleading lasted and made me laugh when he was gone."

Esther caressed his faded hands and said, as if her spirit with his were seeing the future, "He is gone. Will he come again?"

"Yes, Malluch the faithful goes with him and will bring him back when I am ready."

"And when will that be, Father?"

"Not long, not long. He thinks all his witnesses are dead. There is one living who will not fail him, if he be indeed my master's son."

170

"His mother?"

"No, daughter. I will set the witness before him. Till then let us leave the business with the Lord. I am tired. Call Abimelech."

Esther called the servant, and they returned into the house.

32

The Grove of Daphne

When Ben Hur left the great warehouse, it was with the thought that another failure was to be added to the many he had already met in the quest for his people. This one, though, enshrouded him with a sense of utter loneliness on earth, which more than anything else serves to draw from the soul its remaining zest for life.

He made his way to the edge of the landing through the people and the piles of goods and was tempted by the cool shadows darkening the river's depth. The lazy current seemed to stop and wait for him. To balance this seeming spell, the saying of the voyager flashed into his memory—"Better be a worm and feed upon the mulberries of Daphne, than a king's guest." He turned and walked rapidly down the landing and back to the inn.

"The road to Daphne!" the steward said, surprised at the question Ben Hur put to him. "You have not been there before? Well, count this the happiest day of your life. You cannot mistake the road. The next street to the left, going south, leads straight to Mount Sulpius, crowned by the altar of Jupiter and the Amphitheater. Follow it to the third cross street, known as Herod's Colonnade. Turn to your right there and stay on this way through the old city of Seleucus to the bronze gates of Epiphanes. There the road to Daphne begins—and may the gods keep you!"

He gave a few directions concerning his baggage, and Ben Hur set out. The Colonnade of Herod was easily found. Then on to the brazen gates, under a marble portico, he traveled with a multitude mixed of people from all the trading nations of the earth.

It was about the fourth hour of the day when he went through the gate and found himself one of a procession seemingly without end, moving to the famous Grove. The road was divided into separate ways for pedestrians, men on horses, men in chariots. To the right and left of the road were statues on massive pedestals between groups of oak and sycamore trees, and vine-clad summer houses for the comfort of the weary, of whom on the return journey there were always great crowds. The number and variety of spraying fountains were amazing, all gifts of visiting kings and named after them.

In his wretchedness, Ben Hur barely observed the crowd going with him. He treated the processional displays with the same indifference. To tell the truth, besides his self-absorption, he had some of the complacency of a Roman visiting the provinces fresh from the ceremonies that daily swirled round the golden pillar set up by Augustus as the center of the world. It was not possible for the provinces to offer anything new or superior. He pushed forward through the companies of people in his way.

By the time he reached Heracleia, a suburban village between the city and the Grove, he was somewhat spent with exercise and began to seek recreation. Once a pair of goats led by a beautiful woman, who were brilliant with ribbons and flowers, attracted his attention. Then he stopped to look at a snowy white bull of mighty girth, covered with freshly cut vines and bearing a naked child in a basket on its broad back, the image of a young Bacchus, squeezing the juice of ripened berries into a goblet. As he resumed his walk, he wondered whose altars would be enriched by these offerings.

A horse went by with clipped mane, after the fashion of the time, his rider superbly dressed. He smiled to observe the harmony of pride between the man and the brute. He often turned his head after that at hearing the rumble of wheels and the dull thud of hoofs, aware that he was becoming interested in the styles of chariots and charioteers as they rustled past him.

He noticed that the people around him were of all ages, sexes, and all in holiday attire. One company was uniformed in white, another in black. Some bore flags, some smoking censers. Some went slowly, singing hymns. Others stepped to the music of flutes and tambourines. If such people were going to Daphne every day in the year, what a wondrous sight Daphne must be! At last there was a burst of joyous cries, and as people pointed their fingers, he looked and saw the temple gate of the consecrated Grove on the brow of a hill. The hymns swelled to louder strains.

The music quickened, and, borne along by the impulsive current and sharing the common eagerness, he followed them into the place of worship.

He stood upon a broad esplanade paved with polished stone, a restless loud multitude around him in gayest colors. Behind them was the iridescent spray flying crystal-white from fountains. Before him, off to the southwest, dustless paths radiated out into a garden and beyond that into a forest, with a veil of pale blue vapor hanging over it. Ben Hur gazed wistfully, uncertain where to go.

A woman at that moment exclaimed, "Beautiful! But where do we go to now?"

Her companion, wearing a wreath of bays, laughed and answered, "Where do we go to, you pretty barbarian? The question implies an earthly fear. And did we not agree to leave all these behind in Antioch with the dust there? The winds that blow here are the breath of the gods. Let us give ourselves to inhaling the winds."

"But if we should get lost?"

"O you timid woman! No one was ever lost in Daphne, except those on whom her gates close forever."

"And who are they?" she asked, still fearful.

"Those who have yielded to the charms of the place and chosen it for life. Listen! Stand here, and I will tell you whom I speak about."

There was a scurry of sandaled feet upon the marble pavement. The crowd parted, and a group of girls rushed around the speaker and his fair friend and began singing and dancing to the tambourines they brought with them. The woman was scared and clung to the man, who put an arm about her and, with kindled face, kept time to the music with the other and those overhead. The hair of the dancers floated free, and their limbs blushed through the robes of gauze that scarcely draped them. Words may not be used to tell of the sensuousness of the dance. One brief round, and they darted off through the yielding crowd as lightly as they had come.

"Now, what do you think?" cried the man to the woman.

"Who are they?" she asked.

"Devadasi—priestesses devoted to the temple of Apollo. There is an army of them. They create a chorus of celebrations. This is their home. Sometimes they wander off to other cities, but all they bring herein to enrich the house of the divine musician. Shall we go now?"

The next minute the two were gone. Ben Hur took comfort in the assurance that no one was ever lost in Daphne, and he too set out—where, he did not know. A sculpture placed upon a beautiful pedestal in the garden attracted him first. It proved to be the statue of a centaur. An inscription informed the unlearned visitor that it exactly represented Chiron, the beloved of Apollo and Diana, instructed by them in the mysteries of hunting, medicine, music, and prophecy. The inscription also requested the stranger to look out at a certain part of the heavens, at a certain hour on a clear night, and he would behold the dead alive among the stars, where Jupiter had transferred them.

Ben Hur turned away as the white bull was led by. The boy sat in the basket, followed by a procession. After them again, the woman with the goats, and behind her the flute and tambourine players and another procession of gift bringers.

"Where do they go?" asked a bystander.

Another answered, "The bull to Father Jove. The goat—"

"Did not Apollo once keep the flocks of Admetus?"

"Aye, the goat to Apollo!"

A certain accommodation to another's religion comes to us after much familiarity with people of a different faith. Gradually we attain the truth that every creed is maintained by good men who are entitled to our respect, but whom we cannot respect without courtesy to their creed. Ben Hur had arrived at this point. Neither the years in Rome nor those in the galley had made an impression upon his religious faith; he was still a Jew. In his view, nevertheless, it was not wrong to look for the beautiful in the Grove of Daphne.

Yet he was angry—not as one who is irritable from chafing of a mere trifle, nor was his anger like the fool's, pumped from the wells of nothing of substance, to be given up by a reproach or a curse. It was the wrath peculiar to ardent natures rudely awakened by the sudden annihilation of a hope—dream, if you will— in which the choicest happiness was thought to be certainly in reach. In such case nothing will satisfy the passion—the quarrel is with his fate.

In an ordinary mood, Ben Hur would not have come to the Grove alone, or, coming alone, he would have made known his position in the consul's family and would have made a provision against wandering idly around. He would have had all the points of interest in mind and gone to them under guidance. Or, wishing to squander days of leisure in the beautiful place, he would have had a letter in hand to the master of it all, whoever he might be. This would have made him a sightseer, like the shouting herd he was accompanying, but he had no reverence or curiosity for the deities of the Grove. He was a man in the blindness of bitter disappointment, adrift, not waiting for Fate, but seeking it as a desperate challenger.

Every one has known this condition, though perhaps not all in the same degree. Everyone will recognize it as the condition in which he has done brave things with apparent serenity. It would have been fortunate for Ben Hur if the folly that now sought him was but a friendly clown with a whistle and painted cap and not violence with a pitiless pointed sword.

33

The Mulberries of Daphne

Ben Hur entered the woods with the processions. He had not enough interest at first to ask where they were going. Yet he had a vague impression they were moving to the temples, which were the central objects of the Grove and supreme in their attractions.

Soon, as singers dreamily play with a flitting chorus, he began repeating to himself, "Better be a worm and feed on the mulberries of Daphne, than a king's guest." Then with much repetition arose these questions: Was life in the Grove so very sweet? Where was the charm? Did it lie in some tangled depth of philosophy? Or was it something in fact, something on the surface, discernible to the wakeful senses? Every year thousands, forswearing the world, gave themselves to her service here. Did they find the charm? And was it sufficient, when found, to induce forgetfulness profound enough to shut out of mind the many things of life that both sweeten and embitter one—hopes hovering in the near future as well as sorrows from the past?

If the Grove was so good for them, why should it not be good for him? He was a Jew. Could it be that the excellences were for all the world but the children of Abraham? He then bent all his faculties to the task of discovery, unmindful of the singing of the gift bringers and the words of his associates.

In the quest, the sky yielded him nothing. It was very blue and full of twittering swallows. Further on, out of the woods at his right hand, a breeze poured across the road, splashing him with a wave of sweet smells, blended of roses and consuming spices. He stopped, as did others, looking in the direction the breeze came.

"A garden over there?" he said to a man at his elbow.

"No, rather some priestly ceremony being performed—something to Diana or Pan or a deity of the woods." The answer was in his mother tongue.

Ben Hur gave the speaker a surprised look. "A Hebrew?" he asked him.

The man replied with a deferential smile. "I was born within a stone's throw of the marketplace in Jerusalem."

Ben Hur was about to make further speech, when the crowd surged forward, thrusting him out on the side of the walk next the woods and carrying the stranger away. The customary gown and staff, a brown cloth on the head tied by a yellow rope, and a strong Judean face to vouch for the garments, remained in the young man's mind, a kind of composite of the man.

This took place at a point where a path into the woods began, offering a happy escape from the noisy procession. Ben Hur took this opportunity. He walked first into a thicket that from the road appeared closed, impenetrable, a nesting place for wild birds. A few steps, however, allowed him to see the master's hand even there. The shrubs were flowering or fruit bearing. Under the bending branches the ground was covered with bright blooms. Over them the jasmine stretched its delicate bonds. From lilac and rose and lily and tulip, from oleander and strawberry tree, all old friends in the gardens of the valleys about the city of David, the air, lingering or in haste, filled itself with the day and night. There was pure happiness for the nymphs and naiads. Down through the flower-lighted shadows a brook went its course gently by many winding ways.

Out of the thicket came the cry of the pigeon and the cooing of turtle-doves. Blackbirds waited for him and allowed for his coming closer. A nightingale kept its place fearlessly, though he passed in arms' length. A quail ran before him at his feet, whistling to the brood she was leading, and as he paused for them to get out of his way, a figure crawled from a bed of honeyed musk brilliant with balls of golden blossoms.

Ben Hur was startled. Had he, indeed, been permitted to see a satyr at home? The creature looked up at him. He smiled at his own scare. Peace without fear—peace here was a universal condition.

He saw on the ground beneath a citron tree, which spread its gray roots sprawling to receive a branch of the brook, the nest of a titmouse. It hung close to the bubbling water, and the tiny creature looked out of the door of the nest into his eyes. *Truly, the bird is speaking to me,* he thought. *It says, "I am not afraid of you, for the law of this happy place is Love."*

The charm of the Grove seemed obvious to him. He was glad and determined to consider himself as one of the lost in Daphne. In charge of the flowers and shrubs and watching the growth of all of nature everywhere to be seen, could not he forgo the days of his troubled life—forgo them and forget?

But by and by his Jewish nature began to stir within him. The charm might be sufficient for some people. Of what kind were they? Love is delightful—ah! How pleasant as a successor to a wretchedness like his. But was it all there was of life?

There was a difference between him and those who buried themselves contentedly here. They had no duties—they could not have had. But he—

"God of Israel!" he cried aloud, springing to his feet with burning cheeks. "Mother! Tirzah! Cursed be the moment, cursed the place, in which I am happy in the midst of your loss!"

He hurried away through the thicket and came to a stream flowing like a strong river between banks of stones broken at points by gates. A bridge carried the path he was traveling across the stream, and, standing upon it, he saw other bridges, no two of them alike. Under him the water was lying in a deep pool, clear as a shadow. Down a little way it tumbled with a roar over rocks. And bridges and pools and resounding cascades proved that the river was running by permission of a master, exactly as the master would have it, as becomes a servant of the gods.

In front of the bridge he viewed a landscape of wide valleys and irregular heights, with groves and lakes and fanciful houses linked together by white paths and shining streams. The valleys were spread out below so that the river would flood them for refreshment in days of drought, and they appeared as green carpets covered with beds of flowers and flecked with flocks of sheep white as balls of snow. The voices of shepherds following their flocks were heard from far away. As if to explain the sacredness of all he beheld, the altars under the open sky seemed countless. Each had a white-gowned attendant, while processions in white went slowly among them. The half-risen smoke of the altars hung in pale clouds over the devoted places.

Sublime mysteries were hidden behind his first view of all this beauty! In various places the ritual was beginning. His gaze wandered, and he realized that there was peace in the air and an invitation everywhere to come and lie down here and be at rest.

Suddenly a revelation dawned upon him—the Grove was a temple—one far-reaching temple without walls! There was never anything like it! The architect had not stopped to bother about columns and porticos, proportions or interiors, or any other limitation. He had simply made a servant of Nature.

From the bridge Ben Hur went forward into the nearest valley and came to a flock of sheep. The shepherd was a girl, and she beckoned to him. "Come!"

Farther on, the path was divided by an altar—a pedestal of black ebony capped with a slab of white marble and on that a brazier of bronze with a fire. Close by it, a woman, seeing him, waved a willow wand and called him. "Stay!" And the temptation in her smile was that of passionate youth.

Farther on he met one of the processions. At its head was a troop of little girls, nude except that they were covered with garlands, who piped their shrill voices into a song. Then a troop of boys, also nude, their bodies deeply sunbrowned, came dancing to the song of the girls. Behind them came the procession, all women, bearing baskets of spices and sweets to the altars—clad in simple robes. As he went by they held out their hands to him and said, "Stay, and go with us." One, a Greek, sang a verse from Anacreon:

> For today I take or give;
> For today I drink and live;
> For today I beg or borrow;
> Who knows about the silent morrow?

But he went his way indifferently and came next to a luxuriant grove in the heart of the vale at the point where it would be most attractive to the observing eye. Through the foliage he caught the light of a statue, so he turned aside and entered the cool retreat.

The grass was fresh and clean. Here grouped together were palm trees plumed like queens, sycamores overtopping laurels of darker foliage, and evergreen oaks rising verdantly, with cedars vast enough to be kings on Lebanon, and mulberries—all so beautiful it is not an exaggeration to speak of them as blown from the orchards of Paradise.

The statue proved to be a Daphne of wondrous beauty. He hardly had time to more than glance at her face because at the base of the pedestal a girl and a youth were lying upon a tiger's skin asleep in each other's arms. Close by were them were their tools and her basket—flung carelessly upon a heap of faded roses.

The scene startled him. Back in the hush of the perfumed thicket he discovered, as he thought, that the charm of the great Grove was peace without fear and had almost yielded to it. Now, in this sleep at the foot of Daphne—in the day's broad glare—he realized that the law of the place was Love, but love without law. This was the sweet peace of Daphne, and for this kings and princes gave of their revenues.

For this a crafty priesthood manipulated nature—her birds and brooks and lilies, the sanctity of altars, and the fertile power of the sun. Ben Hur felt somewhat sorry for the servants of the great outdoor temple, especially for those who, by personal service, kept it in a state so surpassingly lovely. How they came to this condition was not any longer a mystery. The motive was before him.

Some were caught by the promise held out to their troubled spirits of endless peace in a consecrated abode, to the beauty of which, if they did not have money, they could at least contribute their labor. Many of this crowd were devotees of the unmixed sensualism of the East. In this age, there were in all the earth only two types of people capable of the religious service of the kind referred to—those who lived by the law of Moses and those who lived by the law of Brahma. They alone could tell you, it is better to have a law without love than a love without law.

Ben Hur walked with a quicker step, holding his head higher. While not less sensitive to the delightfulness of all about him, he viewed it with a calmer spirit, but he could not so soon forget how nearly he himself had succumbed to it.

34

The Stadium in the Grove

In front of Ben Hur was a forest of cypress trees, each a column tall and straight as a mast. Walking into the shady precinct, he heard a trumpet and an instant after saw the countryman he had come upon in the road going to the temples lying upon the grass close by. The man arose and came to him.

"I give you peace again," he said pleasantly.

"Thank you," Ben Hur replied, then asked, "Are you going my way?"

"I am heading for the stadium, if that is your way."

"The stadium!"

"Yes. The trumpet you heard was a call for the competitors."

"Good friend," said Ben Hur frankly, "I admit my ignorance of the Grove, and if you will let me be your follower, I will be glad."

"That will delight me. Listen! I hear the wheels of the chariots. They are on the track."

Ben Hur listened a moment, then laying his hand upon the man's arm said, "I am the son of Arrius, the duumvir, and you?"

"I am Malluch, a merchant of Antioch."

"Well, good Malluch, the trumpet and the prospect of diversion excite me. I have some skill in the exercises. In the palaestrae of Rome I am not unknown. Let us go to the course."

Malluch lingered to say quickly, "The duumvir was a Roman, yet I see his son in the garments of a Jew."

"The noble Arrius was my father by adoption," Ben Hur answered.

"Ah! I see and beg your pardon."

Passing through the line of trees, they came to a field with a track laid out upon it, its shape and extent exactly like those of the stadium. The course was of soft earth, rolled and sprinkled, and on both sides bordered by ropes stretched loosely upon upright javelins. For the accommodation of spectators there were several stands shaded by substantial awnings, and they were provided with seats in rising rows.

In one of the stands the two newcomers found places.

Ben Hur counted the chariots as they went by—nine in all. "I commend the fellows," he said with goodwill. "Here in the East I thought they aspired to nothing better than the two, but they are ambitious and play with royal fours. Let us study their performance."

Eight of the fours passed the stand, some walking, others trotting, and all exceptionally well handled. Then the ninth one came galloping.

Ben Hur said, "I have been in the stables of the emperor, Malluch, but, by our father Abraham of blessed memory! I never saw the likes of these."

The last four then swept past. All at once they fell into confusion. Someone on the stand uttered a sharp cry. Ben Hur turned and saw an old man half-risen from an upper seat, his hands clenched and raised, his eyes fiercely bright, his long white beard quivering. Some of the spectators nearest him began to laugh.

"They should respect his beard at least. Who is he?" asked Ben Hur.

"A mighty man from the desert, somewhere beyond Moab, and owner of camels and horses descended, they say, from the racers of the first Pharaoh—Sheik Ilderim by name and title," Malluch replied.

The driver meanwhile tried to quiet the four but without success. Each ineffectual effort worried the sheik even more.

"Run! Fly! Do you hear, my children?" yelled the patriarch shrilly. The question was to his attendants, apparently of the tribe. "Do you hear? They are desert-born, like yourselves. Catch them— quick!"

The plunging of the animals increased. "Accursed Roman!" and the sheik shook his fist at the driver. "Did he not swear he could drive them—swear it by all his brood of illegitimate Latin gods? No, hands off me—off I say! They should run swift as eagles and with the temper of hand-bred lambs. Cursed be the mother of liars who calls him son! See them, the priceless! Let him touch one of them with a lash, and—" The rest of the sentence was lost in a furious grinding of his teeth. "To their heads, some of you, and speak to them—a word, one is enough, from the tent song your mothers sang you. Oh, fool that I was to put trust in a Roman!"

Some of the shrewder of the old man's friends planted themselves between him and the horses. Ben Hur, thinking he understood the sheik, sympathized with him. Far more than mere pride of property—more than anxiety for the result of the race—in his view it was within the realm of possibility for the patriarch to love such animals with a deep tenderness.

They were all bright bays, unspotted, perfectly matched, and very well proportioned. As he looked closer at the horses, Ben Hur read the story of their relation to their master. They had grown up under his eyes, objects of his special care in the day, his visions of pride in the night, with his family at home in the black tent out on the shadeless desert. So that they might win him a triumph over the haughty and hated Romans, the old man had brought his loves to the city, never doubting they would win, if only he could find a trusted expert to take them in hand—not merely one with skill, but with a spirit to which their spirits would respond. Unlike the more reserved people of the West, he could not protest the driver's inability and dismiss him civilly. An Arab and a sheik, he had to explode.

Before the patriarch was done with his expletives, a dozen hands were at the bits of the horses, and they quieted them. About that time, another chariot entered the track. Unlike the others, driver, vehicle, and racers appeared precisely as they would be presented in the circus on the day of final trial.

A chariot of classical renown is simply a dray with low wheels and a broad axle on top of a box open at the tail end. This was the primitive pattern. Artistic genius came along in time and took this rude machine and raised it into a thing of beauty—like that in which Aurora, riding ahead of the dawn, is seen in our imagination.

The ancient jockeys, quite as shrewd and ambitious as their successors of the present, rated their humblest turnout a number two and their best grade a number four. In the latter, they contested in the Olympics and the other festal shows.

The same sharp gamesters preferred to put their horses on the chariot straight across. They termed the two next to the pole yoke-steeds and those on the right and left outside the trace-mates. It was their judgment that, by allowing the fullest freedom of action, the greatest speed was attainable. So the harness used was particularly simple. In fact, there was nothing to it except a collar around the animal's neck. Wanting to hitch up, the masters pinned a narrow wooden yoke, or crosstree, near the end of the pole and, by straps passed through rings at the end of the yoke, buckled the latter to the collar. They hitched to the axle the traces of the yoke-steeds.

The other contestants had been introduced in silence. The last newcomer was more fortunate. While moving toward the stand from which they viewed the scene, his progress was signaled by loud demonstrations of applause and cheers, the effect of which was to center attention upon him exclusively. His yoke-steeds, it was observed, were black, while the trace-mates were snow-white. In conformity to the exacting canons of Roman taste, they had all four been mutilated. That is to say, their tails had been clipped, and, to complete the effect, their shorn manes were divided into knots tied with flaring red and yellow ribbons.

In advancing, the stranger reached a point where the chariot came into view from the stand, and its appearance would of itself have justified the shouting. The wheels were marvels of construction. Stout bands of burnished bronze reinforced the hubs. The spokes were sections of ivory tusks, set in with the natural curve outward. Bronze tires held the frames, which were of shining ebony. The axle, as with the wheels, was tipped with heads of snarling tigers done in brass, and the bed was woven of willow wands gilded with gold.

The coming of the beautiful horses and resplendent chariot drew Ben Hur to observe the driver with increased interest. Ben Hur could not see the man's face or even his full figure. Yet the air and manner were familiar and pricked him keenly with a reminder of a period long gone. Who could it be?

The horses were approaching nearer now, at a trot. From the shouting and the gorgeous display of the turnout, it was thought he might be some favorite official or famous prince. Such an appearance was not inconsistent with exalted rank. Kings often struggled for the crown of leaves that was the prize of victory. Nero and Commodus, it will be remembered, devoted themselves to chariot races.

Ben Hur arose and forced his way down nearly to the railing in front of the lower seat of the stand. He was earnest and eager to discover the identity of the driver.

Immediately the driver was in view. A companion rode with him, a Myrtilus, that is, a man of high estate indulging his passion for the racecourse. Ben Hur could only see the driver, standing erect in the chariot, with the reins passed several times round his body—a handsome figure, scantily covered by a tunic of light red cloth. In the right hand was a whip. In the other, with his arm raised, the four lines for the horses. His pose was graceful and animated. The cheers and applause were received by him with statuesque indifference. Ben Hur stood transfixed. His instinct and memory had served him faithfully—the driver was Messala.

His selection of horses, the magnificence of the chariot, his attitude, and, above all, his cold, sharp, eagle features, imperialized in his countrymen by rule of the world through so many generations, Ben Hur knew Messala unchanged, as haughty, confident, and audacious as ever, the same in ambition and cynicism.

35

The Fountain of Castalia

As Ben Hur descended the steps of the stand, an Arab arose upon the last one at the foot and cried out, "Men of the East and West—listen! The good Sheik Ilderim gives you greeting. With four horses, sons of the favorites of Solomon the wise, he has come up against the best. He needs a mighty man to drive them. Whoever will take them to the sheik's satisfaction, he promises enrichment forever. Here in the city and in the circuses, and wherever the strong most do congregate, this is his offer. So says my master, Sheik Ilderim the Generous." The proclamation awakened a great buzz among the people under the awning. It would be repeated and discussed in all the sporting circles of Antioch by night. Ben Hur, hearing it, stopped and looked hesitatingly from the herald to the sheik.

Malluch thought he was about to accept the offer and was relieved when he turned to him and asked, "Good Malluch, where to now?"

He replied with a laugh, "If you would be like others visiting the Grove for the first time, you will go to hear your fortune told."

"My fortune, you said? Though the suggestion has a flavor of unbelief, let us go to the goddess at once."

"No, son of Arrius, these Apollonians have a better trick than that. Instead of speech with a Pythia or a Sibyl, they will sell you a plain papyrus leaf, hardly dry from the stalk, and ask you to dip it in the water of a certain fountain, when it will show you a verse in which you may hear of your future."

The glow of interest departed from Ben Hur's face. "There are people who have no need to worry themselves about their future," he said, gloomily.

"Then you prefer to go to the temples?"

"The temples are Greek, are they not?"

"They call them Greek."

"The Hellenes were masters of the beautiful in art, but in architecture they sacrificed variety to unbending beauty. Their temples are all alike. What do you call the fountain?"

"Castalia."

"It has repute throughout the world. Let us go."

Malluch kept watch on his companion as they went and saw that for the moment at least his spirits were high. He gave no attention to the people passing. There were no exclamations over the wonders they came upon.

The truth was, the sight of Messala had caused Ben Hur to think. It seemed scarcely an hour ago that strong hands had torn him from his mother, scarcely an hour ago that the Roman had put his seal upon the gates of his father's house. He remembered how, in the galleys, he had had little else to do, aside from labor, than dream dreams of vengeance in all of which Messala was the principal victim. There might be, he used to say to himself, escape for Gratus, but for Messala—never! And to strengthen his resolution, he repeated over and over, *Who pointed us out to the persecutors? And when I begged him for help—not for myself— who mocked me and went away laughing?* And always the dream had the same ending. *The day I meet him, help me, You the good God of my people!—help me to some fitting special vengeance!*

And now the meeting was at hand. Perhaps if he had found Messala poor and suffering, Ben Hur's feeling might have been different. But it was not so. He found him more than prosperous. In the prosperity there was a dash and glitter—like a gleam of sun on gold.

They turned into an avenue of oaks, where the people were going and coming in groups—pedestrians and horsemen, women in litters borne by slaves, and chariots rolling by thunderously.

At the end of the avenue the road descended into a lowland, where there was a precipitous facing of gray rock and an open meadow. Then they came in view of the famous Fountain of Castalia.

Ben Hur saw a jet of sweet water pouring from the crest of a stone into a basin of black marble, where, after much boiling and foaming, it disappeared through a funnel.

By the basin, under a small portico cut in the solid wall, sat an old, bearded, wrinkled priest—a hermit. It was hard to say which was the attraction, the forever sparkling fountain or the priest, forever there. He heard, saw, was seen, but never spoke. Occasionally a visitor extended a hand to him with a coin in it. With a cunning twinkle of the eyes, he took the money and gave a leaf of papyrus in exchange.

The receiver plunged the papyrus into the basin, then, holding the dripping leaf in the sunlight, would be rewarded with a verse inscribed upon it. Before Ben Hur could test the oracle, some other visitors were seen approaching across the meadow, and their appearance caused curiosity from the entire group.

He saw a camel first, very tall and white, leading a driver on horseback. A seat on the animal was crimson and gold and unusually large. Two other horsemen followed the camel with tall spears in hand.

"What a wonderful camel!" said one of the company.

"A prince from afar," another one suggested.

"More likely a king."

"If he were on an elephant I would say he was a king."

A third man had a different opinion. "By Apollo, friends, you can see there are two of them—they are neither kings nor princes. They are women!"

In the midst of the dispute the strangers arrived. No traveler at the fountain, though from the remotest parts, had ever beheld a taller, statelier animal of his kind. Such great black eyes! And such exceedingly fine white hair! Nobody had ever seen the peer of this camel. And how well he suited his housing of silk and all its finery of gold in fringe and gold tassel! The tinkling of silver bells went before him, and he moved lightly, as if not knowing his burden.

But who were the man and woman under the howdah? Every eye questioned them. If the former were a prince or a king, the philosophers of the crowd might not deny the impartiality of time. When they saw the thin, shrunken face buried under an immense turban, skin the hue of a mummy, making it impossible to discover his nationality, they knew the limit of life was equal for the great as well as the insignificant.

The woman was seated in the style of the East, amidst veils

and laces of surpassing fineness. Above her elbows she wore armlets fashioned like coiled snakes and linked to bracelets at the wrist by strands of gold. Her hands showed tapered fingers glittering with rings and stained at the tips till they blushed like the pink of mother-of-pearl. She wore an open headdress, sprinkled with beads of coral and strung with coin pieces called sunlets, half-smothered in the mass of her straight, blue-black hair, of itself an incomparable ornament, not needing the veil that covered it.

From her elevated seat she looked upon the people pleasantly, and apparently she was so intent upon studying them as to be unconscious of the interest she herself was raising. And what was unusual—in violation of the custom among women of rank in public—she looked at them with an open, unveiled face.

It was a fair, youthful face, oval, with the ruddiness of lamplight. The eyes, naturally large, were outlined along the lids with the black paint known throughout the East. She had a small head, classic in shape, set upon a long, graceful neck—the air, we may fancy, happily described by the word *queenly.*

The fair creature spoke to the driver—an Ethiopian of vast brawn and naked to the waist—who led the camel nearer the fountain and told it to kneel. He then received a cup from her hand and filled it at the basin. That instant the sound of wheels and the trampling of horses in rapid motion broke the silence her beauty had imposed, and with a great outcry the bystanders parted in every direction, hurrying to get away.

"This Roman plans to ride us down. Look out!" Malluch shouted to Ben Hur, setting an example of quick flight.

The latter faced the direction from which the sounds came and saw Messala in his chariot pushing the four straight at the crowd. This time the view was near and distinct.

The parting of the company uncovered the camel, which might have been more agile than his kind generally. Yet the hoofs were almost upon him, and he resting with closed eyes, chewed the endless cud with the sense of security bred in him. The Ethiopian wrung his hands out of fear. In the howdah, the old man moved to escape. But he was hampered with age and could not, even in the face of danger, forget the dignity that was clearly his habit. It was too late for the woman to save herself.

Ben Hur stood nearest them, and he called to Messala, "Hold on! Look where you are going! Get back!"

The patrician was laughing in hearty good humor.

Seeing there was but one chance of rescue, Ben Hur stepped in and caught the bits of the left steed and his mate. "Dog of a Roman! Do you care so little for life?" he cried, exerting all his strength.

The two horses reared and drew the others around. The tilting of the pole tilted the chariot. Messala barely escaped a fall, while his complacent Myrtilus rolled back like a clod to the ground. Seeing the peril past, all the bystanders burst into mocking laughter.

The matchless audacity of the Roman then showed itself. Loosing the lines from his body, he tossed them to one side, dismounted, walked round the camel, looked at Ben Hur, and spoke partly to the old man and partly to the woman.

"Pardon, I pray you both. I am Messala," he said. "And by the old Mother of the earth, I swear I did not see you or your camel! As to these good people—perhaps I trusted my skill too much. I sought to get a laugh from them—the laugh is theirs. May it do them good!"

The good-natured, careless look and gesture he threw the bystanders accorded well with the speech. They became quiet to hear what more he had to say. Assured of victory over the offended, he signaled his companion to take the chariot to a safer distance and spoke boldly to the woman.

"You have interest in the good man here, whose pardon, if not granted now, I shall seek with great diligence later—his daughter, I believe."

She made no reply.

"By Pallas, you are beautiful! Beware that Apollo does not mistake you for his lost love. I wonder what land can boast herself to be your mother. Do not turn away. A truce! There is the sun of India in your eyes. In the corners of your mouth Egypt has given her love signs. Do not turn to that slave, fair mistress, before proving merciful to this one. Tell me at least that I am pardoned."

At this point she broke in upon him. "Will you come here?" she asked, looking toward Ben Hur.

"Take the cup and fill it, I pray you," she said to him. "My father is thirsty."

"I am your most willing servant!"

Ben Hur turned, about to do the favor, and was face to face with Messala. Their glances met. The Jew's was defiant; the Roman sparkled with humor.

"O stranger, beautiful as you are cruel!" Messala said, waving his hand to her. "If Apollo does not get you, you will see me again. Not knowing your country, I cannot name a god to commend you to. So, by all the gods, I will commend you to—myself!"

Seeing that the Myrtilus had the four horses composed and ready, he returned to the chariot. The woman looked after him as he moved away, and whatever else there was in her look, there was no displeasure. She received the water, and her father drank. Then she raised the cup to her lips and, leaning down, gave it to Ben Hur with gracefulness.

"Keep it, we ask of you! It is full of blessings, all yours!"

Immediately the camel awoke and got on his feet. He was about to go when the old man called, "Stand here."

Ben Hur went to him respectfully.

"You have served the stranger well today. There is but one God. In his holy name I thank you. I am Balthasar, the Egyptian. In the Great Orchard of Palms, beyond the village of Daphne, in the shade of the palms, Sheik Ilderim the Generous abides in his tents, and we are his guests. Seek us there. You will have welcome sweet with the savor of the grateful."

Ben Hur was left in wonder at the old man's clear voice and reverent manner. As he gazed after the two who were departing, he caught sight of Messala going as he had come, joyous, indifferent, and with a mocking laugh.

36

The Chariot Race Discussed

As a rule, there is no surer way to arouse the dislike of men than to behave well where they have behaved badly. In this instance, happily, Malluch was an exception to the rule. The affair he had just witnessed raised Ben Hur in his mind, since he could not deny him courage. If he could now get some insight into the young man's history, the results of the day would not be all unprofitable to good master Simonides.

He had learned that the subject of his investigation was a Jew and the adopted son of a famous Roman. Another conclusion that might be of importance was beginning to formulate itself in the shrewd mind of the spy—between Messala and the son of the duumvir there was a connection of some kind. But what was it? And how could it be reduced to clear understanding? With all this realization, the ways and means of a solution were not immediate.

In the heat of his perplexity, Ben Hur himself came to his help. He laid his hand on Malluch's arm and drew him out of the crowd, which was already going back to its own concerns with the gray old priest and the mystic fountain.

"Good Malluch," he said, stopping, "may a man forget his mother?"

The question was abrupt and without cause and the kind that leaves the person addressed in a state of confusion. Malluch looked into Ben Hur's face for a hint of meaning but saw, instead, two bright red spots, one on each cheek, and what might have been repressed tears.

Then he answered mechanically, "No! Never!" and a moment after, "If he is an Israelite, never!" And when he was completely recovered, "My first lesson in the synagogue was the Shema. My next was the saying of the son of Sirach, 'Honor your father with your whole soul, and forget not the sorrows of your mother.'"

The red spots on Ben Hur's face deepened. "The words bring my childhood back again. And, Malluch, they prove you to be a genuine Jew. I believe I can trust you."

Ben Hur let go the arm he was holding, caught the folds of the robe covering his own breast, and pressed them close, as if to smother pain.

"My father," he said, "bore a good name and was not without honor in Jerusalem, where he lived. My mother, at his death, was in the prime of womanhood. It is not enough to say of her she was good and beautiful. In her tongue was the law of kindness, and her works were praised in all the gates, and she smiled at days to come. I had a little sister, and she and I were the family, and we were so happy that I have never seen harm in the saying of the old rabbi, 'God could not be everywhere, and so he made mothers.'

"One day an accident happened to a Roman in authority as he was riding past our house at the head of a cohort. The legionnaires burst into the gate and rushed in and seized us. I have not seen my mother or sister since. I cannot say they are dead or living. I do not know what became of them.

"But, Malluch, the man in the chariot over there was present at the separation. He gave us over to the captors. He heard my mother's prayer for her children, and he laughed when they dragged her away. I may hardly say which is deepest in my memory—love or hate. Today I knew him—and Malluch"—he caught the listener's arm again—"and, Malluch, he knows and takes with him now the secret I would give my life for. He could tell if she lives, and where she is, and her condition. If she—no, they—much sorrow has made the two as one—if they are dead, he could tell where they died, and of what, and where their bones await my finding."

"And will he not?"

"No."

"Why?"

"I am a Jew, and he is a Roman."

"But Romans have tongues, and Jews, though ever so despised, have methods to beguile them."

"For such as he? No. And besides, the secret is one of the state. All my father's property was confiscated and divided."

194

Malluch nodded his head slowly, as much as to admit the argument. Then he asked again, "Did he not recognize you?"

"He could not. I was sent to death in life and have been long since accounted dead."

"I wonder that you did not strike him," said Malluch, yielding to a touch of compassion.

"That would have been to forever put him past serving me. I would have had to kill him, and death, you know, keeps secrets better even than a guilty Roman."

The man who, with so much to avenge, could so calmly put such an opportunity aside must be confident of his future or have some better design ready, and Malluch's interest changed with the thought. It ceased to be that of an emissary in duty bound to another. Ben Hur was actually asserting a claim upon him for his own sake. In other words, Malluch was preparing to serve him with good heart and from downright admiration.

After a brief pause, Ben Hur resumed speaking.

"I would not take his life, good Malluch. His possession of the secret is for the present his safeguard. Yet I may punish him, and if you give me help, I will try."

"He is a Roman," said Malluch, without hesitation, "and I am of the tribe of Judah. I will help you. If you choose, put me under oath—under the most solemn oath."

"Give me your hand—that will do," Ben Hur said, with an elated feeling. "What I would charge you with is not difficult, good friend. Neither is it opposed to your conscience. Let us move on."

They took the road that led to the right across the meadow. Ben Hur was first to break the silence.

"Do you know Sheik Ilderim the Generous?"

"Yes."

"Where is his Orchard of Palms? Or rather, Malluch, how far is it beyond the village of Daphne?"

Malluch recalled the generosity of the favor shown him by the woman at the fountain and wondered if he who had the sorrows of a mother in mind was about to forget them for a lure of love. Yet he replied, "The Orchard of Palms lies beyond the village two hours by horse and one by a swift camel."

195

"Thank you. Have the games of which you told me been widely published? And when will they take place?"

The questions, if they did not restore confidence to Malluch, at least stimulated his curiosity.

"Oh yes, they will be of ample splendor. The prefect is rich and could afford to lose his place. Yet, as is the way with successful men, his love of riches in no way is diminished. And to gain a friend at court, if nothing more, he must make do for the Consul Maxentius, who is coming here to make final preparations for a campaign against the Parthians. The money there is in the preparations, the citizens of Antioch know from experience. So they have had permission to join the prefect in the honors intended for the great man. A month ago heralds went to all quarters to proclaim the opening of the circus for the celebration.

"The name of the prefect would be of itself a good guarantee of variety and magnificence, particularly throughout the East. All the islands and the cities by the sea will be assured of the extraordinary and will be here in person or represented by their most famous professionals. The fees offered are royal."

"And the circus—I have heard it is second only to the Maximus."

"At Rome, you mean. Well, ours seats two hundred thousand people. Yours seats seventy-five thousand more. Yours is of marble; so is ours. They are exactly the same in arrangement."

"Are the rules the same?"

Malluch smiled.

"If Antioch dared to be original, son of Arrius, Rome would not be the mistress she is. The laws of the Circus Maximus govern all except in one particular—there are four chariots, which may start at once. Here all start without reference to number."

"That is the practice of the Greeks," said Ben Hur.

"Yes, Antioch is more Greek than Roman."

"So then, Malluch, may I choose my own chariot?"

"Your own chariot and horses. There is no restriction upon either."

Ben Hur's face gave a look of satisfaction.

"One thing more now, O Malluch. When will the celebration be?"

"Tomorrow, and the next day—" the other counted aloud "—then, to speak in the Roman style, if the sea-gods be good, the consul arrives. Yes, the sixth day from this we have the games."

"The time is short, Malluch, but it is enough." The words were spoken decisively. "By the prophets of our old Israel! I will take to the reins again. Stay! One condition—is there assurance that Messala will be a competitor?"

Malluch now saw the plan and all its opportunities for the humiliation of the Roman. And he would not have been a true descendant of Jacob if he had not considered the chances. His voice actually trembled as he said, "Do you have the practice?"

"Fear not, my friend. The winners in the Circus Maximus have held their crowns these three years at my will. Ask them— ask the best of them, and they will tell you so. In the last great games the emperor himself offered me his patronage if I would take his horses in hand and run them against the other entries."

"But you did not?" Malluch spoke eagerly.

"I . . . I am a Jew"—Ben Hur seemed shrinking within himself as he spoke—"and though I have a Roman name, I dared not professionally do a thing to sully my father's name in the cloisters and courts of the Temple. And if I take to the course here, Malluch, I swear it will not be for the prize or the winner's fee."

"Hold—swear not so!" cried Malluch. "The prize is ten thousand sestertii—a fortune for life!"

"Not for me, even if the prefect trebled it fifty times. Better than that, better than all the imperial revenues from the first year of the first caesar—I will make this race to humble my enemy. Vengeance is permitted by the law."

Malluch smiled and nodded as if saying, "Right—trust me a Jew to understand a Jew."

"Messala will drive," he said. "He is committed to the race in many ways—through publication in the streets, baths and theaters, and palace and barracks. His name is on the tablets of every young spendthrift in Antioch."

"In wager, Malluch?"

"Yes, in wager. And every day be comes to practice, as you saw him."

"Ah! And that is the chariot, and those the horses, with which he will make the race? Thank you, Malluch! You have served me well already. I am satisfied. Now be my guide to the Orchard of Palms and give me an introduction to Sheik Ilderim the Generous."

"When?"

"Today. His horses may be engaged tomorrow."

"You like them, then?"

"I saw them an instant only from the stand, when Messala drove up, and I might not look at anything else. Yet I recognized the horses of the blood which is the wonder as well as the glory of the deserts. I never saw that before, except in the stables of Caesar. But once seen they are always known. Tomorrow, I will know them with the same certainty. If all that is said of them be true, and I can bring their spirit under the control of mine, I can—"

"Win the sestertii!" said Malluch, laughing.

"No," answered Ben Hur, as quickly. "I will do what better becomes a man born to the heritage of Jacob—I will humble my enemy in a very public place. But," he added impatiently, "we are losing time. How can we most quickly reach the tents of the sheik?"

Malluch took a moment for reflection.

"It is best to go straight to the village, which is fortunately near by. If two swift camels are found for hire there, we will be on the road only an hour."

The village had palaces with beautiful gardens, interspersed with inns of the princely sort. Camels were happily secured, and the journey to the famous Orchard of Palms began.

37

Ben Hur Hears of Christ

In the course of their journey the friends came to the river, which they followed with the windings of the road, over bold bluffs and into vales, and the land was in full foliage of oak and sycamore and myrtle and perfuming jasmine. The river was bright with slanted sunlight, which would have slept but for ships in endless procession, gliding with the current or bounding under the impulse of oars.

They came to a lake fed by black water from the river. An old palm tree dominated the angle of the inlet. Malluch clapped his hands and shouted, "Look! The Orchard of Palms!"

Ben Hur went into a tract of land without limit and level as a floor. And the palms, as if they knew Ben Hur's thought and would win him after a way of their own, seemed, as he passed under their arches, to stir and sprinkle him with dewy coolness.

The road wound in close parallel with the shore of the lake. It carried the travelers down to the water's edge, and there was a shining expanse on that side by the opposite shore, on which, as on this one, no tree but the palm was found.

"See that," said Malluch, pointing to the place. "Each ring upon its trunk marks a year of its life. Count them from root to branch, and if the sheik tells you the grove was planted before the Seleucidae were heard of in Antioch, do not doubt him."

The palm tree has received honors, beginning with the artists of the first kings, who could find no form in all the earth to serve them so well as a model for the pillars of their palaces and temples.

For the same reason Ben Hur said, "Good Malluch, Sheik Il-derim appeared to be a very common man as I saw him at the stand today. The rabbis in Jerusalem would look down upon him, I fear, as a son of a dog of Edom. How did he come in possession of the Orchard? And how has he been able to hold it in light of the greed of Roman governors?"

"If lineage derives excellence from time, son of Arrius, then old Ilderim is a great man, though he be an uncircumcised Edomite." Malluch spoke warmly. "All his fathers before him were sheiks. One of them—I will not say when he lived or did the good deed—once helped a king who was being hunted with swords. The story says he loaned him a thousand horsemen who knew the paths of the wilderness and its hiding places as shepherds know the scant hills they inhabit with their flocks. They carried him around until the opportunity came, and then they slew the enemy with their spears and set him upon his throne again.

"And the king, it is said, remembered the service, brought the son of the desert to this place, and asked him to set up his tent and bring his family and his herds, for the lake and trees and all the land from the river to the nearest mountains were his and his children's forever. And they have never been disturbed in the possession. The rulers succeeding have found it good policy to keep peace with the tribe to whom the Lord has given increase of men and horses and camels and riches.

"Even the prefect in the citadel overlooking Antioch thinks it a happy day when Ilderim, surnamed the Generous on account of good deeds done all manner of men, traveling as our fathers Abraham and Jacob traveled, comes up to briefly exchange his bitter wells for the pleasantness you see about us."

"How is it, then?" said Ben Hur, who had been listening, not mindful of the slow gait of the camels. "I saw the sheik tear his beard while he cursed himself that he had put trust in a Roman. Caesar, had he heard him, might have said, 'I do not like such a friend as this—take him away.'"

"It would be a shrewd judgment," Malluch replied, smiling. "Ilderim is not a lover of Rome. He has a grievance. Three years ago the Parthians rode across the road from Bozra to Damascus and attacked a caravan laden, among other things, with the incoming tax returns of a district near there. They killed every creature taken, which the censors in Rome could have forgiven if the imperial treasure had been spared. The farmers of the taxes, being charged with the loss, complained to Caesar, and Caesar held Herod liable. Herod seized the property of Ilderim, whom he charged with treasonable neglect of duty. The sheik appealed to

Caesar, and Caesar has given him such an answer as might be expected from an unwinking sphinx. The old man's heart has been aching ever since, and he nurses his wrath and takes pleasure in its daily growth."

"He can do nothing, Malluch."

"Well," said Malluch, "that involves another explanation, which I will give you. But look! The hospitality of the sheik begins early—the children are speaking to you."

The camels stopped, and Ben Hur looked down upon some little girls of the Syrian peasant class, who were offering him their baskets filled with dates. The fruit was freshly gathered and not to be refused. He stooped and took it, and as he did so a man in the tree nearby cried, "Peace to you, and welcome!" They said their thanks to the children, and the friends moved on at such a pace as the animals chose.

"You must know," Malluch continued, pausing now and then to eat a date, "that the merchant Simonides gives me his confidence and sometimes flatters me by taking me into his council. I serve him at his house, and I have made acquaintance with many of his friends, who, knowing my relationship with the host, talk to him freely in my presence. In that way I became somewhat intimate with Sheik Ilderim."

For a moment Ben Hur's attention wandered. There arose before his mind's eye the image, pure, gentle, and appealing, of Esther, the merchant's daughter. Her dark eyes, bright with the peculiar Jewish luster, met his in a modest gaze. He heard her step and her voice as when she approached him with the wine, and he admitted to himself again all the sympathy she showed for him, so plainly that words were unnecessary and so sweetly that words would have been but a detraction. The vision was exceedingly pleasant.

"A few weeks ago," said Malluch, continuing, "the old Arab called on Simonides and found me there. I offered to withdraw, but he himself forbade me. 'Since you are an Israelite,' he said, 'stay, for I have a strange story to tell.' The emphasis on the word *Israelite* excited my curiosity. I remained, and this is in substance his story.

"A good many years ago, three men called at Ilderim's tent

out in the wilderness. They were all foreigners, a Hindu, a Greek, and an Egyptian, and they had come on white camels, the largest he had ever seen. He welcomed them and gave them rest. Next morning they arose and prayed a prayer new to the sheik—a prayer addressed to God and his Son—with much mystery as well. After breaking fast with him, the Egyptian told him who they were and where they had come from.

"Each had seen a star, out of which a voice had told him to go to Jerusalem and ask, 'Where is he that is born King of the Jews?' They obeyed. From Jerusalem they were led by a star to Bethlehem, where they found a newly born child, which they fell down and worshiped. After worshiping him and giving him costly presents and bearing witness to who he was, they went to their camels and fled without delay to the sheik, because if Herod—surnamed the Great—could lay hands upon them, he would certainly kill them. Faithful to his habit, the sheik took care of them and kept them concealed for a year. Then they departed, leaving with him gifts of great value and going their separate ways."

"It is, indeed, a most wonderful story," Ben Hur said at the conclusion. "What did you say they were to ask at Jerusalem?"

"They were to ask, 'Where is he that is born King of the Jews?'"

"Was that all?"

"There was more to the question, but I cannot recall it."

"And they found the child?"

"Yes, and worshiped him."

"It is a miracle, Malluch."

"Ilderim is a grave man, though excitable, as all Arabs are. A lie on his tongue is impossible." Malluch spoke positively.

The camels were forgotten, and, quite as unmindful as their riders, they turned off the road to the grass.

"Has Ilderim heard anything more of the three men?" asked Ben Hur. "What has become of them?"

"Ah, yes, that was the cause of his coming to Simonides that day. Only the night before that day the Egyptian reappeared to him."

"Where?"

"Here at the door of the tent to which we are coming."

"How did he know he is the man?"

"As you knew the horses today—by face and manner."

"By nothing else?"

"He rode the same white camel and called himself by the same name—Balthasar, the Egyptian."

"It is a wonder of the Lord's!" Ben Hur spoke with excitement.

And Malluch, wondering, asked, "Why so?"

"Balthasar, you said?"

"Yes. Balthasar, the Egyptian."

"That was the name the old man gave us at the fountain today."

"It is true," he said. "And the camel was the same—and you saved the man's life."

"And the woman," said Ben Hur, as if speaking to himself, "the woman was his daughter."

He began thinking and seemed to have a vision of the woman, more welcome than that of Esther, if only because it stayed longer with him. But no—

"Tell me again," he said. "Were the three to ask, 'Where is he that is to be King of the Jews?'"

"Not exactly. The words were 'born to be King of the Jews.' Those were the words as the old sheik caught them first in the desert, and he has ever since been waiting the coming of the King. Nor can anyone shake his faith that he will come."

"How—as king?"

"Yes, and bringing the doom of Rome—so says the sheik."

Ben Hur kept silent awhile, thinking and trying to control his feelings.

"The old man is one of many millions," he said slowly, "one of many millions each with a wrong to avenge. And this strange faith, Malluch, is bread and wine to his hope, for who but a Herod may be king of the Jews while Rome endures? But, following the story, did you hear what Simonides said to him?"

"If Ilderim is a grave man, Simonides is a wise one," Malluch replied. "I listened, and he said—but listen! Someone is overtaking us."

The noise grew louder, until presently they heard the rumble of wheels mixed with the beating of horse hoofs. A moment later Sheik Ilderim himself appeared on horseback, followed by a train, among which were the four wine-red Arab horses drawing the chariot. The two friends had outdistanced him, but at the sight of them, he raised his head and spoke kindly.

"Peace to you! Ah, my friend Malluch! Welcome! And tell me you are not going but have just come—that you have something for me from the good Simonides—may the Lord of his fathers keep him for many years to come! Yes, take up the straps, both of you, and follow me. I have bread and the flesh of a young goat. Come!"

They followed him to the door of the tent, where, when they had dismounted, he stood to receive them, holding a platter with three cups filled with a creamy liquor just drawn from a great smoke-stained skin bottle hanging from the central post.

"Drink," he said, heartily, "drink, for this is the draught of the tentmen."

They each took a cup and drank till only the foam remained.

"Enter now, in God's name."

When they went in, Malluch took the sheik aside and spoke to him privately. Then he went to Ben Hur and excused himself.

"I have told the sheik about you, and he will let you try his horses in the morning. He is your friend. Having done for you all I can, you must do the rest and let me return to Antioch. There is one there who has my promise to meet him tonight. I have no choice but to go. I will come back tomorrow prepared, if all goes well in the meantime, to stay with you until the games are over."

With blessings given and received, Malluch set out to return.

38

The Wise Servant and His Daughter

The lower horn of a new moon touched the palace on Mount Sulpius, and two-thirds of the people of Antioch were out on their housetops comforting themselves with the night breeze when it blew and with fans when it failed. Simonides sat in the chair that had come to be a part of him and from the terrace looked down over the river at his ships swinging at their moorings. The wall at his back cast its shadow broadly over the water to the opposite shore. Above him the endless tramp upon the bridge went on.

Esther was holding a plate for him containing his frugal supper—some wheaten cakes light as wafers, some honey, and a bowl of milk, into which he now and then dipped the wafers after dipping them into the honey.

"Malluch is lagging tonight," he said, letting her know his thoughts.

"Do you believe he will come?" Esther asked.

"Unless he has gone to the sea or the desert and is still following him, he will come."

Simonides spoke with quiet confidence.

"He may write," she said.

"Not so, Esther. He would have sent a letter when he found he could not return, and told me so. Because I have not received such a letter, I know he can come, and will."

"I hope so," she said very softly.

Something in the utterance attracted his attention. It might have been the tone; it might have been the wish. The smallest bird cannot light upon the greatest tree without sending a shock to its most distant leaf. Every mind is at times no less sensitive to the most trifling words.

"You wish him to come, Esther?" he asked.

"Yes," she said, lifting her eyes to his.

"Why? Can you tell me?" he persisted.

"Because—" she hesitated, then began again "—because the young man is—" The stop was full.

"Our master. Is that the word?"

"Yes."

"And you still think I should not allow him to go away without telling him to come, if he chooses, and take us—and all we have—all, Esther—the goods, the shekels, the ships, the slaves, and the mighty credit, which is a mantle of cloth of gold and finest silver spun for me by the greatest of the angels of men—success."

She made no answer.

"Does that move you at all? No?" he said, with the slightest taint of bitterness. "Well, I have found, Esther, that the worst reality is never unendurable when it comes out from behind the clouds through which we at first see it darkly. I suppose it will be so with death. And by that philosophy the slavery to which we are going must after a while become sweet.

"It pleases me even now to think what a favored man our master is. The fortune cost him nothing—not an anxiety, not a drop of sweat, not so much as a thought. It attaches to him in his youth. And, Esther, let me waste a little vanity with the reflection—he gets what he could not go into the market and buy with a vast sum—you, my child, my darling. You, blossom from the tomb of my lost Rachel!" He drew her to him and kissed her twice—once for herself, once for her mother.

"Do not say so," she said, when his hand fell from her neck. "Let us think better of him. He knows what sorrow is and will set us free."

"Ah, your instincts are fine, Esther. And you know I lean upon them in doubtful cases where good or bad is to be pronounced of a person standing before you as he stood this morning. But—" his voice rose and hardened "—these limbs upon which I cannot stand, this body drawn and beaten out of human shape, they are not all I bring to him.

"Oh, no! I bring him a soul which has triumphed over torture and Roman malice. Bring him a mind which has eyes to see gold at a distance farther than the ships that Solomon sailed, and power to bring it to hand—yes, Esther, into my palm here for the fingers to grip and keep lest it take wings at some other's word—a mind skilled at scheming."

He stopped and laughed. "Why, Esther, before the new moon, which in the courts of the Temple on the Holy Hill they are at this moment celebrating, passing into its next quarter I could ring the world so as to startle even Caesar. For know you, child, I have that faculty which is better than any one sense, better than a perfect body, better than courage and will and experience, ordinarily the best product of the longest lives—but which even the great do not sufficiently regard—the faculty of drawing men to my purpose and holding them faithfully to its achievement, by which I multiply my worth into hundreds and thousands. So the captains of my ships plow the seas and bring me honest returns. So Malluch follows the youth, our master, and will—"

Just then a footstep was heard upon the terrace. "Ha, Esther! Did I not say so? He is here, and we will have tidings. For my sake, sweet child, my lily just budded—I pray the Lord God, who has not forgotten his wandering sheep of Israel, that the tidings be good and comforting. Now we will know if he will let you go with all your beauty, and me with all my faculties."

Malluch came to the chair.

"Peace to you, good master," he said, with a low bow. "And to you, Esther, most excellent of daughters."

He stood before them deferentially, and the attitude and the address left it difficult to define his relation to them. The one was that of a servant; the other indicated familiarity and friendship. On the other side, Simonides, as was his habit in business, after answering the greeting, went straight to the subject.

"What of the young man, Malluch?"

The events of the day were told quietly and in the simplest words and until he was through there was no interruption. Nor did the listener in the chair so much as move a hand during the narration. Except for his eyes, wide open and bright, and an occasional long-drawn breath, he might have been a statue.

"Thank you, Malluch," he said, heartily, at the conclusion. "You have done well—no one could have done better. Now what do you say of the young man's nationality?"

"He is an Israelite, good master, and of the tribe of Judah."

"You are positive?"

"Very positive."

"He appears to have told you but little of his life."

"He has somewhere learned to be prudent. I might call him distrustful. He baffled all my attempts upon his confidence until we started from the Castalian fountain going to the village of Daphne."

"A place of abomination! Why did he go there?"

"I would say from curiosity, the first motive of the many who go. But, very strangely, he took no interest in the things he saw. Of the temple, he merely asked if it were Grecian. Good master, the young man has a troubled mind from which he would hide, and he went to the Grove, I think, as we go the sepulchers with our dead—he went to bury it."

"That is good, if so," Simonides said in a low voice. Then louder, "Malluch, the poor make themselves poorer as apes of the rich, and the merely rich carry themselves like princes. Did you sees signs of weakness in the youth? Did he display money—coin of Rome or Israel?"

"None, good master."

"Surely, Malluch, where there are so many inducements to folly—so much, I mean, to eat and drink—surely he made you a generous offer of some sort. His age, if nothing more, would warrant that much."

"He neither ate nor drank in my company."

"In what he said or did, Malluch, could you in anyway detect his master purpose? You know they peep through cracks close enough to stop the wind."

"Allow me to understand you," said Malluch, in doubt.

"Well, you know we neither speak nor act, much less decide grave questions concerning ourselves, except as we are driven by a motive. In that respect, what do you make of him?"

"As to that, Master Simonides, I can answer with much assurance. He is devoted to finding his mother and sister—that first. Then he has a grievance against Rome. And as the Messala of whom I told you had something to do with the wrong, the great present object is to humiliate him. The meeting at the fountain furnished an opportunity, but it was put aside as not sufficiently public for revenge."

"Messala is influential," said Simonides thoughtfully.

"Yes, but the next meeting will be in the circus."

"Well—and then?"

"The son of Arrius will win."

"How do you know?"

Malluch smiled. "I am judging by what he says."

"Is that all?"

"No, there is a much better sign—his spirit."

"Yes, but Malluch, his idea of vengeance—what is its scope? Does he limit it to the few who did him the wrong, or does he take in the many? And more—is his feeling but the whim of a sensitive boy, or has it the seasoning of suffering manhood to give it endurance? You know, Malluch, the vengeful thought that has root merely in the mind is but a dream of the idlest sort, which one clear day will dissipate, while the revenge of passion is a disease of the heart, which climbs up, up to the brain and feeds itself on both alike."

Simonides for the first time showed signs of feeling. He spoke rapidly and with clenched hands and the eagerness of a man demonstrating the disease he described.

"My master," Malluch replied, "one of my reasons for believing the young man to be a Jew is the intensity of his hate. It was plain to me that he had himself under control, as was natural, seeing how long he has lived in an atmosphere of Roman jealousy. Yet I saw it blaze—once when he wanted to know Ilderim's feeling toward Rome and again when I told him the story of the sheik and the wise man and spoke of the question, 'Where is he that is born King of the Jews?'"

Simonides leaned forward quickly. "Ah, Malluch, his words—give me his words. Let me judge the impression the mystery made upon him."

"He wanted to know the exact words. Were they 'to be' or 'born to be'? It appeared he was struck by a seeming difference in the effect of the two phrases."

Simonides settled back into his pose of listening judge.

"Then," said Malluch, "I told him Ilderim's view of the mystery—that the King would come with the doom of Rome. The young man's blood rose over his cheeks and forehead, and he said earnestly, 'Who but a Herod can be king while Rome endures?'"

"Meaning what?"

"That the empire must be destroyed before there could be another rule."

Simonides gazed for a time at the ships and their shadows slowly swinging together in the river. When he looked up, it was to end the interview.

"Enough, Malluch," he said. "Go eat, and make yourself ready to return to the Orchard of Palms. You must help the young man in his coming trial. Come to me in the morning. I will send a letter to Ilderim." Then in an undertone, as if to himself, he added, "I may attend the circus myself."

When Malluch, after the customary benediction was given and received, was gone, Simonides took a deep draught of milk and seemed refreshed and relieved.

"Put the meal down, Esther," he said. "It is over."

She obeyed and resumed her place upon the arm of the chair close to him.

"God is good to me," he said fervently. "His habit is to move in mystery, yet sometimes he permits us to think we see and understand him. I am old, dear, and must go. But now, in this eleventh hour, when my hope was beginning to die, he sends me this one with a promise, and I am lifted up. I see the way to a circumstance itself so great that it shall be like a new birth to the whole world. And I see a reason for the gift of my great riches, the end for which they were designed. Truly, my child, I take hold of life anew."

Esther nestled closer to him, as if to bring his thoughts from afar.

"The King has been born," he continued, imagining he was still speaking to her, "and he must be near half of his life. Balthasar says he was a child on his mother's lap when he saw him and gave him presents and worship. And Ilderim believes it was twenty-seven years ago last December when Balthasar and his companions came to his tent asking for a hiding place from Herod.

"Therefore the coming cannot now be long delayed. Tonight, or it may be tomorrow. Holy fathers of Israel, what happiness in the thought! I seem to hear the crash of the falling of old walls and the clamor of a universal change—yes, and for the uttermost joy of men, the earth opens to swallow up Rome, and they look up and laugh and sing that she is not, while we are."

Then he laughed at himself. "Why, Esther, have you ever heard the like? Surely I have in me the passion of a singer and the thrill of Miriam and David. In my thoughts, which should be those of a plain worker in figures and facts, there is a confusion of cymbals clashing and harp strings played loudly, and the voices of a multitude standing around a new-risen throne. I will put the thinking aside for the present. Only when the King comes he will need money and men, for as he was a child born of a woman he will be only a man after all, bound to human ways as you and I are. And for the money he will have need of help, and especially leaders.

"Do you not see a broad road for both me and my master? And at the end of it glory and revenge for us both? And—" he paused, struck with the selfishness of a scheme in which she did not have part, and added, kissing her "—and happiness for your mother's child."

She sat still, saying nothing. Then he remembered the difference in their natures and that they did not delight in the same cause or fear the same thing. He remembered she was but a girl.

"What are you thinking of, Esther?" he said. "If the thought has the form of a wish, give it to me, little one, while the power remains mine. For power, you know, is a fickle thing and always has its wings spread for flight."

She answered with childish simplicity. "Send for him, father. Send for him tonight and do not let him go into the circus."

"Ah!" he said, and again his eyes fell upon the river, where the shadows were deep since the moon had sunk far down behind Sulpius, leaving the city to the distant stars. He was actually touched by a twinge of jealousy. If she should really love the young master—oh no! That could not be. She was too young. But the idea had a firm grip and held him still and cold. She was sixteen. He knew it well. On her last birthday he had gone with her to the shipyard where there was a launch, and the yellow flag that the galley bore to its bridal with the waves had on it "Esther." So they celebrated the day together.

Yet the fact struck him now with great surprise. There are realizations that come to us all painfully, mostly related, such as pertain to ourselves—that we are growing old, for instance, and, more difficult, that we must die. Such a realization crept into his heart, in shadowy form, yet substantial enough to cause him to sigh. It was not enough that she should enter upon her young womanhood only a servant, but she must give her master her affections, the truth and tenderness and delicacy of which he the father so knew so well, because up to now they had all been his own completely. In the pang of the moment the brave old man lost sight of his new scheme and its subject, the miraculous King. By a mighty effort, however, he controlled himself and asked calmly, "Not go into the circus, Esther? Why, child?"

"It is not a place for a son of Israel, father."

"Rabbinical, Esther! Is that all?"

The tone of the inquiry was searching and went to her heart, which began to beat loudly—so loudly she could not answer. A new and strangely pleasant sensation came upon her.

"The young man is to have the fortune," he said, taking her hand and speaking more tenderly. "He is to have the ships and the shekels—all, Esther, all. Yet I did not feel poor, for you were left me, and your love is so like the dead Rachel's. Tell me, is he to have that too?"

She bent over him and laid her cheek against his head.

"Speak, Esther. I will be the stronger for the knowledge. In warning there is strength."

She sat up then and spoke as if she were Truth's holy self.

"Comfort yourself, father. I will never leave you. Though he takes my love, I will be your handmaid ever as now."

And stooping, she kissed him.

"And more," she said, continuing. "He is handsome in my sight, and his voice drew me to him, and I shudder to think of him in danger. Yes, father, I would be more than glad to see him again. Still the love that is unrequited cannot be perfect love, so I will wait for a time, remembering I am your daughter and my mother's."

"A very blessing of the Lord are you, Esther! A blessing to keep me rich, though all else be lost. And by his holy name and everlasting life, I swear you will not suffer."

At his request, a little later, the servant came and brought his chair into the room, where he sat for a time thinking of the coming of the King, while she went off and slept the sleep of the pure.

39

A Roman Orgy

The palace across the river nearly opposite Simonides' place is said to have been completed by the famous Epiphanes. He was a builder whose taste ran to the immense rather than to the classical—an architectural imitator, in other words, imitating the Persians instead of the Greeks.

The wall enclosed the whole island to the water's edge and was built for the double purpose of bulwark against the river and defense against the mob. It was said to have rendered the palace unfit for constant occupancy. The legates abandoned it and moved to another residence built for them on the western ridge of Mount Sulpius, under the temple of Jupiter.

Many flatly denied the bill against the ancient abode. They said, with shrewdness at least, that the real object of the removal of the legates was not a more healthful locality but the assurance given to them by the huge barracks, named citadel, situated just over the way on the eastern ridge of the mount. And the opinion was plausible. Among other pertinent things, it was remarked that the palace was kept in perpetual readiness for use. When a consul, general of the army, king, or visiting official of any kind arrived at Antioch, quarters were at once assigned to him on the island.

The house was spacious, floored with polished marble slabs and lighted in the day by skylights in which colored mica served as glass. The walls were blue, green, Tyrian purple, and gold. Around the room ran a continuous divan of Indian silks and wool of Cashmere. The furniture consisted of tables and stools of Egyptian patterns grotesquely carved.

While Simonides was in his chair perfecting his scheme in aid of the miraculous King, whose coming he had decided was close at hand, Esther was asleep. Across the river by the bridge, through the lion-guarded gate and a number of Babylonian halls and courts, stood the gilded palace.

Five chandeliers hung by sliding bronze chains from the ceiling—one in each corner and in the center one—enormous pyramids of lighted lamps. About the tables, seated or standing, or moving restlessly from one to another, were a hundred persons.

All were young, some of them little more than boys. That they were Italians and mostly Romans was past doubt. They all spoke Latin purely, while each one appeared in the indoor dress of the great capital on the Tiber—that is, in short-sleeved tunic and skirt. On the divan, togas bordered with purple and lacernae lay where they had been carelessly tossed. Sleepers stretched at ease, whether overcome by the heat and fatigue of the sultry day or by Bacchus. The hum of voices was loud and incessant. Sometimes there was an explosion of laughter or a burst of rage. The company was at its favorite games, draughts and dice, and there was the rattle of the tesserae, or ivory cubes, loudly shaken, and the moving of the pieces on the checkered boards.

"Good Flavius," said a player, holding his piece in suspended movement, "you see that lacerna—that one in front of us on the divan. It is fresh from the shop and has a shoulder buckle of gold broad as a palm."

"Well," said Flavius, intent upon his game, "I have seen these before. Yours may not be old, yet, by the girdle of Venus, it is not new! What of it?"

"Only that I would give it to find a man who knows everything."

"Ha! For something cheaper, I will find several here who wear the purple who will take your offer. But play."

"There—check!"

"So, by all the Jupiters! Now, what do you say? Again?"

"Be it so."

"And the wager?"

"A sestertium."

They each drew tablet and stylus and made an agreement. And while they were resetting the pieces, Flavius returned to his friend's remark.

"A man who knows everything! The oracles would die. What would you do with such a monster?"

"He would answer one question, my Flavius, then I would cut his throat."

215

"And the question?"

"I would have him tell me the hour—no, the minute—Maxentius will arrive tomorrow."

"Good play! I have you! And why the minute?"

"Have you ever stood uncovered in the Syrian sun on the dock where he will land? The fires of the Vesta are not so hot. And by our Father Romulus, I would die in Rome. Avernus is here; there, in the square in front of the Forum, I could stand, and, with my hands raised, touch the floor of the gods. By Venus, my Flavius, you fooled me! I have lost. O Fortune!"

"Again?"

"I must have back my sestertium."

"All right."

They played again and again. And when day, stealing through the skylights, began to dim the lamps, it found the two in the same places at the same table, still at the game. Like most of the company, they were military attaches of the consul, awaiting his arrival and amusing themselves in the meantime.

During this conversation a group entered the room and, unnoticed at first, proceeded to the central table. The wine had made no impression upon the leader unless to heighten his handsome qualities. He was a most manly Roman, carrying his head high. His eyes glittered, and he was shrouded in a spotless white toga. He walked in an imperial manner for one who was not Caesar. When at length he stopped and looked over at the players, they all turned to him with a shout.

"Messala! Messala!"

Those in the distant quarters heard the cry and reechoed it where they were. Instantly the groups dissolved and, breaking up games, rushed toward the center of the room.

"Good health to you, Drusus, my friend," he said to the player at his right. "Your health—and your tablets for a moment."

He raised the waxen boards, glanced at the history of wagers, and tossed them down.

"Denarii, only denarii—coins of cartmen and butchers!" he said, with a scornful laugh. "By the drunken Semele, what is Rome coming to when a caesar sits nights waiting a turn of fortune to bring him but a beggarly denarius!"

The Drusus reddened to his brows, but the bystanders interrupted his reply by surging to the table and shouting, "The Messala! The Messala!"

"Men of the Tiber," Messala continued, taking a box with the dice in it from a hand nearby, "who is he most favored of the gods? A Roman. Who is the lawgiver of the nations? A Roman. Who is, by sword's might, the universal master?"

"A Roman, a Roman!" they shouted.

"Yet—" he lingered to catch their ears "—yet there is a better one than the best of Rome."

He raised his patrician head and paused, to sting them with his sneer.

"Did you hear?" he asked. "There is a better than the best of Rome."

"Yes—Hercules!" cried one.

"Bacchus!" yelled a satirist.

"Jove—Jove!" thundered the crowd.

"Name him!" they demanded.

"I will," he said, at the next lull. "It is he who adds the perfection of Rome to the East; he who in addition to the arm of conquest, which is Western, has also the art needful for enjoying dominion, which is Eastern."

"His best is a Roman after all," someone shouted, and there was a great laugh and long applause, an admission that Messala had the advantage.

"In the East," he continued, "we have not gods, only Wine, Women, and Fortune, and the greatest of them is Fortune. Therefore our motto—'Who Dares What I Dare?'—is fit for the Senate, for battle, and for him who, seeking the best, challenges the worst."

His voice dropped into an easy, familiar tone but without giving up the ascendancy he had gained. "In the great chest up in the citadel I have five talents, coin found in the markets, and here are the receipts."

He drew a roll of paper from his tunic and, flinging it on the table, continued amidst breathless silence, every eye watching, every ear listening. "This sum is the measure of what I dare. Who of you dares so much? You are silent. Is it too great? Come, throw me for at least one for the honor of the river by which you were born—Rome East against Rome West! Orontes the barbarous against Tiber the sacred!"

He rattled the dice overhead while waiting. "The Orontes against the Tiber!" he repeated, with a more scornful emphasis.

Then he turned to Drusus, with a laugh heard throughout the palace.

"My friend! Don't be offended because I leveled the caesar in you down to the denarii." His manner was frank and cordial.

Drusus melted in a moment. "By the Nymphae, yes!" he said laughing. "I will throw with you, Messala—for a denarius."

A boy was looking over the table, watching the scene. Suddenly Messala turned to him. "Who are you?" he asked.

The lad drew back.

"No, by Castor! And his brother too! I mean no offense. It is a rule among men, in matters other than dice, to keep the record closest when the deal is least. I need a clerk. Will you serve me?"

The young fellow drew his tablets ready to keep score.

"Hold it, Messala, hold!" cried Drusus. "I do not know if it is ominous to hold the poised dice with a question, but one occurs to me, and I must ask it."

"No, my Drusus, I will make the throw. Thus—" He turned the box upon the table and held it firmly over the dice.

And Drusus asked, "Did you ever see Quintus Arrius?"

"The duumvir?"

"No—his son."

"I did not know he had a son."

"Well, it is nothing," Drusus added, indifferently. "Only, my Messala, Pollux was not more like Castor than Arrius is like you."

Twenty voices took this up. "True, true! His eyes—his face," they cried.

"What!" answered one, disgusted. "Messala is a Roman. Arrius is a Jew."

"You are right," a third exclaimed. "He is a Jew."

There was a promise of a dispute, so Messala interjected, "The wine has not come, my Drusus. As to Arrius, I will accept your opinion of him, so tell me more about him."

"Well, be he Jew or Roman—and, by the great god Pan, I say it not in disrespect of your feelings, my Messala! This Arrius is handsome and brave and shrewd. The emperor offered him favor and patronage, which he refused. He came up in a mysterious way and keeps his distance as if he felt himself better or knew himself worse than the rest of us. In the palaestrae he was unmatched—he played with the blue-eyed giants from the Rhine and the hornless bulls of Sarmatia as if they were willow wisps.

"The duumvir left him vastly rich. He has a passion for arms and thinks of nothing but war. Maxentius admitted him into his family, and he was to have taken to sea with us, but we lost him at Ravenna. Nevertheless he arrived safely. We heard of him this morning. Instead of coming to the palace or going to the citadel, he dropped his baggage at the inn and has disappeared again."

At the beginning of the speech Messala listened with polite indifference. As it proceeded he became more attentive, and at the conclusion he took his hand from the dice-box and called out, "My Caius! Did you hear?"

A youth at his elbow—his comrade in the day's chariot practice—answered, much pleased with the attention, "If I did not, my Messala, I would not be your friend."

"Do you remember the man who caused you to fall today?"

"By the love-locks of Bacchus, have I not a bruised shoulder to help me keep it in mind?" and he seconded the words with a shrug.

"Well, be grateful to the Fates—I have found your enemy. Listen."

So Messala turned to Drusus.

"Tell us more of him who is both Jew and Roman—by Phoebus, a combination to make a Centaur handsome! What garments does he wear, my Drusus?"

"Those of the Jews."

"Did you hear, Caius?" said Messala. "The fellow is young, and he has the face of a Roman. Yet he loves best the garb of a Jew. And in the palaestrae fame and fortune come of arms to throw a horse or tilt a chariot, as the necessity may order. And Drusus, help my friend again. Doubtless this Arrius plays tricks with words, otherwise he could not so confound himself—today a Jew, tomorrow a Roman. But of the rich tongue of the Greeks—can he speak in that as well?"

"With such purity, Messala, he might have been a contestant in the Isthmia."

"Are you listening, Caius?" said Messala. "The fellow is qualified to salute a woman—for that matter, Aristomache herself—in the Greek. And as I keep the count, that is five. What do you say?"

"You have found him, my Messala," Caius answered, "or I am not myself."

"Your pardon, Drusus—and pardon of all—for speaking in riddles this way," Messala said, in his winsome way. "By all the decent gods, I would not strain your courtesy to the point of breaking, but now help me." He put his hand on the dice-box again, laughing. "You did speak, I think, of mystery in connection with the coming of the son of Arrius. Tell me of that."

"It is nothing, Messala, nothing," Drusus replied. "A child's story. When Arrius, the father, sailed in pursuit of the pirates, he was without wife or family. He returned with a boy—the one we spoke of—and the next day adopted him."

"Adopted him?" Messala repeated. "By the gods, Drusus, you do indeed interest me! Where did the duumvir find the boy? And who was he?"

"Who shall answer you that, Messala? Who but the young Arrius himself? In the fight the duumvir—then but a tribune—lost his galley. A returning vessel found him and one other—all of the crew who survived—afloat upon the same plank. I tell you now the story of the rescuers, which has this excellent quality at least—it has never been contradicted. They say, the duumvir's companion on the plank was a Jew—"

"A Jew!" echoed Messala.

"And a slave."

"How, Drusus? A slave?"

"When the two were lifted to the deck, the duumvir was in his tribune's armor, and the other in the outfit of a rower."

Messala arose from leaning against the table. "A galley." He checked the debasing word and looked around, for once in his life at a loss.

Just then a procession of slaves filed into the room, some with great jars of wine, others with baskets of fruit and confections, others with cups and flagons, mostly silver.

Instantly Messala climbed upon a stool. "Men of Tiber," he said, in a clear voice, "let us turn this waiting for our chief into a feast of Bacchus. Who do you choose for master?"

Drusus arose.

"Who shall be master but the giver of the feast?" he said. "Answer, Romans."

They gave their reply in a shout.

Messala took the wreath from his head, gave it to Drusus, who climbed upon the table and, in view of all, solemnly replaced it, making Messala master of the night.

"Some came with me into the room," he said, "who were just risen from table. So that our feast may have the approval of sacred custom, bring me the one who is most overcome by wine."

A din of voices answered, "Here he is, here he is!"

And from the floor where he had fallen a youth was brought forward, so effeminately beautiful he might have passed for the drinking god himself—only the crown would have dropped from his head.

"Lift him upon the table," the master said. But he could not sit.

"Help him, Drusus, as the fair Nyone may yet help you."

Drusus took the drunkard in his arms.

Then addressing the limp figure, Messala said, amidst profound silence, "O Bacchus! Greatest of the gods, be good tonight. And for myself, and these your followers, I vow this wreath"—and from his head he raised it reverently—"I vow this wreath to your altar in the Grove of Daphne."

He bowed, replaced the crown upon his locks, then stooped and uncovered the dice, saying with a laugh, "See, my Drusus, by the ass of Silenus, the denarius is mine!"

There was a shout that set the floor quaking, and the grim Atlantes to dancing, and the orgies began.

40

A Driver for Ilderim's Arabs

Sheik Ilderim was a man of too much importance to go about with only a small entourage. He had a reputation to keep with his tribe, as became a prince and patriarch of the greatest following in all the desert east of Syria. With the people of the cities he had a similar reputation, which was that of one of the richest persons who was not a king in all the East. And, being rich—in money as well as in servants, camels, horses, and flocks of all kinds—he took pleasure in a certain standard that, besides magnifying his dignity with strangers, contributed to his personal pride and comfort. He had three large tents—one for himself, one for visitors, and one for his favorite wife and her women—and six or eight lesser ones, occupied by his servants and such tribal retainers as he had chosen to bring with him as a bodyguard—strong men of proven courage and skillful with bow, spear, and horses.

To be sure, his property of whatever kind was in no danger at the Orchard; yet as the habits of a man go with him to town not less than the country, and, as it is never wise to loosen discipline, so the interior of the tent was devoted to his cows, camels, goats, and whatever property might tempt a lion or a thief.

To do him full justice, Ilderim kept all the customs of his people well, so his life at the Orchard was a continuation of his life in the desert. It was an imitation of the old patriarchal ways— the genuine pastoral life of primitive Israel.

In the morning the caravan arrived at the Orchard. "Here, plant it here," he said, stopping his horse, and thrusting a spear into the ground. He went to a group of three great palm trees and patted one of them as he would have patted his horse's neck or the cheek of his child.

Then, at his call, the women and children came and unfolded the canvas from its packing on the camels. The women had sheared the hair from the brown goats of the flock and twisted it

222

into thread, then woven the thread into cloth. They stitched the cloth together, making a perfect dark-brown roof, though seen from a distance it looked as black as the tents of Kedar. With jests and laughter, the united followers of the sheik stretched the canvas from pillar to pillar, driving the stakes and fastening the cords as they went. And when the walls of open reed matting were put in place—the finishing touch to the building after the style of the desert—they waited the good man's judgment with a hush of anxiety.

He walked in and out, looking at the house in relation to the sun, the trees, and the lake, and said, rubbing his hands with heartiness, "Well done! Make the tent now as you know well, and tonight we will sweeten the bread and the milk with honey, and at every fire there will be a goat. God be with you! There will not be want of sweet water, for the lake is our well. Nor will the donkeys or the least of the flock hunger, for there is green pasture also. God be with you all, my children! Go."

And shouting, the many happy followers went their ways then to pitch their own tents. A few remained to arrange the interior for the sheik. Of these the menservants hung a curtain to the central row of pillars, making two apartments. The one on the right was for Ilderim himself, the other for his horses—his jewels of Solomon—which they led in.

They then erected the arms rack against the middle pillar and filled it with javelins, spears, bows, arrows, and shields. Outside of them hung the master's sword, modeled after the new moon, and the glitter of its blade rivaled the glitter of the jewels bedded in its grip. On the other end they displayed the great man's apparel—his woolen and linen robes, tunics, trousers, and colored kerchiefs. Nor did they cease the work until he pronounced it well done.

In the meantime the women drew out and set up the divan and put a frame together in the shape of three sides of a square, with the opening facing the door, and covered it with cushions and base curtains, and the cushions with a changeable brown-and-yellow striped spread. At the corners they placed pillows and bolsters sacked in blue-and-crimson cloth. Then around the divan they laid a border of carpet and carpeted the inner space as well. They again waited until the master said it was good. Nothing remained then but to bring and fill the jars with water and hang the skin bottles ready for the hand—tomorrow the leben. Every Arab would see why Ilderim should be both happy and generous—in his tent by the lake of sweet waters, under the palms of the Orchard of Palms.

This was the tent Ben Hur approached. Servants were already awaiting the master's direction. One of them took off his sandals. Another unlatched Ben Hur's Roman shoes. Then the two exchanged their dusty outer garments for fresh ones of white linen.

"Enter—in God's name, enter and take rest," said the host heartily, and he led the way to the divan. "I will sit here," he said next, pointing, "and there the stranger will sit."

A woman skillfully piled the pillows as rest for his back. After that they sat upon the side of the divan, while water was brought fresh from the lake, and their feet were bathed and dried with napkins.

"We have a saying in the desert," Ilderim began, stroking his beard and combing it with his slender fingers, "that a good appetite is the promise of a long life. Do you have this?"

"By that rule, good sheik, I will live a hundred years. I am a hungry wolf at your door," Ben Hur replied.

"Well, you will not be sent away like a wolf. I will give you the best of the flocks."

Ilderim clapped his hands. "Seek the stranger in the guest tent, and say I, Ilderim, send him a prayer that his peace may be as incessant as the flowing waters."

The man in waiting bowed.

"Also say," Ilderim continued, "that I have returned with another person for breaking of bread. And, if Balthasar the wise cares to share the loaf, three may partake of it."

The second servant went away.

"Let us take our rest now."

Then Ilderim settled himself upon the divan, as at this time merchants would sit on their rugs in the bazaars of Damascus. When finally at rest, he stopped combing his beard and said gravely, "Because you are my guest and have drunk my wine and are about to taste my salt, you ought not refuse a question: Who are you?"

"Sheik Ilderim," said Ben Hur, calmly enduring his gaze, "I hope you will not think me trifling with your just demand. But was there ever a time in your life when to answer such a question would have hurt you?"

"By the splendor of Solomon, yes!" Ilderim answered. "Betrayal of self is at times as base as the betrayal of a tribe."

"Thanks, good sheik!" Ben Hur exclaimed. "No answer ever became you better. Now I know you only seek assurance to justify the trust I have come to ask and that such assurance is of more interest to you than the affairs of my poor life."

The sheik bowed, and Ben Hur hastened to pursue his advantage. "So if it please you then," he said. "First, I am not a Roman, as the name given to you implies."

Ilderim clasped the beard overflowing his breast and gazed at the speaker with faintly twinkling eyes through his heavy, closed brows.

"In the next place," Ben Hur continued, "I am an Israelite of the tribe of Judah."

The sheik raised his brows a little.

"Nor that only. Sheik, I am a Jew with a grievance against Rome, which compared to yours is no more than a child's squabble."

The old man combed his beard with nervous haste.

"What is more, I swear to you, Sheik Ilderim—I swear by the covenant the Lord made with my fathers—if you but give me the revenge I seek, the money and the glory of the race shall be yours."

Ilderim's face began to beam, and it was almost possible to see the satisfaction taking hold of him.

"Enough!" he said. "If at the root of your tongue there is a lie, Solomon himself would not be safe against you. That you are not a Roman—that as a Jew you have a grievance against Rome and revenge to complete—I believe you, and on that score it is enough. But concerning your skills, what experience have you had in racing with chariots? And the horses—can you make them creatures of your will, to come at your call? To go, if you say it, to the full extreme of their breath and strength? And then, when they are ready to perish, out of the depths of your being compel them to one final exertion that is the mightiest of all?

"The gift, my son, does not belong to every one. Ah, by the splendor of God! I knew a king who governed millions of men and was their perfect master, but he could not win the respect of a horse. Mark! I speak not of the dull brutes who serve slaves—the dead in spirit—but of mine here—the kings of their kind. From a lineage reaching back to the broods of the first pharaoh, my comrades and friends, dwellers in tents, who have added our wits to their instincts and joined our souls to their senses until they know all we know of ambition, love, hate, and contempt. In war they are heroes. In trust they are faithful as women. You, there!"

A servant came forward.

"Let my Arabs come!"

The man drew aside part of the dividing curtain of the tent, exposing a group of horses to view, who lingered a moment where they were as if to make certain of their invitation to come in.

"Come!" Ilderim said to them. "Why do you stand there? What do I have that is not yours? Come, I say!"

They stalked slowly in.

"Son of Israel," the master said, "your Moses was a mighty man, but I must laugh when I think of his allowing your fathers to employ the plodding ox and the dull, slow-natured ass and forbidding them to own horses. Do you think he would have done so had he seen that one, and this?" He laid his hand upon the face of the first to reach him and patted it with infinite pride and tenderness.

"It is a misjudgment, sheik," Ben Hur said warmly. "Moses was a warrior as well as a lawgiver beloved by God, and to follow war is to love all its creatures—these among the rest."

An exquisite head—with large eyes, soft as a deer's and half hidden by the dense forelock, and small ears, sharp-pointed and sloped well forward—approached, its nostrils open and its upper lip in motion. "Who are you?" it asked, as plainly as if it were a man speaking.

Ben Hur recognized one of the four racers he had seen on the course and gave his open hand to the beautiful beast.

"They will tell you—the blasphemers! May their days shorten as they grow fewer!" The sheik spoke with the feeling of a man holding back insults. "They will tell you, I say, that our horses of the best blood are derived from the Nesaean pastures of Persia.

"God gave the first Arab a measureless waste of sand, with some treeless mountains, and here and there a well of bitter waters, and said to him, 'Behold your country!' And when the poor man complained, the Mighty One pitied him and said again, 'Be of cheer! For I will twice bless you above other men.' The Arab heard and gave thanks and with faith set out to find the blessings.

"He traveled across the outer boundaries first and failed. Then he made a path into the desert and went on and on—and in the heart of the waste there was a very beautiful green island and in the heart of the island a herd of camels and another of horses. He took them joyfully and kept them with care for what they were—the best gifts of God. And all the horses of the earth went forth from that green isle, even to the pastures of Nesaea and northward to the dreadful valleys attacked by blasts from the Sea of Chill Winds. Do not doubt the story, or if you do, may an amulet never have charm for an Arab again. No, I will give you proof."

He clapped his hands. "Bring me the records of the tribe," he said to the servant who responded.

Six men appeared with chests of cedar reinforced by bands of brass and hinged and bolted with brass. "No," said Ilderim, when they were all set down by the divan, "I meant not all of them. Only the records of the horses—that one. Open it and take back the others."

The chest was opened, disclosing a group of ivory tablets strung on rings of silver wire. Because the tablets were scarcely thicker than wafers, each ring held several hundred of them.

"I know," said Ilderim, taking some of the rings in his hand—"I know with what care and zeal, my son, the scribes of the Temple in the Holy City keep the names of the newly born, that every son of Israel may trace his line of ancestry to its beginning, though it precedes the patriarchs. My fathers—may the recollection of them be fresh forever!—did not think it was sinful to borrow the idea and apply it even to their servants. So here we have the tablets!"

Ben Hur took the rings and separating the tablets saw they contained rude hieroglyphs in Arabic, burned on the smooth surface by a sharp point of heated metal.

"Can you read them, O son of Israel?"

"No. You must tell me their meaning."

"Each tablet records the name of a horse of the pure blood born to my fathers over hundreds of years, and also the names of sire and dame. Take them, and note their age, that you may the more readily believe."

Some of the tablets were nearly worn away. All were yellow with age.

"In the chest there, I can tell you now, I have the perfect history. Perfect because it is certified as history seldom is—showing from what stock all these are sprung—this one, and that now seeking your notice and caress. Their sires come to us here to eat their measure of barley from our open hand and be talked to as children and, as children, kiss the thanks they cannot speak. And now, O son of Israel, you may believe my statement—if I am a lord of the desert, here are my ministers! Take them from me, and I will become as a sick man left by the caravan to die. Thanks to them, age has not diminished the terror of me on the highways between cities, and it will not as long as I have strength to go with them.

"I could tell you marvels done by their ancestors. In a more favorable time I may do so. For the present, it is enough that they were never overtaken in retreat, nor, by the sword of Solomon, did they ever fail in pursuit! That, mark you, while on the sands and under saddle. But now I am afraid, for they are under the yoke for the first time, and the conditions of success are so many. They have the pride and the speed and the endurance. If I find them a master, they will win. Son of Israel! If you are the man, I swear it shall be a happy day that brought you here. Speak now of yourself."

"I know now," said Ben Hur, "why it is that in the love of an Arab his horse is next to his children. And I know also why the Arab horses are the best in the world. But, good sheik, I would not have you judge me by words alone. As you know, all promises of men sometimes fail. Give me the trial first on some plain near here and put the four into my hand tomorrow."

Ilderim's face beamed again, and he started to speak.

"A moment, good sheik," said Ben Hur. "Let me say more.

From the masters in Rome I learned many lessons, little thinking they would serve me in a time like this. These your sons of the desert, though each have separately the speed of eagles and the endurance of lions, will fail if they are not trained to run together under a yoke. For think, sheik, in every four there is one the slowest and one the swiftest. And while the race is to the slowest, the trouble is always with the swiftest. It was that way today—the driver could not bring the best into harmony with the poorest. My trial may have no better result, but if so, I will tell you of it. That I swear. So, if I can get them to run together, moved by my will, directing the four as one, you will have the sestertii and the crown, and I my revenge. What do you say?"

Ilderim listened, combing his beard the while. At the end he said, with a laugh, "I think better of you, son of Israel. We have a saying in the desert 'If you will cook the meal with words, I will promise an ocean of butter.' You will have the horses in the morning."

At that moment there was a stir at the rear entrance to the tent. "The supper—it is here! And yonder is my friend Balthasar, whom you will know. He has a story to tell that an Israelite should never tire of hearing."

And to the servants he added, "Take the records away and return my jewels to their apartment." And they did as he ordered.

41

The Dowar in the Orchard of Palms

The wise men had been eating their meal at their meeting in the desert during the preparations for the supper in Ilderim's tent. Three rugs were spread on the carpet within the space enclosed by the divan. A table not more than a foot in height was brought and set within the same place and covered with a cloth. Off to one side a portable earthenware oven was operated under the care of a woman whose duty it was to provide the company with bread, or, more precisely, in hot cakes of flour from the handmills grinding continually in a neighboring tent.

Meanwhile, Balthasar was conducted to the divan, where Ilderim and Ben Hur received him. A loose black gown covered him. His step was feeble, and his movements were slow and cautious, apparently dependent upon a long staff and the arm of a servant.

"Peace to you, my friend," said Ilderim respectfully. "Peace and welcome."

The Egyptian raised his head and replied, "And to you, good sheik—to you and yours, peace and the blessing of the one God—God, the true and loving."

The manner was gentle and devout and impressed Ben Hur with a feeling of awe. Also the blessing included in the answering salutation had been partly addressed to him, and while that part was being spoken, the eyes of the aged guest, hollow yet luminous, rested upon his face long enough to stir a new and mysterious emotion, so strong that during the meal he again and again scanned the much wrinkled and bloodless face for his meaning. But always there was an expression that was bland, placid, and trustful as a child's.

"This is he, O Balthasar," said the sheik, laying his hand on Ben Hur's arm, "who will break bread with us this evening."

The Egyptian glanced at the young man and looked again, both surprised and doubting.

Then the sheik continued. "I have promised him my horses for trial tomorrow. If all goes well, he will drive them in the circus."

Balthasar continued to gaze at Ben Hur.

"He came well recommended," Ilderim pursued. "You may know him as the son of Arrius, who was a noble Roman sailor, though"—the sheik hesitated, then resumed, with a laugh—"though he declares himself an Israelite of the tribe of Judah. And, by the splendor of God, I believe what he tells me!"

Balthasar could no longer withhold an explanation. "Today, O most generous sheik, my life was in peril and would have been lost had not a youth, like this one—if, indeed, he is not the very same—intervened when all others fled, and saved me." Then he addressed Ben Hur directly. "Are you the one of whom I speak?"

"I cannot answer you so far," Ben Hur replied, with modest deference. "I am the one who stopped the horses of the insolent Roman when they were rushing upon your camel at the Fountain of Castalia. Your daughter left a cup with me."

From the middle of his tunic he produced the cup and gave it to Balthasar. A glow lit the faded countenance of the Egyptian.

"The Lord sent you to me at the Fountain today," he said, in a trembling voice, stretching his hand toward Ben Hur, "and He sends you to me now. I give Him thanks, for from His favor I have the abundance to give you great reward, and I will. The cup is yours; keep it."

Ben Hur took back the gift, and Balthasar, seeing the bewilderment upon Ilderim's face, related the occurrence at the Fountain.

"What!" said the sheik to Ben Hur. "You said nothing of this to me, when you could not have brought a better recommendation. Am I not an Arab and sheik of my tribe of tens of thousands? And is not he my guest? And is it not in my guest-bond that the good or evil you do him is good or evil done to me? Where should you go for reward but here? And whose hand should give it you but mine?" he said shrilly.

"Good sheik, spare me, I pray. I did not come for reward, great or small. And that I may be released from this judgment, I say the help I gave this excellent man would have been also given to your humblest servant."

"But he is my friend, my guest—not my servant. See the difference in the favor of Fortune?" Then to Balthasar the sheik added, "Ah, by the splendor of God! I tell you again he is not a Roman."

With that he turned away and paid attention to the servants, whose preparations for the supper were about complete.

In Balthasar's devotion to men there had been, it will be remembered, no distinctions. The redemption that had been promised him as a reward—for which he was waiting—was universal. To him, therefore, the assertion sounded somewhat like an echo of himself. He took a step nearer to Ben Hur and spoke to him in an endearing way.

"What did the sheik say I should call you? It was a Roman name, I think."

"Arrius. The son of Arrius."

"Yet you are not a Roman?"

"All my people were Jews."

"Were, you said. Are they not living?"

The question was subtle as well as simple, but Ilderim saved Ben Hur from having to answer. "Come," he said to them, "the meal is ready."

Ben Hur gave his arm to Balthasar and conducted him to the table, where shortly they were all seated on their rugs, Eastern fashion. They washed and dried their hands.

Then the sheik made a sign, the servants stopped, and the voice of the Egyptian arose, quivering with holy feeling. "Father of All—God! What we have comes from You. Take our thanks and bless us, that we may continue to do Your will."

It was the grace the good man had said simultaneously with his brethren Gaspar the Greek and Melchior the Hindu, the speech in diverse tongues from which came the miracle displaying the Divine Presence at the meal in the desert years before.

The table where dinner was laid was rich in the delicacies favorite in the East—in bread hot from the oven, vegetables from the gardens, meats and vegetables, milk, honey, and butter—all eaten or drunk, it should be remarked, without any of the modern accessories—knives, forks, or plates. In this part of the meal little was said, for they were hungry. But when the dessert was served this changed. They washed their hands again, had the lap-cloths shaken out, and, with more food and the sharp edge of their hunger gone, they were disposed to talk and listen.

With such a company—an Arab, a Jew, and an Egyptian, all believers alike in one God—there could be only one subject of conversation, and of the three, he spoke to whom the Deity had made almost a personal appearance, who had seen Him in a star, had heard His voice and had been led so far and so miraculously by His Spirit. What should he talk of but that which he had been called to testify?

42

Balthasar Impresses Ben Hur

The shadows cast over the Orchard of Palms by the mountains at sunset left a sweet margin of violet sky and drowsing earth between the day and night. The latter came early and swift, and in the light of its glow in the tent this evening the servants brought four candlesticks of brass and set them on the corners of the table. There were four branches to each candlestick, and on each branch was a lighted silver lamp and a supply of olive oil. In ample light, the group at dessert continued their conversation, speaking in the Syriac dialect, familiar to all peoples in that part of the world.

The Egyptian told his story of the meeting of the three in the desert and agreed with the sheik that it was in December, twenty-seven years before, when he and his companions were fleeing from Herod and arrived at the tent seeking shelter. The story was heard with intense interest. Even the servants were lingering when they could to catch its details.

Ben Hur received it like a man listening to a revelation of deep concern to all humanity, especially the people of Israel. In his mind an idea was crystalizing that was to change his course of life, if not absorb it absolutely.

As the story proceeded, the impression made by Balthasar upon the young Jew increased. At its conclusion, his feeling was too strong to permit even a doubt of its truth. Indeed, there were only assurances as to the consequences of the amazing event.

This very time was near the opening of the ministry of the son of Mary, the same whom Balthasar left worshipfully in his mother's lap in Bethlehem. He was *a man whom the world could not do without*. A shrewd mind inspired by faith will make much of this statement. Before his time, and since, there have been men indispensable to particular people and periods, but his benefit was to the whole race and for all time, so it is unique and divine.

To Sheik Ilderim the story was not new. He had heard it from the three wise men together under circumstances that left no room for doubt. He had acted upon it seriously, because helping fugitives escape from the anger of the first Herod was dangerous. Now one of the three sat at his table again, a welcome guest and revered friend. Sheik Ilderim certainly believed the story.

Yet, in the nature of things, its mighty central fact could not come home to him with the force and absorbing effect in which it came to Ben Hur. Ilderim was an Arab, whose interest in the consequences was only general. On the other hand, Ben Hur was an Israelite, a Jew, with more than a special interest in the truth of the fact. He took hold of the circumstance from a purely Jewish frame of reference.

From his cradle, let it be remembered he had heard of the Messiah. At the colleges he had been made familiar with all that was known of that Being at once the hope, the fear, and the peculiar glory of the chosen people. The prophets, from the first to the last of the heroic line, foretold him, and the coming had been, and yet was, the theme of endless exposition with the rabbis. In the synagogues, in the schools, in the Temple, on fast-days and feast-days, in public and in private, the teachers kept expounding until all the children of Abraham wherever their lots were cast kept the Messiah in expectation and by that expectation ruled and molded their lives literally and with iron severity. There was much argument among the Jews themselves about the Messiah, but the disputation was all limited to one point and one only—when would He come? There was a unanimity about the Messiah among the chosen people, which was a matter of marvelous agreement—he was to be, when he came, the King of the Jews—their political king, their caesar. By their aid he was to make armed conquest of the earth and then, for their profit and in the name of God, rule forever. On this faith the Pharisees, or Separatists—the latter being a political term—in the precincts and around the altars of the Temple, built a foundation of hope far surpassing the dream of the Macedonian. His but covered the earth; theirs covered the earth and filled the skies. That is to say, in their bold and boundless fantasies of blasphemous egotism, God the Almighty was in effect supposed to serve them and allow them to nail him by the ear to a door as a sign of eternal slavery.

In terms of Ben Hur, two circumstances in his life had kept him in a state comparatively free from the influence and negative effects of the radical faith of his Separatist Jewish countrymen. In the first place, his father followed the faith of the Sadducees, who may, in a general way, be termed the liberals of their time. They had some generally formed opinions that denied the soul. They were strict literalists and rigorous observers of the law as found in the books of Moses. But they held the vast mass of rabbinical additions to those books as counterfeit.

They were unquestionably a sect, yet their religion was more a philosophy than a creed. They did not deny themselves the enjoyments of life and saw many admirable methods and inventions among the Gentile divisions of the race. In politics they were in active opposition to the Separatists. In the natural order of things, these opinions and peculiarities would have descended to the son as certainly and clearly as any portion of his father's estate, and, as we have seen, he was actually in the course of acquiring them when a second saving event took place.

Ben Hur's mind and temperament were affected by five years' influence of affluent life in Rome. He recalled what the great city was then: the meetingplace of the nations both politically and commercially, as well as a place where the indulgence of pleasure without restraint was commonplace. Round and round the golden milestone in front of the Forum—in the gloom of eclipse and in unapproachable splendor—flowed all the active currents of humanity. If excellent manners, refinements in society, attainments of intellect, and glory of achievement made no impression upon him, how could he, as the son of Arrius, go day after day over from the beautiful villa near Misenum into the courts of Caesar and be wholly uninfluenced by what he saw there of kings, princes, ambassadors, hostages, and delegates from every known land, waiting humbly to hear the yes or no that was to make or unmake them? As mere gatherings, to be sure, there was nothing to compare with the gatherings at Jerusalem in celebration of the Passover. Yet when he sat under the purple tent of the Circus Maximus, one of 350,000 spectators, he must have been visited by the thought that possibly there might be some branches of the family of man worthy of divine consideration, if not mercy, even if they were uncircumcised. Some deserved mercy because of their sorrows, and even more by their hopelessness in the midst of sorrows, made fit for brotherhood in the promises of his countrymen.

When the reflection came to him, he could not have been blind to a certain distinction. The wretchedness of the masses, and their hopeless condition, had no relation whatever to religion. Their murmurs and groans were not against their gods or for want of gods. In the oak woods of Britain the Druids had their followers. Odin and Freya maintained their godships in Gaul and Germany. The Persians were still devoted to Ormuzd. In hope of Nirvana, the Hindus moved on patiently in the rayless paths of Brahma. The noble Greek mind, in the depths of philosophy, still sang of the heroic gods of Homer, while in Rome nothing was so common and cheap as gods.

According to whim, the masters of the world, because they were masters, carried their worship and offerings indifferently from altar to altar, and delighted in the pandemonium they had created. Their discontent, if they were discontented, was with the number of gods. For, after borrowing all the divinities of the earth, they began to deify their caesars and devote to them both altars and holy service. No, the unhappy condition was not from religion, but from bad government and revolution and countless tyrannies. The prayer—everywhere alike, in Lodinum, Alexandria, Athens, Jerusalem—was for a king to conquer, not a god to worship.

After two thousand years, it can be said that in terms of religion there was no relief from the universal confusion except from some God who could prove Himself a true God, and a masterful one, and come to the rescue. But the people of the time, even the discerning and philosophical, could find no hope except in crushing Rome. That done, relief would follow in restoring and reorganizing individual societies. Therefore, they prayed, conspired, rebelled, fought, and died, drenching the soil with blood and tears—yet always failing nonetheless.

Ben Hur was in agreement with the mass of men of his time who were not Romans. The five years' residence in the capital gave him an opportunity to see and study the miseries of the subjugated world. He believed fully that the evils that afflicted it were

237

political and were to be cured only by the sword. He was going to make himself ready for a part in that great day to provide the heroic remedy. By practice of arms he was a perfect soldier, but war has its higher callings, and he who would fight successfully in them must know more than to defend himself with shield and thrust with spear. In those great fields of war the general finds his task: to make himself preeminent. The consummate captain is a fighting man armed with an army. He was swayed by the reflection that the vengeance he dreamed of, in connection with his grievances, would be more surely found in some of the ways of war than in any pursuit of peace.

The feelings with which he listened to Balthasar can now be understood. Balthasar's story touched two of the most sensitive areas of his being, and they rang within him. His heart beat fast when, searching himself, he found no doubt either that the recital was true in every detail or that the child so miraculously found was the Messiah. Marveling that Israel was unaware of the revelation and that he had never heard of it before that day, two questions occurred to him, in whose answers he hoped to receive all that was desirable to know: Where was the child now? And what was his mission?

With apologies for the interruptions, he attempted to draw out the perspective of Balthasar, who was quite willing to speak.

43

Christ Is Coming—Balthasar

"If only I could answer you," Balthasar said, in his earnest and devout way. "Oh, if I knew where he is, how quickly I would go to him! The seas would not prevent me, nor the mountains."

"You have tried to find him, then?" asked Ben Hur.

A smile flitted across the face of the Egyptian.

"The first task I charged myself with after leaving the shelter given to me in the desert"—Balthasar cast a grateful look at Ilderim—"was to learn what became of the child. But a year passed, and I dared not go up to Judea in person, for Herod still held the throne and was as bloody-minded as ever. In Egypt, upon my return, there were a few friends who believed the wonderful things I told them of what I had seen and heard—a few who rejoiced with me that the Redeemer was born—a few who never tired of the story.

"Some of them came up with me looking for the child. They went first to Bethlehem and found the inn, but the steward—he who sat at the gate the night of the birth and the night we came following the star—was gone. The king had taken him away, and he was seen no more."

"But they found some proofs, surely," said Ben Hur eagerly.

"Yes, proofs written in blood—a village in mourning, mothers still crying for their little ones. You must know, when Herod heard of our flight, he sent down and slew the youngest-born of the children of all the families of Bethlehem. Not one escaped. The faith of my messengers was confirmed, but they came to me saying the child was dead, slain with the other innocents."

"Dead!" exclaimed Ben Hur, aghast. "Dead, you say?"

"No, my son, I did not say so. I said my messengers told me the child was dead. I did not believe the report then; I do not believe it now."

"I see—you have some special knowledge."

239

"Not so," said Balthasar, dropping his gaze. "The Spirit was to go with us no farther than to the child. When we came out of the house, after we had seen the babe and our presents were given, we looked immediately for the star. But it was gone, and we knew we were left to ourselves. The last inspiration of the Holy One—the last I can recall—was that which sent us to Ilderim for safety."

"Yes," said the sheik, fingering his beard nervously. "You told me you were sent to me by a Spirit—I remember it."

"I have no special knowledge," Balthasar continued, observing the dejection of Ben Hur, "but, my son, I have given the matter much thought—thought continuing through years, inspired by faith, which, I assure you, calling upon God as a witness, is as strong in me now as in the hour I heard the Spirit calling me by the shore of the lake. If you will listen to me, I will tell you why I believe the child is living."

Both Ilderim and Ben Hur appeared to summon all their faculties that they might understand as well as hear. The interest reached the servants, who drew near to the divan and stood listening. Throughout the tent there was a profound silence.

"We three believe in God." Balthasar bowed his head as he spoke. "And He is the truth. The hills may turn to dust and the seas be drunk dry by south winds, but His word shall stand, because it is the truth."

He uttered this in a solemn manner.

"The Voice, which was his, speaking to me by the lake, said, 'Blessed are you, O son of Mizraim! Redemption comes. With two others from the remote parts of the earth you will see the Savior.' I have seen the Savior—blessed be his name! But the redemption, which was the second part of the promise, is yet to come. Do you see now? If the child is dead, there is no agent to bring the redemption about, and the word is nothing, and God—no, I dare not say it!"

He threw up his hands in horror. "Redemption was the work for which the child was born. And so long as the promise abides, not even death can separate him from his work until it is fulfilled. Take that now as one reason for my belief, then give me further attention." The good man paused.

"Will you not taste the wine? It is at your hand—see," said Ilderim respectfully.

Balthasar drank and, seeming refreshed, continued. "The Savior I saw was born of woman, in nature like us, and subject to all our ills—even death. That is the first consideration. Ponder next the work set apart for him. Was it not a performance for which only a grown man is fitted? A wise man, both firm and strong—a man, not a child? To become this he had to grow as we grow. Remember the dangers his life was subject to in the meantime—the long period between childhood and maturity. The existing powers were his enemies. Herod was his enemy, and what would Rome have been? And as for Israel—that he should not be accepted by Israel was the motive for cutting him off. Do you see now? What better way was there to watch him grow than by placing him into obscurity? So I say to myself and to my listening faith, which is never moved except by a yearning of love—I say he is not dead, but lost. And since his work remains undone, he will come again. There you have the reasons for my belief. Are they not good reasons?"

Ilderim's small Arab eyes were bright with understanding, and Ben Hur, lifted from his dejection, said heartily, "I, at least, may not object to them. What else, pray?"

"Have you not heard enough, my son? Well," he began, in a calmer tone, "seeing that the reasons were good—more plainly, seeing it was God's will that the child should not be found—I settled my faith into patience and waited." He raised his eyes, full of holy trust, and broke off abstractedly—"I am waiting now. He lives, keeping well his mighty secret. Though I cannot go to him, nor name the hill or the valley of his abiding place, he lives. It may be as the fruit in blossom, it may be as the fruit just ripening, but by the certainty there is in the promise and reason of God, I know he lives."

A thrill of awe struck Ben Hur—a thrill that was merely the dying of his half-entertained doubt. "Where do you think he is?" he asked in a low voice, hesitating, like one who feels the pressure of a sacred silence upon his lips.

Balthasar looked at him kindly and replied, though his mind was not entirely freed from its abstraction. "In my house on the

Nile, so close to the river that the passersby in boats see it and its reflection in the water at the same time—in my house, a few weeks ago, I sat thinking. A man thirty years old, I said to myself, would have his fields of life all plowed and his planting well done, for after that it is summertime, with space scarce enough to ripen his sowing. The child, I said further, is now twenty-seven—his time to plant must be at hand.

"I asked myself, as you here asked, my son, and answered by coming here, as to a good resting-place close by the land your fathers had from God. Where else should he appear, if not in Judea? In what city should he begin his work, if not in Jerusalem? Who should be first to receive the blessings he is to bring, if not the children of Abraham, Isaac, and Jacob—the children of the Lord? If I were bidden to go seek him, I would search well the hamlets and villages on the slopes of the mountains of Judea and Galilee falling eastwardly into the valley of the Jordan. He is there now. Standing in a door or on a hilltop, only this evening he saw the sun set one day nearer to the time when he himself will become the light of the world."

Balthasar ceased, with his hand raised and finger pointing as if at Judea. All the listeners, even the dull servants outside the divan, moved by his fervor, were startled as if by a majestic presence suddenly apparent within the tent. Nor did the sensation die away at once. Those at the table sat a while thinking. The spell was finally broken by Ben Hur.

"I see, good Balthasar," he said, "that you have been much, if not strangely, favored. I see, also, that you are a wise man indeed. It is not in my power to tell how grateful I am for the things you have told me. I am warned of the coming of great events and borrow somewhat from your faith. Complete the obligation by telling me further of the mission of the one you are waiting for and for whom from this night on I too shall wait as a believing son of Judah. He is to be a Savior, you said. Is he not to be King of the Jews also?"

"My son," said Balthasar, in his benign way, "the mission is still a purpose in the heart of God. All I think about it is taken from the words of the Voice in connection with the prayer to which they were an answer. Shall we refer to them again?"

"You are the teacher."

"The cause of my unrest," Balthasar began calmly, "which made me a preacher in Alexandria and in the villages of the Nile, which drove me at last into the solitude where the Spirit found me, was the fallen condition of men, due to, as I believed, the loss of the knowledge of God. I sorrowed for my kind—not of one class, but all of them. They were so utterly fallen it seemed to me there could be no redemption unless God himself would make it his work. And I prayed for him to come, that I might see him. 'Your good works have conquered. Redemption comes. You shall see the Savior,' the Voice spoke, and with the answer I went up to Jerusalem rejoicing. Now, who is the redemption for? For all the world. And how shall it be accomplished? Strengthen your faith, my son.

"Men say, I know, that there will be no happiness until Rome is destroyed. That is to say, the ills of the time are not, as I once thought, from ignorance of God but from the poor government of rulers. Do we need to be told that human governments are never in favor of religion? How many kings have you heard of who were better than their subjects?

"No, the redemption cannot be for a political purpose—to pull down rulers and powers and vacate their places merely so that others may take them and enjoy them. If that were its only purpose, the wisdom of God would cease to be supreme. I tell you, though it may only be the saying of the blind to the blind, he who comes is to be a Savior of souls. The redemption means that God appears once more on earth, and righteousness appears."

Disappointment showed plainly on Ben Hur's face—his head dropped, and if he was not convinced, he yet felt himself incapable that moment of disputing the views of the Egyptian.

But not Ilderim. "By the splendor of God!" he cried, impulsively, "the judgment does away with all custom. The ways of the world are fixed and cannot be changed. There must be a leader in every community clothed with power, or else there is no reform."

Balthasar received this comment gravely. "Your wisdom, good sheik, is of the world. You do forget that it is from the ways of the world we are to be redeemed. Seeking men as subjects is the ambition of a king. The soul of a man for its salvation is the desire for God."

Ilderim, though silenced, shook his head, unwilling to believe.

Ben Hur took up the argument for him. "Father—I call you such by permission," he said."Who did you ask for at the gates of Jerusalem?"

The sheik gave him a grateful look.

"I was to ask of the people," said Balthasar, quietly, "Where is he that is born King of the Jews?"

"And you saw him in the house in Bethlehem?"

"We saw and worshiped him and gave him presents—Melchior gave him gold; Gaspar gave him frankincense; and I gave him myrrh."

"When you speak of fact, O Father, to hear you is to believe," said Ben Hur. "But in matter of opinion, I cannot understand the kind of king you would make of the child—I cannot separate the ruler from his powers and duties."

"Son," said Balthasar, "we have the habit of studying closely the things that lie close at our feet, giving only a glance at the great objects in the distance. You see now but the title—King of the Jews. If you will lift your eyes to the mystery beyond it, the stumbling block will disappear. The title is only a word. Your Israel has seen better days—days in which God endearingly called the people His people and dealt with them through prophets. Now, if in those days He promised them the Savior I saw—promised him as King of the Jews—the appearance must be according to the promise.

"You see the reason of my question at the gate! It may be you are also regarding the dignity of the child. If so, think—what does it mean to be a successor of Herod by the world's standard of honor? Could not God make his beloved better? If you can think of the almighty Father wanting a title and stooping to borrow the inventions of men, why was I not bidden to ask for a caesar at once? Oh, for the person of whom we speak, look higher, I implore you! Ask rather when he whom we await shall be king. For I do tell you, my son, that is the key to the mystery, which no man shall understand without the key."

Balthasar raised his eyes devoutly. "There is a kingdom on the earth, though it is not of it—a kingdom of wider bounds than the earth—wider than the sea and the earth, though they are rolled together as finest gold. Its existence is a fact as our hearts are facts, and we journey through it from birth to death without seeing it. Nor shall any man see it until he has first known his own soul. For the kingdom is not for him, but for his soul. There is glory in its dominion such as has not entered the imagination."

"What you say, Father, is a riddle to me," said Ben Hur. "I never heard of such a kingdom."

"Nor did I," said Ilderim.

"And I cannot tell you more about it," Balthasar added, humbly dropping his eyes. "What it is, what it is for, how it may be reached, none can know until the child comes to take possession of it as his own. He brings the key of the unseen gate, which he will open for his beloved, among whom will be included all who love him, for only the redeemed will be included."

After that there was a long silence, which Balthasar accepted as the end of the conversation. "Good sheik," he said, in his placid way, "tomorrow or the next day I will go up to the city for a time. My daughter wishes to see the preparations for the games. I will speak further about the time of our going. And, my son, I will see you again. To you both, peace and good night."

They all arose from the table. The sheik and Ben Hur gazed at the Egyptian until he was led out of the tent.

"Sheik Ilderim," said Ben Hur then, "I have heard strange things tonight. Give me permission, I pray, to walk by the lake that I may think of them."

"Go, and I will come after you."

They washed their hands again. Then at a sign from the master, a servant brought Ben Hur his shoes, and he went out.

44

The Kingdom—Spiritual or Political?

Up a little way there was a cluster of palms, which provided shade half in the water and half on the land. A song from the branches was a song of invitation. Ben Hur stopped beneath to listen. At any other time the notes of the bird would have driven his thoughts away. But the story of the Egyptian was a cause of wonder. He carried it, and like a laborer there was to him no music in the sweetest music until mind and body were happily brought to rest.

The night was quiet. Not a ripple broke upon the shore. The old stars of the East were all out, each in its accustomed place, and there was summer everywhere—on the land, on the lake, and in the sky. Ben Hur's imagination was stirred, his feelings aroused, his will all unsettled. The palms, the sky, the air seemed to him like the distant south zone into which Balthasar had been driven by despair for the souls of men. He feared, yet wished and even waited for, the meaning to these things. When at last his feverish mood was cooled, permitting him to calm himself, he was able to think.

His scheme of life has been explained. In reflecting about it up till now there had been one gap that he had not been able to bridge or fill up—one so broad he could see but vaguely to the other side of it. When, finally, he had graduated a captain as well as a soldier, to what goal should he address his efforts? Revolution he thought of, of course. But the processes of revolution have always been the same, and to lead men into them there have always been required, first, a cause or pretense to enlist adherents; and second, an end, or something as a practical achievement. As a rule he fights well who has wrongs to right. But he fights vastly better who, with wrongs as a spur, has steadily before him a glorious result—a result in which he can find balm for wounds, compensation for valor, remembrance and gratitude in the event of death.

To determine the worth of either the cause or the end, it was necessary that Ben Hur should study the followers to whom he looked when all was ready for action. Very naturally, they were his countrymen. The wrongs of Israel were done to every son of Abraham, and each person was a cause vastly holy and inspiring.

Yes, the cause was there, but the end—what should it be? The hours and days he had given to this part of his scheme were past calculation and all with the same conclusion—a dim and uncertain idea of national liberty. Was it sufficient? He could not say no, for that would have been the death of his hope. And he shrank from saying yes, because his judgment taught him better.

He could not assure himself even that Israel was able single-handed to successfully combat Rome. He knew the resources of that great enemy. He knew her skill was superior to her resources. A universal alliance might suffice, but that was impossible, except for a hero who would come from one of the suffering nations and by martial successes accomplish a victory to fill the whole earth. What glory to Judea if she could prove to be the Macedonia of the new Alexander! Under the rabbis, valor was possible but not discipline. And then the taunt of Messala in the garden of Herod—"All that you conquer in the six days you lose on the seventh."

The hero might be discovered in his day, or he might not. God only knew. There did not need to be any lingering upon the effect of Malluch's skeleton recital of the story of Balthasar. He heard it with a bewildering satisfaction—a feeling that here was the solution for the trouble—here was the perfect hero found at last. And he a son of the lion tribe and King of the Jews! Behind the hero was the world in arms.

The king implied a kingdom. He was to be a warrior as glorious as David, a ruler as wise and magnificent as Solomon. The kingdom was to be a power against which Rome was to dash itself to pieces. There would be colossal war and the agonies of death and birth. Then finally there would be peace, meaning, of course, Judean dominion of the world forever.

Ben Hur's heart beat hard because for that instant he had a vision of Jerusalem as the capital of the world and Zion the site of the throne of the Universal Master.

To the enthusiast it seemed a rare fortune that the man who

had seen the King was at the tent to which he was going. He could see him there and hear him and learn of the coming change, especially all he knew of the time of its happening. If it were at hand, the campaign with Maxentius should be abandoned, and he would go and begin organizing and arming the tribes, so that Israel might be ready when the great day of the restoration began to break.

Now, as we have seen, Ben Hur had the marvelous story from Balthasar himself. Was he satisfied? There was a shadow upon him deeper than that of the cluster of palms—the shadow of a great uncertainty, which pertained more to the kingdom than the King.

What of this kingdom? And what is it to be? Ben Hur asked himself. Thus the questions arose early that were to follow the child to the end and survive him on earth—incomprehensible in his day and a puzzle to all who do not or cannot understand that every man is two in one—a deathless soul and a mortal body.

"What is it to be?" he asked.

The child himself answered, but for Ben Hur there were only the words of Balthasar. "On the earth, yet not of it—not for men, but for their souls—a dominion, nevertheless, of unimaginable glory." The hapless youth found the phrases only the darkening of a riddle.

"The hand of man is not in this effort," he said despairingly. "Nor has the king of such a kingdom any use for men. Neither toilers, counselors, nor soldiers. The earth must die or be made new, and new principles for government must be discovered—something besides force. But what?"

He could not see it. The power there is in love had not yet occurred to any man; much less had one come speaking of government and its objects. Love is better and mightier than force.

In the midst of his reverie a hand was laid upon his shoulder.

"I have a word to say, O son of Arrius," said Ilderim, stopping by his side. "A word, and then I must return, for the night is fleeting."

"I give you welcome, sheik."

"As to the things you have heard recently," said Ilderim, almost without pause, "believe them except that which relates to the King and kingdom the child will set up when he comes. As to this, keep an open mind until you hear Simonides the merchant—a good man here in Antioch, to whom I will make you known. The Egyptian gives you an entry to his dreams that are too good for the earth. Simonides is wiser; he will bring you the sayings of your prophets, giving you the chapter and verse, so you cannot deny that the child will be King of the Jews in fact—he will, by the splendor of God! A king as Herod was, only better and far more magnificent. And then, you see, we will taste the sweetness of vengeance. I have said it. Peace to you!"

"Stay—sheik!"

If Ilderim heard his call, he did not stay.

"Simonides again!" said Ben Hur bitterly. "Simonides here, Simonides there. I wish to be rid of my father's servant—at least to hold onto that which is mine—yet he is richer, if indeed he be not wiser, than the Egyptian. By the covenant! It is not to the faithless a man should go to find a faith to keep, and I will not go to them. But I hear singing—and the voice a woman's—or an angel's! It comes this way."

Down the lake came a woman singing. Her voice floated along the hushed water and was melodious as a flute, and it grew louder each instant. Immediately the dipping of oars was heard in slow measure. A little later the words were distinguishable—words in purest Greek, best fit for all the tongues of the day for the expression of a passionate grief.

The Lament

I sigh as I sing for the story land
    Across the Syrian sea.
The odorous winds from the musky sand
    Were breaths of life to me.
They play with the plumes of the whispering palm
    For me, alas! No more;
Nor more does the Nile in the moonlit calm
    Moan past the Memphian shore.
O Nilus! Thou god of my fainting soul!
    In dreams thou come to me;
And, dreaming, I play with the lotus bowl,
    And sing old songs to thee;

And hear from afar the Memnonian strain,
And calls from dear Simbel;
And wake to a passion of grief and pain
That e'er I said—Farewell!

At the conclusion of the song the singer was past the cluster of palms. The last word—"farewell"—floated past Ben Hur, weighted with all the sweet sorrow of parting. The passing of the boat was like the passing of a deeper shadow into the deeper night.

Ben Hur drew a long breath hardly distinguishable from a sigh.

"I know her by the song—the daughter of Balthasar. How beautiful it was! And how beautiful she is!"

He recalled her large eyes curtained slightly by her drooping lids, the oval cheeks and rosy, rich, full lips, and all the grace of the tall, slender figure. "How beautiful she is!" he repeated. And his heart answered by quickening its movement.

Then, almost in the same instant, another face, younger and quite as beautiful—as well as more childlike and tender—appeared out of the lake. "Esther!" he said, smiling. "As I wished, a star has been sent to me."

He turned and went slowly back to the tent. His life had been crowded with griefs and with vengeful preparations—too much crowded for love. Was this the beginning of a happy change?

And if a strong influence went with him into the tent, whose was it? Esther had given him a cup. So had the Egyptian. And both had come to him at the same time under the palms. Who?

45

Messala Takes the Wreath Off his Head

The morning after the party in the palace, the couch was covered with young patricians. Maxentius would come, and the city would gather to receive him. The legion would descend from Mount Sulpius in the glory of their armor. There might be ceremonial splendors to impress the most notable ever before seen or heard of in the gorgeous East. Yet the many patricians will continue to sleep on the divan where they had fallen or been carelessly tossed by indifferent slaves. The idea that they would be able to take part in the reception that day was about as possible as for the figures in the studio of a modern artist to rise and do a waltz.

Not all, however, who participated in the orgy were in this shameful condition. When dawn began to peer through the skylights of the palace, Messala arose and took the wreath from his head, as a sign that the reveling was at an end. Then he gathered his robe about him, gave a last look at the scene, and without a word departed for his quarters. Cicero the orator could not have retired with more gravity from a nightlong senatorial debate.

Three hours afterward two couriers entered his room, and they each received a dispatch from his own hand, sealed and in duplicate, consisting chiefly of a letter to Valerius Gratus, the procurator, still resident in Caesarea. The importance attached to the speedy and certain delivery of the paper was evident. One courier was to travel over land, the other by sea, and both were to make the utmost haste. The letter read as follows:

Antioch, XII. Kal. Jul.
Messala to Gratus

O my Midas!

I pray you take no offense at the address, seeing it is one of love and gratitude.

O my Midas!

I have to relate to you an astonishing event, which, though as yet somewhat of a guess, will, I do not doubt, justify your instant attention.

Allow me first to revive your memory. Remember, a good many years ago, a family of a prince of Jerusalem, incredibly ancient and vastly rich—by the name of Ben Hur. If your memory is ailing, there is, if I am not mistaken, a wound on your head that may help you to remember the circumstance.

Next, to arouse your interest. In punishment of the attempt on your life—may all the gods forbid it should ever prove to have been an accident—the family was seized and disposed of, their property confiscated, O my Midas! As the action had the approval of our Caesar, who was as just as he was wise—may there be flowers upon his altars forever!—there should be no shame in referring to the sums that were realized to us both from that source, and it is not possible that I could ever cease to be grateful to you, certainly not while I continue, as at present, in the uninterrupted enjoyment of the task that fell to me.

In vindication of your wisdom—a quality for which, as I am now advised, the son of Gordius, to whom I have boldly likened you, was never distinguished among men or gods—I recall further that you did away with the family of Hur, both of us at the time supposing the plan we established to be the most effective one possible for our purposes, which were silence on the part of the victims and delivery over to inevitable but natural death. You will remember what you did with the mother and sister of the criminal. Yet, if I now yield to a desire to learn whether they be living or dead, I know, from knowing your nature, O my Gratus, that you will pardon me as one scarcely less amiable than yourself.

What is more immediately essential, however, I bring to your remembrance that the actual criminal was sent to the galleys as a slave for life—the sentence was carried out. And that may serve to make the event that I am about to relate even more astonishing. I saw and read the receipt for his body delivered to the tribune commanding the galley.

You may begin now to give me more special attention, O my most excellent Phrygian!

Because of the limit of life as a galley slave, the outlaw that we disposed of should be dead. And if you will excuse a momentary weakness, O most virtuous and tender of men! I loved him in childhood. Because he was very handsome, I used in much admiration to call him my Ganymede. He ought in right to have fallen in the arms of the most beautiful daughter of the family. Feeling, however, that he was certainly dead, I have lived a full five years in calm and innocent enjoyment of the fortune for which I am in a degree indebted to him. I make the admission of indebtedness without intending it to diminish my obligation to you.

Last night, while acting as master of the feast for a party in Rome—their extreme youth and inexperience appealed to my compassion—I heard an interesting story. Maxentius, the consul, as you know, comes today to conduct a campaign against the Parthians. There is among the ambitious who are to accompany him a son of the late duumvir Quintus Arrius. I had occasion to inquire about him in particular. When Arrius set out in pursuit of the pirates, whose defeat gained him his final honors, he had no family. But when he returned from the expedition, he brought back with him an heir. The son and heir of whom I speak is the one you sent to the galleys—the very Ben Hur who should have died at his oar five years ago—returned now with fortune and rank and possibly as a Roman citizen too. Well, you are too firmly seated to be alarmed, but I, O my Midas! I am in danger—no need to tell you of what. Who should know, if you do not?

When Arrius, the father by adoption of this apparition from the arms of the most beautiful of the Oceanides joined battle with the pirates, his vessel was sunk, and only two of all her crew escaped drowning—Arrius himself and this one, his heir.

The officers who took them from the plank on which they were floating say the associate of the unfortunate tribune was a young man who, when lifted to the deck, was in the costume of a galley slave.

This should be convincing, to say the least. But lest you scoff again, I tell you, O my Midas! That yesterday, by good fortune—I have a vow to Fortune because of this—I met the mysterious son of Arrius face to face. And I declare now that, though I did not then recognize him, he is the very Ben Hur who was my friend for years—the very Ben Hur who, if he be a man, though of the commonest grade, must this very moment of my writing be thinking of vengeance—for so would I were I he—vengeance not to be satisfied short of life. Vengeance for country, mother, sister, self, and—I say it last, though you may think it should be first—for fortune lost.

By this time, O my good benefactor and friend! My Gratus! In consideration of your sestertia in peril, their loss being the worst that could happen to one of your high estate—I quit calling you after the foolish old King of Phrygia—by this time, I say (meaning after having read me so far), I have faith to believe you have ceased scoffing and are ready to think what ought to be done in such an emergency.

It is rude to ask you now what shall be done. Rather let me say I am your client. Or better yet, you are my Ulysses, whose part it is to give me sound direction.

And I am pleased to think that I will see you when this letter is put into your hand. I see you read it once, your face was grave, and then again, and you smiled. Then hesitation ended and your judgment made, it is wisdom like Mercury's, promptness like Caesar's.

The sun is now fairly risen. An hour from now two messengers will depart from my door, each with a sealed copy. One of them will go by land, the other by sea. I regard it as that important that you should be early and particularly informed of the appearance of our enemy in this part of our Roman world.

I will await your answer here.

Ben Hur's coming and going will of course be regulated by his master, the consul, who, though he exerts himself without rest day and night, he cannot get away for less than a month. You know what a task it is to assemble and provide for an army destined to operate in a desolate, townless country.

I saw the Jew yesterday in the Grove of Daphne. If if he is not there now, he is certainly in the neighborhood, so it is easy for me to keep an eye on him. Indeed, I would say, with the most positive assurance, that he is to be found at the Orchard of Palms, under the tent of the traitor Sheik Ilderim, who cannot escape our strong hand for long. Do not be surprised if Maxentius, as his first move, places the Arab on a ship bound for Rome.

I am very particular about the whereabouts of the Jew because it will be important to you, O illustrious one! When you come to consider what is to be done, remember that in every scheme involving human action there are always three elements to be taken into account— time, place, and means.

If you say this is the place, have then no hesitancy in trusting the business to your most loving friend, who would be your best scholar as well.

Messala

46

Ilderim's Arabs Under the Yoke

About the time the couriers departed from Messala's door with the dispatches (it was still the early morning hour), Ben Hur entered Ilderim's tent. He had taken a plunge into the lake, breakfasted, and appeared now in a sleeveless undertunic.

The sheik saluted him from the divan. "I give you peace, son of Arrius," he said, with admiration, for in truth he had never seen a more perfect illustration of glowing, powerful, confident manhood. "I give you peace and good will. The horses are ready. And you?"

"The peace you give me, good sheik, I give you in return. I thank you for so much good will. I am ready."

Ilderim clapped his hands. "I will have the horses brought. Be seated."

"Are they yoked?"

"No."

"Then allow me to serve myself," said Ben Hur. "It is necessary that I make the acquaintance of your Arab horses. I must know them by name, sheik, that I may speak to them individually. I must also know their temper, for they are like people. If bold, I need to scold them; if timid, the better for praise and flattery. Let the servants bring me the harness."

"And the chariot?" asked the sheik.

"I will let the chariot alone today. In its place, let them bring me a fifth horse, if you have it. He should be barebacked and as swift as the others."

Ilderim's wonder was aroused, and he summoned a servant immediately. "Ask them to bring the harness for the four," he said. "The harness for the four, and the bridle for Sirius."

Ilderim then arose. "Sirius is my love, and I am his, O son of Arrius. We have been comrades for twenty years—in the tent, in battle, in all the ways of the desert we have been comrades. I will show him to you."

Going to the dividing curtain, he held it, while Ben Hur passed under. The horses came to him in a group. One with a small head, luminous eyes, the neck like the segment of a bent bow, and a mighty chest, curtained thickly by a mane as soft and wavy as a female's locks. He whinnied low and gladly at sight of him.

"Good horse," said the sheik, patting the dark-brown cheek. "Good horse, good morning." Turning then to Ben Hur, he added, "This is Sirius, father of the four here. Mira, the mother, awaits our return. She is too precious to be chanced in a region where there is a stronger hand than mine. And I much doubt—" he laughed as he spoke "—O son of Arrius, if the tribe could endure her absence. She is their glory. They worship her. If she galloped over them, they would laugh. Ten thousand horsemen, sons of the desert, will ask today, 'Have your heard of Mira?' And to the answer, 'She is well,' they will say, 'God is good! Blessed be God!'"

"Mira, Sirius—names of stars, are they not, O sheik?" asked Ben Hur, going to each of the four and to the sire, offering his hand.

"And why not?" replied Ilderim. "Were you ever out on the desert at night?"

"No."

"Then you cannot know how much we Arabs depend upon the stars. We borrow their names in gratitude and give them in love. My fathers all had their Miras, as I have mine. And these children are stars nonetheless. There, you see, is Rigel and there Antares. That one is Atair, and the one you go to now is Aldebaran, the youngest of the brood, but none the worse because of that. He will carry you against the wind till it roars in your ears like Akaba. And he will go where you say, son of Arrius—yes, by the glory of Solomon! He will take you to the lion's jaws if you dare so much."

The harness was brought to them. Ben Hur equipped the horses with his own hands and led them out of the tent and there attached the reins.

"Bring me Sirius," he said. An Arab could not have better sprung to seat on the horse's back.

"And now the reins." They were given to him and carefully separated.

"Good sheik," he said, "I am ready. Let a guide go before me to the field, and send some of your men with water."

There was no trouble in starting. The horses were not afraid. Already there seemed a tacit understanding between them and the new driver, who had performed his part calmly and with the confidence that always produces assurance. Ben Hur sat upon Sirius instead of standing in a chariot.

Ilderim's spirit arose. He combed his beard and smiled with satisfaction as he muttered, "He is not a Roman, no, by the splendor of God!" He followed on foot, the entire entourage of the tent—men, women, and children—following him, participants in his nomadic life, if not in his confidence.

The field, when reached, proved ample and well fitted for the training, which Ben Hur began immediately by driving the four slowly at first in perpendicular lines and then in wide circles. Advancing further in the course, he next put them into a trot. Later progressing, he drove them into a gallop. Finally he shortened the circles and then later drove right and left and forward, without a break. An hour was filled with this process. Slowing the gait to a walk, he drove up to Ilderim.

"The work is done, there is nothing now but to practice," he said. "I give you joy, Sheik Ilderim, that you have such servants as these. See," he continued, dismounting and going to the horses, "see, the gloss of their red coats is without spot. They breathe as lightly as when I began. It will be great joy, and I will take it hard if"—he turned his flashing eyes upon the old man's face—"if we have not the victory and our—"

He stopped, flushed, and bowed. At the sheik's side he observed for the first time, Balthasar, leaning upon his staff, and two women closely veiled. At one of the latter he looked a second time, saying to himself, with a flutter of his heart, *It is she—the Egyptian!*

Ilderim picked up his broken sentence. "The victory and our revenge!" Then he said, "I am not afraid. I am glad. Son of Arrius, you are the man. Be the end like the beginning, and you will see of what stuff is the lining of the hand of an Arab who is able to help you."

"I thank you, good sheik," Ben Hur replied modestly. "Let the servants bring drink for the horses." With his own hands he poured the water.

Remounting Sirius, he renewed the training, going as earlier from a walk to a trot to a gallop. Finally, he pushed the steady racers into a run, gradually quickening it to full speed. The performance then became exciting, and there was applause for the slight holding of the reins and admiration for the four, which were the same, whether they flew forward or wheeled in curved patterns. In their action there was unity, power, grace, all without effort of labor. The admiration was unmixed with pity, which would have been as well bestowed upon swallows in their evening flight.

In the midst of the exercises, and the attention they received from all the bystanders, Malluch entered the ground, seeking the sheik. "I have a message for you, O sheik," he said, waiting a moment he supposed favorable for the speech. "A message from Simonides, the merchant."

"Simonides!" answered the Arab. "It is well. May Abaddon conquer all his enemies."

"He asked me to first give you the holy peace of God," Malluch continued, "and then this dispatch, with the prayer that you read it the instant of receipt."

Ilderim, standing in his place, broke the sealing of the package delivered to him and from a wrapping of fine linen took two letters, which he proceeded to read.

Simonides to Sheik Ilderim

O friend!
First assure yourself of a place in my inner heart.
There is in your tent a youth of fair presence, calling himself the son of Arrius, and such he is by adoption.
He is very dear to me.
He has a wonderful history, which I will tell you. Come thou today or tomorrow, that I may tell you the history and have your counsel.
In the meantime, favor all his requests, as long as they are not against honor. Should there be need of reparation, I am bound to you for it.
That I have interest in this youth, keep private.

258

Remember me to your other guest. He, his daughter, yourself, and all whom you may choose to be of your company, must depend on me at the circus the day of the games. I have seats already engaged.

To you and all yours, peace.

What should I be but your friend?

Simonides

O friend!

Out of the abundance of my experience, I send you a word.

There is a sign that all persons not Romans, and who have monies or goods subject to seizure, accept as warning—that is, the arrival at a seat of power of some high Roman official charged with authority.

Today the Consul Maxentius comes. Be warned!

Another word of advice. A conspiracy to be set against you, O friend, must include the Herods as parties. You have great properties in their dominions. So keep watch.

This morning send for your trusty keepers of the roads leading south from Antioch and ask them to search every courier going and coming. If they find private dispatches relating to you or your affairs, you should see them!

You should have received this yesterday, though it is not too late, if you act promptly.

If couriers left Antioch this morning, your messengers know the byways and can get before them with your orders. Do not hesitate.

Burn this after reading.

Your friend,
Simonides

Ilderim read the letters a second time and refolded them in the linen wrap and put the package under his tunic.

The exercises in the field continued only a little longer—in all, about two hours. At their conclusion, Ben Hur brought the four horses to a walk and drove to Ilderim.

"With leave, sheik," he said, "I will return your Arabs to the tent and bring them out again this afternoon."

Ilderim walked to him as he sat on Sirius and said, "I give them to you, son of Arrius, to do with as you will until after the games. You have done with them in two hours what the Roman—may jackals gnaw his bones fleshless!—could not in as many weeks. We will win—by the splendor of God, we will win."

259

At the tent Ben Hur remained with the horses while they were being cared for. Then, after a plunge in the lake and a cup of wine with the sheik, whose flow of spirits was royally exuberant, he dressed himself in his Jewish garb again and walked with Malluch on into the Orchard.

There was much conversation between the two, but it was not all important. One part, however, must not be overlooked.

"I will give you," Ben Hur said, "an order for my property stored in the inn this side of the river by the Seleucian Bridge. Bring it to me today, if you can. And good Malluch—if I do not overtask you—"

Malluch heartily expressed his willingness to be of service.

"Thank you, Malluch" said Ben Hur. "I will take you at your word, remembering that we are brethren of the old tribe and that the enemy is a Roman. First, then—as you are a man of business, which I much fear Sheik Ilderim is not—"

"Arabs seldom are," said Malluch gravely.

"No, I do not challenge their shrewdness, Malluch. It is well, however, to look after them. To save a forfeit or hinderance in connection with the race, you would put me perfectly at rest by going to the office of the circus and seeing that he has complied with every preliminary rule. And if you can get a copy of the rules, the service may be of great use to me. I would like to know the colors I am to wear and particularly the number of the gate I am to occupy at the starting. If it be next to Messala's on the right or left, it is good. If not, and you can have it changed so as to bring me next to the Roman, do so. Do you have a good memory, Malluch?"

"It has never failed me, son of Arrius, where the heart helped it as now."

"I will venture, then, to charge you with one further service. I saw yesterday that Messala was proud of his chariot, as he might be, for the best of Caesar's scarcely surpass it. Can you not make its display an excuse that will enable you to find if it is light or heavy? I would like to have its exact weight and measurements— and, Malluch, though you fail in all else, bring me exactly the height his axle stands above the ground.

"You understand, Malluch? I do not wish him to have any actual advantage of me. I do not care for his splendor. If I beat him, it will make his fall the harder and my triumph the more complete. If there are important advantages, I want them."

"I see!" said Malluch. "A line dropped from the center of the axle is what you want."

"You have it. And be glad, Malluch—it is the last of my orders. Let us return to the tent."

At the door of the tent they found a servant replenishing the smoke-stained bottles of freshly made wine and stopped to refresh themselves. Shortly afterwards Malluch returned to the city.

During their absence a well-mounted messenger had been dispatched with orders as suggested by Simonides. He was an Arab and carried nothing written.

47

The Arts of Cleopatra

"Iras, the daughter of Balthasar, sends me with a greeting and a message," said a servant to Ben Hur, who was resting in the tent.

"Give me the message."

"Would it please you to accompany her upon the lake?"

"I will carry the answer myself. Tell her so."

His shoes were brought to him, and in a few minutes Ben Hur sallied out to find the fair Egyptian. The shadow of the mountains was creeping over the Orchard of Palms in advance of night. Far off through the trees came the tinkling of sheep bells, the lowing of cattle, and the voices of the herdsmen bringing their charges home. Life at the Orchard, it should be remembered, was in all respects as pastoral as life on the bare meadows of the desert.

Sheik Ilderim had witnessed the exercises of the afternoon, which were a repetition of those of the morning. After which he went to the city to answer the invitation of Simonides. He thought to return in the night, but, considering the immensity of the field to be talked over with his friend, it was hardly possible.

Ben Hur, left alone, had seen his horses cared for. He cooled and purified himself in the lake, exchanged the field garb for his customary all-white vestments, as became a Sadducean of pure blood, dined early, and, thanks to the strength of youth, was recovered well from the violent exertion he had undergone.

It is neither wise nor honest to detract from beauty as a quality. There cannot be a refined soul that is insensible to its influence. Beauty is of itself a power, and it was now drawing Ben Hur.

The Egyptian was a wonderfully beautiful woman to him—with a beautiful face and form. In his thoughts she always appeared to him as he saw her at the fountain, and he felt the influence of her words even sweeter because of the tearful expression of gratitude to him. Her eyes were the large, soft, black, and al-mond-shaped eyes of her nation—eyes that spoke more than is found in the greatest wealth of words. Ben Hur's recurring thought of her was of a figure tall, slender, graceful, refined, wrapped in rich and floating robes, wanting only an imaginative mind to make her, like the Shulamite, terrible as an army with banners.

In other words, as she returned to his fancy, the whole pas-sionate Song of Solomon came with her, inspired by her pres-ence. With this sentiment and that feeling, he was going to see if in reality she actually justified them. It was not love that was influ-encing him so far but admiration and curiosity, which just might be the heralds of love.

The landing was a simple affair, consisting of a short stair-way and a platform bordered by some lampposts. At the top of the steps he paused, curious at what he saw.

A boat rested lightly as an eggshell upon the clear water. An Ethiopian—the camel driver at the Castalian fountain—occupied the rower's place, his blackness intensified by a shining white liv-ery. The boat was cushioned and carpeted in brilliant Tyrian red.

The Egyptian herself sat on the rudder seat, sunk in Indian shawls and the most delicate veils and scarfs. Her arms were bare to the shoulder, and not only faultless in their shape, they com-pelled attention to them. Her hands, the fingers even, seemed en-dowed with graces and meaning. Each was an object of beauty. The shoulders and neck were protected from the evening air by an ample scarf, which nevertheless did not hide them.

Ben Hur paid no attention to these details in the glance he gave her. There was simply an impression made upon him, and, like strong light, it was a sensation rather than sight. "Your lips are like a thread of scarlet; your temples are like a piece of pomegran-ate within your locks. Rise up, my love, my fair one, and come away, for lo! The winter is past, the rain is over and gone; the flowers appear on the earth; the time of the singing of birds is come, and the voice of the turtle is heard in the land"—such was the impression she made upon him, translated into words.

"Come," she said, observing him stop, "come, or I shall think you are a poor sailor."

The red of his cheeks deepened. Did she know anything of

his life upon the sea? He descended to the platform at once. "I was afraid," he said, as he took the vacant seat before her.

"Of what?"

"Of sinking the boat," he replied smiling.

"Wait until we are in deeper water," she said, giving a signal to the black, who dipped the oars, and they were off.

If love and Ben Hur were enemies, the latter was never more at mercy. The Egyptian sat where he could not help but see her, she whom he had already engrossed in memory as his ideal Shulamite from the Song of Solomon. With her eyes giving light to his, the stars might come out, and he would not see them, and in fact they did. The night might fall with unrelieved darkness everywhere else; her look would give him illumination. And then, given both youth and such companionship, there is no situation in which the fancy takes such complete control as upon tranquil waters under a calm night sky, warm with summer. It is easy at such a time to glide slowly out of the commonplace into the romantic.

"Give me the rudder," he said.

"No," she replied. "Did I not ask you to ride with me? I am indebted to you and would begin to pay you back. You may talk and I will listen, or I will talk and you will listen. That choice is yours. But it shall be mine to choose where we go and the way there."

"And where may that be?"

"You are alarmed again."

"O fair Egyptian, I only asked you the main question of every captive."

"Call me Egypt."

"I would rather call you Iras."

"You may think of me by that name, but call me Egypt."

"Egypt is a country and has many people."

"Yes! And such a country!"

"I see. It is to Egypt we are going."

"I wish we were! I would be so glad!" She sighed as she spoke.

"You do not care for me then," he said.

"Ah, by that I know you were never there."

"I never was."

"Oh, it is the land where there are no unhappy people, the desire of all the rest of the earth, the mother of all the gods, and therefore supremely blessed. There, O son of Arrius, there you will find an increase of happiness, and the wretched drink once of the sweet water of the sacred river and laugh and sing, rejoicing like children."

"Are not the very poor with you there as elsewhere?"

"The very poor in Egypt are the very simple in wants and ways," she replied. "They have no wish beyond having enough, and how little that is a Greek or a Roman cannot know."

"But I am neither Greek nor Roman."

She laughed. "I have a garden of roses, and in the midst of it is a tree, and its bloom is the richest of all. Where did it come from, do you think?"

"From Persia, the home of the rose."

"No."

"From India, then."

"No."

"Ah! One of the isles of Greece."

"I will tell you," she said. "A traveler found it perishing by the roadside on the plain of Rephaim."

"Oh, in Judea!"

"I put it in the earth that was left bare by the receding Nile, and the soft south wind blew over the desert and nursed it, and the sun kissed it in pity, after which it could only grow and flourish. I stand in its shade now, and it thanks me with much perfume. As with the roses, so with the men of Israel. Where shall they reach perfection but in Egypt?"

"Moses was but one of millions."

"No, there was a reader of dreams. Will you forget him?"

"The friendly pharaohs are dead."

"Ah, yes! The river by which they lived sings to them in their tombs. Yet the same sun tempers the same air to the same people."

"Alexandria is but a Roman town."

"She has but exchanged scepters. Caesar took the sword from her and in its place left learning. Go with me to the Brucheium, and I will show you the college of nations; to the Serapeion and see the perfection of architecture; to the library and read the immortals; to the theater and hear the heroics of the Greeks and Hindus; to the quay and count the triumphs of commerce.

"Descend with me into the streets, O son of Arrius, and, when the philosophers have gone and taken with them the masters of all the arts and all the gods have their devotees and nothing remains of the day but its pleasures, you shall hear the stories that have amused men from the beginning and the songs that will never die."

As he listened, Ben Hur was carried back to the night when, in the summerhouse in Jerusalem, his mother, in much the same poetry of patriotism, explained the departed glories of Israel. "I see now why you wish to be called Egypt. Will you sing me a song if I call you by that name? I heard you last night."

"That was a hymn of the Nile," she answered, "a lament that I sing when I would fancy I smell the breath of the desert and hear the surge of the dear old river. Let me rather give you an idea from the Indian mind. When we get to Alexandria, I will take you to the corner of the street where you can hear it from the daughter of the Ganga, who taught it to me. Kapila, you should know, was one of the most revered of the Hindu sages."

She sang a song, and Ben Hur did not have time to express his thanks for the song before the bottom of the boat grated upon the underlying sand, and the next moment the bow ran upon the shore.

"A quick voyage, O Egypt!" he cried.

"And a briefer stay!" she replied, as with a strong push the black sent them shooting into the open water again.

"You will give me the rudder now."

"Oh, no," said she, laughing. "To you, the chariot; to me, the boat. We are merely at the lake's end, and the lesson is that I must not sing anymore. Having been to Egypt, let us now go to the Grove of Daphne."

"Without a song on the way?" he said.

"Tell me something of the Roman from whom you saved us yesterday," she asked.

The request put Ben Hur in an unpleasant mood. "I wish this

were the Nile," he said, evasively. "The kings and queens, having slept so long, might come down from their tombs and ride with us."

"They were of the colossi and would sink our boat. The pygmies would be preferable. But tell me of the Roman. He is very wicked, is he not?"

"I cannot say."

"Is he of noble family and rich?"

"I cannot speak of his riches."

"How beautiful his horses were! And the bed of his chariot was gold and the wheels ivory. And his audacity! The bystanders laughed as he rode away—they who were so nearly under his wheels!"

She laughed at the recollection.

"They were rabble," said Ben Hur bitterly.

"He must be one of the monsters who are said to be growing up in Rome—Apollos who is as ravenous as Cerberus. Does he reside in Antioch?"

"He is from the East somewhere."

"Egypt would suit him better that Syria."

"Hardly," Ben Hur replied. "Cleopatra is dead."

That instant the lamps burning before the door of the tent came into view.

"Ah, then, we have not been to Egypt. I have not seen Karnak or Philae or Abydos. This is not the Nile. I have only imagined a son of India and been boating in a dream."

"Mourn rather that you have not seen the Rameses pharoahs at Abu Sumbul, which makes it so easy to think of God, the maker of the heavens and earth. Or why should you mourn at all? Let us go on to the river. And I cannot sing—" she laughed "—because I have said I would not, yet I can tell you stories of Egypt."

"Go on! Yes, till morning comes, and the evening, and the next morning!" he said vehemently.

"Of what shall my stories be? Of the mathematicians?"

"Oh, no."

"Of the philosophers?"

"No, no."

"Of the magicians?"

"If you will."

"Of war?"

"Yes."

"Of love?"

"Yes."

They whiled the hours away with conversation and stories. As they stepped ashore, she said, "Tomorrow we go to the city."

"But you will be at the games?" he asked.

"Oh, yes."

"I will send you my colors." With that they parted.

48

Messala on Guard

Ilderim returned to the tent the next day about the third hour. As he dismounted, a man whom he recognized as of his own tribe came to him and said, "O sheik, I was asked to give you this package, with request that you read it at once. If there is an answer, I was to await your directions."

Ilderim gave the package his immediate attention. The seal was already broken. The address ran *To Valerius Gratus at Caesarea.*

"Abaddon take him!" growled the sheik, at discovering a letter in Latin.

Had the letter been in Greek or Arabic, he could have read it. As it was, the most he could make out was the signature in bold Roman letters—MESSALA—upon which his eyes twinkled.

"Where is the young Jew?" he asked.

"In the field with the horses," a servant replied.

The sheik replaced the papyrus in its envelopes and, tucking the package under his girdle, remounted the horse. That moment a stranger made his appearance, coming, apparently, from the city.

"I am looking for Sheik Ilderim, also named the Generous," the stranger said. His language and attire was that of a Roman.

What he could not read, he could still speak, so the old Arab answered, with dignity, "I am Sheik Ilderim."

The man looked away and, returning his gaze, said with forced composure, "I heard you had need of a driver for the games."

Ilderim's lip under the white moustache curled contemptuously. "Go your way," he said. "I have a driver."

He turned to ride away, but the man lingered and spoke again. "Sheik, I am a lover of horses, and they say you have the most beautiful in the world."

The old man was touched. He drew in his rein, as if on the point of yielding to the flattery, but finally replied, "Not today, not today. Some other time I will show them to you. I am too busy just now."

He rode to the field, while the stranger went to town again, with a smiling countenance. He had accomplished his mission.

And every day thereafter, down to the great day of the games, a man—sometimes two or three men—came to the sheik at the Orchard, pretending to seek an engagement as driver.

In this way Messala kept watch over Ben Hur.

49

Ilderim and Ben Hur Deliberate

The sheik waited, well satisfied, until Ben Hur drew his horses off the field at noon, for he had seen them, after being put through all the other paces, all four run at full speed as if the four were one.

"This afternoon, O sheik, I will give Sirius back to you." Ben Hur patted the neck of the old horse as he spoke. "I will give him back and ride the chariot."

"So soon?" Ilderim asked.

"With horses such as these, good sheik, one day is enough. They are not afraid. They have a man's intelligence, and they love the exercise. This one"—he shook a rein over the back of the youngest of the four—"you called him Aldebaran, I believe—is the swiftest. Traveling only once around a stadium he would lead the others three times his length."

Ilderim pulled his beard and said, with twinkling eyes. "Aldebaran is the swiftest, but what of the slowest?"

"This is the one." Ben Hur shook the rein over Antares. "This is he. But he will win, for—look, sheik—he will run his utmost all day. And, as the sun goes down, he will reach his swiftest."

"Right again," said Ilderim.

"I have only one fear, sheik."

The sheik became very serious.

"In his greed to triumph, a Roman cannot keep his honor pure. In all of the games—mark you—their tricks are unlimited. In chariot racing their cheating extends to everything—from horse to driver, from driver to master. Therefore, good sheik, look carefully at all you have. From this day till the trial is over, let no stranger so much as see the horses. If you would be perfectly safe, do more— keep watch over them with armed guards as well as a sleepless eye. Then I will have no fear of the outcome."

At the door of the tent they dismounted. "What you say shall

271

be done. By the splendor of God, no hand shall come near them unless it belongs to one of the faithful. Tonight I will set watches. But, son of Arrius"—Ilderim brought out the package and opened it slowly, while they walked to the divan and seated themselves— "son of Arrius, look at this and help me with your Latin."

He passed the letter to Ben Hur. "There. Read—and read aloud, translating what you find into the tongue of your fathers. Latin is an abomination."

Ben Hur was in good spirits and began the reading lightheartedly. "'Messala to Gratus!'" He paused. A premonition quickened his pulse.

Ilderim observed his agitation. "Well, I am waiting."

Ben Hur asked for pardon and recommenced reading the paper, which was one of the duplicates of the letter dispatched so carefully to Gratus by Messala the morning after the revel in the palace.

The paragraphs in the beginning were remarkable only as further proof that the writer had not outgrown his habit of mockery. When they were passed, and Ben Hur came to parts intended to refresh the memory of Gratus, his voice trembled, and twice he stopped to regain his self-control. By a strong effort he continued. "'I recall further'" he read, "'that you did away with the family of Hur'"—there the reader again paused and drew a long breath— "'both of us at the time supposing the plan we established to be the most effective one possible for our purposes, which were silence on the part of the victims and delivery over to inevitable but natural death.'"

Here Ben Hur broke down utterly. The paper fell from his hands, and he covered his face. "They are dead—dead. I alone am left."

The sheik had been a silent but not unsympathetic witness of the young man's suffering. Now he arose and said, "Son of Arrius, it is for me to beg your pardon. Read the paper by yourself. When you are strong enough to read the rest of it to me, send word, and I will return." He went out of the tent, and nothing in all his life proved him to be a better man.

Ben Hur flung himself on the couch and gave in to his feelings, and he wept. When somewhat recovered, he recollected that a portion of the letter remained unread, and, taking it once again, he resumed the reading. "You will remember," the passage read, "what you did with the mother and sister of the criminal. Yet, if I now yield to a desire to learn whether they be living or dead—"

Ben Hur gasped, and read again and then again, and at last cried aloud. "He does not know they are dead. He does not know it! Blessed be the name of the Lord! There is yet hope." He finished the sentence and was strengthened by it and went on bravely to the end of the letter.

"They are not dead," he said, after reflection. "They are not dead, or he would have heard of it."

A second reading, more careful than the first, confirmed this opinion. Then he sent for the sheik.

"In coming to your hospitable tent, O sheik," he said, calmly, when the Arab was seated and they were alone, "it was not in my mind to speak of myself further than to assure you I had sufficient training to be entrusted with your horses. I declined to tell you my history. But the circumstances that have sent this paper to my hand and given it to me to be read are so strange that I feel compelled to trust you with everything.

"And I am even more inclined to do so by the knowledge conveyed that both of us are threatened by the same enemy, and it is needful that we make common cause against him. I will read the letter and give you an explanation. Then you will not wonder why I was so moved. If you thought me weak or childish, you will then excuse me."

The sheik held his peace, listening closely, until Ben Hur came to the paragraph in which he was particularly mentioned— "'I saw the Jew yesterday in the Grove of Daphne,'" said the passage, "'and if he is not there now, he is certainly in the neighborhood, so it is easy for me to keep an eye on him. Indeed, I would say, with the most positive assurance, that he is to be found at the Orchard of Palms.'"

"Ah!" exclaimed Ilderim, in such a tone that one might hardly say he was more surprised than angry. At the same time, he clutched his beard.

"'At the Orchard of Palms,'" Ben Hur repeated, "'under the tent of the traitor Sheik Ilderim.'"

"Traitor! I?" the old man cried, in a shrill tone, while lip and beard quivered with ire and the veins swelled on his forehead and neck as if they would burst.

"Yet a moment, sheik," said Ben Hur. "This is Messala's opinion of you. Hear his threat." And he read on. "'—under the tent of the traitor Sheik Ilderim, who cannot escape our strong hand for long. Do not be surprised if Maxentius, as his first move, places the Arab on ship bound for Rome.'"

"To Rome! Me—Ilderim—sheik of ten thousand horsemen with spears—me to Rome!" He leaped rather than rose to his feet, his arms outstretched, his fingers spread and curved like claws, his eyes glittering like a serpent's.

"O God! No, by all the gods except of Rome! When shall this insolence end? A freeman I am. My people are free. Must we die slaves? Or worse, must I live like a dog, crawling to a master's feet? Must I lick his hand, lest he lash me? What is mine is not mine. I am not my own, for the breath of my body must be beholden to a Roman. Oh, if I were young again! Oh, could I shake off twenty years—or ten—or five!"

He ground his teeth and clenched his fists over his head. Then, coming up with another idea, he walked away and back again to Ben Hur swiftly and caught his shoulder with a strong grasp.

"If I were as you, son of Arrius—as young, as strong, as practiced in arms—if I had a motive spurring me on to revenge, a motive like yours, great enough to make hate sacred—Let's do away with disguise on your part and on mine! Son of Hur, I say—"

At that name the flow of Ben Hur's blood stopped. Surprised, bewildered, he gazed into the Arab's eyes, which were now close to his and fiercely bright.

"Son of Hur, I say, were I in your condition, with half your wrongs, carrying about memories like yours, I would not, I could not, rest."

Never pausing, his words following each other like a torrent, the old man swept on. "To all my grievances, I would add those of the world and devote myself to vengeance. From country to country I would go firing all mankind. No war for freedom would be without me fighting. There would be no battle against Rome in which I would not play a part. I would turn Parthian, if I could do no better. If men failed me, still I would not give up.

"By the splendor of God! I would herd with wolves and make friends common enemies. I would use every weapon. As long as my victims were Romans, I would rejoice in slaughter. Mercy I would not ask. Mercy I would not give. To the flames would go everything Roman. To the sword would go every Roman born. At night I would pray the gods, the good and the bad alike, to lend me special terrors—storms, drought, heat, cold, and all the nameless poisons they let loose in air, all the thousand things of which men die on sea and on land. Oh, I could not sleep. I—"

The sheik stopped for lack of breath, panting and wringing his hands. And, safe to say, of all the passionate outbursts Ben Hur retained only a vague impression brought about by the fiery eyes, piercing voice, and rage too intense for coherent expression.

For the first time in years, the youth had heard himself addressed by his proper name. One man at least knew him and acknowledged it without demanding proof of identity, and he was an Arab fresh from the desert!

How did he come by his knowledge? The letter? No. It told of the cruelties his family had suffered. It told the story of his own misfortunes, but it did not say he was the very victim whose escape from doom was the theme of this heartless narrative. That was the explanation he told the sheik would follow after the reading of the letter. He was pleased, with a sense of hope restored, yet he kept an air of calmness.

"Good sheik, tell me how you came by this letter."

"My people watch the roads between the cities," Ilderim answered bluntly. "They took it from a courier."

"Are they known to be your people?"

"No. To the world they are robbers, whom it is mine to catch and slay."

"Again, sheik. You call me son of Hur—my father's name. I did not think I was known to a person on earth. How did you come by the knowledge?"

Ilderim hesitated, but he answered, "I know you, yet I am not free to tell you more."

"Someone holds you in restraint?"

The sheik kept quiet and walked away. But, observing Ben Hur's disappointment, he came back and said, "Let us say no more about the matter now. I will go to town. When I return, I may talk to you fully. Give me the letter."

Ilderim rolled the papyrus carefully, restored it to its envelope, and became once more full of energy. "What do you say?" he asked, while waiting for his horse and retinue. "I told you what I would do, were I you, and you have made no answer."

"I intended to answer, sheik, and I will." Ben Hur's countenance and voice changed. "All you have said in terms of revenge I will do—all at least within the power of man. I devoted myself to vengeance long ago. Every hour of the five years past, I have lived with no other thought. I have taken no respite, I have had no pleasures of youth. The attractions of Rome were not for me. I wanted her to educate me for revenge. I resorted to her most famous masters and professors—not those of rhetoric or philosophy. I had no time for them. The arts essential to a fighting man were my desire. I associated with gladiators and with winners of prizes in the circus, and they were my teachers. The drill masters in the great camp accepted me as a scholar and were proud of my attainments in their field.

"Sheik, I am a soldier, but the things that I dream of require me to be a captain. With that thought, I have taken part in the campaign against the Parthians. When it is over, then, if the Lord spares my life and strength, then"—he raised his clenched hands and spoke vehemently—"then I will be a Roman-taught enemy. Then Rome shall account to me in Roman lives for her ills. You have my answer, sheik."

Ilderim put an arm over his shoulder and kissed him, saying passionately, "If your God does not favor you, son of Hur, it is because He is dead. You take this from me—I swear you will have my hands and their fullness—men, horses, camels, and the desert for preparation. I swear it! Enough for the present. You will see or hear from me before night."

Turning abruptly off, the sheik was speedily on the road to the city.

276

50

Training the Four

The intercepted letter was conclusive in terms of a number of points of great interest to Ben Hur. It had the effect of a confession that the writer was a party to the putting away of his family with murderous intent; that he had sanctioned the plan adopted for the purpose; that he had received a portion of the proceeds of the confiscation and was still enjoying his part; that he dreaded the unexpected appearance of what he was pleased to call the chief criminal and accepted it as a menace; that he contemplated such further action as would keep him secure in the future and was ready to do whatever his accomplice in Caesarea might advise.

Now that the letter had reached the hand of him who was really its subject, it was a notice of danger to come as well as a confession of guilt. So when Ilderim left the tent, Ben Hur had much to think about, requiring immediate action. His enemies were as clever and powerful as any in the East. If they were afraid of him, he had greater reason to be afraid of them. He strove earnestly to reflect rationally upon the situation, but could not. His feelings constantly overwhelmed him.

There was a certain qualified pleasure in the assurance that his mother and sister were alive, and it mattered little that the foundation of the assurance was only a guess. It seemed as if discovery were now close at hand, since there was one person who could tell him where they were. These were mere feelings. Underlying them was a superstitious fancy that God was about to intervene in his behalf, in which case faith whispered to him to stand still.

Occasionally, referring to the words of Ilderim, he wondered where the Arab gathered his information about him. Not from Malluch certainly; nor from Simonides, whose interests, all selfish, would keep him mute. Could Messala have been the informant? No. Disclosure might be dangerous in that area.

Conjecture was futile. At the same time, as often as Ben Hur was kept from the solution, he was consoled with the thought that whoever the person with the knowledge might be, he was a friend and, because of this, would reveal himself in good time. A little more waiting and a little more patience were the only solution. Possibly the errand of the sheik was to see that the letter might bring about a full disclosure of truth.

He would have been patient if only he could have believed Tirzah and his mother were waiting for him under circumstances that permitted hope on their part as strong as his.

He wandered far through the Orchard, pausing now where the date gatherers were busy, yet not too busy to offer him their fruit and talk with him. Then he stopped under the great trees to watch the nesting birds or hear the bees swarming about the berries bursting with honeyed sweetness and filling all the green and golden spaces with the music of their beating wings.

He lingered the longest by the lake, however. He looked upon the water and its sparkling ripples, with its sensuous life, thinking of the Egyptian and her marvelous beauty and of floating with her here and there through the night made brilliant by her songs and stories. He might not forget the charm of her manner, the lightness of her laugh, the flattery of her attention, the warmth of her hand upon his hand, which was on the tiller of the boat.

From her it was but a short way to Balthasar and the strange things that he had witnessed, unrelated to any law of nature—and from the wise man, again, to the King of the Jews, whom the good man with such patience was by faith holding in holy promise.

This brought the distance of the King even nearer. His mind stayed there, finding in the mysteries of that person a satisfaction that answered much for everything else he was seeking. Because, perhaps, nothing is so easy as denying an idea that is not agreeable to our wishes, so he rejected the definition given by Balthasar of the kingdom the King was coming to establish. A kingdom of souls, if not intolerable to the Sadducean faith, seemed to him only an abstraction drawn from the depths of a devotion too ideal.

The kingdom of Judea, on the other hand, was more than comprehensible. It had once been and, if only for that reason, might be again. And it suited his pride to think of a new kingdom broader in its domain, richer in power, and of a more unapproachable splendor than the old one—of a new king wiser and mightier than Solomon—a new king under whom, especially, he could find both service and revenge. In that mood he returned to the tent.

The midday meal was disposed of, and to further occupy himself Ben Hur had the chariot rolled out into the sunlight. He gave a careful inspection of the vehicle. No point or part of it escaped him. With a pleasure that will be better understood later, he saw that the pattern was Greek, in his judgment preferable to the Roman in many respects. It was wider between the wheels, and lower and stronger, and the disadvantage of greater weight would be more than compensated by the greater endurance of his Arab horses. Speaking generally, the carriage-makers of Rome built almost solely for the games, sacrificing safety to beauty and durability to grace. The chariots of Achilles and "the king of men," designed for war and all its extreme tests, still ruled the tastes of those who met and struggled for the crowns Isthmian and Olympic.

Next he brought the horses and, hitching them to the chariot, drove to the field of exercise, where, hour after hour, he practiced them racing under the yoke. When he went away in the evening, it was with a restored spirit and a fixed purpose to defer action in the matter of Messala until the race was won or lost. He could not forgo the pleasure of meeting his adversary under the eyes of the East. That there might be other competitors did not seem to enter his thought. His confidence in the result was absolute. He had no doubt of his own skill, and as to the four horses, they were his full partners in the glorious game.

"Let him look to it! Antares! Aldebaran! Shall he not, O honest Rigel, and you, Atair, king among coursers, shall he not beware of us? Good hearts!"

After nightfall, Ben Hur sat by the door of the tent waiting for Ilderim, who had not yet returned from the city. He was not impatient, or vexed, or doubtful. The sheik would be heard from, at least.

Indeed, whether it was from satisfaction with the performance of the four, or the refreshment there is in cold water succeeding bodily exercise, or supper partaken with royal appetite, the young man was in good humor verging upon elation. He felt himself in the hands of a Providence that was no longer his enemy. At last there was a sound of horse's feet coming rapidly, and Malluch rode up.

"Son of Arrius," he said, cheerily, after salutation, "I salute you for Sheik Ilderim, who requests you to mount and go to the city. He is waiting for you."

Ben Hur asked no questions but went in where the horses were feeding. Aldebaran came to him, as if offering his service. He played with him lovingly, but passed on and chose another, not of the four—they were sacred to the race. Very shortly the two were on the road, going swiftly and in silence.

Some distance below the Seleucian Bridge, they crossed the river by a ferry and, riding far round on the right bank and recrossing by another ferry, entered the city from the west. The detour was long, but Ben Hur accepted it as a precaution for which there was good reason.

They rode down to Simonides' landing, and in front of the great warehouse under the bridge, Malluch drew in the reins. "We are here," he said. "Dismount."

Ben Hur recognized the place. "Where is the sheik?" he asked.

"Come with me. I will show you."

A watchman took the horses, and almost before he realized it, Ben Hur stood once more at the door of the house, listening to the response from within.

"In God's name, enter."

51

Simonides Renders Account

Malluch stopped at the door, and Ben Hur entered alone. The room was the same in which he had formerly interviewed Simonides, except now, close by the armchair there was a polished bronze rod set on a broad wooden pedestal, rising higher than a tall man, holding burning lamps of silver on sliding arms. The light was clear, bringing into view the paneling on the walls, the cornice with its row of gilded balls, and the dome was dully tinted with violet mica.

Within a few steps, Ben Hur stopped.

Three persons were present, looking at him—Simonides, Ilderim, and Esther.

He glanced hurriedly from one to another as if to find an answer to the question half-formed in his mind: *What business can these three have with me?* He became calm, with all of his senses alert, for the question was succeeded by another, *Are they friends or enemies?* Finally, his eyes rested upon Esther.

The men returned his look kindly. In her face there was something more than kindness—something too spiritual for definition, which went to his inner consciousness.

In the back of his mind there was a comparison in which the Egyptian arose and set herself over against the gentle Jewess. It lived but an instant and, as is the habit of such comparisons, passed away without a conclusion.

"Son of Hur." The guest turned to the speaker.

"Son of Hur," said Simonides, repeating the address slowly and with distinct emphasis, "take the peace of the Lord God of our fathers—take it from me." He paused, then added, "From me and mine."

The speaker sat in his chair, with his royal head, bloodless face, and masterful air. Under the influence, visitors forgot the broken limbs and distorted body of the man. The full black eyes gazed out under the white brows steadily but not sternly. A moment later, he crossed his hands upon his breast. The action, taken with the greeting, could not be misunderstood, and was not.

"Simonides," Ben Hur answered, much moved, "the holy peace you give is accepted. As son to father, I return it to you. Only let there be perfect understanding between us." He sought delicately to put aside the submission of the merchant and, in place of the relation of master and servant, substitute one higher and holier.

Simonides let his hands fall and, turning to Esther, said, "A seat for the master, daughter."

She hastened and brought a stool and stood looking from one to the other—from Ben Hur to Simonides, from Simonides to Ben Hur. And they waited, each declining the superiority that initial speech would imply.

When finally the pause began to be embarrassing, Ben Hur advanced and gently took the stool from her and, going to the chair, placed it at the merchant's feet. "I will sit here," he said.

His eyes met hers—only for an instant—but both were pleased. He recognized her gratitude, she his generosity and forbearance.

Simonides bowed his acknowledgment. "Esther, child, bring me the paper," he said with a breath of relief.

She went to a panel in the wall, opened it, took out a roll of papyri, and brought it to him.

"You speak well, son of Hur," Simonides began, while unrolling the sheets. "Let us understand each other. In anticipation of the demand—which I would have made had you refused it—I have here a statement covering everything necessary to the understanding required. I could see only two points involved—the property first, and then our relationship. The statement is explicit regarding both. Will it please you to read it now?"

Ben Hur received the papers but glanced at Ilderim.

"No," said Simonides, "the sheik will not deter you from reading. The account—such you will find it—is by nature requiring a witness. In the attesting place at the end you will find, when you come to it, the name *Ilderim, Sheik.* He knows everything. He is your friend. All he has been to me, that will he be to you also."

Simonides looked at the Arab, nodding pleasantly, and the latter gravely returned the nod, saying, "You have spoken well."

Ben Hur replied, "I know already the excellence of his friendship and have yet to prove myself worthy of it." Immediately he continued, "Later, Simonides, I will read the papers carefully. For the present, take them, and if you are not too weary, give me their substance."

Simonides took back the roll. "Here, Esther, stand by me and receive the sheets, lest they fall into disarray."

She took her place by his chair, letting her right arm fall lightly across his shoulder, so that, when he spoke, the account seemed to have been given by both of them jointly.

"This," said Simonides, drawing out the first leaf, "shows the money I had of your father's, being the amount saved from the Romans. There was no property saved, only money, and the robbers would have secured that except for our Jewish custom of bills of exchange. The amount saved, being sums I drew from Rome, Alexandria, Damascus, Carthage, Valentia, and elsewhere within the circle of trade, was one hundred and twenty talents of Jewish money."

He gave the sheet to Esther and took the next one.

"With that amount—one hundred and twenty talents—I charged myself. Now here are my credits. I use the word, as you will see, with reference to the proceeds gained from the use of the money." From separate sheets he then read amounts, which, fractions omitted, were as follows:

By ships	60 talents
By goods in store	110 talents
By cargoes in transit	75 talents
By camels, horses, etc.	20 talents
By warehouses	10 talents
By bills due	54 talents
By money on hand and subject to draft	224 talents
Total	553 talents

"To these now, to the five hundred and fifty-three talents gained, add the original capital I had from your father, and you have six hundred and seventy-three talents! All yours, making you, O son of Hur, the richest person in the world."

He took the papyri from Esther and, reserving one, rolled them and offered them to Ben Hur. The pride perceptible in his manner was not offensive. It might have been from a sense of duty well done; it might have been for Ben Hur. "And there is nothing," he added, dropping his voice, but not his eyes "there is nothing now you may not do."

The moment was one of absorbing interest to all present. Simonides crossed his hands upon his breast again. Esther was anxious; Ilderim nervous. A man is never so on trial as in the moment of excessive good fortune.

Taking the roll, Ben Hur arose, struggling with emotion. "All this is to me as a light from heaven, sent to drive away a night that has been so long that I feared it would never end, and so dark I had lost the hope of seeing," he said with a deep voice. "I give first thanks to the Lord, who has not abandoned me, and next to you, Simonides. Your faithfulness outweighs the cruelty of others and redeems our human nature. If there is nothing I cannot do, so be it. Shall any man in my hour of such mighty privilege be more generous than I? Serve me as a witness now, Sheik Ilderim. Hear my words as I shall speak them and remember. And you, Esther, good angel of this good man! Hear also."

He stretched his hand with the roll to Simonides. "The things these papers take into account—all of them, ships, houses, goods, camels, horses, money, the least as well as the greatest—I give back to you, O Simonides, making them all yours and sealing them to you and yours forever."

Esther smiled through her tears. Ilderim pulled his beard rapidly, his eyes glistening like beads of jet. Simonides alone was calm.

"Sealing them to you and yours forever," Ben Hur continued, with better control of himself, "with one exception, and upon one condition."

The breath of the listeners waited upon his words. "The hundred and twenty talents that were my father's you shall return to me."

Ilderim's countenance brightened. "And you shall join me in the search of my mother and sister, holding all yours subject to the expense of discovery, even as I will hold mine."

Simonides was much affected. Stretching out his hand, he said, "I see your spirit, son of Hur, and I am grateful to the Lord that He has sent you to me as you are. If I served your father well in life and his memory afterwards, do not be afraid of my defaulting in your service."

Exhibiting, then, the reserved sheet, he continued. "You have not all the account. Take this and read aloud."

Ben Hur took the supplement and read it. "Statement of the servants of Hur, rendered by Simonides, steward of the estate.

1. Amrah, Egyptian, keeping the palace in Jerusalem
2. Simonides, the steward, in Antioch
3. Esther, daughter of Simonides."

Now in all his thoughts of Simonides, not once had it entered Ben Hur's mind that by the law a daughter followed the parent's condition. In all his visions of her, the sweet-faced Esther had figured as the rival of the Egyptian and an object of possible love. He shrank from the revelation so suddenly brought to him and looked at her blushing.

And blushing, she dropped her eyes before him.

Then he said, while the papyrus rolled itself together, "A man with six hundred talents is indeed rich and may do what he pleases. But rarer than money, more priceless than the property, is the mind that amassed the wealth and the heart it could not corrupt when amassed. Simonides—and you—fair Esther—fear not. Sheik Ilderim here shall be witness that in the same moment you were declared my servants, that moment I declared you free. And what I declare, that will I put in writing. Is this not enough? Can I do more?"

"Son of Hur," said Simonides, "truly you make servitude light. I was wrong. There are some things you cannot do. You cannot make us free by law. I am your servant forever, because I went to the door with your father one day, and in my ear the awl marks yet abide."

"Did my father do that?"

285

"Do not judge him," cried Simonides quickly. "He accepted me as a servant of that class because I asked him to do so. I never repented of the step. It was the price I paid for Rachel, the mother of my child here—for Rachel, who would not be my wife unless I became what she was."

"Was she a servant forever?"

"Even so."

Ben Hur walked the floor because of a powerless wish. "I was rich before," he said, stopping suddenly. "I was rich with the gifts of the generous Arrius. Now this greater fortune comes, and the mind that achieved it. Is there not a purpose of God in it all? Counsel me, Simonides! Help me to see the right and do it. Help me to be worthy of my name, and what you are in law to me, that will I be to you in fact and deed. I will be your servant forever."

Simonides' face actually glowed. "O son of my dead master! I will do better than help. I will serve you with all my mind and heart. I have not a body. It perished in your cause. But with mind and heart I will serve you. I swear it, by the altar of our God and the gifts upon the altar! Only make me formally what I have assumed to be."

"Name it," said Ben Hur eagerly.

"As steward, the care of the property will be mine."

"Count yourself steward now. Or will you require it in writing?"

"Your word simply is enough. It was so with your father, and I will not ask more from the son. And now, if the understanding be complete—" Simonides paused.

"It is with me," said Ben Hur.

"And you, daughter of Rachel, speak!" said Simonides, lifting her arm from his shoulder.

Esther, left alone, stood a moment, her color coming and going. Then she went to Ben Hur and said with a sweet womanliness, "I am not better than my mother was, and, as she is gone, I pray you, O my master, let me care for my father."

Ben Hur took her hand and led her back to the chair, saying, "You are a good daughter. Have your will."

Simonides replaced her arm upon his neck, and there was silence for a time in the room.

52

Spiritual or Political—Simonides Argues

Simonides looked up, no less a master. "Esther," he said, quietly, "the night is going fast. And, lest we become too weary for that which is before us, let the refreshments be brought."

She rang a bell. A servant answered with wine and bread, which she passed round.

"The agreement, my good master," continued Simonides, when all were served, "is not perfect in my sight. From now on our lives will run on together like rivers that have met and joined their waters. I think their flowing will be better if every cloud is blown from the sky above them. You left my door the other day with what seemed to be a denial of the claims that I have just allowed in the broadest terms. But it was not so, indeed it was not. Esther is witness that I recognized you, and that I did not abandon you, let Malluch state his case."

"Malluch!" exclaimed Ben Hur.

"One bound to a chair, like me, must have many far-reaching hands if he would move the world from which he is so cruelly barred. I have many such, and Malluch is one of the best of them. And, sometimes,"—he cast a grateful glance at the sheik—"sometimes I borrow from others' goodness of heart, like Ilderim the Generous—good and brave. Let him tell you if I either denied or forgot you."

Ben Hur looked at the Arab. "This is he, good Ilderim, this is he who told you of me?"

Ilderim's eyes twinkled as he nodded his answer.

"How, O my master," said Simonides, "may we without trial tell what a man is? I knew you. I saw your father in you. But what kind of man you were I did not know. There are people to whom fortune is a curse in disguise. Were you one of them? I sent Malluch to find out for me, and in my service he was my eyes and ears. Do not blame him. He brought me a report of you that was all good."

"I do not," said Ben Hur heartily. "There was wisdom in your goodness."

"The words are very pleasant to me," said the merchant with feeling, "very pleasant. My fear of misunderstanding is laid to rest. Let the rivers run on now as God may give them direction."

After a time he continued. "I am compelled now by truth. The weaver sits weaving and, as the shuttle flies, the cloth increases and the figures grow and the dreams continue meanwhile. So to my hands the fortune grew, and I wondered at the increase and asked myself about it many times. I could see a hidden hand not my own was with the enterprises I set going. The storms that heaped the seashore with wrecks blew my ships sooner into port. Strangest of all, I, so dependent on others, held to a place like a dead person, had never a loss by an agent—never. The weather stooped to serve me, and all my servants, in fact, were faithful."

"It is very strange," said Ben Hur.

"So I kept saying. Finally, O my master, I came to agree with your opinion—God was in it—and like you I asked, What can His purpose be? Intelligence is never wasted. Knowledge like God's never takes place except with design. I have held the question in heart these many years, waiting for an answer. I felt sure, if God were in it, some day, in His own good time, in His own way, He would show me His purpose, making it clear as a white house upon a hill. And I believe He has done so."

Ben Hur listened, alert with every faculty.

"Many years ago, with my people—your mother was with me, Esther, beautiful as morning over old Mount Olivet—I sat by the wayside north of Jerusalem, near the Tombs of the Kings, when three men passed by riding great white camels, like none that had ever been seen in the Holy City. The men were strangers and from far countries. The first one stopped and asked me a question, 'Where is he that is born King of the Jews?' As if to increase my wonder, he went on to say, 'We have seen his star in the east and have come to worship him.'

"I could not understand but followed them to the Damascus Gate. And of every person they met on the way—of the guard at the gate, even—they asked the question. All who heard it were amazed like me. In time I forgot the circumstance, though there was much talk of it as an indication of the Messiah. What children we are, even the wisest! When God walks the earth, His steps are often centuries apart. Have you seen Balthasar?"

"And heard him tell his story," said Ben Hur.

"A miracle!" cried Simonides. "As he told it to me, my good master, I seemed to hear the answer I had so long waited for. God's purposes burst upon me. The King will be poor when he comes—poor and friendless, without a following, without armies, without cities or castles, a kingdom to be set up, and Rome to be reduced and blotted out.

"See, O my master! You flushed with strength, you trained to bear arms and fight, you blessed with riches—see the opportunity the Lord has sent you! Shall not His purpose be yours? Could a man be born to a more perfect glory?"

Simonides made a very strong argument for this course of action.

"But the kingdom!" Ben Hur answered eagerly. "Balthasar says it is to be a kingdom of souls."

The pride of the Jewish people was as strong in Simonides as in Ben Hur, and therefore he had a slightly contemptuous smile as he began his reply. "Balthasar has been a witness of wonderful things—of miracles, my master. And when he speaks of them, I bow in agreement, for he has personally seen and heard. But he is a son of Mizraim and not even a proselyte to our Jewish faith. He may hardly be supposed to have special knowledge so that we must bow to him in a matter of God's dealing with our Israel. The prophets had their light from heaven directly, as he had his— many to one, and Jehovah is always the same forever. I must believe the prophets. Bring me the Torah, Esther."

He proceeded to speak without waiting for her.

"May the testimony of a whole people be slighted, my master? Though you travel from Tyre, which is by the sea in the north, to the capital of Edom, which is in the desert to the south, you will not find a follower of the Shema, an alms-giver in the Temple, or anyone who has ever eaten of the lamb of the Passover, to tell you the kingdom the King is coming to build for the children of the covenant is not of this world, like our father David's kingdom. Now, where did they get the faith, you ask? We will see presently."

Esther then returned, bringing a number of scrolls carefully enveloped in dark-brown linen lettered quaintly in gold.

"Keep them, daughter, to give to me as I call for them," the father said, in the tender voice he always used in speaking to her, and continued his argument. "There are too many, my good master—too many, indeed—for me to repeat to you the names of the holy men who, in the providence of God, succeeded the prophets. They were only a little less favored than the prophets—the seers who have written and the preachers who have taught since the Captivity—the very wise who borrowed their lights from the lamp of Malachi, the last of his line, and whose great names Hillel and Shammai never tired of repeating in the schools.

"Will you ask them the nature of the kingdom? The Lord of the sheep in the Book of Enoch—who is he? Who but the King of whom we are speaking? A throne is set up for him. He will strike the earth, and the other kings are to be shaken from their thrones and the enemies of Israel to be flung into a cavern of fire flaming with pillars of fire.

"Also the singer of the Psalms of Solomon said, 'Behold, O Lord, and raise up to Israel their king, the son of David, at the time you know, O God, to rule Israel, your children. . . . And he will bring the peoples of the heathen under his yoke to serve him. . . . And he shall be a righteous king taught of God . . . for he shall rule all the earth by the word of his mouth forever.'

"And last, though not least, hear the words of Ezra, the second Moses, in his visions of the night and ask him who is the lion with human voice that says to the eagle—which is Rome—'You have loved liars and overthrown cities of the industrious and destroyed their walls, though they did you no harm. Therefore, be gone, that the earth may be refreshed and recover itself and hope in the justice and piety of him who made her.' Thus, the eagle of Rome is no more. Surely, my master, son of Hur, the testimony of these prophets should be enough! But the way to the fountain's head is open. Let us go up to it at once. Some wine, Esther, and then the Torah."

"Do you believe the prophets, master?" he asked, after drinking. "I know you do, for they influenced the faith of all your relatives. Esther, give me the book that has in it the visions of Isaiah."

He took one of the rolls that she had unwrapped for him and read, "'The people that walked in darkness have seen a great light; they that dwell in the land of the shadow of death, upon them has the light shined. . . . For unto us a child is born, unto us a son is given; and the government shall be upon his shoulder. . . . Of the increase of his government and peace there shall be no end, upon the throne of David and upon his kingdom, to order it and to establish it with judgment and with justice from henceforth even forever.' Do you believe the prophets, my master? Now, Esther, the word of the Lord that came to Micah."

She gave him the roll he asked for. "'But you,'" he began reading, "'but you, Bethlehem Ephrath, though you be little among the thousands of Judah, yet out of you shall he come forth unto me that is to be ruler in Israel.' This was he, the very child Balthasar saw and worshiped in the cave. Do you believe the prophets, O my master? Give me, Esther, the words of Jeremiah."

Receiving that roll, he read as before, "'Behold, the days come, said the Lord, that I will raise unto David a righteous branch, and a king shall reign and prosper and shall execute judgment and justice in the earth. In his days Judah shall be saved, and Israel shall dwell safely.' As a king he shall reign— as a king, my master! Do you believe the prophets? Now, daughter, the roll of the sayings of that son of Judah in whom there was no blemish."

She gave him the book of Daniel. "Hear, my master," he said. "'I saw in the night visions, and behold, one like the Son of man came with the clouds of heaven. . . . And there was given him dominion, and glory, and a kingdom, that all people, nations, and languages should serve him; his dominion is an everlasting dominion, which shall not pass away, and his kingdom that which shall not be destroyed.' Once again I ask, do you believe the prophets, O my master?"

"It is enough. I believe," cried Ben Hur.

"What then?" asked Simonides. "If the King comes to this world poor, will not my master, out of his abundance, give him help?"

"Help Him? To the last shekel and the last breath. But why speak of his coming poor?"

"Give me, Esther, the word of the Lord as it came to Zechariah," said Simonides.

She gave him one of the rolls. "Hear how the King will enter Jerusalem." Then he read, "'Rejoice greatly, O daughter of Zion. . . . Behold, your King comes unto you with justice and salvation; lowly and riding upon an ass, and upon a colt, the foal of an ass.'"

Ben Hur looked away.

"What do you see, O my master?"

"Rome!" he answered gloomily—"Rome and her legions. I have dwelt with them in their camps. I know them."

"Ah!" said Simonides. "You will be a master of legions for the King, with millions to choose from."

"Millions!" cried Ben Hur.

Simonides sat a moment thinking. "The question of power should not trouble you," he next said.

Ben Hur gave him a questioning look.

"You were seeing the lowly King in the act of coming to his own," Simonides answered. "Seeing Him on the right hand, and on the left the brassy legions of Caesar, and you were asking, What can he do?"

"That is correct."

"O my master!" Simonides continued, "you do not know how strong our Israel is. You think of him as a sorrowful old man weeping by the rivers of Babylon. But go up to Jerusalem next Passover and stand on the Xystus, or in the Street of Barter, and see him as he is.

"The promise of the Lord to father Jacob coming out of Padan-Aram was a law under which our people have not ceased multiplying—not even in captivity. They grew under the foot of the Egyptian. The grip of the Roman has only nurtured them. Now they are indeed 'a nation and a company of nations.' Nor that only, my master. To measure the strength of Israel—which is, in fact, measuring what the King can do—you shall not hold solely by the rule of natural increase but add the other important element—I mean the spread of the faith, which will carry you to the far end of the whole known world.

"Further, there is a habit, I know, to think and speak of Jerusalem as Israel, which may be compared to our finding an embroidered fragment and holding it up as a magisterial robe of Caesar's. Jerusalem is only a stone in the Temple, or the heart in the body.

"Turn from regarding the legions, strong though they are, and count the hosts of the faithful waiting for the old summons, 'To your tents, O Israel!'—count the many in Persia, children of those who chose not to return with the remnant. Count the brethren who swarm the markets of Egypt and farther Africa. Count the Hebrew colonists making a profit in the West—in the courts of Spain, for example. Count those of the pure blood and proselytes in Greece and in the isles of the sea and here in Antioch and, for that matter, those of that city lying accursed in the shadow of the unclean wall of Rome herself. Count the worshipers of the Lord dwelling in tents along the deserts next to us, and so on. Separate those who annually send gifts to the Holy Temple in acknowledgment of God, that they may be counted also.

"And when you have done counting, lo, a census of the swords that await you. A kingdom ready-made for the one who is to do 'judgment and justice in the whole earth'—in Rome not less than in Zion. You have the answer: what Israel can do, that the King can do."

It operated upon Ilderim like the blowing of a trumpet. "Oh, that I had back my youth!" he cried, starting to his feet.

Ben Hur sat still. The speech, he saw, was an invitation to devote his life and fortune to the mysterious Being who was tangibly as much at the center of a great hope with Simonides as with the devout Egyptian. The idea was not a new one but had come to him repeatedly—once while listening to Malluch in the Grove of Daphne, afterwards more distinctly while Balthasar was giving his idea of what the kingdom was to be. Still later in the walk through the old Orchard, it had risen almost, if not quite, into a resolve to action. At such times it had come and gone only as an idea, accompanied by various feelings.

"But not now. A master had it under control, a master was planning it. Already He had exalted it into a brilliant cause with possibilities that were infinitely holy. The effect was as if a door so far unseen had suddenly opened flooding Ben Hur with light and beckoning him to a task that had been his one perfect dream—a service reaching far into the future and rich with the rewards of a duty well done and prizes to sweeten and soothe his ambition. One more influence was needed.

"Let us concede all you say, O Simonides," said Ben Hur, "that the King will come and his kingdom shall be as Solomon's. Assume I am also ready to give myself and all I have to him and his cause. Even more, say that I should do God's purpose in the ordering of my life and in your quick amassing of an astonishing fortune. Then what? Shall we proceed like blind men building what they cannot see? Shall we wait till the King comes? Or until he sends for me? You have age and experience on your side. Answer me."

Simonides answered at once. "We have no choice. None. This letter"—he produced Messala's letter as he spoke—"this letter is the signal for action. We are not strong enough to resist the alliance proposed between Messala and Gratus. We do not have the influence at Rome nor the force here. They will kill you if we wait. They are not merciful—look at me and judge." He shuddered at the terrible recollection.

"O my good master," he continued, recovering himself, "how strong are you in your purposes and goals?"

Ben Hur did not understand him.

"I remember how pleasant the world was to me in my youth," Simonides proceeded.

"Yet," said Ben Hur, "you were capable of a great sacrifice."

"Yes. For love."

"Has not life other motives as strong?"

Simonides shook his head. "There is ambition."

"Ambition is forbidden a son of Israel."

"What about revenge?"

The spark dropped upon the flaming passion. The man's eyes gleamed; his hands shook. He answered, quickly, "Revenge is a Jew's by right. It is the law."

"A camel, even a dog, will remember a wrong," cried Ilderim.

Directly Simonides picked up the broken thread of his thought.

"There is a work for the King, which should be done in advance of his coming. We may not doubt that Israel is to be his right hand, but it is a hand of peace, without cunning in war. Of the millions, there is not one trained band, not even a captain. The mercenaries of the Herods I do not count, for they are kept only to crush us.

"The condition is as the Roman would have it. His policy has worked well for his tyranny, but the time of change is at hand, when the shepherd shall put on armor and take up the spear and sword, and the feeding flocks shall be turned to fighting lions. Some one, my son, must have the place next to the King at his right hand. Who shall it be, if not he who does this work well?"

Ben Hur's face flushed at the prospect, though he said, "I see. But speak plainly. A deed to be done is one thing. How to do it is another."

Simonides sipped the wine Esther brought him and replied. "The sheik and you, my master, shall be principal players, each with a part. I will remain here, carrying on as now and watchful that the spring does not go dry. You will go to Jerusalem, and then to the wilderness, and begin numbering the fighting men of Israel and dividing them into tens and thousands and choosing captains and training them and in secret places hoarding arms, for which I shall keep you supplied.

"Beginning over in Perea, you will go then to Galilee, where it is only a step to Jerusalem. In Perea, the desert will be at your back and Ilderim in reach of your hand. He will watch the roads, so that nothing shall pass without your knowledge. He will help you in many ways. Until the ripening time no one shall know what we have planned. Mine is only a servant's part. I have spoken to Ilderim. What do you say?"

Ben Hur looked at the sheik.

"It is as he says, son of Hur," the Arab responded. "I have given my word, and he is content with it. But you will have my oath, binding to me, and the ready hands of my tribe, and whatever serviceable thing I have."

The three—Simonides, Ilderim, Esther—gazed at Ben Hur intently. "Every man," he answered, at first sadly, "has a cup of pleasure poured for him, and sooner or later it comes to his hand, and he drinks it—every man but me. I see, Simonides, and you, generous sheik—I see where the proposal goes. If I accept and enter upon the course, farewell to peace and the hopes that cluster around it. The doors I might enter and the gates of quiet life will shut behind me, never to open again, for Rome keeps them all. Her outlaws and hunters will follow me, and in the tombs near cities and the dismal caverns of remotest hills, I must eat my crumbs and find my home."

They all turned to Esther, who hid her face upon her father's shoulder, sobbing.

"I did not think of you, Esther," said Simonides gently, for he himself was deeply moved.

"It is good, Simonides," said Ben Hur. "A man bears a hard doom better, knowing there is pity for him. Let me go on."

They listened again.

"I was about to say," he continued, "I have no choice, but take the part you assign me, and by remaining here I will meet an untimely death. I will go to the work at once."

"Shall we sign agreements?" asked Simonides, directed by his own business practices.

"I rest upon your word," said Ben Hur.

"And I," Ilderim answered.

The treaty was simply concluded that was to alter Ben Hur's life. And almost immediately the latter added, "It is done then."

"May the God of Abraham help us!" Simonides exclaimed.

"One word now, my friends," Ben Hur said, more cheerfully. "By your leave, I will be my own until after the games. It is not probable Messala will set peril on foot for me until he has given the procurator time to answer him. And that cannot be in less than seven days from the sending of his letter. Meeting him in the circus is a pleasure I would buy at whatever risk."

Ilderim, well pleased, assented readily, and Simonides, intent on business, added, "It is well, for the delay will give me time to do you a good turn. I understood you are speaking of an inheritance derived from Arrius. Is it in property?"

"A villa near Misenum and houses in Rome."

"I suggest, then, the sale of the property and safe deposit of the proceeds. Give me an account of it, and I will have authorities drawn and send an agent on the mission right away. We will hold off the imperial robbers at least this once."

"You shall have the account tomorrow."

"Then, if there is nothing more, the work of the night is done," said Simonides.

Ilderim combed his beard, complacently saying, "And well done."

"The bread and wine again, Esther. Sheik Ilderim will make us happy by staying with us till tomorrow, or at his pleasure. And you, my master—"

"Let the horses be brought," said Ben Hur. "I will return to the Orchard. The enemy will not discover me if I go now, and"—he glanced at Ilderim—"the four will be glad to see me."

As the day dawned, he and Malluch dismounted at the door of the tent.

53

Esther and Ben Hur

On the next night, about the fourth hour, Ben Hur stood on the terrace of the great warehouse with Esther. Below them on the landing was much activity and shifting of packages and boxes and shouting of men, who looked, in the light of the crackling torches kindled in their aid, like the laboring genies of the fantastic Eastern tales. A galley was being loaded for instant departure. Simonides had not yet come from his office, where, at the last moment he would deliver to the captain of the vessel instructions to proceed without stop to Ostia, the seaport of Rome and, after landing a passenger there, continue leisurely to Valentia, on the coast of Spain.

This passenger was the agent going to dispose of the estate derived from Arrius the duumvir. When the lines of the vessel were cast off and her voyage begun, Ben Hur would be committed irrevocably to the work undertaken the night before. If he was disposed to change his mind regarding the agreement with Ilderim, a little time was allowed him to give notice and break it off. He was still master and had only to say the word.

This may have been the thought in his mind. He was standing with folded arms, looking upon the scene in the manner of a man debating with himself. Young, handsome, rich, but recently from the patrician circles of Roman society, it is easy to think of the world seeking him with appeals not to give more to dangerous duty or ambition with outlaws involved.

We can even imagine the arguments with which he was pressed: the hopelessness of contention with Caesar; the uncertainty regarding everything connected with the king and his coming; the ease, honors, estate, and goods in market; and strongest of all, the senses newly acquired of home, with friends to make it delightful. Only those who have been long desolate wanderers can know the power there was in this appeal.

The world is always cunning enough of itself, always whispering to the weak, *Stay, take your ease,* always presenting the sunny side of life—the world was in this instance helped by Ben Hur's companion.

"Were you ever at Rome?" he asked.

"No," Esther replied.

"Would you like to go?"

"I do not think so."

"Why not?"

"I am afraid of Rome," she answered, with a perceptible tremor of the voice.

He looked at her then—or rather down upon her, for at his side she appeared little more than a child. In the dim light he could not see her face distinctly. Even the form was shadowy. But again he was reminded of Tirzah, and a sudden tenderness fell upon him—just so the lost sister stood with him on the housetop the calamitous morning of the accident to Gratus. Poor Tirzah! Where was she now?

Esther benefited from this feeling. He could never look upon her as his servant, if not his sister, and that she was his servant in fact would make him always the more considerate and gentle toward her.

"I cannot think of Rome," she continued, recovering her voice and speaking in her quiet, womanly way, "I cannot think of Rome as a city of palaces and temples and crowded with people. She is to me a monster who has possession of one of the beautiful lands and lies there luring men to ruin and death—a monster that it is not possible to resist—a ravenous beast gorging with blood. Why—" She faltered and stopped.

"Go on," said Ben Hur reassuringly.

She drew closer to him, looked up again, and said, "Why must you make her your enemy? Why not rather make peace with her and be at rest? You have had many ills, and borne them. You have survived the snares laid for you by foes. Sorrow has consumed your youth. Is it well to live so now the remainder of your days?" The girlish face under his eyes seemed to come nearer as the pleading went on.

He stooped toward it and asked, softly, "What would you have me do, Esther?"

299

She hesitated a moment, then asked, in return, "Is the property near Rome a residence?"

"Yes."

"And pretty?"

"It is beautiful—a palace in the midst of gardens and shell-strewn walks; fountains without and within; statues in the shady nooks, hills all around covered with vines, and so high that Neapolis and Vesuvius are in sight, and the sea is an expanse of purpling blue dotted with restless sails. Caesar has a country seat nearby, but in Rome they say the old Arrian villa is the prettiest."

"And the life there—is it quiet?"

"There was never a summer day, never a moonlit night, more quiet, except when visitors come. Now that the old owner is gone, and I am here, there is nothing to break the silence—nothing, unless it be the whispering of servants, or the whistling of happy birds, or the noise of fountains at play. It is changeless, except as day by day old flowers fade and fall, and new ones bud and bloom, and the sunlight gives way to the shadow of a passing cloud.

"The life, Esther, was all too quiet for me. It made me restless by always keeping present a feeling that I, who have so much to do, was dropping into idle habits and tying myself with silken chains, and after a while—and not a long while either—would end with nothing done."

She looked off over the river.

"Why did you ask?" he said.

"My good master—"

"No, Esther—do not call me that. Call me friend—brother, if you will. I am not your master and will not be. Call me brother."

He could not see the flush of pleasure that reddened her face or the glow of the eyes that went out lost in the void above the river.

"I cannot understand," she said, "the nature that prefers the life you are going to—a life of—"

"Of violence, and it may be of blood," he said, completing the sentence.

"Yes," she added, "the nature that could prefer that life to what might be found in the beautiful villa."

"Esther, you are mistaken. There is no preference. The Roman is not so kind. I am going out of necessity. To stay here is to die. And if I go there, the end will be the same—a poisoned cup or a judge's sentence obtained by perjury. Messala and the procurator Gratus are rich with the plunder of my father's estate, and it is more important to them to keep their gains now than was their getting them in the first place. A peaceable settlement is out of reach, because of the confession it would imply.

"And then, Esther, if I could buy them, I do not know that I would. I do not believe peace possible to me. No, not even in the sleepy shade and sweet air of the marble porches of the old villa—no matter who might be there to help me bear the burden of the days or by what patience of love she gave me. Peace is not possible to me while my people are lost, for I must be alert to find them. If I find them, and they have suffered wrong, shall not the guilty suffer for it? If they are dead by violence, shall the murderers escape? Oh, I could not sleep for dreams! Nor could the holiest love, by any strategy, lull me to a rest that my conscience would not strangle."

"Is it so bad, then?" she asked. "Can nothing be done?"

Ben Hur took her hand. "Do you care so much for me?"

"Yes," she answered simply.

The hand was warm, and in the palm of his it was lost. He felt it tremble. Then the Egyptian came to his mind, so much the opposite of this little one, so tall, so audacious, with a cunning flattery, a ready wit, a wonderful beauty, as well as a bewitching manner. He carried the hand to his lips and gave it back.

"You shall be another Tirzah to me, Esther."

"Who is Tirzah?"

"The little sister the Romans stole from me and whom I must find before I can rest or be happy."

Just then a gleam of light flashed across the terrace and fell upon the two. Looking around they saw a servant push Simonides in his chair out of the door. They went to the merchant, and afterwards they talked of him.

Immediately the lines of the galley were cast off, and she swung around and, midst the flashing of torches and the shouting of joyous sailors, hurried off to the sea—leaving Ben Hur committed to the cause of the King who was to come.

54

Posted for the Race

The day before the games, in the afternoon, all Ilderim's racing property was taken to the city and put in quarters adjoining the circus. The good man carried along with it a great deal of property, with servants, mounted and armed retainers, horses in leading, driven cattle, camels laden with baggage. His leaving from the Orchard was not unlike a tribal migration. The people along the road did not fail to laugh at his procession, yet he was not in the least offended by their rudeness. If he was under surveillance, as he had reason to believe, the informer would describe the semi-barbarous show with which he came up to the races.

The Romans would laugh; the city would be amused; but what did he care? The next morning the pageant would be far on the road to the desert. Every movable thing of value belonging to the Orchard would be going with it—everything except what was essential to the success of his four. He was, in fact, starting home. His tents were folded. In twelve hours all would be out of the reach of whoever might pursue. A man is never safer than when he is laughed at, and the shrewd old Arab knew it.

Neither he nor Ben Hur overestimated the influence of Messala. It was their opinion, however, that he would not begin active measures against them until after the meeting in the circus. If defeated there, especially if defeated by Ben Hur, they might instantly look for the worst he could do. He might not even wait for advice from Gratus. With this in view, they planned their course and were prepared to take themselves out of harm's way. They rode together now in good spirits, calmly confident of success on the next day.

On the way, they came upon Malluch, who was waiting for them. The faithful friend gave no sign that made it possible to infer any knowledge on his part of the relationship so recent between Ben Hur and Simonides, or of the treaty between them and Ilderim. He exchanged greetings as usual and produced a paper, saying to the sheik, "I have here the notice of the master of the games, just issued, in which you will find your horses published for the race. You will also find in it the order of exercises. Without waiting, good sheik, I congratulate you on your victory."

He gave the papers to him and, leaving the worthy to master them, turned to Ben Hur. "To you also, son of Arrius, my congratulations. There is nothing now to prevent your meeting Messala. Every condition preliminary to the race is complied with. I have the assurance from the master himself."

"I thank you, Malluch," said Ben Hur.

Malluch proceeded. "Your color is white, and Messala's scarlet and gold. The good choices are visible already. Boys are now hawking white ribbons along the streets. Tomorrow every Arab and Jew in the city will wear them. In the circus you will see the white fairly divide the galleries with the red."

"The galleries—but not the tribunal over the Porta Pompae."

"No. The scarlet and gold will rule there. But if we win—" Malluch chuckled with the pleasure of the thought "—if we win, how the dignitaries will tremble! They will bet, of course, according to their scorn of everything not Roman—two, three, five to one on Messala, because he is a Roman."

Dropping his voice yet lower, he added, "It ill becomes a Jew of good standing in the Temple to put his money on such a hazard. Yet, in confidence, I will have a friend next behind the consul's seat to accept offers of three to one, or five, or ten—the madness may go to such height. I have put six thousand shekels to his order for the purpose."

"No, Malluch," said Ben Hur, "a Roman will wager only in his Roman coin. Suppose you find your friend tonight and place to his order sestertii in such amount as you choose. And look, Malluch—let him be instructed to seek wagers with Messala and his supporters: Ilderim's four against Messala's."

Malluch reflected a moment. "The effect will be to center interest upon your contest."

"The very thing I seek, Malluch."

"I see."

"Yes, Malluch. If you would serve me perfectly, help me to fix the public eye upon our race—Messala's and mine."

Malluch spoke quickly. "It can be done."

"Then let it be done," said Ben Hur.

"Enormous wagers offered will answer. If the offers are accepted, all the better." Malluch turned his eye watchfully upon Ben Hur.

"I shall have back the equivalent of his robbery," said Ben Hur, partly to himself. "Another opportunity may not come. And if I could break his fortune as well as his pride! Our father Jacob could take no offense."

A look of determined will knit his handsome face, giving emphasis to his further speech. "Yes, it shall be. Listen, Malluch! Don't stop in your offer of sestertii. Advance them to talents, if there are any who dare so much. Five, ten, twenty talents. Yes, fifty, if the wager is with Messala himself."

"It is a mighty sum," said Malluch. "I must have security."

"So you will. Go to Simonides and tell him I wish the matter to be arranged. Tell him my heart is set on the ruin of my enemy and that the opportunity has such excellent promise that I choose such hazards. On our side be the God of our fathers! Go, good Malluch. Let this not slip."

Malluch, greatly delighted, gave him a parting word and started to ride away, but then returned. "Your pardon," he said to Ben Hur. "There was another matter. I could not get near Messala's chariot myself, but I had another view it. From his report, its hub stands quite a palm higher from the ground than yours."

"A palm! So much?" cried Ben Hur joyfully.

Then he leaned over to Malluch. "As you are a son of Judah, Malluch, and faithful to your kin, get a seat in the galley over the Gate of Triumph, down close to the balcony in front of the pillars and watch when we make the turns there. Watch carefully."

At that moment a cry burst from Ilderim. "By the splendor of God! What is this?" He drew near Ben Hur with a finger pointing to the notice.

"Read it," said Ben Hur.

"No, you'd better."

Ben Hur took the paper, which was signed by the prefect of the province. It informed the public that there would be first a procession of extraordinary splendor, that the procession would be succeeded by the customary honors to the god Consus, and then the games would begin: running, leaping, wrestling, boxing, each in the order stated. The names of the competitors were given, with their several nationalities and schools of training, the trials in which they had been engaged, the prizes won, and the prizes now offered.

The sums of money were also stated, in illuminated letters, telling of the departure of the day when the simple wreath of pine or laurel was fully enough for the victor, hungering for glory as something better than riches, and content with the former.

Ben Hur sped over these parts of the program. At last he came to the announcement of the race. He read it slowly. Lovers of the heroic sports were assured they would certainly be gratified by an Orestean struggle unparalleled in Antioch. The city offered the spectacle in honor of the consul. One hundred thousand sestertii and a crown of laurel were the prizes. Then followed the particulars. The entries were six in all—fours only permitted. The competitors would be turned into the course together. Each four then received description.

I. Four of Lysippus the Corinthian—two grays, a bay, and a black; entered at Alexandria last year, and again at Corinth, where they were winners. Lysippus, driver. Color, yellow.

II. Four of Messala of Rome—two white, two black; victors of the Circensian as exhibited in the Circus Maximus last year. Messala, driver. Colors, scarlet and gold.

III. Four of Cleanthes the Athenian—three gray, one bay; winners at the Isthmian last year. Cleanthes, driver. Color, green.

IV. Four of Dicaeus the Byzantine—two black, one gray, one bay; winners this year at Byzantium. Dicaeus, driver. Color, black.

V. Four of Admetus the Sidonian—all grays; thrice entered at Caesarea, and thrice victors. Admetus, driver. Color, blue.

VI. Four of Ilderim, Sheik of the Desert—all bays; first race. Ben Hur, a Jew, driver. Color, white.

Ben Hur, a Jew, driver! Why that name instead of Arrius?

Ben Hur raised his eyes to Ilderim. He had found the cause of the Arab's outcry. Both rushed to the same conclusion. The hand was the hand of Messala!

55

Making the Wagers

Evening had hardly arrived in Antioch, where, in the center of the city, flowed currents of people reveling in the rituals of Bacchus and Apollo. Great indulgence was seen in the great roofed streets covered with literally miles of porticos carved in marble, polished to a high finish. Darkness and rest were not permitted anywhere. The singing, the laughter, and the shouting were incessant and blended together like the roar of waters dashing through hollow grottoes, confused by a multitude of echoes.

The many nationalities represented, though they might have amazed a stranger, were not peculiar to Antioch. Of the various missions of the great empire, one seems to have been the great fusion of people. Accordingly, whole nations rose up and went at pleasure, taking with them their customs, speech, and gods. Where they chose, they engaged in business, built houses, erected altars, and were what they had been at home.

There was a peculiarity, however, that could not have failed the notice of an onlooker this night in Antioch. Nearly everyone wore the colors of one or other of the charioteers announced for tomorrow's race. Sometimes it was in form of a scarf or a badge, often a ribbon or a feather. Whatever the form, it signified the wearer's partiality. Green meant a friend of Cleanthes the Athenian and black an adherent of the Byzantine. This was according to a custom, old probably as the day of the race of Orestes, showing the absurd yet appalling extremities to which men allow their follies to drag them.

There were three colors primarily—green, white, and a mixture of scarlet and gold. Going from the streets to the palace on the island we find the five great chandeliers in the saloon are freshly lighted. The assembly was much the same as that described in connection with the place. The divan had its group of sleepers and still the tables resounded with the rattle and clash of dice. Yet the greater part of the group were not doing anything. They walked around or yawned or paused as they passed each other to exchange idle chatter. Will the weather be fair tomorrow? Are the preparations for the games complete? Do the laws of the circus in Antioch differ from the laws of the circus in Rome?

The truth is, the young men were suffering boredom. Their heavy work was done, that is, their tablets were covered with memoranda of wagers—wagers on every contest: the running, the wrestling, the boxing, on everything but the chariot race. They cannot find anybody who will hazard so much as a denarius with them against Messala.

There were no colors in the saloon but his, and no one thought of his defeat. They said, Is he not perfect in his training? Did he not graduate from an imperial school? Were not his horses winners at the Circensian in the Circus Maximus? And then—ah, yes! He is a Roman!

In a corner, at ease on the divan, Messala himself could be seen. Around him, sitting or standing, were his admirers, plying him with questions. There was, of course, but one topic.

Drusus and Cecilius entered. "Ah!" cried the young prince, throwing himself on the divan at Messala's feet. "By Bacchus, I am tired!"

"Why?" asked Messala.

"Up the street—to the Omphalus, and beyond—there are rivers of people—never so many in the city before. They say we will see the whole world at the circus tomorrow."

Messala laughed scornfully. "The idiots! They never beheld a Circensian with Caesar for a master. But, my Drusus, what found you?"

"Nothing."

"You forget," said Cecilius.

"What?" asked Drusus.

"The procession of whites."

"Whites!" cried Drusus, half-rising. "We met a faction of whites." He fell back lazily.

"Cruel Drusus—please go on," said Messala.

"Scum of the desert they were, my Messala, and garbage eaters from Jacob's Temple in Jerusalem. What had I to do with them?"

"No," said Cecilius, "Drusus is afraid you will laugh, but I am not, my Messala."

"Speak, then."

"We stopped the faction and—"

"Offered them a wager," said Drusus, relenting. He laughed, then continued. "And one fellow with not enough skin on his face to make a worm for a cap stepped forth and said yes. I drew my tablets. 'Who is your man?' I asked. 'Ben Hur the Jew,' he said. Then I: 'What shall it be? How much?' He answered, 'Ah—' Excuse me, Messala. By Jove's thunder, I cannot go on for laughter!" The listeners leaned forward.

Messala looked to Cecilius. "A shekel," said the latter. "A shekel!" A burst of scornful laughter followed the repetition.

"And what did Drusus say?" asked Messala.

An outcry by the door brought about a rush to that quarter, and, as the noise continued and grew louder, even Cecilius went off, pausing only to say, "The noble Drusus, my Messala, put up his tablet and—lost the shekel."

"A white!"

"Let him come!"

"This way, this way!"

These and like exclamations filled the room, stopping other discussion. The dice players quit their games. The sleepers awoke, rubbed their eyes, drew their tablets, and hurried to the common center.

"I offer you—"

"And I—"

The person so warmly received was the respectable Jew, Ben Hur's fellow voyager from Cyprus. He entered, grave, quiet, and observant. His robe was spotlessly white. So was the cloth of his turban. Bowing and smiling at the welcome, he moved slowly toward the central table. Arriving there, he drew his robe about him in a stately manner, took a seat, and waved his hand. The gleam of a jewel on a finger helped achieve the silence that ensued.

"Most noble Romans—I salute you!" he said.

"Easy, by Jupiter! Who is he?" asked Drusus.

"A dog of Israel—Sanballat by name—supplier for the army. Residence, Rome. Vastly rich. He spins mischief finer than spiders spin their webs. Come—by the girdle of Venus! Let us catch him!"

Messala arose as he spoke and, with Drusus, joined the mass crowded around the supplier.

"It came to my mind on the street," said the supplier, producing his tablets and opening them on the table with an impressive air of business, "that there was great discomfort in the palace because offers on Messala were going without takers. The gods, you know, must have sacrifices, and here I am. You see my color; let us get to the matter at hand. Odds first, amounts next. What will you give me?" The audacity of this remark seemed to stun his hearers.

"Hurry!" he said. "I have an engagement with the consul."

The prod was effective. "Two to one," cried half-a-dozen in a voice.

"What!" exclaimed Sanballat, astonished. "Only two to one, and your man is a Roman!"

"Take three, then."

"Three you say—only three—and mine but a dog of a Jew! Give me four."

"Four it is," said a boy, stung by the taunt.

"Five—give me five," cried the oddsmaker instantly. A profound stillness fell upon the assembly.

"The consul—your master and mine—is waiting for me." The silence became awkward.

"Give me five—for the honor of Rome, five."

"Five let it be," said someone in answer.

There was a sharp cheer and a commotion, and Messala himself appeared. "Five let it be," he said.

And Sanballat smiled and prepared to write it down. "If Caesar dies tomorrow," he said, "Rome will not be entirely without. There is at least one other with the spirit to take his place. Give me six."

"Six it is," answered Messala.

There was another shout louder than the first.

"Six it is," repeated Messala. "Six to one—the difference between a Roman and a Jew. And, having found it, now, redeemer of the flesh of swine, let us get on with it. The amount—and quickly. The consul may send for you, and I will then be left empty."

Sanballat took this comment coolly and wrote and offered the writing to Messala.

"Read, read!" everybody demanded. And Messala read:

Chariot race. Messala of Rome, in wager with Sanballat, also of Rome, says he will beat Ben Hur, the Jew. Amount of wager, twenty talents. Odds to Sanballat, six to one.
Witnesses:

Sanballat

There was no noise nor motion. Each person seemed held frozen in the pose the reading found him. Messala stared at the memorandum, while everyone's eyes opened wide, staring at him. He felt their gaze and thought rapidly. Only a short time ago he had stood in the same place and in the same way admonished the countrymen around him. They would remember it. If he refused to sign, his hero image was lost.

But he could not sign. He was not worth one hundred talents, nor the fifth part of the sum. Suddenly his mind became a blank. He stood speechless. The color fled from his face. An idea at last came to him.

"You Jew!" he said. "Where do you have twenty talents? Show me."

Sanballat's provoking smile deepened. "There," he replied, offering Messala a paper.

"Read it!" the voices arose all around. Again Messala read:

At Antioch, Tammuz 16th day.
The bearer, Sanballat of Rome, has now to his order with me fifty talents, coin of Roman.

Simonides

"Fifty talents!" echoed the throng in amazement.

Then Drusus came to the rescue. "By Hercules!" he shouted, "the paper lies, and the Jew is a liar. Who but Caesar has fifty talents at his command? Down with the insolent white!"

The cry was angrily repeated. Yet Sanballat kept his seat, and his smile grew more exasperating the longer he waited.

Finally Messala spoke. "Hush! One to one, my countrymen— for love of our ancient Roman name." The timely action recovered his dominance of the crowd.

"You circumcised dog!" he continued, to Sanballat, "I gave you six to one, did I not?"

"Yes," said the Jew quietly.

"Well, give me now the fixing of the amount."

"With reserve, if the amount is trifling, have your way," answered Sanballat.

"Write, then, five in place of twenty."

"Have you so much?"

"By the mother of the gods, I will show you receipts."

"No, the word of so brave a Roman must pass. Only make the sum even—six make it, and I will write."

"Write it that way."

And they exchanged writings.

Sanballat immediately arose and looked around him, a sneer in place of his smile. No man better than he knew those with whom he was dealing.

"Romans," he said, "another wager, if you dare! Five talents against five talents that the white will win. I challenge you as a group."

They were again surprised.

"What!" he cried louder. "Shall it be said in the circus tomorrow that a dog of Israel went into the parlor of the palace full of Roman nobles—among them the close friends of Caesar—and laid five talents before them as a challenge, and they did not have the courage to take it up?" The sting was unendurable.

"Be done with us, insolent one!" said Drusus. "Write the challenge and leave it on the table. And tomorrow, if we find you have indeed so much money to bet on such a hopeless cause, I promise it shall be taken."

Sanballat wrote again and, rising, said, unmoved as ever, "See, Drusus, I leave the offer with you. When it is signed, send it to me any time before the race begins. I will be found with the consul in a seat over the Porta Pompae. Peace to you. Peace to all." He bowed and departed, uncaring of the shouts of derision that pursued him out of the door.

In the night the story of the prodigious wager flew along the streets and over the city, and Ben Hur, lying with his four horses, was told of it and also that Messala's whole fortune was on the race. And he slept ever so soundly.

56

The Circus

The circus at Antioch stood on the south bank of the river, nearly opposite the island, differing in no way from the plan of such buildings in general. In the purest sense, the games were a gift to the public. Consequently, everybody was free to attend, and, vast as the holding capacity of the structure was, so fearful were the people, on this occasion, that there should be no room for them, that early the day before the opening of the exhibition they took up all the vacant spaces in the vicinity. Their temporary shelter appeared as an army in waiting.

At midnight the entrances were opened wide, and the rabble, surging in, occupied the quarters assigned to them, from which nothing less than an earthquake or an army with spears could have dislodged them. They dozed the night away on the benches and breakfasted there, and there the close of the exercises found them patient and curious, as in the beginning.

The better people, when their seats were secured, began moving toward the circus about the first hour of the morning. The noble and very rich among them were distinguished by litters and retinues of liveried servants.

By the second hour, the flow from the city was an unbroken and innumerable stream. The legion, in full force and with all its standards on exhibit, descended from Mount Sulpius. When the rear of the last cohort disappeared by the bridge, Antioch was literally abandoned—not that the circus could hold the multitude, but that the multitude had gone out to it.

A great concourse on the river shore witnessed the consul come across from the island in a royal barge. As the great man landed and was received by the legion, the martial ceremony for one brief moment transcended the attraction of the circus.

At the third hour, the audience was assembled. At last, a flourish of trumpets called for silence, and instantly the gaze of more than a hundred thousand persons was directed toward the eastern section of the building.

Out of the Porta Pompae over in the east came a mixed sound of voices and harmonized instruments. Presently the chorus of the procession with which the celebration began came forth. The master of the games and civic authorities of the city, givers of the games, followed in robes and garlands. Then the gods came, some on platforms carried by men, others in great, gorgeously decorated four-wheel carriages. Next were the contestants of the day, each in the costume exactly as he would run, wrestle, leap, box, or drive.

Slowly crossing the arena, the procession proceeded to make a complete circuit of the course. The display was beautiful and imposing. Approval went before it in shouts, as the water rises and swells in front of a boat in motion. If the dumb, figured gods made no sign of appreciation of the welcome, the master of the games and his associates received it gladly.

The reception of the athletes was even more demonstrative, for there was not a man in the assembly who had not wagered something on them, though perhaps only a farthing. And it was noticeable, as the classes moved by, that the favorites among them were speedily singled out. Either their names were loudest in the uproar, or they were more profusely showered with wreaths and garlands tossed to them from the balcony.

If there was a question as to the popularity with the public of the several games, it was now put to rest. To the splendor of the chariots and the excellent beauty of the horses, the charioteers added the personality necessary to perfect the charm of their display. Their tunics of the finest woolen texture represented the assigned colors. A horseman accompanied each of them except Ben Hur, who, for some reason—possibly distrust—had chosen to go alone. They were all helmeted but him.

As they approached, the spectators stood upon the benches, and there was a deepening of the general clamor. One might detect the shrill piping of women and children. At the same time, the wreaths flying from the balcony thickened into a storm and, striking the men, dropped into the chariot beds, which were threatened to be filled to the top. Even the horses had a share in the ovation. It was made apparent that some of the drivers were more in favor than others. And nearly every individual on the benches, women and children as well as men, wore a color, most frequently a ribbon upon the chest or hair—whether green, yellow, or blue, but mainly of white and scarlet-and-gold.

In a modern assembly called together as this one was, particularly where there are sums gambled upon a race, a preference would be decided by the qualities or performance of the horses. Here, however, nationality was the rule. If the Byzantine and Sidonian found small support, it was because their cities were barely represented on the benches. The Greeks, though very numerous, were divided between the Corinthians and the Athenians, leaving only a scant showing of green and yellow.

Messala's scarlet and gold would have been only a little better if the citizens of Antioch had not joined the Romans by adopting the color of their favorite. Then there were left the country people, or Syrians, Jews, and Arabs. The latter, from faith in the blood of the sheik's four, blended largely with hate of the Romans, whom they desired above all things to see beaten and humbled, mounted the white standard. They made the most noisy, and probably most numerous, faction of all.

As the charioteers moved on in the circuit, the excitement increased. At the second goal, where especially in the galleries the white was the ruling color, the people dispersed their flowers and split the air with screams.

"Messala! Messala!"

"Ben Hur! Ben Hur!"

These were their cries. After the passage of the procession, the various factions took their seats and resumed conversation.

"By Bacchus! Was not he handsome?" exclaimed a woman, whose Roman citizenship was betrayed by the colors flying in her hair.

"And how splendid his chariot!" replied a neighbor, of the same loyalty. "It is all ivory and gold. Jupiter grant he wins!"

The notes on the bench behind them were entirely different. "A hundred shekels on the Jew!" The voice was high and shrill.

"No, do not be rash," whispered a friend to the speaker. "The children of Jacob are not expert at Gentile sports, which are accursed in the sight of the Lord."

"True, but have you ever seen one who is more cool and assured? And what an arm he has!"

"And what horses!" said a third.

"And for that," a fourth one added, "they say he has all the tricks of the Romans."

A woman finished the compliments. "Yes, and he is even handsomer than the Roman."

Encouraged by these comments, the follower shrieked again, "A hundred shekels on the Jew!"

"You fool!" answers an Antiochian, from a bench on the edge of the balcony. "Don't you know there are fifty talents laid against him, six to one, on Messala? Put up your shekels, lest Abraham rise and strike you."

"You donkey of Antioch! Cease your braying. Don't you know it was Messala betting on himself?"

Thus the controversy was not always good-natured.

When the march was ended and the procession returned to the Porta Pompae, Ben Hur knew he had his prayer heard. The eyes of the East were upon his contest with Messala.

57

The Start

About three o'clock the program was concluded, except the chariot race. The master of the games, wisely considerate of the comfort of the people, chose that time for a recess. At once the restaurants were opened and all who could hastened to the portico outside where the restauranteurs had their quarters. Those who remained talked, gossiped, and consulted their tablets, and, all distinctions forgotten, remained in two classes—the winners, who were happy, and the losers, who were grim.

Now, however, a third class of spectators, composed of citizens who desired only to witness the chariot race, partook of the recess and came in to take their reserved seats. By so doing they hoped to attract the least attention. Among these were Simonides and his party, whose places were in the vicinity of the main entrance on the north side, opposite the consul.

As the four hearty servants carried the merchant in his chair up the aisle, curiosity grew. Then someone called his name. Those nearby it heard it and passed it on along the benches to the west. Many climbed on seats to get a view of the man of whom common report had created a romance mixed with good and bad fortune the like had never been known or heard of before.

Ilderim was also recognized and warmly greeted. But nobody knew Balthasar or the two women who followed him and were closely veiled. The people respectfully made way for the party, and the ushers seated them in close speaking distance of each other down by the railing overlooking the arena. For comfort they sat upon cushions and had stools for footrests. The women were Iras and Esther.

Upon being seated, the latter cast a frightened look at the circus and drew her veil closer about her face. The Egyptian, letting her veil fall upon her shoulders, viewed the scene with a certain unconsciousness of being stared at.

The newcomers generally were still making their first examination of the great spectacle, beginning with the consul and his attendants, when some workmen ran in and began to stretch a chalked rope across the arena from balcony to balcony in front of the pillars of the first goal.

About the same time, six men came in through the Porta Pompae and occupied a post, one in front of each stall. There was a prolonged hum of voices in every quarter.

"See! The green goes to number four on the right. The Athenian is there."

"And Messala—yes, he is number two."

"The Corinthian—"

"Watch the white! See, he crosses over and stops. Number one it is—number one on the left."

"No, the black stops there, and the white at number two."

"So it is."

The gatekeepers were dressed in tunics colored like those of the competing charioteers, so, when they took their stations, everybody knew the particular stall in which his favorite was at that moment waiting.

"Did you ever see Messala?" the Egyptian asked Esther.

The Jewess shuddered as she answered no. If Messala was not her father's enemy, the Roman was Ben Hur's.

"He is beautiful as Apollo."

As Iras spoke, her large eyes brightened, and she shook her jeweled fan. Esther looked at her and thought, *Is he, then, so much handsomer than Ben Hur?*

The next moment she heard Ilderim say to her father, "Yes, his stall is number two on the left of the Porta Pompae."

Thinking it was of Ben Hur he spoke, her eyes turned that way. Taking the briefest glance at the gate, she drew the veil close and muttered a little prayer.

Then Sanballat came to the party. "I have just from the stalls, sheik," he said, bowing gravely to Ilderim, who began combing his beard, while his eyes glittered with eager curiosity. "The horses are in perfect condition."

Ilderim replied simply, "If they are beaten, I hope it is by someone other than Messala."

Turning then to Simonides, Sanballat drew out a tablet, saying, "I bring you also something of interest. I reported, you will remember, the wager concluded with Messala last night and stated that I left another that, if taken, was to be delivered to me in writing today before the race began. Here it is."

Simonides took the tablet and read the memorandum carefully. "Yes," he said, "their emissary came to ask me if you had bet a certain amount of money with me. Keep the tablet nearby. If you lose, you know where to come. If you win, friend, see to it! See that the signers do not escape. Hold them to the last shekel. That is what they would do with us."

"Trust me," replied the supplier.

"Will you not sit with us?" asked Simonides.

"You are very good," the other responded. "But if I leave the consul, the young Romans over there will boil over. Peace to you all."

Finally the recess came to an end. The trumpeters blew a call and those absent rushed back to their places. At the same time, some viewers appeared in the arena and, climbing upon the division wall, went to a wall near the second goal at the west end and placed upon it seven wooden balls. Then returning to the first goal, upon that wall there they set up seven other pieces of wood hewn to represent dolphins.

"What shall they do with the balls and fishes, sheik?" asked Balthasar.

"Have you never attended a race?"

"Never before, and I hardly know why I am here."

"Well, they are to keep count. At the end of each round you will see one ball and one fish taken down."

The preparations were now complete, and presently a trumpeter in gaudy uniform arose by the master of the games, ready to blow the signal of commencement promptly at his order. Straightway the stir of the people and the hum of their conversation died away. Every face nearby and every face in the lessening perspective, turned to the east, as all eyes settled upon the gates of the six stalls that shut in the competitors.

The unusual flush upon his face gave proof that even Simonides had caught the universal excitement.

Ilderim pulled his beard nervously.

"Look for the Roman," said the fair Egyptian to Esther, who did not hear her because, with close-drawn veil and beating heart, she sat watching for Ben Hur.

The structure containing the stalls was situated midway on the course, on the starting side of the first goal. Every stall was an equal distance from the starting line, or chalked rope. The trumpet sounded short and sharp, and the starters, one for each chariot, leaped down from behind the pillars of the goal, ready to give assistance if any of the four horses became unmanageable.

The trumpet blew again, and all the gatekeepers threw the stalls open. The mounted attendants of the charioteers appeared first, five in all, because Ben Hur rejected the service. The chalked line was lowered to let them pass, then raised again. They were beautifully mounted, yet they were scarcely observed as they rode forward because all the time the trampling of eager horses and the voices of the eager drivers were heard behind them in the stalls, so no one would even look away for an instant from the gaping doors.

The chalked line up was again, and the gatekeepers called their men. Instantly the ushers on the balcony waved their hands and shouted with all their strength, "Down! Down!" One might as well have whistled to hold back a storm.

Coming forth from each stall, like missiles in a volley from a great many guns, rushed the six fours, and the vast assembly arose. Electrified and leaping upon the benches, they filled the circus and the air above it with yells and screams. This was the time for which they had so patiently waited! This was the moment of supreme interest treasured up in their talk and dreams since the proclamation of the games!

"He has come—there—look!" cried Iras, pointing to Messala.

"I see him," answered Esther, looking at Ben Hur.

The veil was withdrawn. For an instant the little Jewess was brave. An idea of the joy there is in doing a heroic deed under the eyes of a multitude occurred to her, and she understood forever after how, at such times, the souls of men, in the frenzy of performance, laugh at death or forget it utterly.

The competitors were now under view from nearly every part of the circus, yet the race had not begun. They had first to make the chalked line successfully.

The line was stretched for the purpose of equalizing the start. If it were dashed at, the upheaval of man and horses would be seen. On the other hand, to approach it timidly was to chance the possibility of being thrown behind in the beginning of the race, and that meant certain forfeit of the great advantage always sought for—the position next to the division wall on the inner line of the course.

The spectators knew thoroughly this trial and its perils and consequences, and if the opinion of old Nestor, uttered when he handed the reins to his son, were true:

> "It is not strength, but art, obtained the prize,
> And to be swift is less than to be wise."

Everyone on the benches looked for a warning of the winner, and they breathlessly watched for the result. The arena swam in a dazzle of light. Yet each driver looked first for the rope, then for the coveted inner line. Thus, all six were aiming at the same point and speeding furiously, and a collision seemed inevitable. Also, what if the master of the games, at the last moment, dissatisfied with the start, should withhold the signal to drop the rope? Or not give the signal in time?

The crossing was about two hundred and fifty feet in width. A quick eye, steady hand, and unerring judgment were required. If one looked away or his mind wandered or a rein slipped, he was lost. What a great attraction to the assembly of the thousands over the spreading balcony!

The spectators viewed Messala's chariot, rich with ivory and gold. They saw the drivers, erect and statuesque, undisturbed by the motion of the chariots, their limbs naked, and fresh and ruddy with the healthful polish of the baths. In their right hands were goads, suggestive of dreadful torture. In their left hands the reins passed taut from the ends of the carriage poles. They saw the fours, heads tossing, nostrils flaring, and legs pounding the ground with a crushing impact like hammers—every muscle of the rounded bodies glowing with glorious life.

The competitors each started on the shortest line for the position next to the wall. Yielding would be like giving up the race, and who dared to yield? The cries of encouragement from the balcony were indistinguishable and indescribable—a roar that had the same effect upon all the drivers.

The fours neared the rope together and then the trumpeter by the master's side blew a signal vigorously. Seeing the action the judges dropped the rope—and not an instant too soon, for the hoof of one of Messala's horses struck it as it fell. Nothing daunted, the Roman shook his long lash, loosed the reins, leaned forward, and with a triumphant shout took the wall.

"Jove with us!" yelled all the Roman faction in a frenzy of delight.

As Messala turned in, the bronze lion's head at the end of his axle caught the foreleg of the Athenian's right-hand trace-mate, flinging the horse over against its yokefellow. Both staggered, struggled, and lost their headway. The ushers had their will, at least in part. The thousands held their breath with horror. Only up where the consul sat was there shouting.

"Jove with us!" screamed Drusus frantically.

"He wins! Jove with us!" answered his associates, seeing Messala speed on. Tablet in hand, Sanballat turned to them. A crash from the course below stopped his speech, and he looked that way.

Messala had now passed, and the Corinthian was the only contestant on the Athenian's right, so on that side the latter tried to turn his broken four. Then, as ill-fortune would have it, the wheel of the Byzantine, who was next on the left, struck the tailpiece of his chariot, knocking his feet from under him. There was a crash, a scream of rage and fear, and the unfortunate Cleanthes fell under the hoofs of his own steeds, which was a terrible sight.

Esther covered her eyes.

The Corinthian swept on, as well as the Byzantine and the Sidonian. Sanballat looked for Ben Hur and turned again to Drusus and his coterie. "A hundred sestertii on the Jew!" he cried.

"Taken!" answered Drusus.

"Another hundred on the Jew!" shouted Sanballat.

Nobody appeared to hear him. He called again.

The situation below was too absorbing, and they were too busy shouting, "Messala! Messala! Jove with us!"

When the Jewess tried to look again, a party of workmen was removing the horses and broken chariot. Another party was taking away the man himself, and every bench occupied by a Greek was vocal with prayers for vengeance. Suddenly she dropped her hands. Ben Hur was unhurt at the front, driving freely forward along with the Roman! Behind them, in a group, followed the Sidonian, the Corinthian, and the Byzantine. The race was on. The souls of the racers were in it.

58

The Race

When the dash for the position began, Ben Hur was on the extreme left of the six. For a moment, like the others, he was half blinded by the light in the arena. Yet he managed to catch sight of his antagonists and discern their purpose. He gave one searching look at Messala, who was more than an antagonist to him. The air of passionless pride characteristic of the fine patrician face was there as of old and so was the Italian beauty, which the helmet increased. But it may have been a jealous fancy or the effect of the brassy shadow in which the features were cast at the moment. Still the Israelite thought he saw the soul of the man as through a dark glass—cruel, cunning, and desperate, not so excited as determined—a soul in a tension of watchfulness and fierce resolve.

Ben Hur let his own resolution harden to a similar temper. At whatever cost, indeed at all costs, he would humble this enemy! Pride, friends, wagers, honor—everything that can be thought of as a possible interest in the race was lost in this one deliberate purpose. Even regard for life should not hold him back. Yet there was no passion on his part, no blinding rush of heated blood from his heart to his brain, no impulse to fling himself upon Fortune, for he did not believe in Fortune. To the contrary, he had his plan, and, confiding in himself, he settled to the task as one never more observant, never more capable.

When he was not even halfway across the arena, he saw Messala's rush would, if there was not a collision and the rope fell, give him the wall. He ceased to doubt that the rope would fall, and, further, it came to him in a sudden flash of insight that Messala knew it was to be let drop at the last moment by prearrangement with the master of the games so that he could safely reach that point in the contest. What more Romanlike than of the official to lend himself to a countryman who, besides being so popular, had also so much at stake? There could be no other reason for the

323

confidence with which Messala pushed his four forward the instant his competitors were prudently checking their fours in front of the obstruction—no other reason except madness.

It is one thing to see a necessity and another to act upon it. Ben Hur yielded the wall for the time being. The rope fell, and all the fours except his sprang into the course under an urgency of both command and lash. He drew hard to the right and, with all the speed of his Arab horses, darted across the trails of his opponents, his angle of movement had the purpose of losing the least time and gaining the greatest possible advance. So, while the spectators were cringing at the Athenian's mishap, and the Sidonian, Byzantine, and Corinthian were striving with such skill as they possessed to avoid involvement in the ruin, Ben Hur swept around and took the course neck and neck with Messala, though on the outside.

The marvelous skill shown in making the change from the extreme left across to the right without appreciable loss did not fail the sharp eyes on the benches. The circus seemed to rock with prolonged applause. Esther clasped her hands in glad surprise, and Sanballat, smiling, offered his hundred sestertii a second time without a taker. Then the Romans began to doubt, thinking Messala might have found an equal, if not a master, and that he was an Israelite!

And now, racing together side by side, a narrow space between them, the two neared the second goal. The pedestal of the three pillars, viewed from the west, was a stone wall in the form of a half circle, around which the course and opposite balcony were bent in an exact parallel. Making this turn was considered in all respects the most telling test of a charioteer. It was, in fact, the very feat in which Orestes failed.

A hush fell over all the circus, so that for the first time in the race the rattle and clang of the cars plunging after the tugging steeds were distinctly heard. Then, it would seem, Messala observed Ben Hur and recognized him, and at once the audacity of the man manifested itself in an astonishing manner.

"Down Eros, up Mars!" he shouted, whirling his lash with practiced hand and whipping the excellent Arabs of Ben Hur like they had never known. The blow was seen in every quarter, and the amazement was universal. The silence deepened. Up on the benches behind the consul the boldest held his breath, waiting for the outcome. Only a moment later down from the balcony, as thunder falls, burst the indignant cry of the people.

The four sprang forward frightened. No hand had ever been laid upon them except in love. They had been nurtured ever so tenderly. And as they grew, their confidence in man became a lesson beautiful to see. What should such dainty creatures do under such indignity but leap as from death?

They sprang forward as with one impulse, and forward leaped the chariot. Where did Ben Hur get the large hand and mighty grip that helped him manage so well? Where but from the oar with which so long he fought the sea? And what was the jolt of the floor under his feet to the dizzy lurch with which in time past the trembling ship yielded to the beat of staggering billows, drunk with their power?

So he kept his place and gave the four free rein and called to them in a soothing voice, trying merely to guide them round the dangerous turn. Before the fever of the people began to abate, he had the mastery back. Not that only, but, on approaching the first goal, he was again side by side with Messala, carrying with him the sympathy and admiration of everyone who was not a Roman. So clearly was the hostile feeling shown, so vigorous its cry, that Messala, even with all his boldness, felt it unsafe to trifle any further.

As the chariots whirled round the goal, Esther caught sight of Ben Hur's face—a little pale and held higher, yet otherwise calm and placid.

Immediately a man climbed on the platform at the west end of the division wall and took down one of the conical wooden balls. A dolphin on the east platform was taken down at the same time.

In the same way, the second ball and second dolphin disappeared, and then the third ball and third dolphin. Three rounds were concluded, and still Messala held the inside position and still Ben Hur moved with him side by side; still the other competitors followed as before. The contest began to have the appearance of one of the double races that became so popular in Rome during the later Caesarean period—Messala and Ben Hur in the first place, the Corinthian, Sidonian, and Byzantine in the second.

Meantime the ushers succeeded in returning the multitude to their seats, though the clamor continued to run the rounds, keeping, as it were, even pace with the rivals in the course below.

In the fifth round the Sidonian succeeded in getting a place outside Ben Hur but lost it immediately. The sixth round was entered without a change of relative position.

Gradually the speed had been quickened—gradually the blood of the competitors warmed with the work. Men and beasts seemed to know alike that the final crisis was near, bringing the time for the winner to assert himself.

The interest that from the beginning had centered chiefly in the struggle between the Roman and the Jew, with an intense and general sympathy for the Jew, was fast changing to anxiety on his account. On all the benches the spectators bent forward motionless, except as their faces turned to follow the contestants. Ilderim remained still, and Esther forgot her fears.

"A hundred sestertii on the Jew!" cried Sanballat to the Romans under the consul's awning. There was no reply.

"A talent—or five talents, or ten. You choose!" He shook his tablets at them defiantly.

"I will take your sestertii," answered a Roman youth, preparing to write.

"Do not," interjected a friend.

"Why?"

"Messala has reached his utmost speed. See him lean over his chariot rim, the reins loose as flying ribbons. Then look at the Jew."

The first one looked. "By Hercules!" he replied, his face fell. "The dog throws all his weight on the bits. I see! If the gods do not help our friend, he will be run away with by the Israelite. No, not yet. Look! Jove with us!"

The cry, swelled by the sound of every Latin tongue, shook the very covering over the consul's head.

If it was true that Messala had attained his utmost speed, the effort was paying off, slowly but certainly he was beginning to forge ahead. His horses were running with their heads low down.

From the balcony their bodies appeared actually to skim the earth. Their nostrils showed blood-red in expansion. Their eyes seemed to be straining in their sockets. Certainly the good steeds were doing their best! How long could they keep the pace? It was only the beginning of the sixth round. On they dashed. As they neared the second goal, Ben Hur turned in behind the Roman's car.

The joy of Messala's faction reached its bound. They screamed and howled and tossed their colors, and Sanballat filled his tablets with wagers.

Malluch, in the lower gallery over the Gate of Triumph, found it hard to remain cheerful. He had cherished the vague hint dropped to him by Ben Hur of something to happen in the turn by the western pillars. It was the fifth round, yet that something had not come. And he had said to himself, *The sixth will bring it*, but Ben Hur was hardly holding a place at the tail of his enemy's rear.

Over in the east end, Simonides' party held their peace. The merchant's head was bent low. Ilderim dropped his brows till there was nothing of his eyes but an occasional sparkle of light. Esther scarcely breathed. Iras alone appeared glad.

Along the home stretch Messala was leading, and right behind him was Ben Hur. Messala, fearful of losing his place, hugged the stony wall with a perilous clasp. If he moved a foot to the left, he would be dashed to pieces. Yet, when the turn was finished, no man, looking at the wheel tracks of the two chariots, could have said, Here went Messala, there the Jew. They left only one trace behind them.

As they whirled by, Esther saw Ben Hur's face again, and it was whiter than before. Simonides, shrewder than Esther, said to Ilderim, the moment the rivals turned into the course, "I am no judge, good sheik, if Ben Hur is not about to execute some crafty design. His face had that look."

Ilderim answered, "Did you see how clean they were, and fresh? By the splendor of God, friend, they have not even been running hard ! But now watch!"

One ball and one dolphin remained on the platforms. And all the people drew a long breath, for the beginning of the end was at hand.

First, the Sidonian gave the scourge to his four, and smarting with fear and pain they dashed desperately forward, promising for a brief time to go to the front. The effort ended only in promise. Next, the Byzantine and Corinthian each made the trial with a similar result. Then they were practically out of the race. After that, with perfect readiness, all of the factions except the Romans joined their hope in Ben Hur and openly expressed their feelings.

"Ben Hur! Ben Hur!" they shouted, and the blended voices of the many rolled overwhelmingly over the consular stand. From the benches above him as he passed the sentiment descended in fierce cries.

"Speed on, Jew!"

"Take the wall now!"

"On! Loose the Arabs! Give them rein and a scourge!"

"Let him not have the next turn on you again. Now or never!"

Over the balustrade they stooped low, stretching their hands imploringly to him. Either he did not hear, or could not do better, for halfway round the course he was still following. At the second goal there was still no change.

And now, to make the turn, Messala began to draw in his lefthand steeds, an act that necessarily slackened their speed. His spirit was high. More than one altar was richer for his vows. The Roman genius was still the leader. Only six hundred feet away, three more pillars, were fame, increase of fortune, promotions, and a triumph immeasurably sweetened by hate, all in store for him!

That moment Malluch, in the gallery, saw Ben Hur lean forward over his Arabs and give them the reins. Out flew the many-folded lash in his hand. Over the backs of the startled steeds it writhed and hissed, and, though it did not fall, there were both sting and menace in its quick snap.

As the man went from quiet to relentless action, his face blushed, his eyes gleamed. He seemed to exert his will along the reins, and instantly not one, but the four as one, answered with a leap that landed them alongside the Roman's chariot.

Messala, on the perilous edge of the goal, heard, but dared not look to see what this awakening meant. He received no sign from the people. Above the noises of the race there was only one voice, and that was Ben Hur's.

In the old Aramaic, as the sheik himself would do, he called to the Arabs. "On, Atair! On, Rigel! What, Antares! Do you linger now? Good horse. On, Aldebaran! I hear them singing in the tents. I hear the children singing and the women—singing of the stars, of Atair, Antares, Rigel, Aldebaran, victory! And the song will never end. Well done! Home tomorrow, under the black tent—home! On, Antares! The tribe is waiting for us, and the master is waiting! 'Tis done! We have overthrown the proud. The hand that smote us is in the dust. Ours the glory! Steady! The work is done. Rest!"

At the moment chosen for this dash, Messala was moving in a circle round the goal. To pass him, Ben Hur had to cross the track, and good strategy required the movement to be in a forward direction, that is, on a similar circle limited to the least possible increase. The thousands on the benches understood it all. The signal was given, and the magnificent responded. They saw the four close in just outside Messala's outer wheel. Ben Hur's inner wheel was behind the other's car.

Then they herd a crash loud enough to send a thrill through the circus, and, quicker than thought itself, out over the course a spray of shining white and yellow splinters flew. The bed of the Roman's chariot toppled down on its right side. There was a rebound as the axle hit the hard earth, then another. Then the car split into pieces, and Messala, entangled in the reins, pitched forward headlong.

To increase the horror of the sight by making death certain, the Sidonian, who occupied the wall right behind, could not stop or turn out. He drove into the wreck full speed, then over the Roman, and into the latter's four, all mad with fear. Out of the turmoil, the fighting of the horses, the resounding of blows, the murky cloud of dust and sand, he crawled, in time to see the Corinthian and Byzantine go on down the course after Ben Hur, who had not been an instant delayed.

The people arose and leaped upon the benches and shouted and screamed. Those who looked that way caught glimpses of Messala, now under the trampling of the fours, now under the abandoned cars. He was still. They thought he was dead.

But by far the greater number followed Ben Hur in his flight. They had not seen the cunning touch of the reins by which, turning a little to the left, he caught Messala's wheel with the iron-shod point of his axle and crushed it. But they had seen the transformation of the man, and they felt the heat and glow of his spirit, the heroic resolution, the maddening energy of action with which, by look, word, and gesture, he so suddenly inspired his Arabs. And such running! It was like the long leaping of lions in harness. Except for the lumbering chariot, it seemed the four were flying. When the Byzantine and Corinthian were halfway down the course, Ben Hur turned the first goal.

And the race was won!

The consul rose. The people shouted themselves hoarse. The master of the games came down from his seat and crowned the victors.

The fortunate man among the boxers was a low-browed, yellow-haired Saxon, of such a barbaric face as to attract a second look from Ben Hur, who recognized a teacher who had been a favorite of his at Rome. The young Jew looked up and beheld Simonides and his party on the balcony. They waved their hands to him. Esther kept her seat, but Iras arose and gave him a smile and a wave of her fan—favors not less intoxicating to him because they would have fallen to Messala had he been the victor.

The procession was then formed and, amidst the shouting of the multitude that had had its will, went out of the Gate of Triumph. And the day was over.

59

The Invitation of Iras

Ben Hur tarried across the river with Ilderim. At midnight, as previously determined, they would take the road that the caravan, then thirty hours out, had pursued.

The sheik was happy. His offers of gifts had been royal, but Ben Hur had refused everything, insisting that he was satisfied with the humiliation of his enemy. The generous dispute continued for a while.

"Think," the sheik would say, "what you have done for me. In every black tent down to the Akaba and to the ocean, the renown of my Mira and her children will go. They who sing of them will magnify me and forget that I am at the wane of life. And all the masterless spears will come to me, and my sword-hands will multiply past counting. You do not know what it is to have such a sway of commerce and immunity from kings. Yes, by the sword of Solomon! If my messenger seeks favor for me of Caesar, that he will get. Yet nothing?"

And Ben Hur would answer, "No, sheik, have I not your hand and heart? Let your increase of power and influence go to the King who comes. In the work I am going to, I may have great need. Saying no now will allow me to ask of you with better grace later."

In the middle of controversy of this kind, two messengers arrived—Malluch and one unknown. The former was admitted first.

The good fellow did not attempt to hide his joy over the events of the day. "But, coming to that with which I am charged," he said, "the master Simonides sends me to say that, upon the ending of the games, some of the Roman faction hastened to protest paying the prize money."

Ilderim started up, crying, in his shrillest tones, "By the splendor of God! The East shall decide whether the race was fairly won."

"No, good sheik," said Malluch, "the master has paid the money."

"'Tis well."

"When they said Ben Hur struck Messala's wheel, the master laughed and reminded them of the blow the Arabs had at the turn of the goal."

"And what of the Athenian?"

"He is dead."

"Dead!" cried Ben Hur.

"Dead!" echoed Ilderim. "What fortune these Roman monsters have! Messala escaped?"

"Escaped—yes, O sheik, with his life, but it shall be a burden to him. The physicians say he will live but never walk again."

Ben Hur looked silently up to heaven. He had a vision of Messala, chair-bound like Simonides and, like him, going around on the shoulders of servants. Simonides had abode well, but what would Messala do with his pride and ambition?

"Simonides also asked me to say," Malluch continued, "Sanballat is having trouble. Drusus, and those who signed with him, referred the question of paying the five talents they lost to the Consul Maxentius, and he had referred it to Caesar. Messala also refused his losses, and Sanballat, in imitation of Drusus, went to the consul, where the matter is still in consideration. The better Romans say the protestors should not be excused, and all the adverse factions join with them. The city rings with scandal."

"What does Simonides say?" asked Ben Hur.

"The master laughs and is well pleased. If the Roman pays, he is ruined. If he refuses to pay, he is dishonored. The imperial policy will decide the matter. To offend the East would be a bad beginning with the Parthians. To offend Sheik Ilderim would be to antagonize the desert, over which lie all Maxentius's lines of operation. So Simonides asked me to tell you not to worry. Messala will pay."

Ilderim was at once restored to his good humor. "Let us be off now," he said, rubbing his hands. "The business will do well with Simonides. The glory is ours. I will order the horses."

"Wait," said Malluch. "I left a messenger outside. Will you see him?"

"By the splendor of God! I forgot him."

Malluch left and was succeeded by a lad of gentle manners and delicate appearance, who knelt upon one knee and said, "Iras, the daughter of Balthasar, well known to good Sheik Ilderim, has entrusted me with a message to the sheik, who, she says, will do her great favor by receiving her congratulations on account of the victory of the four."

"The daughter of my friend is kind," said Ilderim, with sparkling eyes. "Do give her this jewel as a sign of the pleasure I have from her message." He took a ring from his finger as he spoke.

"I will do as you say, O sheik," the lad replied. "The daughter of the Egyptian charged me to speak more. She prays the good Sheik Ilderim to send word to the youth Ben Hur that her father has taken residence for a time in the palace of Idernee, where she will receive the youth after the fourth hour tomorrow. And if, with her congratulations, Sheik Ilderim will accept her gratitude for this other favor done, she will be ever so pleased."

The sheik looked at Ben Hur, whose face was suffused with pleasure. "What will you do?" he asked.

"By your leave, O sheik, I will see the fair Egyptian."

Ilderim laughed and said, "Shall not a man enjoy his youth?"

Then Ben Hur answered the messenger. "Say to her who sent you that I, Ben Hur, will see her at the palace of Idernee, wherever that may be, tomorrow at noon."

The lad arose and, with a silent salute, departed.

At midnight Ilderim took to the road, having arranged to leave a horse and a guide for Ben Hur, who was to follow him.

60

In the Palace of Idernee

Going the next day to fill his appointment with Iras, Ben Hur turned from the Omphalus, which was in the heart of the city, into the Colonnade of Herod and came shortly to the palace of Idernee.

From the street he passed first into a foyer, on the sides of which were stairways under a cover, leading up to a portico. Winged lions sat by the stairs. In the middle there was a gigantic fountain spouting water over the floor. The lions, walls, and floor were reminders of the Egyptians: everything, even the balustrading of the stairs, was of massive gray stone.

Above the vestibule and covering the landing of the steps arose the portico, a pillared area, so light, so exquisitely proportioned, it was at that period hardly possible to conceive of except by a Greek. Of marble snowy white substance, its effect was that of a lily dropped carelessly upon a great bare rock.

Ben Hur paused in the shade of the portico to admire its tracery and finish and the purity of its marble. Then he passed on into the palace. Ample folding doors stood open to receive him. The passage into which he first entered was high, but somewhat narrow. Red tiling covered the floor, and the walls were tinted to match. Yet this plainness was a sign of something more beautiful to come.

He moved on slowly. Soon he would be in the presence of Iras. She was waiting for him with song and story. She was sparkling, fanciful, capricious—with smiles and glances that lent voluptuous suggestion to her whispers. She had sent for him the evening of the boat ride on the lake in the Orchard of Palms, and he was going to her in the beautiful palace of Idernee. He was happy and dreamful.

The passage brought him to a closed door, where he paused. And as he did so, the broad leaves began to open of themselves, without creak or sound of a lock. Standing in the shade of the dull passage and looking through the doorway, he beheld the atrium of a Roman house, roomy and rich, with a fabulous degree of magnificence.

How large the chamber was cannot be stated, because of the deception there is in realizing exact proportions. Its depth was vistalike, something never to be said of another interior. When he stopped to view it and looked down upon the floor, he was standing upon the breast of the goddess Leda, represented as caressing a swan. And, looking farther, he saw the whole floor was similarly laid in mosaic pictures of mythological subjects. There were stools and chairs with separate designs and an exquisitely composed work of art. The articles of furniture were duplicated on the floor distinctly, as if they floated upon unrippled water.

Even the figures upon the paneling of the walls and the fresco of the ceiling were reflected on the floor. The ceiling curved up toward the center, where there was an opening through which the sunlight poured and the sky, ever so blue, seemed within reach of the hand. The gilded pillars supporting the roof at the edges of the opening shone like flame where the sun struck them, and their reflections beneath seemed to stretch to infinite depth. There were quaint and curious candelabra, statues, and vases, the entirety making an interior that would have well furnished the house on the Palatine Hill that Cicero bought of Crassus.

Still in his dreamy state, Ben Hur sauntered about, charmed by all he beheld, and waited. He did not mind a little delay. When Iras was ready she would come or send a servant. In every well-regulated Roman house the atrium was the reception chamber for visitors.

He stood under the opening in the roof and pondered the sky and its azure depth. Then, leaning against a pillar, he studied the light and shade and its effects. Yet nobody came. He wondered why Iras stayed for so long. At last he woke to a consciousness of the silence that held the house in thrall, and the thought of it made him uneasy and distrustful.

Still he put the feeling off with a smile and a promise. "She is giving the last touch to her eyes, or she is arranging a wreath for me. She will come soon, more beautiful of the delay!" He sat down then to admire a candelabrum. He listened even as he looked at the pretty object—he listened, but there was not a sound. The palace was still as a tomb.

There might be a mistake. No, the messenger had come from the Egyptian, and this was the palace of Idernee. Then he remembered how mysteriously the door had opened, so soundlessly.

He went to the same door. Though he walked ever so lightly, the sound of his steps were loud and harsh, and he shrank from it. He was getting nervous. The cumbersome Roman lock resisted his first effort to raise it. The blood chilled in his cheek—he wrenched it with all his might but in vain, for the door was not even shaken. A sense of danger seized him, and for a moment he stood indecisive.

Who in Antioch had the motive to do him harm? Messala!

And this palace of Idernee? He had seen Egypt in the foyer, Athens in the snowy portico, but here in the atrium was Rome. Everything about him betrayed Roman ownership. True, the house was on the great thoroughfare of the city, a very public place in which to do him violence, but for that reason it was more in line with the audacious genius of his enemy. The atrium underwent a change. With all its elegance and beauty, it was no more than a trap. Apprehension painted it in black.

There were many doors on the right and left of the atrium, leading, doubtless, to bedrooms. He tried them, but they were all firmly fastened. Knocking might bring a response. Afraid to make an outcry, he went to a couch and, lying down, tried to reflect.

All too plainly he was a prisoner, but for what purpose? And by whom?

If the work was Messala's! He sat up, looked about, and smiled defiantly. There were weapons in every table. But birds had been starved in golden cages. That would not happen to him! The couches would serve him as battering rams. He was strong, and there was an increase of might in both rage and despair!

Messala himself could not come. He would never walk again. He was a cripple like Simonides. Still he could move others. And there were others everywhere able to be moved by him. Ben Hur arose and tried the doors again. Once he called out. The room echoed so that he was startled. With such calmness as he could assume, he made up his mind to wait a time before attempting to break out.

In such a situation the mind has its ebb and flow of fear, with periods of peace between. At length—how long he could not have said—he came to the conclusion that the affair was an accident or mistake. The palace certainly belonged to somebody. It must have care and keeping, and the keeper would come. The evening or the night would bring him. So concluding, he waited patiently. The evening or the night would bring him. Patience!

Half an hour passed—a much longer period to Ben Hur—when the door that had admitted him opened and closed noiselessly as before and without attracting his attention.

That moment he was sitting at the farther end of the room. A footstep startled him. *At last she has come!* he thought with a throb of relief and pleasure, and he arose.

The step was heavy and accompanied with the grind and clang of coarse sandals. The gilded pillars were between him and the door. He advanced quietly and leaned against one of them. He heard the voices of men—one of them rough and guttural. What was said he could not understand, as the language was not of the East or South of Europe.

After a general survey of the room, the strangers crossed to their left and were brought into Ben Hur's view—two men, one very stout, both tall, and both in short tunics. They did not have the air of masters of the house or domestics. Everything they saw appeared wonderful to them. Everything they stopped to examine they touched. They were common men. The atrium seemed profaned by their presence. At the same time, their leisurely manner and the assurance with which they proceeded pointed to some right or business. If business, with whom?

With much conversation they sauntered this way and that, all the time gradually approaching the pillar by which Ben Hur was standing. Off a little way, where a slanted gleam of the sun fell with a glare upon the mosaic of the floor, there was a statue that attracted their notice. In examining it, they stopped in the light.

Ben Hur recognized the tall, stout stranger as the Northman whom he had known in Rome and seen crowned only the day before in the circus as the winning fighter. When he saw the man's face, scarred with the wounds of many battles, and filled with ferocious passions, when he surveyed the fellow's naked limbs, marvels of exercise and training, and his shoulders of Herculean breadth, a thought of personal danger chilled every vein. A sure instinct warned him that the opportunity for murder was too perfect to have come by chance. And here now were the murderers, and their business was with him.

He turned an anxious eye upon the Northman's comrade— young, black-eyed, black-haired, and altogether Jewish in appearance. He observed, also, that both the men were in the costume that professionals of their class were in the habit of wearing in the arena. Putting the several circumstances together, Ben Hur could no longer be in doubt. He had been lured into the palace with an evil design. Out of reach of aid, in this splendid privacy, he was to die!

At a loss as to what to do, he gazed at each man and was able to see that he had entered upon a new life, different from the old in one regard: in the old life he had been the victim of violence done to him, but from now on he was to be the aggressor.

Only yesterday he had found his first victim. To those of the Christian nature this would have brought the weakness of remorse. No so with Ben Hur. His spirit had its emotions from the teachings of the first lawgiver, not the last and greatest one. He had dealt punishment, not wrong, to Messala. By permission of the Lord, he had triumphed, and he derived faith from the circumstance—faith, the source of all rational strength, especially strength in peril.

Nor did the influence stop there. The new life appeared to him as a mission just begun, holy as the King to come was holy, and certain as the coming of the King was certain—a mission in which force was lawful if only because it was unavoidable. Should he, on the very threshold of such an errand, be afraid?

He undid the sash around his waist and, baring his head and casting off his white Jewish gown, stood out in an undertunic like those of his enemy and was ready in body and mind. Folding his arms, he placed his back against the pillar and calmly waited.

The examination of the statue was brief. Immediately the Northman turned and said something in the unknown tongue, then both looked at Ben Hur. A few more words, and they advanced toward him.

"Who are you?" he asked, in Latin.

The Northman gave a smile, which did not relieve his face of its brutalism, and answered, "Barbarians."

"This is the palace of Idernee. Who do you seek? Stand and answer." The words were spoken with earnestness.

The strangers stopped, and in his turn the Northman asked, "Who are you?"

"A Roman."

The giant laid his head back upon his shoulders.

"I have heard how a god once came from a cow licking a salted stone, but not even a god can make a Roman of a Jew." When the laugh was over, he spoke to his companion again, and they moved nearer.

"Hold!" said Ben Hur, leaving the pillar. "One word."

They stopped again. "A word!" replied the Saxon, folding his immense arms across his breast and relaxing the menace beginning to blacken his face. "A word! Speak."

"You are Thord the Northman."

The giant opened his blue eyes.

"You were a teacher in Rome."

Thord nodded.

"I was your student."

"No," said Thord, shaking his head. "By the beard of Irmin, I have never had a Jew to make a fighting man of."

"But I will prove my saying."

"How?"

"You came here to kill me."

"That is true."

"Then let this man fight me singly, and I will demonstrate the proof on his body."

A gleam of humor shone in the Northman's face. He spoke to his companion, who answered. Then he replied with the naïveté of a child, "Wait until I say begin."

He pushed a couch out on the floor and proceeded leisurely to stretch his burly form upon it. When perfectly at ease, he said, simply, "Now begin."

Without ado, Ben Hur walked over to his antagonist.

"Defend yourself," he said.

The man put up his hands.

As the two confronted each other in this approved position, there was no discernible inequality between them. On the contrary, they were as alike as brothers. To the stranger's confident smile Ben Hur showed an earnestness that, had his skill been known, would have been accepted as fair warning of danger. Both knew the combat was to be mortal.

Ben Hur feinted with his right hand. The stranger warded, slightly advancing his left arm. Before he could return to the guard position, Ben Hur caught him by the wrist in a grip that years at the oar had made as terrible as a vise. The surprise was complete and no time given to think it through. To throw himself forward, to push the arm across the man's throat and over his right shoulder and turn him to the front left side, to strike surely with the ready left hand the bare neck under the ear—these were only divisions of the same movement. No need of a second blow. The man fell heavily, without a cry, and lay still.

Ben Hur turned to Thord.

"What! By the beard of Irmin!" the latter cried, in astonishment, rising to a sitting posture. Then he laughed.

"I could not have done it better myself." He viewed Ben Hur coolly from head to foot and, rising, faced him with undisguised admiration.

"It was my trick—the trick I have practiced for ten years in the schools of Rome. You are not a Jew. Who are you?"

"You knew Arrius the duumvir."

"Quintus Arrius? Yes, he was my patron."

"He had a son."

"Yes," said Thord, his battered features lighting dully. "I knew the boy. He would have made a king gladiator. Caesar offered him his patronage. I taught him the very trick you played on this one here—a trick impossible except to a hand and arm like mine. It has won me many a crown."

"I am that son of Arrius."

Thord drew nearer and viewed him carefully. Then his eyes brightened with genuine pleasure, and, laughing, he held out his hand. "He told me I would find a Jew here—a dog of a Jew—whom by killing I was serving the gods."

"Who told you so?" asked Ben Hur, taking the hand.

"Messala."

"When, Thord?"

"Last night."

"I thought he was hurt."

"He will never walk again. He told me on his bed between groans."

It was a vivid portrayal of hate in a few words, and Ben Hur saw that the Roman, if he lived, would still be capable and dangerous and follow him unrelentingly. Revenge remained to sweeten the ruined life. Thus the reason to cling to the fortune that he lost in the wager with Sanballat.

Ben Hur thought through the possibilities with a distinct foresight of the many ways in which it would be possible for his enemy to interfere with him in the work he had undertaken for the King who was coming. Why not resort to the Roman's methods? The man hired to kill him could be hired to strike back. It was in his power to offer higher wages. The temptation was strong. Half yielding, he chanced to look down at his late antagonist lying still, with white upturned face, so like himself. A light came to him, and he asked, "Thord, what was Messala to give you for killing me?"

"A thousand sestertii."

"You shall have them yet. If you do now what I tell you, I will add three thousand more to the sum."

The giant reflected aloud. "I won five thousand yesterday. From the Roman one—six. Give me four, good Arrius—four more—and I will stand firm for you, though old Thor, my namesake, strike me with his hammer. Make it four, and I will kill the lying patrician, if you say so. I have only to cover his mouth with my hand this way."

He illustrated the process by clapping his hand over his own mouth.

"I see," said Ben Hur. "Ten thousand sestertii is a fortune. It will enable you to return to Rome and open a wine shop near the Great Circus and live well." The very scars on the giant's face glowed afresh with the pleasure the picture gave him.

"I will make it four thousand," Ben Hur continued, "and in what you shall do for the money there will be no blood on your hands, Thord. Hear me now. Did not your friend here look like me?"

"I would have said he was an apple from the same tree."

"Well, if I put on his tunic and dress him in these clothes of mine and you and I go away together, leaving him here, can you not get your sestertii from Messala all the same? You have only to make him believe it is me that is dead."

Thord laughed till the tears ran down his face. "Ten thousand sestertii were never won so easily. And a wine shop by the Great Circus! All for a lie without blood in it! Give me your hand, son of Arrius. Get on now, and if you ever come to Rome, do not fail to ask for the wine shop of Thord the Northman. By the beard of Irmin, I will give you the best, though I borrow it from Caesar!"

They shook hands again, after which the exchange of clothes was done. It was arranged then that a messenger should go at night to Thord's lodging place with the four thousand sestertii.

When they were done, the giant knocked at the front door. It opened to him, and, leaving the atrium, he led Ben Hur into an adjoining room, where the latter completed his attire from the coarse garments of the dead fighter. They separated immediately in the Omphalus.

"Don't fail, son of Arrius, to visit the wine shop near the Great Circus! By the beard of Irmin, there never was fortune gained so cheap. The gods keep you."

Upon leaving the atrium, Ben Hur gave a last look at the other man as he lay in the Jewish vestments and was satisfied. The likeness was striking. If Thord kept faith, the cheat on Messala was a secret to endure forever.

At night, in the house of Simonides, Ben Hur told the good man all that had taken place in the palace of Idernee, and it was agreed that after a few days public inquiry should be set about for the discovery of the whereabouts of the son of Arrius. Eventually the matter was to be carried boldly to Maxentius. Then, if the mystery did not come out, Messala and Gratus would be at rest and happy, and Ben Hur free to go to Jerusalem to search for his lost people.

As he left, Simonides sat in his chair out on the terrace overlooking the river and gave his farewell and the peace of the Lord with the blessing of a father. Esther went with the young man to the head of the steps.

"If I find my mother, Esther, you shall go to her at Jerusalem and be a sister to Tirzah." And with these words he kissed her. Was it only a kiss of peace?

He crossed the river next to the late quarters of Ilderim, where he found the Arab who was to serve him as guide. The horses were brought out.

"This one is yours," said the Arab.

Ben Hur looked, and to his amazement it was Aldebaran, the swiftest and brightest of the sons of Mira and, next to Sirius, the beloved of the sheik. And he knew the old man's heart came to him along with the gift.

The corpse in the atrium was taken up and buried at night. As part of Messala's plan, a courier was sent off to Gratus to please him by the announcement of Ben Hur's death—this time an event beyond question.

Before long a wine shop was opened near the Circus Maximus, with the inscription over the door *Thord the Northman.*

61

The Tower of Antonia—Cell No. VI

It was now thirty days from the night Ben Hur left Antioch to go out with Sheik Ilderim into the desert. A great change had taken place—great at least as respecting the fortunes of the hero Ben Hur. Valerius Gratus had been succeeded by Pontius Pilate.

The removal cost Simonides exactly five talents in Roman money paid by hand to Sejanus, who was then in the height of power as an imperial favorite. The purpose was to help Ben Hur by lessening his exposure while in and around Jerusalem and attempting to discover his family. The faithful servant put the winnings from Drusus and his associates to such pious uses, all of whom, having paid their wagers, became at once the enemies of Messala, whose repudiation was still an unsettled question in Rome.

Brief as the time was, already the Jews knew that the change of rulers was not for the better. The cohorts sent to relieve the garrison of Antonia made their entry into the city by night, so the next morning the first sight that greeted the people resident in the neighborhood were the walls of the old Tower decorated with military ensigns, consisting of busts of the emperor mixed with eagles and globes.

A passionate multitude marched to Caesarea, where Pilate was lingering, and implored him to remove the detested images. Five days and nights they approached his palace gates. At last he appointed a meeting with them in the circus. When they were gathered, he encircled them with soldiers. Instead of resisting, they offered him their lives and convinced him. He recalled the images and ensigns to Caesarea, where Gratus, with more consideration, had kept such abominations to the Jews housed during the eleven years of his reign.

The worst of men once in a while vary their wickedness by doing good deeds. Such was the case with Pilate. He ordered an inspection of all the prisons in Judea and a return of the names of the persons in custody, with a statement of the crimes for which they had been charged. Doubtless the motive was one common with officials just installed—dread of past responsibility. The people, however, thinking of the good that might come from the measure, gave him credit and for a period were comforted. The relations were astonishingly good.

Hundreds of persons were released against whom there were no accusations. Many others came to light who had long been accounted dead. Yet more amazing, there were openings of dungeons not merely unknown by the people but actually forgotten by the prison authorities. With one instance we now have to deal with, and, strange to say, it occurred in Jerusalem.

The Tower of Antonia, which will be remembered as occupying two-thirds of the sacred area on Mount Moriah, was originally a fortress built by the Macedonians. Afterwards, John Hyrcanus turned it into a defense of the Temple, and in his day it was considered impregnable.

But when Herod came with his bolder genius, he strengthened its walls and extended them, leaving a vast edifice that included everything necessary for the stronghold he intended to last forever, such as offices, barracks, armories, and prisons of all types. He leveled the solid rock and tapped it with deep excavations and built over them, connecting the whole great mass with the Temple by a beautiful colonnade. From the roof one could look down over the courts of the sacred structure.

In such condition the Tower fell at last out of his hands into the Romans', who were quick to see its strength and advantages and convert it to their uses. All through the administration of Gratus it had been a garrisoned citadel and underground prison terrifying to rebels. There was woe when the cohorts poured from its gates to suppress disorder! Woe to a Jew who passed the same gates going in under arrest!

The order of the new procurator requiring a report of the persons in custody was received at the Tower of Antonia and promptly executed, and two days had gone since the last unfortunate was brought up for examination. The tabulated statement, ready for forwarding, lay on the table of the tribune in command. In five minutes more it would be on the way to Pilate, visiting in the palace up on Mount Zion.

The tribune's office was spacious and cool and furnished in a style suitable to the dignity of the commandant of an important post. Looking in upon him about the seventh hour of the day, the officer appeared weary and impatient. When the report was dispatched, he would go to the roof of the colonnade for air and exercise and the amusement of watching the Jews over in the courts of the Temple. His subordinates and clerks shared his impatience.

In the time of waiting, a man appeared in a doorway leading to an adjoining apartment. He rattled a bunch of keys, each heavy as a hammer, and at once attracted the chief's attention.

"Ah, Gesius! Come in," the tribune said.

As the newcomer approached the table where the chief sat in an easy chair, everybody present looked at him and, observing a certain expression of alarm on his face, became silent so that they might hear what he had to say.

"Tribune!" he began, bending low, "I fear to tell you what news I bring you."

"Another mistake, Gesius?"

"If I could persuade myself it is only a mistake, I would not be afraid."

"A crime, then—or, worse, a breach of duty. You may laugh at Caesar, or curse the gods and live, but if the offense is to the eagles—you know the result, Gesius. Go on!"

"It is now about eight years since Valerius Gratus selected me to be keeper of the prisoners here in the Tower," said the man, deliberately. "I remember the morning I began the duties of my office. There had been a riot the day before and fighting in the streets. We slew many Jews and suffered on our side. The affair resulted, it was said, from an attempt to assassinate Gratus, who had been knocked from his horse by a tile thrown from a roof. I found him sitting where you now sit, tribune, his head swathed in bandages. He told me of my selection and gave me these keys, numbered to correspond with the numbers of the cells. They were the badges of my office, he said, and not to be parted with.

"There was a roll of parchment on the table. Calling me to

him, he opened the roll. 'Here are diagrams of the cells,' he said. There were three of them. 'This one,' he went on, 'shows the arrangement of the upper floor. This second one gives you the second floor. And this last is of the lower floor. I give them to you in trust.' I took them from his hand, and he said, further, 'Now you have the keys and the diagrams. Go immediately and acquaint yourself with the whole arrangement. Visit each cell and see to its condition. When anything is needed for the security of a prisoner, order it according to your judgment, for you are the master under me and no one else.'

"I saluted him and turned to go away. He called me back. 'I forgot,' he said. 'Give me the diagram of the third floor.' I gave it to him, and he spread it upon the table. 'Here, Gesius,' he said, 'see this cell.' He laid his finger on the one numbered V. 'There are three men confined in that cell, desperate characters, who by some means got hold of a state secret and suffer for their curiosity, which'—he looked at me severely—'in such matters is worse than a crime. Accordingly, they are blind and tongueless and are placed there for life. They shall have nothing but food and drink, to be given to them through a hole, which you will find in the wall covered by a slide. Do you hear, Gesius?' I made him answer. 'It is well,' he continued.

" 'One thing more that you will not forget'—he looked at me threateningly—'the door of their cell—cell number V on the same floor—this one, Gesius'—he put his finger on the particular cell to impress my memory—'shall never be opened for any purpose, neither to let one in nor out, not even yourself.' 'But if they die?' I asked. 'If they die,' he said, 'the cell shall be their tomb. They were put there to die and be lost. The cell is leprous. Do you understand?' With that he let me go."

Gesius stopped and from the breast of his tunic drew three parchments, all much yellowed by time and use. Selecting one of them, he spread it upon the table before the tribune, saying, simply, "This is the lower floor." The whole company looked at it.

PASSAGE				
V	IV	III	II	I

347

"This is exactly, O tribune, as I had it from Gratus. See, there is cell number V," said Gesius.

"I see," the tribune replied. "Go on now. The cell was leprous, he said."

"I would like to ask you a question," remarked the keeper modestly.

The tribune assented.

"Had I not a right, under the circumstances, to believe the diagram a true one?"

"What else could you do?"

"Well, it is not a true one."

The chief looked surprised.

"It is not a true one," the keeper repeated. "It shows only five cells upon that floor, but there are six."

"Six, you say?"

"I will show you the floor as it is—or as I believe it to be." Upon a page of his tablets Gesius drew a diagram and gave it to the tribune.

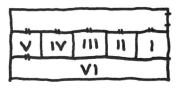

"You have done well," said the tribune, examining the drawing and thinking that the narrative was at an end. "I will have the diagrams corrected, or, better, I will have a new one made and given to you. Come for it in the morning." Saying this, he arose.

"But hear me further, O tribune."

"Tomorrow, Gesius, tomorrow."

"That which I have to tell you will not wait."

The tribune good-naturedly resumed his chair.

"I will hurry," said the keeper humbly, "only let me ask another question. Had I not a right to believe Gratus in what he further told me as to the prisoners in cell number V?"

"Yes, it was your duty to believe there were three prisoners in the cell—prisoners of state—blind and without tongues."

"Well," said the keeper, "that was not true either."

"No!" said the tribune, with returning interest.

"Hear and judge for yourself, tribune. As required I visited all the cells, beginning with those on the first floor and ending with those on the lower. The order that the door of number V should not be opened had been respected. Through all the eight years food and drink for three men had been passed through a hole in the wall. I went to the door yesterday, curious to see the wretches who, against all expectation, had lived so long. The locks refused the key. We pulled a little, and the door fell down, rusted from its hinges. Going in, I found only one man, old, blind, tongueless, and naked. His hair dropped in stiffened mats below his waist. His skin was like the parchment there. He held his hands out, and the fingernails curled and twisted like the claws of a bird. I asked him where his companions were. He shook his head in denial. Thinking to find the others, we searched the cell. The floor was dry. So were the walls. If three men had been shut in there and two of them had died, at least their bones would have endured."

"So you think—"

"I think, tribune, there has been only one prisoner there in the eight years."

The chief regarded the keeper sharply and said, "Be careful! You are saying that Valerius lied."

Gesius bowed but said, "He might have been mistaken."

"No, he was right," said the tribune warmly. "By your own statement he was right. Did you not say that for eight years food and drink had been furnished for three men?"

The bystanders approved the shrewdness of their chief.

Yet Gesius did not seem shaken in his thinking. "You have only half the story, tribune. When you have it all, you will agree with me. You know what I did with the man. I sent him to the bath and had him shorn and clothed, then took him to the gate of the Tower and told him to go free. I washed my hands of him.

"Today he came back and was brought to me. By signs and tears he at last made me understand he wished to return to his cell, and so I ordered it. As they were leading him off, he broke away and kissed my feet and, by piteous dumb signs, insisted I should go with him, and I went. The mystery of the three men stayed in my mind. I was not satisfied with it. Now I am glad I yielded to his entreaty."

The whole company at this point became very still.

"When we were in the cell again and the prisoner knew it, he caught my hand eagerly and led me to a hole similar to that through which we passed him his food. Though large enough to push your helmet through, it escaped me yesterday. Still holding my hand, he put his face to the hole and gave a beastlike cry. A sound came faintly back. I was astonished and drew him away and called out, 'What is here!' At first there was no answer. I called again and received back these words, 'Be praised, O Lord!' Yet more astonishing, tribune, the voice was a woman's. And I asked 'Who are you?' and received this reply: 'A woman of Israel, entombed here with her daughter. Help us quickly or we die.' I told them to be of cheer and hurried here to know your will."

The tribune arose hastily. "You were right, Gesius," he said, "and I see now. The diagram was a lie and so was the tale of the three men. There have been better Romans than Valerius Gratus."

"Yes," said the keeper. "I gleaned from the prisoner that he had regularly given the women of the food and drink he had received."

"It is accounted for," replied the tribune. And observing the faces of his friends and reflecting how well it would be to have witnesses, he added, "Let us rescue the women. Come, all of us."

Gesius was pleased. "We will have to pierce the wall," he said. "I found where a door had been, but it was filled solidly with stones and mortar."

The tribune stayed to say to a clerk, "Send workmen after me with tools. Make haste, but hold the report, for I see it will have to be corrected." In a short time they were gone.

350

62

The Lepers

"A woman of Israel, entombed here with her daughter. Help us quickly, or we die." This was the reply Gesius, the keeper, had from the cell that appeared on his amended diagram as VI. It was the mother of Ben Hur and Tirzah, his sister.

The morning of their seizure, eight years before, they had been carried to the Tower, where Gratus proposed to kill them. He had chosen the Tower for a better purpose, especially cell VI, because, first, it could be lost better than any other. Second, it was infected with leprosy. For these prisoners were not to be put in a safe place but in a place to die. They were taken down by slaves in the nighttime when there were no witnesses of the deed. Then, in completion of the savage task, the same slaves walled up the door, after which they were themselves separated and sent away never to be heard of again.

To avoid the accusation that might result in a distinction between the infliction of punishment and the commission of a double murder, Gratus preferred putting his victims where natural death was certain, though slow. So that they might linger along, he selected a convict who had been made blind and tongueless and put him in the only connecting cell, there to serve them with food and drink. Under no circumstances could the poor wretch tell the tale or identify either the prisoners or their doomsman. So, with a cunning partly due to Messala, the Roman, under color of punishing a brood of assassins, paved the way to confiscation of the estate of the Hurs, of which no portion ever reached the imperial coffers.

As the last step in the scheme, Gratus summarily removed the old keeper of the prisons, not because he knew what had been done—for he did not—but because, knowing the underground floors as he did, it would be next to impossible to keep the transaction from him. Then with masterly ingenuity the procurator had new diagrams drawn for delivery to a new keeper, with the omission, as we have seen, of cell VI. The instructions given to the new keeper, taken with the omission of the diagram, accomplished the plan—the cell and its unhappy tenants were all lost.

What may be told of the life of the mother and daughter during the eight years must have a relation to their culture and previous habits. Conditions are pleasant or grievous to us according to our past circumstances and temperaments. It is not extreme to say, if there was a sudden exit of all men from the world, heaven as prefigured in the Christian sense would not be a heaven to the majority.

On the other hand, neither would everyone suffer equally. If the mind possesses more intelligence, the capacity of the soul for pure enjoyment is also increased. How much better, therefore, if the soul is saved! If it is lost, however, the cultivation of enjoyment is to no effect. Its capacity for enjoyment in the case of salvation is also the measure of its capacity to suffer damnation. Therefore, repentance must be something more than mere remorse for sins. The soul must undergo a change of nature to be made fit for heaven.

To form an adequate idea of the suffering endured by the mother of Ben Hur, think of her spirit and its sensibilities more than the conditions of her confinement. It was not what the conditions were but how she was affected by them. It was in anticipation of this thought that the scene in the summerhouse on the roof of the family palace was given so fully before the separation of the family of Hur. Recall the serene, happy, luxurious life in the princely house and contrast it with the existence in the lower dungeon of the Tower of Antonia. With remembrance of these unfortunate women as they were, let us go down and see them as they are.

The cell VI was in the form that Gesius drew it on his diagram. Little idea can be realized of its dimensions other than it was a roomy, roughened interior, with ledged and broken walls and floors.

In the beginning, the site of the Macedonian Castle was separated from the site of the Temple by a narrow but deep cliff somewhat in shape of a wedge. The workmen, wishing to hew out a series of chambers, made their entry in the north face of the cleft and worked their way in, leaving a ceiling of natural stone. Delving further, they formed cells V, IV, III, II, I with no connection with number VI except through number V. In the same way, they constructed the passage and stairs to the floor above. The process of the work was the same as that found in carving out the Tombs of the Kings, to be seen a short distance north of Jerusalem. Only when the cutting was done, cell VI was enclosed on its outer side by a wall of formidable stones, in which, for ventilation, narrow openings were left sculpted like modern portholes. Herod, when he took hold of the Temple and Tower, put a yet more massive facing upon this outer wall and shut up all the openings except one, which still admitted a little fresh air and a ray of light not strong enough to redeem the room from darkness. This was cell VI.

The two women were grouped close by the small opening. One was seated, the other half reclining against her. There was nothing between them and the bare rock. The light, slanting upwards, struck them with a ghastly effect, and one could not avoid seeing that they were without covering. At the same time love was still alive, for the two were in each other's arms. Riches take wings, comforts vanish, hope withers away, but love stays with us. God is love.

The stony floor was polished shining smooth where the two were located. Who shall say how much of the eight years they had spent in that space there in front of the opening, nursing their hope of rescue by that timid yet friendly ray of light? When the brightness came creeping in, they knew it was dawn. When it began to fade, they knew the world was hushing for the night, which could not be anywhere so long and utterly dark as with them.

The world! Through that crevice, as if it were broad and high as a king's gate, they went to the world in their thoughts and passed their weary time walking up and down as spirits do, looking and asking, the one for her son, the other for her brother. On the seas they sought him, and on the islands of the seas. Today he was in this city, tomorrow in that other. And everywhere, and at all times, he was a flitting sojourner, for, as they lived waiting for him, he lived looking for them. How often their thoughts passed each other in the endless search, his coming, theirs going! It was such sweet flattery for them to say to each other, "While he lives, we shall not be forgotten. As long as he remembers us, there is hope!" The strength one can gain from little can only be known when one has been subjected to the trial.

Their sorrows had clothed them with a sort of sanctity. It is clear that they had undergone a change of appearance not to be accounted for only by the long confinement. The mother had been beautiful as a woman, the daughter beautiful as a child. Not even love could say as much now. Their hair was long, unkempt, and strangely white. One shrank from them and shuddered with an indefinable repulsion, though the effect may have been the result of an illusory glazing of the light, glimmering dismally through the unhealthy murk. Or they may have been enduring the tortures of hunger and thirst, not having had anything to eat or drink since their servant, the convict, was taken away—that is, since yesterday.

Tirzah, reclining against her mother in a half embrace, moaned piteously.

"Be quiet, Tirzah. They will come. God is good. We have been mindful of Him and not forgotten to pray at every sounding of the trumpets over in the Temple. The light, you see, is still bright. The sun in standing in the south sky yet, and it is hardly more than the seventh hour. Somebody will come to us. Let us have faith. God is good."

The mother's words were simple and effective, although Tirzah was no longer a child due to the eight years being added to the thirteen she had attained when last we saw her. "I will try and be strong, mother," she said. "Your suffering must be as great as mine. And I do so want to live for you and my brother! But my tongue burns, my lips scorch. I wonder where he is, and if he will ever find us!"

Their voices sounded sharp and unnatural. The mother drew the daughter closer to her breast and said, "I dreamed about him last night and saw him plainly, Tirzah, as I see you. We must believe in dreams, you know, because our fathers did. The Lord spoke to them so often in that way. I thought we were in the Women's Court just before the Gate Beautiful. There were many women with us. And he came and stood in the shade of the Gate and looked here and there, at this one and that. My heart beat strong. I knew he was looking for us and stretched my arms to him and ran, calling him. He heard me and saw me, but he did not know me. In a moment he was gone."

"Would it be possible, Mother, to meet him in fact? We are so changed."

"It might be so. But—" The mother's head drooped, and her face knitted as with a wrench of pain. Recovering, however, she went on. "But we could make ourselves known to him."

Tirzah threw up her arms and moaned again. "Water, mother, water, though only a drop."

The mother stared around in blank helplessness. She had named God so often and so often promised in His name that the repetition was beginning to have a mocking effect upon her. A shadow passed before her, dimming the dim light, and she thought of death as very near, waiting to come in as her faith went out. Hardly knowing what she did, speaking aimlessly, she said again, "Patience, Tirzah. They are coming—they are almost here."

She thought she heard a sound over by the little trap in the partition wall where they held all their communication with the world. And she was not mistaken. A moment, and the cry of the convict rang through the cell. Tirzah heard it also, and they both arose, still holding each other.

"Praise to the Lord forever!" exclaimed the mother, with the fervor of restored faith and hope.

"Ho, there!" they heard next, and they replied, "Who are you?"

The voice was strange. What did it matter? Except from Tirzah, they were the first and only words the mother had heard in eight years. The reaction was mighty—from death to life—and so instantly!

"A woman of Israel, entombed here with her daughter. Help us quickly, or we die!"

"Be of good cheer. I will return."

The women sobbed aloud. They were found. Help was coming. From wish to wish hope flew as the twittering swallows fly. They were found. They would be released. And restoration would follow—restoration to all they had lost—home, society, property, son, and brother! The scanty light glazed them with the glory of the day, and, forgetful of pain and thirst and hunger and of the menace of death, they sank upon the floor and cried, holding tightly to each other the while.

This time they did not have long to wait. Gesius, the keeper, had told his tale methodically, but finished it at last. The tribune was prompt.

"Within there!" he shouted through the trap.

"Here!" said the mother, rising.

Directly she heard another sound in another place, as of blows on the wall—ringing blows delivered with iron tools. She did not speak, nor did Tirzah, but they listened, knowing well the meaning of it all—that a way to liberty was being made for them. In the same way men buried a long time in deep mines hear the coming of rescuers, heralded by the thrust of bar and hammer of pick. They answer gratefully with heart throbs, their eyes fixed upon the spot from which the sounds come, and they cannot look away lest the work should cease and they return to despair.

The arms outside were strong, the hands skillful, the will strong. Each instant the blows sounded more plainly. Now and then a piece fell with a crash, and liberty came nearer. Suddenly the workmen could be heard speaking. Then—happiness! Through a crevice flashed a red ray of torches. Into the darkness it cut incisive as a brilliant diamond, beautiful as if from a spear of the morning.

"It is he, mother! He has found us at last!" cried Tirzah, with the quickened hope of youth.

But the mother answered meekly, "God is good!"

A block fell inside, and another—then a great mass, and the door was open. A man covered with mortar and stone dust stepped in and stopped, holding a torch over his head. Two or three others followed with torches and stood aside for the tribune to enter.

The tribune stopped, because they fled from him—not with fear, but shame. From the obscurity of their partial hiding he heard these words, which were the saddest, most despairing the human tongue could utter. "Do not come near us—unclean, unclean!"

The men flared their torches while they stared at each other.

"Unclean, unclean!" came from the corner again, a slow, sorrowful wail. With such a cry we can imagine a spirit vanishing from the gates of Paradise, while looking back.

So the widow and mother performed her duty and in the moment realized that the freedom she had prayed for and dreamed of, fruit of scarlet and gold seen from afar, was but an apple of Sodom in the hand. She and Tirzah were lepers.

"These four are accounted as dead—the blind, the leper, the poor, and the childless." This is what the Talmud says. That is, to be a leper was to be treated as one who is dead—to be excluded from the city as a corpse; to be spoken to by the best beloved only from a distance; to dwell with only lepers; to be utterly unprivileged; to be denied the rites of the Temple and the synagogue; to go about in rent garments and with covered mouth, except when crying, "Unclean, unclean!"; to find home in the wilderness or in abandoned tombs; to become a materialized specter of Gehenna; to be at all times not only a living offense to others but also a breathing torment to oneself; afraid to die, yet without hope except in death.

Once—she might not tell the day or year, for down in the haunted hell even time was lost—once the mother had felt a dry scab in the palm of her right hand, a trifle that she tried to wash away. It clung to her hand stubbornly, yet she thought little of the sign till Tirzah complained that she, too, was attacked in the same way. The supply of water was scant, and they denied themselves drink that they might use it for the sores. Finally the whole hand was attacked. The skin cracked open, the fingernails loosened from the flesh. There was not much pain, rather a steadily increasing discomfort. Later their lips began to parch and seam. One day the mother, who was cleanly next to godliness and struggled against the impurities of the dungeon with all her ingenuity, thinking the enemy was taking hold of Tirzah's face, led her to the light and, feeling a terrible dread, realized that the young girl's eyebrows were white as snow.

Oh, the anguish of that assurance! The mother was speechless for a while and paralyzed, capable of only one thought—leprosy!

When she began to think as a mother would, it was not of herself but her child, and her motherlike tenderness turned to courage, and she prepared for the last sacrifice of perfect heroism. She buried her knowledge in her heart. Being hopeless herself, she redoubled her devotion to Tirzah, and with wonderful ingenuity and tireless effort continued to keep the daughter ignorant of what they were plagued with, and even continued to hope that it was nothing. She repeated her little games and retold her stories, inventing new ones and listening with much pleasure to the songs she heard from Tirzah, while on her wasting lips the psalms of the singing king David served to bring the soothing balm of forgetfulness and keep alive in them both the recollection of the God who would seem to have abandoned them.

Slowly, steadily, with horrible certainty, the disease spread, after a while bleaching their heads white, eating holes in their lips and eyelids, and covering their bodies with scales. Then it went to their throats, making their voices shrill, then to their joints, hardening the tissues and cartilage—slowly and, as the mother well knew, past remedy, it was affecting their lungs and arteries and bones, at each advance making the sufferers more and more loathsome. So it would continue till death, which might still be years ahead.

Another day of dread later came—the day the mother, under the necessity of duty, at last told Tirzah the name of their ailment, and the two, in agony and despair, prayed that the end might come quickly.

Still, as is the force of habit, these so afflicted grew in the course of time to not merely speak resignedly of their disease but viewed the hideous transformation of their bodies as a matter of course and despite this clung to their existence.

One tie to earth remained to them. Not aware of their own loneliness, they kept up a strong spirit by talking and dreaming of Ben Hur. The mother promised reunion with him to the sister, and she to the mother, not doubting, either of them, that he was equally faithful to them and would be equally overjoyed at their meeting. They found pleasure with the spinning of this slender thread and excused their painful suffering. They were comforting themselves the moment Gesius called them, at the end of twelve hours' fasting and thirst.

The torches flashed with a red light through the dungeon, and liberty had come.

"God is good," the widow cried—not for what had been, but for what was. In thankfulness for present mercy, nothing so affects us as losing the sight of past ills.

The tribune came immediately to the corner where she had fled, and suddenly a sense of duty struck the mother and immediately the awful warning was spoken: "Unclean, unclean!"

Not all the selfishness of joy over the prospect of freedom could keep her blind to the consequences of her release, now that it was at hand. The old happy life could never be lived again. If she went near the house called home, it would be to stop at the gate and cry, "Unclean, unclean!" She must go around with the yearnings of love alive in her breast as strong as ever, and more sensitive as well, because it could not be returned.

The boy of whom she had thought so constantly and with all sweet promises such as mothers find their purest delight in, must at meeting her stand at a distance. If he held out his hands to her and called, "Mother," because of her love for him she must answer, "Unclean!" She was spreading her long tangled locks, bleached unnaturally white, in front of Tirzah, who must continue to be her only partner for the rest of her life. Yet the brave woman accepted her fate.

The tribune heard it with a tremor but held his place. "Who are you?" he asked.

"Two women dying of hunger and thirst. Yet"—the mother did not falter—"do not come near us, nor touch the floor or the wall. Unclean, unclean!"

"Give me your story, woman, and your name, when you were put here, by whom, and for what reason."

"There was at one time in Jerusalem a prince named Ben Hur, the friend of all generous Romans and who had Caesar for his friend. I am his widow, and this one with me is his child. How can I tell you why we were put here, when I do not know, unless it was because we were rich? Valerius Gratus can tell you who our enemy was and when our imprisonment began. I cannot. See the way we have been reduced—oh, see, and have pity!"

The air was heavy with the smoke of the torches, yet the Roman called one of the torch bearers to his side and wrote the answer nearly word for word. It was terse and comprehensive, containing a history, an accusation, and a prayer. No common person would have made it, and he could only pity and believe.

"You will have relief, woman," he said, closing the tablets. "I will send you food and drink."

"And clothing and purifying water, we ask you, generous Roman!"

"As you wish," he replied.

"God is good," said the widow, sobbing. "May His peace abide with you!"

"And further," he added, "I cannot see you again. Make preparation, and tonight I will have you taken to the gate of the Tower and set you free. You know the law. Farewell."

He spoke to the men and went out the door.

Very shortly some slaves came to the cell with a large bucket of water, a basin and napkins, a platter of bread and meat, and some women's garments. Setting them down within reach of the prisoners, they went away.

About the middle of the first watch, the two were conducted to the gate and walked into the street. So the Roman left them, and they were once more free in the city of their fathers.

They looked up to the stars, twinkling merrily as of old, then they asked themselves, "What next? And where to?"

63

Jerusalem Again

Around the hour Gesius, the keeper, made his appearance before the tribune in the Tower of Antonia, a man was climbing the eastern face of Mount Olivet. The road was rough and dusty, and vegetation on that side burned brown, for it was the dry season in Judea. It was good that the traveler had youth and strength, not to speak of the cool flowing garments with which he was clothed.

He proceeded slowly, looking often to his right and left, not with the vexed, anxious expression that marks a man going forward uncertain of the way, but rather the air with which one approaches an old acquaintance after a long separation—half pleasure, half inquiry, as if he were saying, "I am glad to be with you again. Let me see how you have changed."

The traveler was Ben Hur, and the spectacle was Jerusalem. Not the Holy City of today, but the Holy City of Herod—the Holy City of the Christ. Beautiful yet, as seen from old Olivet, what must it have been then?

Ben Hur went to a stone and sat down and, stripping his head of the white handkerchief that served as a covering, viewed the city at leisure.

The same has been done often since by a great variety of persons, under unusual circumstances, by Romans, by Muslims, by the Crusader, all conquerors, by many a pilgrim from the great New World, which awaited discovery nearly fifteen hundred years after the time of our story. But probably only Ben Hur had sensations so keenly poignant, so sadly sweet and yet proudly bitter. He was stirred by the recollections of his countrymen, their triumphs and struggles, their history, which is the history of God. The city was built by them as a lasting testimony of their crimes and devotion, their weakness and genius, and their religion.

Though he had seen Rome and was familiar with it, he was

gratified. The sight filled him with a measure of pride that would have made him drunk with vainglory except for this thought: princely as the property was, it did not any longer belong to his countrymen. The worship in the Temple was allowed by the permission of strangers. The hill where David dwelled contained an office in which the chosen of the Lord were wrung for taxes and scourged for strong faith. These were the griefs of patriotism common to every Jew of the period. But Ben Hur brought a personal history with him that gave the spectacle of Jerusalem special significance.

A country of hills changes little. Where the hills are of rock, not at all. The scene Ben Hur viewed is the same now, except as regards the city. Down to the dry bed of the Cedron the greenery extended, refreshing to one's vision. Olivet ceased there, and Moriah began—a wall white as snow, established by Solomon and completed by Herod. Up the wall the eye climbed course by course along the rocks composing it—up to Solomon's Porch, which was as the pedestal of the monument. Lingering there a moment, one's eye went next to the Gentile's court, then to the Israelite's Court, then to the Women's Court, then to the Court of the Priests, each a pillared tier of white marble, one above the other in terraced progression.

Over them all a crown infinitely sacred and beautiful and majestic in proportions, covered with beaten gold! The Tent, the Tabernacle, the Holy of Holies. The Ark was not there, but Jehovah was—in the faith of every child of Israel He was there as a personal Presence. As a temple and a monument, none of man's buildings approached that superlative sight.

Now, not a stone of it remains upon another. When shall the rebuilding be begun? Every pilgrim asks this who has stood where Ben Hur was, knowing that the answer is in the heart of God, whose secrets are marvelous in their safeguarding. And then the third question, What about him who foretold the ruin that has so certainly fallen upon Jerusalem?

And still Ben Hur's eyes climbed up—up over the roof of the Temple to the hill of Zion, consecrated to sacred memories, inseparable from the anointed kings. He knew the Cheesemonger's Valley dipped deep down between Moriah and Zion; that it was spanned by the Xystus; that there were gardens and palaces in its depths. But over them all his thought soared with his vision to the great buildings on the royal hill—the house of Caiaphas, the Central Synagogue, the Roman Praetorim, all relieved against Gareb, purpling in the distance.

And when in the midst of them he singled out the palace of Herod, how could he not but think of the King Who Was Coming, to whom he was devoted, whose path he wished to prepare, whose empty hands he dreamed of filling? And his fancy ran forward to the day the new King should come to claim his own and take possession of it—of Moriah and its Temple; of Zion and its towers and palaces; of Antonia, towering darkly just to the right of the Temple; of the millions in Israel who would assemble with palm branches and banners, to rejoice because the Lord had conquered and given them the world.

Men speak of dreaming as if it were a phenomenon of night and sleep. They should know better. All results achieved by us are self-promised, and all self-promises are made in the dreams we have when awake.

The sun stooped low in its course. The flaring disk seemed for a while to perch on the far summit of the mountains in the west, brazening all the sky above the city and rimming the walls and towers with the brightness of gold. Then it disappeared with a plunge. The quiet turned Ben Hur's thoughts homeward. There was a point in the sky a little north of the front side of the Holy of Holies where he gazed. Under it, straight as a lead-line would have dropped, lay his father's house, if the house still stood.

The mellowing influences of the evening mellowed his feelings, and, putting his ambitions aside, he thought of the duty that was bringing him to Jerusalem. Out in the desert while with Ilderim, a messenger had come one evening with the news that Gratus was removed from power and Pontius Pilate sent to take his place.

Messala was disabled and believed him to be dead. Gratus was powerless and gone. Why should Ben Hur defer a search any longer for his mother and sister? There was nothing to fear now. If he himself could not see into the prisons of Judea, he could examine them with the eyes of others. If the lost were found, Pilate could have no motive in holding them in custody—none, at least, that could not be overcome by bribes.

If found, he would carry them to a place of safety, and then, in a calmer mind, his conscience at rest, after this one first duty done, he could give himself more completely to the king who was coming. He resolved at once to complete his plan. That night he had discussed it with Ilderim and obtained his assent. Three Arabs came with him to Jericho, where he left them and the horses and proceeded alone and on foot. Malluch was to meet him in Jerusalem.

Ben Hur's scheme, it should be observed, was still a generality. In view of the future, it was advisable to keep himself in hiding from the authorities, particularly the Romans. Malluch was shrewd and trustworthy, the very man to charge with the duty of the investigation.

Where to begin was the first point. He did not have a clear idea about it. His wish was to begin with the Tower of Antonia. The gloomy tower was planted over a labyrinth of prison cells, which, even more than the strong garrison, were a terror to the Jewish imagination. A burial of his mother and sister might be possible there. Besides, in such a dire strait, the natural inclination is to start searching at the place where the loss occurred, and he could not forget that his last sight of his loved ones was as the guard pushed them along the street in the direction to the Tower. If they were not there now, but had been, some record of the fact must remain, a clue that had only to be followed faithfully to the end.

With this inclination there at least was a hope that he could not give up. From Simonides, he knew Amrah, the Egyptian nurse, was living. It will be remembered that the faithful woman, the morning the calamity overtook the Hurs, broke from the guard and ran back into the palace, where, along with other servants, she had been sealed up. During the years following, Simonides kept her supplied, so she was there now, the sole occupant of the great house, which, with all his offers, Gratus had not been able to sell.

The story of its rightful owners was sufficient to secure the property from strangers, whether purchasers or mere occupants.

People going to and fro passed it with whispers. Its reputation was that of a haunted house, probably because of the infrequent glimpses of poor old Amrah, who was seen sometimes on the roof or in the latticed window. Certainly no more constant spirit ever lived than she, nor was there ever a tenement so shunned and fit only for ghostly occupation. Now, if he could get to her, Ben Hur fancied she could give him knowledge that, though faint, might yet be serviceable. Anyhow, the sight of her in that place, so endeared to him from memory, would be a pleasure next to finding the objects of his search.

So first of all things, he would go to the old house and look for Amrah. He arose shortly after the sunset and began to descend the Mount by the road that, from the summit, bends a little north of east. Down nearly at the foot, close by the bed of the Cedron, he came to the intersection with the road leading south to the village and the pool of Siloam. There he walked along with a herdsman driving some sheep to market. He spoke to the man and joined him and in his company passed by Gethsemane on into the city through the Fish Gate.

64

Ben Hur at His Father's Gate

It was dark when, parting with the driver inside the gate, Ben Hur turned into a narrow lane leading to the south. A few of the people whom he met greeted him. The rocks on the pavement were rough. The houses on both sides were low, dark, and cheerless. The doors were all closed. Occasionally, from the roofs he heard women crooning to children. The loneliness of his situation, the night, the uncertainty cloaking the reason for his coming, all made him cheerless. With his feelings sinking lower and lower, he came directly to the deep reservoir now known as the Pool of Bethesda, in which the water reflected the overarching sky. Looking up, he saw the northern wall of the Tower of Antonia, a black, frowning heap reared into the dim, steel-gray sky. He halted as if challenged by a threatening sentinel.

The Tower stood up high and seemed vast, resting apparently upon sure foundations, and he was forced to acknowledge its strength. If his mother were there in a living burial, what could he do for her? By his own strong hand, nothing. An army might beat the stony face with a battering ram—and be laughed at. The gigantic southeast turret looked down in the self-containment of a hill. And he thought, cunning is so easily baffled. And God, always the last resort of the helpless—God is sometimes so slow to act!

In doubt and misgiving, he turned into the street in front of the Tower and followed it slowly on the west side.

Over in Bezetha he knew there was an inn, where it was his intention to seek lodging while in the city. But just now he could not resist the impulse to go home. His heart drew him that way.

The old formal salutation that he received from the few people who passed him had never sounded so pleasant. Soon, all the eastern sky began to silver and shine, objects that before were invisible in the west—chiefly the tall towers on Mount Zion—emerged from a shadowy depth and put on a spectral distinct-

366

ness, floating, as it were, above the yawning blackness of the valley below, like castles in the air.

He came, at length, to his father's house.

At the gate on the north side of the old house Ben Hur stopped. In the corners the wax used in the sealing was still plainly seen, and across the valves was the board with the inscription

"THIS IS THE PROPERTY
OF THE EMPEROR."

Nobody had gone in or out of the gate since the dreadful day of the separation. Should he knock as of old? It was useless, he knew, yet he could not resist the temptation. Amrah might hear and look out of one of the windows on that side.

Taking a stone, he mounted the broad stone step and tapped three times. A dull echo replied. He tried again, louder than before, and again, pausing each time to listen. The silence was mocking. Retiring into the street, he watched the windows. But they, too, were lifeless. The parapet on the roof was defined sharply against the brightening sky. Nothing could have stirred upon it that would be unseen by him, and nothing stirred.

From the north side he passed to the west, where there were four windows, which he watched long and anxiously but with little effect. At times his heart swelled with impotent wishes. At others, he trembled at the deceptions of his own fancy. Amrah made no sign—not even a ghost stirred.

Silently, then, he crept around to the south. There, too, the gate was sealed and inscribed. The mellow splendor of the August moon, pouring over the crest of Olivet, since called the Mount of Offense, brought the lettering boldly out. He read it and was filled with rage. All he could do was to wrench the board from its nailing and hurl it into the ditch. Then he sat upon the step and prayed for the new King and that his coming might be hastened. As his blood cooled, without realizing, he yielded to the fatigue of long travel in the summer heat, sank down lower, and at last slept.

About that time two women came down the street from the direction of the Tower of Antonia, approaching the palace of the

Hurs. They advanced stealthily, with timid steps, pausing often to listen. At the corner of the rugged edifice, one said to the other, in a low voice, "This is it, Tirzah!"

And Tirzah, after a look, caught her mother's hand and leaned upon her heavily, sobbing, but silent.

"Let us go on, my child, because"—the mother hesitated and trembled; then, with an effort to be calm, continued—"because when morning comes they will expel us from the gate of the city to—return no more."

Tirzah sank almost to the stones. "Ah, yes!" she said, between sobs. "I forgot. I had the feeling of going home. But we are lepers and have no home. We belong to the dead!"

The mother stooped and raised her tenderly, saying, "We have nothing to fear. Let us go on." Indeed, lifting their empty hands, they could have run upon a legion and put it to flight.

Creeping in close to the rough wall, they glided on like two ghosts till they came to the gate, where they also paused. Seeing the board, they stepped upon the stone in the recent tracks of Ben Hur and read the inscription: "This is the property of the Emperor." Then the mother clasped her hands and with upraised eyes moaned in unutterable anguish.

"What now, mother? You scare me!"

And the answer was, presently, "Oh, Tirzah, the poor are dead! He is dead!"

"Who, Mother?"

"Your brother! They took everything from him—everything—even this house!"

"Poor!" said Tirzah vacantly.

"He will never be able to help us."

"And then, Mother?"

"Tomorrow, my child, we must find a seat by the wayside and beg alms as the lepers do. Beg, or—"

Tirzah leaned upon her again and said, whispering, "Let us—let us die!"

"No!" the mother said firmly. "The Lord has appointed our times, and we are believers in the Lord. We will wait on Him even in this. Come away!"

She caught Tirzah's hand as she spoke and hastened to the

west corner of the house, keeping close to the wall. No one was in sight there. They moved on to the next corner and shrank from the moonlight, which lay exceedingly bright over the whole south front and along a part of the street.

The mother's will was strong. Casting one look back and up to the windows on the west side, she stepped out into the light, drawing Tirzah close to her. And the extent of their affliction was then to be seen—on their lips and cheeks, in their bleary eyes, in their cracked hands, especially in the long, snaky stiff locks, like their eyebrows ghastly white. Nor was it possible to have discovered which was mother and which was daughter. Both seemed ancient.

"Hush!" said the mother. "There is someone lying upon the step—a man. Let us go around him."

They crossed to the opposite side of the street quickly and, in the shade there, moved on till just before the gate, where they stopped.

"He is asleep, Tirzah!" The man was very still.

"Stay here, and I will try the gate."

Saying this, the mother stole noiselessly across and attempted to touch the wicket. She never knew if it yielded, for that moment the man sighed and, turning restlessly, shifted the handkerchief on his head in such a manner that his face was left upturned and fair in the broad moonlight. She looked down at it and wondered, then looked again, stooping a little, arose, and clasped her hands and raised her eyes appealingly to heaven. An instant later, she ran back to Tirzah.

"As the Lord lives, the man is my son—your brother!" she said in an awe-inspiring whisper.

"My brother? Judah?"

The mother caught her hand eagerly. "Come!" she said in the same forced whisper. "Let us look at him together—once more—only once—then help Your servants, Lord!"

They crossed the street hand in hand, ghostly quick, ghostly still. When their shadows fell upon him, they stopped. One of his hands was lying out upon the step palm up. Tirzah fell upon her knees and would have kissed it, but the mother drew her back.

"Not on your life! Unclean, unclean!" she whispered. Tirzah shrank from him, as if he were the leprous one.

Ben Hur was as handsome as a man could be. His cheeks and forehead were swarthy from exposure to the desert sun and air, yet under the light moustache the lips were red, the teeth shone white, and the soft beard did not hide the full roundness of his chin and throat. How beautiful he appeared to his mother's eyes! How mightily she yearned to put her arms about him and take his head upon her bosom and kiss him, as had been her habit in his happy childhood! Where did she get the strength to resist the impulse?

Her mother love, which, if observed well, has this unlikeness to any other love: it is tender to the object, it can be infinitely tyrannical toward itself, and that is where all its power of self-sacrifice originates. Not for restoration to health and fortune, not for any blessing of life, not for life itself, would she have left her leprous kiss upon his cheek! But she must touch him. In that instant of finding him she must renounce him forever. How bitter, how hard it was. Let some other mother go through this! She knelt down and, crawling to his feet, touched the soul of one of his sandals with her lips, yellow though it was with the dust of the street—and touched it again and again. And her very soul was in her kisses.

He stirred and tossed his hand. They moved back but heard him mutter in his dream. "Mother! Amrah! Where is—" He fell off into deep sleep.

Tirzah stirred wistfully. The mother put her face in the dust, struggling to suppress a sob so deep and strong that it seemed her heart was bursting. She wished almost he might waken.

He had asked for her. She was not forgotten. In his sleep he was thinking of her. Was this not enough to console her?

Then the mother beckoned to Tirzah, and they arose. Taking one more look, as if to print his image upon their minds, hand in hand they recrossed the street. Back in the shade of the wall, they removed themselves and knelt, looking at him, waiting for him to wake—waiting for some revelation that they knew nothing about. Nobody has yet given us a measure for the patience of a love like theirs.

By and by, while he was yet sleeping, another woman appeared at the corner of the palace. The two in the shade saw her plainly in the light—a small figure, much bent, dark-skinned, gray-haired, dressed neatly in servant's garb and carrying a basket full of vegetables.

At the sight of the man upon the step the newcomer stopped. Then, as if deciding, she walked on—very lightly as she drew near the sleeper. Walking around him, she went to the gate, slid the wicket latch easily to one side and put her hand in the opening. One of the broad boards in the left valve swung ajar without noise. She put the basket through and was about to follow, when, yielding to curiosity, she lingered to have one look at the stranger whose face was below her in full view.

The spectators across the street heard a low exclamation and saw the woman rub her eyes as if to regain their clarity, bend down closer, gaze wildly around, look at the sleeper, stoop and raise his hand, and kiss it fondly—which they wished to do but dared not.

Awakened by the action, Ben Hur instinctively withdrew the hand. As he did so, his eyes met the woman's. "Amrah! O Amrah, is it you?" he said.

Her good heart made no answer in words, but she put her arms around his neck, crying for joy. He gently pushed her arms away and lifting the dark face wet with tears, kissed it. His joy was only a little less than hers. Then his mother and sister across the way heard him say, "Mother—Tirzah—O Amrah, tell me of them! Speak, I pray you!"

Amrah only cried again.

"You have seen them, Amrah. You know where they are. Tell me they are at home."

Tirzah moved, but the mother, discerning her purpose, caught her and whispered, "Do not go—not for life itself. Unclean, unclean!"

Her love was directed to his good. Though both their hearts broke, he should not become what they were, and she conquered. Meantime Amrah, so entreated, only wept all the more.

"Were you going in?" he asked, then, seeing the board swung back. "Come, then. I will go with you." He arose as he spoke. "The Romans—be the curse of the Lord upon them! The Romans lied. The house is mine. Rise, Amrah, and let us go in."

A moment later they were gone, leaving the two in the shade to view the gate staring blankly at them—the gate that they might not ever enter again. They nestled together in the dust.

They had done their duty. Their love was proven.

Next morning they were found and driven out of the city with stones.

"Begone! You are of the dead. Go to the dead!" With their doom ringing in their ears, they went away.

65

The Tomb Above the King's Garden

Nowadays travelers in the Holy Land looking for the famous place with the beautiful name, the King's Garden, descend the bed of the Cedron or the curve of Gihon and Hinnom as far as the old well of En-rogel, take a drink of the sweet living water, and stop, having reached the extent of the interesting sights. They look at the great stones where the well is circled and ask about its depth, smile at the primitive method of drawing up the water, and have some pity on the ragged wretch who manages the process. Turning around, they are enraptured with both Mount Moriah and Zion, which slope toward them from the north, one ending in Ophel, the other in what used to be the site of the city of David.

In the background, far up in the sky, the tops of the sacred places are visible: the Haram, with its graceful dome; and the stalwart remains of Hippicus, defiant even in its ruins. When that view has been enjoyed and is impressed upon their memories, the travelers glance at the Mount of Offense standing in rugged stateliness at their right hand and then at the Hill of Evil Counsel over on the left, in which, if they are filled with scriptural history and in rabbinical traditions, they will not be overcome by superstitious fear.

The second morning after the preceding incidents, Amrah drew near the well of En-rogel and seated herself upon a stone. One familiar with Jerusalem, looking at her, would have said she was the favorite servant of some well-to-do family. She brought with her a water jar and a basket, the contents of the latter covered with a snow-white napkin. Placing them on the ground at her side, she loosened the shawl that fell from her head, knit her fingers together in her lap, and gazed demurely up to where the hill dropped steeply down into the Aceldama and the Potter's Field.

It was very early, and she was the first to arrive at the well. Soon, however, a man came bringing a rope and a leather bucket.

Greeting the little dark-faced woman, he undid the rope, attached it to the bucket, and waited on customers. Others who chose to do so might draw water for themselves. He was a professional in the business and would fill the largest jar the stoutest woman could carry.

Amrah sat still and had nothing to say. Seeing the jar, the man asked after a while if she wished it to be filled. She answered him civilly, "Not now," so he gave her no more attention. When the dawn finally appeared over Olivet, his patrons began to arrive, and he had all he could handle to attend to them. All the time she stayed in her seat, looking intently up at the hill.

Her custom had been to go to market after nightfall. Stealing out unobserved, she would seek the shops over by the Fish Gate in the east, make her purchases of meat and vegetables, and return and shut herself in again.

She had nothing to tell Ben Hur of her mistress or Tirzah. He would have had her move to a place less lonesome, but she refused. She would have had him live in his own room again, which was just as he had left it. But the danger of discovery was too great, and he wished above all things to avoid inquiry. He would come and see her as often as possible. Coming in the night, he would also go away in the night.

She was satisfied and at once tried to figure ways to make him happy. It did not occur to her that he was a man now. Nor did it enter her mind that he might have lost his boyish tastes. To please him, she tried to go on her old round of services for him. He used to be fond of sweets. She remembered the things in that line that delighted him most, and she resolved to make them and have a supply always ready when he came. Could anything be happier? So the next night, earlier than usual, she crept out with her basket and went over to the Fish Gate Market. Wandering around, seeking the best honey, she happened to hear a man telling a story.

The narrator was one of the men who had held torches for the commandant of the Tower of Antonia when, down in cell VI, the Hurs were found. The particulars of the discovery were all told, and she heard them, with the names of the prisoners, and the widow's account of herself.

The feelings with which Amrah listened to the recital were consistent with the devoted creature she was. She made her purchases and returned home as if in a dream. What happiness she had in store for her boy! She had found his mother!

She put the basket away, both laughing and crying. Suddenly she stopped and thought. It would kill him to be told that his mother and Tirzah were lepers. He would go through the awful city over on the Hill of Evil Counsel—into each infected tomb without rest, asking for them, and the disease would catch him, and their fate would be his. She wrung her hands. What should she do?

Like many before her, and many since, she derived inspiration, if not wisdom, from her devotion and came to a single conclusion.

The lepers, she knew, were accustomed on mornings to come down from their sepulchral homes in the hill and take a supply of water for the day from the well of En-rogel. Bringing their jars, they would set them on the ground and wait, standing far away until they were filled. The mistress and Tirzah must come to the well, for the law was unchangeable and allowed no distinctions. A rich leper was no better than a poor one.

So Amrah decided not to speak to Ben Hur of the story she had heard but go alone to the well and wait. Hunger and thirst would drive the unfortunates there, and she believed she could recognize them at sight. If not, they might recognize her.

Meantime Ben Hur came, and they talked much. Tomorrow Malluch would arrive. Then the search should be immediately begun. He was impatient to begin it. To amuse himself he would visit the sacred places in the vicinity. The secret weighed heavily on the woman, but she held her peace.

When he was gone she busied herself in the preparation of good things to eat, applying her utmost skill to the work. At the approach of day, as signaled by the stars, she filled the basket, selected a jar, and took the road to En-rogel, going out by the Fish Gate, which was the earliest one open, and arrived as scheduled.

Shortly after sunrise, when business at the well was most pressing, and the drawer of water most hurried, when, in fact, half a dozen buckets were in use at the same time, everybody making haste to get away before the cool of the morning melted into the heat of the day, the tenants of the hill began to appear and move about the doors of their tombs. Somewhat later they were found in groups, with many young children. A number of them came momentarily around the turn of the bluff—women with jars upon their shoulders, old and very feeble men hobbling along on staffs and crutches. Some leaned upon the shoulders of others. A few—the utterly helpless—lay like heaps of rags upon litters. Even that community of supreme sorrow had a light of love to make life endurable and attractive. Distance softened without entirely veiling the misery of the outcasts.

From her seat by the well Amrah kept watch upon the ghostly groups. She scarcely moved. She imagined more than once she saw those she sought. She had no doubt that they were there upon the hill. She knew that they must come down near her. When the people at the well were all served they would come.

Now at the base of the bluff there was a tomb, which had more than once attracted Amrah by its wide opening. A stone of large dimensions stood near its mouth. The sun shone into it in the hottest hours of the day, and it seemed altogether uninhabitable by anything living.

From there and greatly to her surprise, the patient Egyptian saw two women coming, one half-supporting and half-leading the other. They were both white-haired. Both looked old, but their garments were not rent, and they gazed about them as if the locality was new. The witness below thought she even saw them shrink in a terrified way at the spectacle offered by the hideous assembly they participated in. They were slight reasons to make her heart beat faster, and she draw her attention to them exclusively.

The two remained by the stone for a while. Then they moved slowly, painfully, and with much fear toward the well, where several voices were raised to stop them. Yet they kept on. The one who drew water picked up some pebbles and prepared to drive them back. The company cursed them. The greater company on the hill shouted shrilly, "Unclean, unclean!"

Surely, thought Amrah of the two, as they kept coming, *they are strangers to the language of lepers.*

She arose and went to meet them, taking the basket and jar. The alarm at the well immediately subsided.

"What a fool," one said laughing."What a fool to give good bread to the dead in that way!"

"And to think of her coming so far!" said another. "I would at least make them meet me at the gate."

Amrah, with a better motive, proceeded. What if she should be mistaken! Her heart rose into her throat. And the farther she went the more doubtful and confused she became. Four or five yards from where they stood waiting for her she stopped.

It was the mistress she loved, whose hand she had so often kissed in gratitude, whose image of matronly loveliness she had treasured in memory so faithfully! And there was the Tirzah she had nursed through babyhood, whose pains she had soothed, whose sports she had shared. There was the smiling, sweet-faced, songful Tirzah, the light of the great house, the promised blessing of her old age! Her mistress, her darling—they were like this? The soul of the woman sickened at the sight.

"These are old women," she said to herself. "I never saw them before. I will go back." She turned away.

"Amrah," said one of the lepers.

The Egyptian dropped the jar and looked back, trembling. "Who called me?" she asked.

"Amrah."

The servant's wondering eyes settled on the speaker's face. "Who are you?" she cried.

"We are the ones you are seeking."

Amrah fell upon her knees. "O my mistress! As I have made your God my God, I praise Him because He has led me to you!"

And the poor overwhelmed creature began moving forward upon her knees.

"Stay, Amrah! Do not come not nearer. Unclean, unclean!"

The words were enough. Amrah fell upon her face, sobbing so loud the people at the well heard her. Suddenly she rose on her knees again.

"O my mistress, where is Tirzah?"

"Here I am, Amrah, here! Will you bring me a little water?"

The habits of the servant toward her master returned. Pulling back the coarse hair that had fallen over her face, Amrah arose and went to the basket and uncovered it.

"See," she said, "here are bread and meat."

She would have spread the napkin upon the ground, but the mistress spoke again.

"Do not, Amrah. Those people over there may stone you and refuse us a drink. Leave the basket with me. Take up the jar and fill it and bring it here. We will carry them to the tomb with us. For this day you will then have rendered all the service that is lawful. Hurry, Amrah."

The people who watched all this made way for the servant and even helped her fill the jar, so strong was the grief her face showed.

"Who are they?" a woman asked.

Amrah meekly answered, "They used to be good to me."

Raising the jar upon her shoulder, she hurried back. In forgetfulness she would have gone to them, but the cry "Unclean, unclean! Beware!" stopped her. Placing the water by the basket, she stepped back and stood off a little way.

"Thank you, Amrah," said the mistress, taking the articles into her possession. "This is very good of you."

"Is there nothing more I can do?" asked Amrah.

The mother's hand was upon the jar, and she was feverish with thirst. Yet she paused and, rising, said firmly, "Yes, I know that Judah has come home. I saw him at the gate the night before last, asleep on the step. I saw you wake him."

Amrah clasped her hands. "O my mistress! You saw it and did not come!"

"That would have killed him. I can never take him in my arms again. I can never kiss him anymore. O Amrah, you love him, I know!"

"Yes," said the true heart, bursting into tears again and kneeling. "I would die for him."

"Prove to me what you say, Amrah."

"I am ready."

"Then you shall not tell him where we are or that you have seen us—only that, Amrah."

"But he is looking for you. He has come from afar to find you."

"He must not find us. He shall become what we are. Hear this Amrah. You shall serve us as you have this day. You shall bring us the little we need—not long now—not long. You shall come every morning and evening like this, and"—the voice trembled, the strong will almost broke down—"and you shall tell us of him, Amrah. But you shall say nothing of us to him. Do you hear?"

"Oh, it will be so hard to hear him speak of you and see him going about looking for you—to see all his love and not tell him so much as that you are alive!"

"Can you tell him we are well, Amrah?" The servant bowed her head in her arms.

"No," the mistress continued. "Then be silent altogether. Go now, and come this evening. We will look for you. Till then, farewell."

"The burden will be heavy, mistress, and hard to bear," said Amrah.

"It would be much harder to see him as we are," the mother answered as she gave the basket to Tirzah. "Come again this evening," she repeated, taking up the water and starting for the tomb.

Amrah waited kneeling until they had disappeared. Then she took the road sorrowfully home.

In the evening she returned, and after that it became her custom to serve them in the morning and evening, so that they wanted for nothing that they needed. The tomb, though stony and desolate, was less cheerless than the cell in the Tower had been. Daylight gilded its door, and it was in the beauty of the world. Also one can wait death with so much more faith out under the open sky.

66

A Trick of Pilate's—The Combat

The morning of the first day of October, Ben Hur arose from his couch in the inn dissatisfied with the whole world.

Little time had been lost in discussion upon the arrival of Malluch. He began the search at the Tower of Antonia, searching boldly, by directly inquiring of the commanding tribune. He gave the officer a history of the Hurs and all the particulars of the accident of Gratus, describing the affair as being completely without evil intentions. The object of the quest now, he said, was to the feet of Caesar, if any of the unhappy family were discovered alive to carry a petition, seeking restitution of the estate and the return to their civil rights. Such a petition, he had no doubt, would result in an investigation by the imperial order, a proceeding of which the friends of the family had no fear.

In reply the tribune stated the circumstances of the discovery of the women in the Tower and permitted a reading of the memorandum he had taken of their account of themselves. When he requested a copy, he even permitted that. Malluch then hurried to Ben Hur.

It is useless to attempt a description of the effect the terrible story had upon the young man. The pain was not relieved by tears or passionate outcries. It was too deep for any expression. He sat still for a long time, with a pale face and laboring heart. Now and then, as if to show the thoughts that were most poignant, he muttered, "Lepers, lepers! They—my mother and Tirzah—they are lepers! How long, how long, O Lord?"

One moment he was torn by a virtuous rage of sorrow, the next by a longing for vengeance, which, it must be admitted, was scarcely less virtuous.

Finally he arose. "I must look for them. They may be dying."

"Where will you look?" asked Malluch.

"There is only one place for them to go."

Malluch intervened and finally prevailed, in order to have the planning of the further attempt entrusted to him. Together they went to the gate over on the side opposite the Hill of Evil Counsel, from time immemorial the leper's begging ground. There they stayed all day, giving alms, asking for the two women, and offering rich rewards for their discovery. They did this repeatedly day after day through the remainder of the fifth month and all of the sixth. There was diligent scouring of the dreaded city on the hill by lepers to whom the rewards offered were mighty incentives, for they were only dead as proclaimed in the law. Over and over again the gaping tomb down by the well was invaded and its tenants subjected to inquiry, but they kept their secret secure. The result was failure. And now, the morning of the first day of the seventh month, the extent of the additional information gained was that, not long before, two leprous women had been stoned from the Fish Gate by the authorities. A little pressing for clues, together with some shrewd comparison of dates, led to the sad assurance that the sufferers were the Hurs and left the same old questions darker than ever. Where were they? And what had become of them?

"It was not enough that my people should be made lepers," said the son, with an intense bitterness. "That was not enough. No! They must be stoned from their native city! My mother is dead! She has wandered into the wilderness! Tirzah is dead! I alone am left. And for what? How long, O God, Lord God of my fathers, how long shall this Rome endure?"

Angry, hopeless, and vengeful, he entered the courtyard of the inn and found it crowded with people who had come in during the night. While he ate his breakfast, he listened to some of them. He was specially attracted to one party. They were mostly young, active, and hardy men, with a provincial manner. In their look, a certain indefinable air, there was a spirit that did not belong to the lower orders of Jerusalem, the spirit thought by some to be the peculiar nature of life in mountainous districts, but which may be traced to a life of healthful freedom. He figured they were Galileans, in the city for various purposes, but chiefly to take part in the Feast of Trumpets, set for that day. They were objects of interest, coming from the region in which he hoped to find the ready support in the work he was shortly about to do.

While observing them, his mind thinking ahead of great achievements possible for a legion of such spirits disciplined in the severe Roman style, a man came into the court, his face flushed, his eyes filled with excitement.

"Why are you here?" he said to the Galileans. "The rabbis and elders are going from the Temple to see Pilate. Come, make haste, and let us go with them."

They surrounded him in a moment. "To see Pilate! For what?"

"They have discovered a conspiracy. Pilate's new aqueduct is to be paid for with the money of the Temple."

"What! With the sacred treasure?"

They repeated the question to each other with flashing eyes.

"It is Corban—money belonging to God. Let him touch a shekel of it if he dare!"

"Come," cried the messenger. "The procession is by this time across the bridge. The whole city is following after. We may be needed. Hurry!"

As if the thought and the act were one, there was a quick discarding of useless garments, and the party stood bareheaded and in the short, sleeveless undertunics they were used to wearing as reapers in the field and boatmen on the lake—the garb in which they climbed the hills following the herds and plucked the ripened vintage, careless of the sun. Lingering only to tighten their girdles, they said, "We are ready."

Then Ben Hur spoke to them.

"Men of Galilee," he said, "I am a son of Judah. Will you take me in your company?"

"We may have to fight," they replied.

"Oh, then, I will surely not be the first to run away!"

They accepted the response in good humor, and the messenger said, "You seem brave enough. Come along."

Ben Hur took off his outer garments. "You think there may be fighting?" he asked quietly, as he tightened his girdle.

"Yes."

"With whom?"

"The guard."

"Legionnaires?"

"Who else can a Roman trust?"

"What do you have to fight with?"

They looked at him silently.

"Well," he continued, "we will have to do the best we can, but shouldn't we choose a leader? The legionnaires always have one and are so able to act with one mind."

The Galileans stared more curiously, as if the idea were new to them.

"Let us at least agree to stay together," he said. "Now I am ready, if you are."

"Yes, let us go."

The inn, it should not be forgotten, was in Bezetha, the new town, and to get to the Praetorium, as the Romans fashioned the palace of Herod on Mount Zion, the party had to cross the low-lands north and west of the Temple. By streets running north and south, with intersections hardly up to the dignity of alleys, they passed rapidly around the Akra district to the Tower of Mariamne, where the way was short to the grand gate of the walled heights. In going, they overtook people like themselves stirred to anger by news of the proposed desecration. When finally they reached the gate of the Praetorium, the procession of elders and rabbis had gone in with a great following, leaving a greater crowd clamoring outside.

A centurion watched the entrance with the guard drawn up fully armed under the beautiful marble battlements. The sun struck the soldiers squarely on the helm and shield, but they kept their ranks, indifferent to its dazzle and to the sounds of the rabble. Through the open bronze gates a current of citizens poured in, while a much smaller group poured out.

"What is going on?" one of the Galileans asked one who was leaving.

"Nothing," was the reply. "The rabbis are in front of the door of the palace asking to see Pilate. He refused to come out. They have sent one to tell him they will not go away till he has heard them. They are waiting."

"Let us go in," said Ben Hur in his quiet way, seeing what his companions probably did not—that there was not only a disagreement between the rabbis and the governor but an argument and a serious question as to who would have his will.

Inside the gate there was a row of trees in leaf, with seats under them. The people, whether going or coming, carefully avoided the shade cast gratefully upon the white, clean-swept pavement, for, strange as it may seem, a rabbinical ordinance, alleged to have been derived from the law, permitted no green thing to be grown within the walls of Jerusalem. Even the wise king, it was said, wanting a garden for his Egyptian bride, was constrained to plant it down in the meetingplace of the valleys above En-rogel.

The front of the palace shone through the treetops. Turning to the right, the party proceeded a short distance to a spacious square on the west side where the residence of the governor stood. An excited multitude filled the square. Every face was directed toward a portico built over a broad doorway, which was closed. Under the portico there was another array of legionnaires.

The throng was so close that the friends could not well have advanced if this had been their desire. They therefore remained in the rear, observers of what was going on. Around the portico they could see the high turbans of the rabbis, whose impatience communicated at times to the mass behind them. A cry was heard: "Pilate, if you are a governor, come forth!"

Once a man coming out pushed through the crowd, his face red with anger.

"Israel is of no account here," he said, in a loud voice. "On this holy ground we are no better than dogs of Rome."

"Will he not come out, do you think?"

"Come? Has he not three times refused?"

"What will the rabbis do?"

"As at Caesarea—camp here till he gives them ear."

"He will not dare touch the treasure, will he?" asked one of the Galileans.

"Who can say? Did not a Roman profane the Holy of Holies? Is there anything sacred from Romans?"

An hour passed and, though Pilate gave them no answer, the rabbis and crowd remained. Noon came, bringing a shower from the west, but no change in the situation, except that the multitude was larger and much noisier, and the feeling was more decidedly angry. The shouting was almost continuous. "Come forth!" The cry sometimes had disrespectful words.

Meanwhile Ben Hur held his Galilean friends together. He believed the pride of the Roman would eventually get the better of his discretion and that the end could not be far off. Pilate was only waiting for the people to furnish him an excuse for a resort to violence.

And at last the end came. In the midst of the assembly the sound of blows was heard, followed instantly by yells of pain and rage and a very furious commotion. The venerable men in front of the portico were aghast. The common people in the rear at first pushed forward. In the center, the effort was made to get out. And for a short time the pressure of opposing forces was terrible. A thousand voices made an inquiry, all at once. No one had time to answer, and the surprise speedily became panic.

Ben Hur kept his senses. "You cannot see," he said to one of the Galileans.

"No."

"I will raise you up." He caught the man about the middle and lifted him bodily.

"What is it?"

"I see now," said the man. "There are some armed with clubs, and they are beating the people. They are dressed like Jews."

"Who are they?"

"Romans, as the Lord lives! Romans in disguise. Their clubs fly like flails! There, I saw a rabbi struck down—an old man! They spare nobody!"

Ben Hur let the man down. "Men of Galilee," he said, "it is a trick of Pilate's. Now, if you do what I say, we will get even with the club men."

The Galilean spirit arose. "Yes!" they answered.

"Let us go back to the trees by the gate, and we may find the planting of Herod, though unlawful, has some good in it after all. Come!"

They ran back all of them fast as they could, and, by throwing their united weight upon the limbs, tore them from the trunks. In a brief time they, too, were armed. Returning, at the corner of the square they met the crowd rushing madly for the gate. Behind, the clamor continued—a medley of shrieks and groans.

"To the wall!" Ben Hur shouted. "To the wall! And let the herd go by!"

So, clinging to the masonry at their right hand, they escaped the force of the rush and little by little made headway until, at last, the square was reached.

"Keep together now and follow me!"

By this time Ben Hur's leadership was in full force. As he pushed into the seething mob his party closed ranks. And when the Romans, clubbing the people and enjoying it as they struck them down, came hand to hand with the Galileans, lithe of limb, eager for the fray and equally armed, they were in turn surprised. Then the shouting was close and fierce, the crash of sticks rapid and deadly, the advance furious as hate could make it.

No one performed his part as well as Ben Hur, whose training served him admirably. Not only did he know how to strike and guard, but his long arms, perfect action, and incomparable strength helped him also to success in every encounter. He was at the same time a fighting man and leader. The club he wielded was of good length and weighty, so he only needed to strike a man once. He seemed to have an eye for each combat of his friends and the faculty of being at the right moment exactly where he was most needed. In his fighting cry there was inspiration for his party and alarm for his enemies. Thus surprised and equally matched, the Romans at first retreated but finally turned their backs and fled to the portico. The impetuous Galileans would have pursued them to the steps, but Ben Hur wisely restrained them.

"Stay, my men!" he said. "The centurion yonder is coming with the guard. They have swords and shields. We cannot fight them. We have done well. Let us get back and out of the gate while we may."

They obeyed him, though slowly, for they frequently had to step over their countrymen lying where they had been felled, some writhing and groaning, some praying for help, others mute as the dead. But the fallen were not all Jews. In that there was consolation.

The centurion shouted to them as they went off. Ben Hur laughed at him and replied in his own tongue, "If we are dogs of Israel, you are jackals of Rome. Remain here, and we will come again."

The Galileans cheered and, laughing, went on.

Outside the gate there was a multitude the like of which Ben Hur had never seen, not even in the circus at Antioch. The house-tops, the streets, the slope of the hill, appeared densely covered with people wailing and praying. The air was filled with their cries.

The party was permitted to pass without challenge by the outer guard. But hardly were they out before the centurion in charge at the portico appeared and in the gateway called to Ben Hur, "You, insolent one! Are you a Roman or a Jew?"

Ben Hur answered, "I am a son of Judah, born here. What do you want with me?"

"Stay and fight."

"Singly?"

"As you wish!"

Ben Hur laughed derisively. "O brave Roman! Worthy son of the bastard Roman Jove! I have no arms."

"You will have mine," the centurion answered. "I will borrow from the guard here."

The people in hearing distance of the speech became silent. Only lately Ben Hur had beaten a Roman under the eyes of Antioch. Now he could beat another one under the eyes of Jerusalem, and the honor might be vastly profitable to the cause of the new King. He did not hesitate. Going frankly to the centurion, he said, "I am willing. Lend me your sword and shield."

"And the helm and breastplate?" asked the Roman.

"Keep them. They might not fit me."

The arms were as frankly delivered, and immediately the centurion was ready. All this time the soldiers in rank close by the gate never moved; they simply listened. As to the multitude, only when the combatants advanced to begin the fight the question sped from mouth to mouth, "Who is he?" And no one knew.

Now the Roman supremacy in arms lay in three things—submission to discipline, the legionary formation of battle, and a peculiar use of the short sword. In combat, they never struck or cut. From first to last they thrust—they advanced and retired thrusting, and generally their aim was at the foreman's face. All this was well known to Ben Hur.

As they were about to engage he said, "I told you I was a son of Judah, but I did not tell you that I am Roman-taught. Defend yourself!"

At the last word Ben Hur closed with his antagonist. A moment, standing foot to foot, they glared at each other over the rims of their embossed shields. Then the Roman pushed forward and feinted an underthrust. The Jew laughed at him. A thrust at the face followed. The Jew stepped lightly to the left. Quick as the thrust was, the step was quicker. Under the lifted arm of the foe he slid his shield, advancing it until the sword and sword-arm were both caught on its upper surface. Another step, this time forward and left, and the man's whole right side was offered to the point. The centurion fell heavily on his breast, clanging upon the pavement, and Ben Hur had won. With his foot upon his enemy's back, he raised his shield overhead, a gladiatorial custom, and saluted the impassive soldiers at the gate.

When the people realized the victory, they went mad. On the houses far as the Xystus, fast as the word could fly, they waved their shawls and handkerchiefs and shouted. If he had consented, the Galileans would have carried Ben Hur off upon their shoulders.

To a petty officer who then advanced from the gate he said, "Your comrade died like a soldier. I leave him unspoiled. Only his sword and shield are mine."

With that he walked away. He spoke to the Galileans off a little, "Brethren, you have behaved well. Let us now separate, lest we be pursued. Meet me tonight at the inn in Bethany. I have something to propose to you of great interest to Israel."

"Who are you?" they asked him.

"A son of Judah," he answered simply.

A throng eager to see him surged around the party.

"Will you come to Bethany?" he asked.

"Yes, we will come."

"Then bring with you this sword and shield, that I may know you." Pushing brusquely through the increasing crowd, he speedily disappeared.

At the insistence of Pilate, the people went up from the city and carried away their dead and wounded, and there was great mourning for them. But their grief was greatly lightened by the victory of the unknown champion, who was sought everywhere and extolled by every one. The faint spirit of the nation was revived by his brave deed. In the streets and even up in the Temple, amidst the solemnities of the feast, old tales of the Maccabees were told again, and thousands shook their heads, whispering wisely, "A little longer, brethren, and Israel will come to her own. Let there be faith in the Lord, and patience."

In this way Ben Hur obtained leadership over many in Galilee and paved the way to greater services in the cause of the King who was coming.

67

Jerusalem Goes Out to a Prophet

The meeting took place in the inn of Bethany as planned. From there Ben Hur went with the Galileans into their country, where his exploits in the old marketplace gave him fame and influence. Before the winter was over, he raised three legions and organized them similar to the Roman pattern. He could have had as many more, for the martial spirit of that gallant people never slept. The task, however, required careful secrecy from both Rome and Herod Antipas.

Contenting himself for the present with the three, he attempted to train and educate them for battle. For that purpose he carried the officers over into the lava beds of Trachonitis and taught them the use of arms, particularly the javelin and sword and the maneuvering peculiar to the Roman legionary formation. Later he sent them home as teachers. And soon the training became a pastime of the people.

As may be realized, the task called for patience, skill, zeal, and faith on his part—qualities that inspire others—and a man never possessed them in greater degree or used them to better effect. How he labored! And with utter denial of self! Yet with all this he would have failed but for the support he had from Simonides, who provided him with arms and money, and from Ilderim, who kept watch and brought supplies. And still he would have failed except for the genius of the Galileans.

Four tribes were under that name—Asher, Zebulon, Issachar, and Napthali—and the districts originally set apart for them. The Jew born in sight of the Temple despised their brethren of the north, but the Talmud itself has said, "The Galilean loves honor and the Jew money."

Hating Rome as fervently as they loved their own country, in every revolt they were first in the field and last to leave it. One hundred fifty thousand Galilean youths perished in the final war with Rome. For the great festal days they went up to Jerusalem marching and camping like armies. Yet they were even tolerant to heathenism. In Herod's beautiful cities, which were Roman in all things, in Sepphoris and Tiberias especially, they took pride, and in building them they gave their loyal support. They had for fellow citizens men from the outside world everywhere and lived in peace with them. To the glory of the Hebrew name they contributed poets such as the singer of the Song of Songs and prophets like Hosea.

To a people so proud, brave, devoted, and imaginative, a tale like the coming of the King was all-powerful. That he was coming to put down Rome would have been sufficient to enlist them in the scheme proposed by Ben Hur. But when, besides, they were assured he was to rule the world, more mighty than Caesar, more magnificent than Solomon, and that the rule was to last forever, the appeal was irresistible, and they joined themselves to the cause, body and soul.

They asked Ben Hur where he received his authority for the sayings, and he quoted the prophets and told them of Balthasar in waiting over in Antioch. And they were satisfied, for it was the old much-loved legend of the Messiah, familiar to them almost as the name of the Lord, the long-cherished dream with a time set for its realization. The King was not merely coming now; he was at hand.

The winter months rolled by for Ben Hur, and spring came, with glad showers blown over the summering sea in the west. By that time he had toiled so earnestly and successfully that he could say to himself and his followers, "Let the good King come. He has only to tell us where he will have his throne set up. We have the swords to keep it for him."

And in all his dealings with the many men, they knew him only as a son of Judah and by that name.

One evening, over in Trachonitis, Ben Hur was sitting with some of his Galileans at the mouth of the cave in which he was stationed, when an Arab courier rode to him and delivered a letter. Breaking the package, he read:

Jerusalem, Nisan IV

A prophet has appeared who men say is Elias. He has been in the wilderness for years, and to our eyes he is a prophet. And so is his speech. He has a burden for one much greater than himself, who, he says, is to come soon and for whom he is now waiting on the eastern shore of the River Jordan. I have been to see and hear him, and the one he is waiting for is certainly the King you are awaiting. Come and judge for yourself.

All Jerusalem is going out to the prophet. The many people on the shore where he lives appear to be like Mount Olivet in the last days of the Passover.

Malluch

Ben Hur's face flushed with joy. "By this word, my friends," he said, "our waiting is at end. The herald of the King has appeared and announced him." Upon hearing the letter read, they also rejoiced at the promise it held out.

"Get ready now," he added, "and in the morning set your faces homeward. When you have arrived there, send word to those under you and bid them to be ready to assemble as I may direct. For myself and you, I will go see if the King is indeed at hand and send you a report. Let us, in the meantime, live in the pleasure of the promise."

Going into the cave, he addressed a letter to Ilderim and another to Simonides, giving notice of the news received and of his purpose to go up immediately to Jerusalem. He dispatched the letters by swift messengers. When night fell, and the stars providing direction came out, he mounted and with an Arab guide set out for the Jordan, intending to find the track of the caravans between Rabbath-Ammon and Damascus.

The guide was sure and Aldebaran swift. By midnight the two were out and speeding southward.

68

Nooning by the Pool—Iras

It was Ben Hur's purpose to turn aside at the break of day and find a safe place in which to rest. But dawn overtook him while out in the desert, and he kept on, the guide promising to bring him after a while to a valley shut in by great rocks, where there was a spring, some mulberry trees, and food in plenty for the horses.

As he rode, thinking of the wondrous events so soon to happen and of the changes they were to bring about in the affairs of men and nations, the guide, always on the alert, called attention to the appearance of strangers behind them. Everywhere around the desert stretched away in waves of sand, slowly yellowing in the growing light and with no green thing visible. Over on the left, but still far off, a range of low mountains extended. In the vacancy of such a waste an object in motion could not long continue to be a mystery.

"It is a camel with riders," the guide said, directly.

"Are there any others behind?" said Ben Hur.

"It is alone. No, there is a man on horseback—the driver, probably."

A little later Ben Hur himself could see that the camel was white and unusually large, reminding him of the wonderful animal he had seen bring Balthasar and Iras to the fountain in the Grove of Daphne. There could be no other like it. Thinking then of the fair Egyptian, his stride became slower and finally fell into a trot, until finally he could discern a curtained tent and two persons seated within it.

What if they were Balthasar and Iras! Should he make himself known to them? But it could not be. This was the desert—and they were alone. But while he debated the question the long swinging stride of the camel brought its riders up to him. He heard the ringing of the tiny bells and saw the rich housings that had been so

393

attractive to the crowd at the Castalian fount. He also saw the Ethiopian, always attendant upon the Egyptians. The tall camel stopped close by his horse, and Ben Hur, looking up, saw Iras herself under the raised curtain looking down at him, her great swimming eyes bright with astonishment.

"The blessing of the true God upon you!" said Balthasar.

"And to you and yours be the peace of the Lord," Ben Hur replied.

"My eyes are weak with years," said Balthasar, "but they approve of that son of Hur whom lately I knew as an honored guest in the tent of Ilderim the Generous."

"And you are that Balthasar, the wise Egyptian, whose speech concerning holy things in expectation is having so much to do with finding me in this desert place. What are you doing here?"

"He is never alone who is where God is—and God is everywhere," Balthasar answered, gravely. "But in the sense of your meaning, there is a caravan a short way behind us going to Alexandria. And as it is to pass through Jerusalem, I thought it best to seek its company as far as the Holy City, where I am going.

"This morning, however, discontented with its slow movement—slower because of a Roman cohort accompanying it—we rose early and got this far in advance. We are not afraid of robbers along the way, for I have here a seal of Sheik Ilderim. Against beasts of prey, God is our sufficient trust."

Ben Hur bowed and said, "The good sheik's seal is a safeguard wherever the wilderness extends, and the lion shall be swift that overtakes this king of his kind."

He patted the neck of the camel as he spoke.

"Yet," said Iras, with a smile, which the youth noticed, whose eyes had turned several times to her during the exchanges with the elder, "yet even he would be better if he would break his fast. Kings have hunger and headaches. If you are indeed the Ben Hur of whom my father has spoken, and whom it was my pleasure to have known as well, you will be willing, I am sure, to show us some path near to living water, that with its sparkle we may grace a morning's meal in the desert."

Ben Hur hastened to answer. "Fair Egyptian, I give you my

sympathy. If you can bear suffering a little longer, we will find the spring you ask for, and I promise that its draught shall be as sweet and cooling as that of the more famous Castalia. With you permission, we will make haste."

"I give you the blessing of the thirsty," she replied, "and offer you in return a bit of bread from the city ovens, dipped in fresh butter from the dewy meadows of Damascus."

"A most rare favor. Let us go on."

Having said this, Ben Hur rode forward with his guide, but one of the inconveniences of traveling with camels is that it interrupts polite conversation.

After a while the party came to a shallow streambed, which was somewhat soft from recent rains and steep in its descent. Momentarily, it widened, and the sides became bluffs ribbed with rocks scarred by floods rushing to the lower depths ahead. Finally, from a narrow passage the travelers entered a spreading vale that was very delightful. The water channels wound here and there, defined by crisp white shingling and appearing like threads tangled among islands green with grasses and fringed with reeds. The bases of the boundary walls were cloaked with clambering vines, and under a leaning cliff over on the left the mulberry grove had planted itself, disclosing the spring that the party was seeking. There the guide conducted them, careless of the whistling partridges and lesser birds of brighter hues who were roused from the reedy undergrowth.

The water started from a crack in the cliff that some loving hand had enlarged into an arched cavity. Graven over it in bold Hebraic letters was the word *God*. The engraver had no doubt drunk there and tarried many days and given thanks in that durable form. From the arch the stream ran merrily over a flag spotted with bright moss and leaped into a glassy, clear pool. From there it stole away between grassy banks, nursing the trees before it vanished in the thirsty sand. A few narrow paths were noticeable around the margin of the pool; otherwise the space around was untrodden turf.

The horses were then turned loose, and from the kneeling camel the Ethiopian assisted Balthasar and Iras. The old man, turning his face to the east, crossed his hands reverently upon his breast and prayed.

"Bring me a cup," Iras said, with some impatience.

From the seat on the camel the slave brought her a crystal goblet. Then she said to Ben Hur, "I will be your servant at the fountain."

They walked to the pool together. He would have dipped the water for her, but she refused his offer and, kneeling, held the cup to be filled by the stream itself. Still not content, when it was cooled and overrunning, she offered him the first drink.

"No," he said, putting the graceful hand aside and seeing only the large eyes half-hidden beneath the arches of the upraised brows, "allow the service to be mine, I pray."

She persisted in having her way. "In my country, son of Hur, we have a saying, 'Better a cupbearer to the fortunate than a minister to a king.'"

"Fortunate!" he said.

There was both surprise and inquiry in the tone of his voice and in his look, and she said quickly, "The gods give us success as a sign by which we may know them to be on our side. Were you not a winner in the circus?"

His cheeks began to flush.

"That was one sign, and there is another. In a combat with swords, you slew a Roman."

His embarrassment deepened—not so much for the triumphs themselves as for the flattery in the fact that she had followed his career with interest. A moment, and the pleasure was followed by a reflection. The combat, he knew, was well known throughout the East, but the name of the victor had been given to a very few—Malluch, Ilderim, and Simonides. Could they have made a confidante of the woman? So he was confused.

Seeing it, she arose and holding the cup over the pool, said, "O gods of Egypt! I thank you for a discovered hero—thanks that the victim in the Palace of Idernee was not my king of men. And so, holy gods, I pour and drink."

She returned to the stream part of the contents of the cup. The rest she drank. When she took the crystal from her lips, she laughed at him.

"O son of Hur, is it a fashion of the very brave to be so easily overcome by a woman? Take the cup now, and see if you cannot find a happy word in it for me!"

He took the cup and stood to refill it.

"A son of Israel has no gods whom he can drink to," he said, playing with the water to hide his amazement. What more did the Egyptian know about him? Had she been told of his relations with Simonides? And there was the treaty with Ilderim—had she knowledge of that also? He was filled with mistrust. Somebody had betrayed his secrets, and they were serious. And, besides, he was going to Jerusalem, the place where such intelligence possessed by an enemy might be most dangerous to him, his associates, and the cause. But was she an enemy?

When the cup was fairly cooled, he filled it and arose, saying, with affected indifference, "Most fair, were I an Egyptian or a Greek or a Roman, I would say"—he raised the goblet overhead as he spoke—"You better gods! I give thanks that there are still left to the world, despite its wrongs and sufferings, the charm of beauty and the combat of love, and I drink to her who best represents them—to Iras, loveliest of the daughters of the Nile!"

She laid her hand softly upon his shoulder.

"You have offended against the law. The gods you have drunk to are false gods. Shall I not tell the rabbis on you?"

"Oh," he replied, laughing, "that is very little to tell for one who knows so much else that is really important."

"I will go further—I will go to the little Jewess who makes the roses grow and the shadows flame in the house of the great merchant over in Antioch. To the rabbis I will accuse you of lack of remorse. To her—"

"Well, to her?"

"I will repeat what you have said to me under the lifted cup, with the gods for witnesses."

He was still a moment, as if waiting for the Egyptian to go on. With his imagination he saw Esther at her father's side listening to the letters he had forwarded—sometimes reading them. In her presence he had told Simonides of the story of the affair in the Palace of Idernee. She and Iras were acquainted. This one was shrewd and worldly; the other was simple and affectionate and therefore easily won. Simonides could not have broken faith—nor Ilderim—for even if not bound by honor, there was no one, unless it might be himself, to whom the consequences of exposure were more serious and certain. Could Esther have been the Egyptian's informant? He did not accuse her, yet a suspicion was sown with the thought. Before he could think through this completely, Balthasar came to the pool.

"We are greatly indebted to you, son of Hur," he said, in his grave manner. "This vale is very beautiful. The grass, the trees, the shade invite us to stay and rest, and the spring here has the sparkle of diamonds in motion and sings to me of a loving God. It is not enough to thank you for the enjoyment we find. Come, sit with us and taste our bread."

"Allow me first to serve you."

With that Ben Hur filled the goblet and gave it to Balthasar, who lifted his eyes in thanksgiving.

Immediately the slave brought napkins, and after washing their hands and drying them, the three seated themselves in Eastern style under the tent that years before had served the Wise Men at the meeting in the desert. And they ate heartily of the good things taken from the camel's pack.

69

The Life of a Soul

The tent was cozily beneath a tree where the gurgle of the stream was constantly within hearing. Overhead the broad leaves hung motionless on their stems. The delicate reed stalks off in the pearly haze stood up arrow straight. Occasionally a home-returning bee shot humming near the shade, and a partridge, creeping from the pond, drank, whistled to his mate, and ran away. The restfulness of the vale, the freshness of the air, the garden beauty seemed to have affected the spirits of the elder Egyptian. His whole manner was unusually gentle, and as often as he bent his eyes upon Ben Hur conversing with Iras, they softened with pity.

"When we overtook you, son of Hur," he said, at the conclusion of the meal, "it seemed your face was also turned toward Jerusalem. May I ask, without offense, if you are going so far?"

"I am going to the Holy City."

"For the need to spare myself prolonged toil, I will further ask you, Is there a shorter road than that by way of Rabbath-Ammon?"

"A rougher route, but shorter, lies by Geresa and Rabbath-Gilead. It is the one I plan to take."

"I am impatient," said Balthasar. "Lately my sleep has been visited by dreams—or rather by the same dream in repetition. A voice—it is nothing more—comes and tells me, 'Hurry, arise! He whom you have so long awaited is at hand.'"

"You mean he that is to be King of the Jews?" Ben Hur asked, gazing at the Egyptian in wonder.

"Even so."

"Then you have heard nothing of him?"

"Nothing, except the words of the voice in the dream."

"Here, then, are tidings to make you as glad as they made me." From his gown Ben Hur drew the letter he received from Malluch.

The hand the Egyptian held out trembled violently. He read aloud, and as he read his feelings intensified. The limp veins in his neck swelled. At the conclusion he raised his suffused eyes in thanksgiving and prayer. He asked no questions, yet had no doubts.

"You have been very good to me, O God," he said. "Let me, I pray you, see the Savior again and worship him, and your servant will be ready to go in peace."

The words, the manner, and the fervor of the simple prayer touched Ben Hur with a sensation new and abiding. God never seemed so actual and so nearby. It was as if He were there bending over them or sitting at their side—a Friend whose favors were to be had by the most unceremonious asking—a Father to whom all His children were alike in love—Father, not more of the Jew than of the Gentile—the universal Father, who needed no intermediates, no rabbis, priests, or teachers. The idea that such a God might send mankind a Savior instead of a king appeared to Ben Hur in a new light and so plain that he could almost discern both the greater need of such a gift and its consistency with the nature of such a Deity. So he could not resist asking, "Now that he has come, O Balthasar, you still think he is to be a Savior and not a king?"

Balthasar gave him a look as thoughtful as it was tender.

"How shall I understand you?" he asked, in return. "The Spirit, which was the star that was my guide of old, has not appeared to me since I met you in the tent of the good sheik. That is to say, I have not seen or heard it as I formerly did. I believe the voice that spoke to me in my dreams was it, but other than that I have no revelation."

"I will recall the difference between us," said Ben Hur, with deference. "You were of the opinion that he would be a king, but not as Caesar is. You thought his sovereignty would be spiritual, not of the world."

"Oh, yes," the Egyptian answered; "and I am of the same opinion now. I see the divergence in our faith. You are going to meet a king of men, I am going to meet a Savior of souls."

He paused with the look often seen when people are struggling, with great effort, to disentangle a thought that is either too high for quick discernment or too subtle for simple expression.

"Let me try, o son of Hur," he said directly, "and help you to a clearer understanding of my belief. Then it may be, seeing how the spiritual kingdom I expect him to set up can be more excellent in every sense than anything of mere caesarean splendor, you will better understand the reason of the interest I take in the mysterious person we are going to welcome.

"I cannot tell you when the idea of a soul in every man had its origin. Most likely the first parents brought it with them out of the garden in which they had their first dwelling. We all know, however, that it has never entirely perished from our minds. Some nations lost it entirely, but not all. In some ages it dulled and faded. In others it was overwhelmed with doubts, but in great goodness God kept sending us at times mighty intellects and prophets to reassure us back to faith and hope.

"Why should there be a soul in every man? Look, son of Hur, at the necessity of such a device. To lie down and die and be no more forever—time never was when man wished for such an end. Nor has the man ever lived who did not in his heart hope for something better. The monuments of the nations are all protests against nothingness after death. So are statues and their inscriptions.

"So is history. The greatest of our Egyptian kings had his effigy cut out of a hill of solid rock. Day after day he went with a host in chariots to see the work. At last it was finished. Never was an effigy so grand and so enduring. It looked like him—the features were his, faithful even to his expression. Now we may think of him saying in that moment of pride, 'Let Death come. There is an afterlife for me!' He had his wish. The statue is there still.

"But what is the afterlife he secured? Only a recollection by men—a glory unsubstantial as moonshine on the brow of the great bust, a story in stone—nothing more. Meantime, what has become of the king? There is an embalmed body up in the royal tombs that once was his—an effigy not so fair to look at as the other out in the desert. But where, son of Hur, where is the king himself? Is he fallen into nothingness? Two thousand years have gone since he was a man alive as you and I are. Was his last breath the end of him?

"To say yes would be to accuse God. Let us rather accept His better plan of attaining life after death for us—actual life, I mean—something more than a place in mortal memory, life with

401

movement, sensation, knowledge, power, and all appreciation, life eternal, though it may be with changes of our condition. You ask what God's plan is? The gift of a soul to each of us at birth, with His simple law—there shall be no immortality except through the soul. In that law we see the necessity of which I spoke.

"See me as I am—weak, weary, old, shrunken in body. Look at my wrinkled face, think of my failing senses, listen to my high-pitched voice. What happiness to me is the promise that when the tomb opens, as soon it will, to receive the wornout husk I call myself, the now viewless doors of the universe, which is but the palace of God, will swing wide to receive me, a liberated, immortal soul!

"I wish I could tell of the ecstasy there must be in that life to come! Do not say I know nothing about it. This much I know, and it is enough for me—the being of a soul implies conditions of divine superiority. In such a being there is no dust, nor any impure thing. It must be finer than air, more impalpable than light, purer than essence—it is life in absolute purity.

"What now, son of Hur? Knowing so much, shall I dispute with myself or you about the unnecessaries—about the form of my soul? Or where it is to abide? Or whether it eats or drinks? Or is winged, or wears this or that? No. It is more important to trust in God. Everything beautiful in this world is all from His hand, declaring the perfection of taste. He is the author of all form. He clothes the lily, He colors the rose, He distills the dewdrop, He makes the music of nature. In a word, He prepared us for this life and imposed its conditions. They are such a guarantee to me that, trustful as a little child, I leave to Him the formation of my soul and every arrangement for the life after death. I know He loves me."

The good man stopped and drank, and the hand carrying the cup to his lips trembled.

Both Iras and Ben Hur shared his emotion and remained silent. A light was breaking upon Ben Hur. He was beginning to see, as never before, that there might be a spiritual kingdom of more import to men than any earthly empire and that after all a Savior would indeed be a more godly gift than the greatest king.

"I might ask you now," said Balthasar, continuing, "whether this human life, so troubled and brief, is preferable to the perfect and everlasting life designed for the soul? But take the question, and think of it for yourself, formulating this: Supposing both to be equally happy, is one hour more desirable than one year? From that thought then advance to the final question, What are seventy years on earth compared to all eternity with God? By and by, son of Hur, thinking in this way, you will be filled with the meaning of the fact I present to you next, to me the most amazing of all events and in its effects the most sorrowful it is that the very idea of life as a soul is a light almost gone out in the world. Here and there, to be sure, a philosopher may be found who will talk to you of a soul, likening it to a principle. But because philosophers take nothing upon faith, they will not go the length of admitting a soul to be a being, and on that account its purpose is compressed darkness to them.

"By the sign as I see it, God meant to make us to know ourselves created for another and a better life, being in fact the greatest need of our nature. But into what a habit the nations have fallen! They live for the day, as if the present were everything, and go about saying, 'There is no tomorrow after death, or, if there is, since we know nothing about it, it is a care unto itself.' So when Death calls them, 'Come,' they may not enter into enjoyment of the glorious afterlife because of their unfitness. That is to say, the ultimate happiness of man was everlasting life in the society of God.

"For my part, speaking with the holiness of truth, I would not give one hour of life as a soul for a thousand years of life as a man."

Here the Egyptian seemed to become unconscious of companionship and spoke of philosophical questions.

"This life has its problems," he said, "and there are men who spend their days trying to solve them. But what are they compared to the problems of the hereafter? What can be compared to knowing God? God, who lined the void with shores and lit the darkness and out of nothing appointed the universe. All places would be opened. I would be filled with divine knowledge. I would see all glories, taste all delights. I would revel in this state. And, if at the end of the hour, it should please God to tell me, 'I take you into

My service forever,' the furthest limit of desire would be passed, after which the attainable ambitions of this life and its joys of whatever kind would only be like the tinkling of little bells." Balthasar paused to recover from the great ecstasy of this feeling.

And to Ben Hur it seemed the speech had been the delivery of a sublime soul speaking for itself.

"I ask your pardon, son of Hur," the good man continued, with a bow. The gravity of his speech was relieved by the tender look that followed it. "I meant to leave the life of a soul and its conditions and pleasures to your own reflection. The joy of the thought has caused much speech. I set out to show, though ever so humbly, the reason for my faith. It grieves me that words are so weak. But you will discover the truth.

"Consider first the excellence of the existence that is reserved for us after death, and give heed to the feelings that the thought is sure to awaken in you—because they are your own soul stirring, doing what it can to urge you to go the right way. Consider next that the afterlife has become so obscured as to justify calling it a lost light. If you find it, rejoice, son of Hur—rejoice as I do, though at a loss for words. For then, besides the great gift that is to be given to us, you will have found the need of a Savior so infinitely greater than the need of a king, and the one we are going to meet will no longer be to you a warrior with a sword or a monarch with a crown.

"How shall we know him by sight? If you continued in your belief as to his character—that he is to be a king as Herod was—of course, you will keep on until you meet a man clothed in purple and with a scepter. On the other hand, the one I look for will be poor, humble, undistinguished—a man appearing as other men, and the sign by which I will know him will be never so simple. He will offer to show me and all mankind the way to eternal life—the beautiful, pure Life of the soul."

The company sat a moment in silence, which was broken by Balthasar.

"Let us arise now," he said, "and go forward again. What I have said has caused in me a return of an impatience to see him who is always in my thought, and if I seem to hurry you, O son of Hur—and you, my daughter—that is my excuse."

At his signal the slave brought them wine in a skin bottle. They poured it and drank and, shaking out the lap-cloths, arose.

While the slave restored the tent and wares to the box, and the Arab brought up the horses, the three washed themselves in the pool.

In a little while they were retracing their steps, intending to overtake the caravan if it had passed them by.

70

Ben Hur Keeps Watch with Iras

The caravan, stretched out upon the desert, was picturesque. As it moved, however, it was like a lazy serpent. By and by its stubborn dragging became intolerable to Balthasar, patient as he was, so at his suggestion the party determined to go on by themselves.

Ben Hur found a certain charm in Iras's presence. If she looked down upon him from her high place, he made haste to get near her. If she spoke to him, his heart beat rapidly. The desire to please her was a constant impulse. Even common objects on the way became interesting the moment she called attention to them. A black swallow in the air that she pointed to went off in a halo. If a bit of quartz or a flash of mica was seen to sparkle in the drab sand under the sun, at a word he turned aside and brought it to her. And if she threw it away in disappointment, far from thinking of the trouble he had been put to, he was sorry it proved so worthless and kept a lookout for something better—a ruby, perhaps a diamond. So the purple of the far mountains became intensely deep and rich if she called attention to it with an exclamation of praise. And when, now and then, the curtain of the tent fell down, it seemed a sudden dullness had dropped from the sky, shrouding all the landscape. Disposed to be this way, yielding to her sweet influence, what shall save him from the dangers there are of close companionship with the fair Egyptian on the solitary journey they were embarking upon?

For there is no logic in love, nor the least mathematical certainty. It is simply inevitable that she shall shape the end result who wields the greatest influence.

There were signs, too, that Iras knew well the influence she was exercising over him. From some place among her belongings she had earlier in the morning drawn a covering of golden coins and adjusted it so that the gleaming strings fell over her forehead and upon her cheeks, blending lustrously with her flowing blue-black hair. From the same safe deposit she had also produced articles of jewelry—rings for her fingers and ears, bracelets, a necklace of pearls—also, a shawl embroidered with threads of fine gold—which she softened with a scarf of Indian lace skillfully folded about her throat and shoulders.

And so arrayed, she plied Ben Hur with countless pleasantries of speech and manner, showering him with smiles, laughing in flutelike sounds—and all the while following him with glances, now melting tenderly, now sparkling bright. By this kind of play Marc Antony forfeited his glory, yet she who brought about his ruin was really not half so beautiful as her countrywoman.

Noon came to them and then the evening. The sun, going down behind a spur of the old Bashan, left the party halted by a pool of clear water out in the Abilene Desert. There the tent was pitched, the supper eaten, and preparations made for the night.

The second watch was Ben Hur's. He was standing with his spear in hand, within arm's reach of the dozing camel, looking now and again at the stars covering the veiled land. The stillness was intense. Only after long spells a warm breath of wind would blow past, but without disturbing him, for still he entertained thoughts of the Egyptian, remembering her charms, wondering and debating how she came by his secrets, the uses she might make of them, and the course he should pursue with her. And through all the debate Love stood off only a short distance—a strong temptation.

At the very moment he was most inclined to yield to the allurement, a very fair hand even in the moonless gleaming was laid softly upon his shoulder. The touch thrilled him. He started, turned—and she was there.

"I thought you were asleep," he said presently.

"Sleep is for old people and little children, and I came out to look at my friends, the stars of the south—those now holding the curtains of midnight over the Nile. But confess that you are surprised!"

He took the hand that had fallen from his shoulder and said, "Well, was it by an enemy?"

"Oh, no! To be an enemy is to hate, and hating is a sickness that Isis will not allow to come near me. She kissed me, you should know, on the heart when I was a child."

"Your speech does not sound in the least like your father's. Are you not of his faith?"

"I might have been"—she laughed low—"I might have been had I seen what he has. I may be when I get old like him. There should be no religion for youth, only poetry and philosophy, and no poetry except that which is the inspiration of wine and mirth and love, and no philosophy that does not give an excuse for follies that cannot outlive a season. My father's God is too awful for me. I failed to find Him in the Grove of Daphne. He was never heard of as present in the courts of Rome. But, son of Hur, I have a wish."

"A wish! Where is he who could say no to it?"

"I will try you."

"Tell it then."

"It is very simple. I wish to help you." She drew closer as she spoke.

He laughed and replied lightly, "O Egypt! I came near saying dear Egypt! Does not the sphinx abide in your country?"

"Well?"

"You are one of its riddles. Be merciful, and give me a little clue to help me understand you. In what do I need help? And how can you help me?"

She took her hand from him and, turning to the camel, spoke to it endearingly and patted its large head as if it were a thing of beauty.

"O you last and swiftest and stateliest of the herds of Job! Sometimes you, too, go stumbling because the way is rough and stony and the burden is grievous. How is it that you know the kind intent by a word and always answer me gratefully, though the help offered is from a woman? I will kiss you, you royal brute!" She stooped and touched the camel's broad forehead with her lips, saying immediately, "Because in your intelligence there is no suspicion!"

Ben Hur, restraining himself, said calmly, "The reproach has not failed its mark, Egypt! I seem to say no. May it not be because I am under the seal of honor and by my silence cover the lives and fortunes of others?"

"May be!" she said, quickly. "It is so."

He shrank a step and asked, his voice sharp with amazement, "What do you know?"

She answered, after a laugh, "Why do men deny that the senses of women are sharper than theirs? Your face has been under my eyes all day. I had but to look at it to see you bore some weight in your mind, and, to find the weight, what had I to do more than recall your debates with my father? Son of Hur"—she lowered her voice and, going nearer, spoke so that her breath was warm upon his cheek—"son of Hur! He you are going to find is to be the King of the Jews, is he not?"

His heart beat fast and hard.

"A King of the Jews like Herod, only greater," she continued.

He looked away into the night, up to the stars. Then his eyes met hers and lingered there. And her breath was on his lips, she was so near.

"Since morning," she said, further, "we have been having visions. Now if I tell you mine, will you serve me as well? What! Silent still?"

She pushed his hand away and turned as if to go, but he caught her and said eagerly, "Stay—stay and speak!"

She went back and, with her hand upon his shoulder, leaned against him. And he put his arm around her and drew her close, very close. In the caress was the promise she asked.

"Speak, and tell me your visions, dear Egypt! A prophet—no, not the Tishbite, not even the Lawgiver—could have refused a request of yours. I am at your will. Be merciful—merciful, I pray."

The entreaty passed apparently unheard, for looking up and nestling in his embrace, she said, slowly, "The vision that followed me was of magnificent war—war on land and sea—with clashing of arms and rush of armies, as if Caesar and Pompey had come again, and Octavius and Antony. A cloud of dust and ashes arose and covered the world, and Rome was not there anymore. All dominion returned to the East. Out of the cloud came another race of heroes, and there were vast domains and brighter crowns for giving away than were ever known. And, son of Hur, while the vision was passing, and after it was gone, I kept asking myself, 'What shall he not have who served the King earliest and best?'"

Again Ben Hur recoiled. The question was the very question that had been with him all day. Then he fancied he had the clue he wanted.

"So," he said, "I have you now. The domains and crowns are the things you would help me obtain. I see! And there never was such a queen as you would be, so shrewd, so beautiful, so royal—never! But, dear Egypt! By the vision as you describe it to me the prizes are all of war, and you are but a woman, though Isis did kiss you on the heart. And crowns are starry gifts beyond your power of help unless, indeed, you have a way to make them more certain than that of the sword. If so, Egypt, show it to me, and I will walk in it, if only for your sake."

She removed his arm and said, "Spread your cloak upon the sand—here, so I can rest against the camel. I will sit and tell you a story that came down the Nile to Alexandria, where I had it."

He did as she said, first planting the spear in the ground near by.

"And what shall I do?" he asked, when she was seated. "In Alexandria is it customary for the listeners to sit or stand?"

From the comfortable place where she was seated she answered, laughing, "The audiences of storytellers are willful, and sometimes they do as they please."

Without more ado he stretched himself upon the sand and put her arm about his neck.

"I am ready," he said. And immediately she began.

How the Beautiful Came to the Earth

You must know, in the first place, that Isis was—and, for that matter, she may yet be—the most beautiful of deities, and Osiris, her husband, though wise and powerful, was sometimes stung with jealousy of her, for only in their loves are the gods like mortals.

The palace of the Divine Wife was of silver, crowning the tallest mountain in the moon, and from there she passed often to the sun, in the heart of which, a source of eternal light, Osiris kept his palace of gold, too bright for man to look at.

One time—there are no days with the gods—while she was pleasantly with him on the roof of the golden palace, she chanced to look, and afar, just on the edge of the universe, saw Indra passing with an army of simians, all carried upon the backs of flying eagles. He, the

410

Friend of Living Things—this Indra is called with much love—was returning from his final war with the hideous Rakshakas—returning victorious, and in his suite were Rama, the hero, and Sita, his bride, who next to Isis herself was the most beautiful.

And Isis arose and took off her girdle of stars and waved it to Sita—waved it in glad salute. And instantly, between the marching host and the two on the golden roof, night fell and shut out the view. But it was not night—only the frown of Osiris.

Now Isis had eyes large as those of the white cow that in the temple eats sweet grasses from the hands of the faithful even while they say their prayers. And her eyes were the color of the cow's and quite as tender. She arose and said, smiling as she spoke, so that her look was little more than the glow of the moon in the hazy harvest month, "Farewell, my good lord. You will call me soon, I know, for without me you cannot make the perfectly happy creature of which you were thinking, any more"—and she stopped to laugh, knowing well the truth of the saying—"any more, my lord, than you yourself can be perfectly happy without me."

"We will see," he said.

And she went her way and took her needles and her chair and sat watching and knitting on the roof of the silver palace .

And the will of Osiris, at labor of his mighty breast, was as the sound of the mills of all the other gods grinding at once, so loud that the near stars rattled like seeds in a parched pod. Some dropped out and were lost. And while the sound kept on she waited and knitted. She did not lose a stitch the entire time.

Soon a spot appeared in the space over toward the sun, and it grew until it was as great as the moon, and then she knew a world was intended. But when, growing and growing, at last it cast her planet in the shade, all except the little point lighted by her presence, she knew how very angry he was. Yet she continued to knit, assured that the end would be as she had said.

And the earth came into being, at first only a cold gray mass hanging listless in the hollow void. Later she saw it separate into divisions—here a plain, there a mountain, yonder a sea, all still without a sparkle. And then, by a riverbank, something moved, and she stopped her knitting in wonder. The something arose and lifted its hands to the sun in sign of knowledge of where it had its being. And this First Man was beautiful to see. And about him were the creations we call nature—the grass, the trees, birds, beasts, even the insects and reptiles.

And for a time the man went about happy in his life. It was easy to see how happy he was. And in the lull of the sound of his laboring Isis heard a scornful laugh and soon the words, blown across from the sun, "Your help, indeed! Here is a creature who is perfectly happy!"

411

And Isis started knitting again, for she was as patient as Osiris was strong, and if he could work she could wait. And wait she did, knowing that mere life is not enough to keep anyone content.

Soon the Divine Wife could see a change in the man. He grew listless and kept to one place by the river and looked up once in a while, always with a moody face. Interest was dying in him. And she made sure of it, even while she was saying to herself, *The creature is sick of his existence,* there was a roar of the creative will at work again. In a twinkling, the earth, up to now a thing of the coldest gray, flamed with colors—the mountains swam in purple, the plains bearing grass and trees turned green, the sea blue, and the clouds varied in infinite ways. And the man sprang up and clapped his hands, for he was cured and happy again.

And Isis smiled and knit away, saying to herself, *It was well thought and will do a little while; but mere beauty in a world is not enough for such a being. My lord must try again.*

With the last word, his thunder shook the moon, and, looking, Isis dropped her knitting and clapped her hands. For up to now everything on the earth but the man had been fixed to a given place. Now all living things, and much that was not living, received the gift of motion. The birds took to wing joyously; beasts great and small went about, each in its way; the trees shook their branches, nodding to the enamored winds; the rivers ran to the seas; and the seas tossed in their beds and rolled in crested waves and with surging and ebbing painted the shores with glistening foam; and above all the clouds floated like unanchored sailed ships.

And the man rose up happy as a child. Osiris was pleased, so that he shouted, "See how well I am doing without you!"

The good wife took up her work and answered quietly, "It was well thought, my lord—and will serve for a while."

And as before, so again. The birds in flight, the running rivers, the seas in tumult ceased to amuse him.

And Isis waited, saying, "Poor creature! He is more wretched than ever."

Osiris stirred, and the noise of his will shook the universe. The sun in its central seat alone stood firm. And Isis looked, but saw no change.

Then, while she was smiling, assured that her lord's last invention was finished, suddenly the creature arose and seemed to listen. And his face brightened, and he clapped his hands for joy, for sounds were heard for the first time on earth. The winds murmured in the trees; the birds sang, each a kind of song of its own, the rivulets running to the rivers became many harpers with harps of silver strings all tinkling together; and the rivers running to the seas surged on in solemn accord. There was music, music everywhere and all the time. So the man could only be happy.

Yet there was no element of beauty except Form and Light. Now, indeed, Osiris was done. And if the creature should again fall off into wretchedness, her help must be asked. And her fingers flew—even ten stitches she took at once.

And the man was happy a long time. Indeed, he would never tire again. But Isis knew better, and she waited and at last saw signs of the end. Sounds became familiar to him, and in their range, from the chirping of the cricket under the roses to the roar of the seas and the bellow of the clouds in the storm, there was nothing unusual. And he pined and sickened and moped by the river and at last fell down motionless.

Then Isis spoke in pity.

"My lord," she said, "the creature is dying."

But Osiris, though seeing it all, held his peace.

"Shall I help him?" she asked.

Osiris was too proud to speak. Then Isis took the last stitch in her knitting and, gathering her work in a roll of brilliance, flung it off so that it fell close to the man. And he, hearing the sound of the fall so near by, looked up. A Woman—the First Woman—was stooping to help him! She reached a hand to him. He caught it and arose and was never again miserable, but evermore happy!

"Such, son of Hur, is the beginning of the creation, as they tell it on the Nile." She paused.

"A clever invention," he said directly, "but it is imperfect. What did Osiris do afterwards?"

"Oh, yes," she replied. "He called the Divine Wife back to the sun, and they went on pleasantly together, each helping the other."

"And shall I not do as the first man did?"

He carried the hand resting upon his neck to his lips. "In love!" he said. His head dropped softly into her lap.

"You will find the King," she said, placing her other hand caressingly upon his head. "You will go on and find the King and serve him. With your sword you will earn his richest gifts, and his best soldier will be my hero."

He turned his face and saw hers close above. In all the sky there was that moment nothing so bright to him as her eyes, enshadowed though they were. Then he sat up, put his arms around her, and kissed her passionately, saying, "O Egypt, Egypt! If the King has crowns for gifts, one shall be mine, and I will bring it and put it here over the place my lips have marked. You shall be a queen—my queen—no one more beautiful! And we will be so happy!"

"And you will tell me everything and let me help you in all things?" she said, kissing him in return.

The question chilled his fervor. "Is it not enough that I love you?" he asked.

"Perfect love means perfect faith," she replied. "But never mind—you will know me better."

She took her hand from him and arose. Moving away, she stopped by the camel and touched its front face with her lips. "O noblest of your kind! That, because there is no suspicion in your love." In another instant, she was gone.

71

At Bethabara

The third day of the journey at noon the party rested by the river Jabbok, where there were a hundred or more men, mostly of Peraea, resting themselves and their beasts. They had hardly dismounted before a man came to them with a pitcher of water and a bowl and offered them a drink.

They received the attention with much courtesy, and he said, looking at the camel, "I am returning from the Jordan, where just now there are many people from distant parts, traveling as you are, illustrious friend, but they had none the equal of your servant here. A very noble animal. May I ask of what breed he comes from?"

Balthasar answered and then sought to rest. But Ben Hur, more curious, responded further to the remark. "At what place on the river are the people?" he asked.

"At Bethabara."

"It used to be a lonesome ford," said Ben Hur. "I cannot understand how it can have become of such interest."

"I see," the stranger replied, "you too are from abroad and have not heard the good tidings."

"What tidings?"

"Well, a man has appeared out of the wilderness—a very holy man—with his mouth full of strange words, which take hold of all who hear them. He calls himself John the Nazirite, son of Zacharias, and says he is the messenger sent before the Messiah."

Even Iras listened closely while the man continued. "They say this John has spent his life from childhood in a cave down by En-gedi, praying and living more strictly than the Essenes. Crowds go to hear him preach. I went to hear him with the rest."

"Have all these, your friends, been there?"

"Most of them are going. A few are leaving."

"What does he preach?"

"A new doctrine—one never before taught in Israel, as all say. He calls it repentance and baptism. The rabbis do not know what to make of him—nor do we. Some have asked him if he is the Christ, others if he is Elijah. But to them all he has the answer, 'I am the voice of one crying in the wilderness, "Make straight the way of the Lord!"'"

At this point the man was called away by his friends. As he was going, Balthasar spoke. "Good stranger!" he said, "tell us if we shall find the preacher at the place you left him."

"Yes, at Bethabara."

"Who should this Nazirite be?" said Ben Hur to Iras, "if not the herald of our King?"

In a short time he had come to regard the daughter as more interested in the mysterious person he was looking for than the aged father! Nevertheless, the latter half-arose with a positive glow in his sunken eyes and said, "Let us hurry. I am not tired." They turned away to help the slave.

There was little conversation between the three at the stopping-place for the night west of Ramoth-Gilead.

"Let us arise early, son of Hur," said the old man. "The Savior may come, and we will not be there."

"The King cannot be far behind his herald," Iras whispered, as she prepared to take her place on the camel.

"Tomorrow we will see!" Ben Hur replied, kissing her hand.

Next day about the third hour, out of the pass through which, skirting the base of Mount Gilead, they had journeyed since leaving Ramoth, the party came upon the barren steppe east of the sacred river. They saw opposite them the upper limit of the old palm lands of Jericho, stretching off to the hill country of Judea. Ben Hur's blood ran quickly, for he knew the ford was close at hand.

"Content yourself, good Balthasar," he said. "We are almost there."

The driver quickened the camel's pace. Soon they caught sight of booths and tents and tethered animals, then of the river, then of a multitude gathered down close by the bank, and still another multitude on the western shore.

Knowing that the preacher was preaching, they made greater

haste. Yet, as they were drawing near, suddenly there was a commotion in the crowd, and it began to break up and disperse.

They were too late!

"Let us stay here," said Ben Hur to Balthasar. "The Nazirite may come this way."

The people were too intent upon what they had heard and too busy in discussion to notice the newcomers. When a few hundred had gone by, and it seemed the opportunity to even see the Nazirite was lost, up the river not far away they saw a person coming toward them of such an unusual appearance that they forgot everything else.

Outwardly the man was rude and uncouth, even savage. Over a thin, gaunt face of the color of brown parchment, over his shoulders and down his back below the middle, fell a covering of sunscorched hair. His eyes were burning bright. His entire right side was naked, the color of his face and quite as thin. A shirt of the coarsest camel's hair—coarse as Bedouin tent cloth—clothed the rest of his person to the knees, gathered at the waist by a broad girdle of untanned leather. His feet were bare. A pouch, also of untanned leather, was fastened to the girdle. He used a knotted staff to help him walk. His movement was quick, decisive, and strangely watchful. Every once in a while he tossed the unruly hair from his face and peered around as if searching for somebody.

The fair Egyptian surveyed the son of the desert with surprise, not to say with disgust. Then, raising the curtain of the tent, she spoke to Ben Hur, who rested his horse near by.

"Is he the herald of your King?"

"It is the Nazirite," he replied, without looking up.

In truth, he himself was more than disappointed, despite his familiarity with the ascetic colonists in En-gedi—their dress, their indifference to all worldly opinion, and their commitment to vows that brought about every imaginable suffering in their body and separated them absolutely from others of their kind as if they had not been born of the same nature. He had been told on his way there to look for a Nazirite whose simple description of himself was as a Voice from the Wilderness.

Still Ben Hur's dream of the King was so great and so much had influenced all thought of him that he never doubted to find in

417

his forerunner some sign or token of the godliness and royalty he was announcing. Gazing at the savage figure before him, the long trains of courtiers whom he had been used to seeing in the baths and in imperial corridors at Rome arose before him, forcing a comparison. Shocked, shamed, and bewildered, he could only answer, "It is the Nazirite."

With Balthasar it was very different. The ways of God, he knew, were not as men would want them to be. He had seen the Savior as a child in a manger and was prepared because of this for the rude and simple in connection with the Divine reappearance. So he kept to his seat, with his lips moving in prayer. He was not expecting a king.

In this time of such interest to the newcomers, another man had been sitting by himself on a stone at the edge of the river, thinking most probably of the sermon he had been hearing. Now, however, he arose and walked slowly up from the shore, in a direction to take him across the line the Nazirite was pursuing and bring him near the camel.

And the two—the preacher and the stranger—kept on until they came, the former within twenty yards of the animal, the latter within ten feet. Then the preacher stopped and flung the hair from his eyes, looked at the stranger, and threw up his hands as a signal to all the people in sight. And they also stopped, each listening intently, and when the hush was perfect, slowly the staff in the Nazirite's hand came down and pointed at the stranger.

All those who before were only listeners were watching intently also.

At the same instant and with the same feeling, Balthasar and Ben Hur fixed their gaze upon the man pointed out, and both had the same impression, only in a different degree. He was moving slowly toward them in a clear space a little in front of them. His form was slightly above the average in stature and slender, even delicate. His actions were calm and deliberate, like that common to men given to serious thought about grave subjects.

His costume was a full-sleeved undergarment reaching to the ankles and an outer robe. On his left arm he carried the usual handkerchief for his head, the red fillet swinging loose down his side. Except for the fillet and a narrow border of blue at the lower edge of the outer robe, his attire was of linen yellowed with dust and road-stains. The only exception were the tassels, which were blue and white, as prescribed by law for rabbis. His sandals were of the simplest kind. He was without pouch or girdle or staff.

These points of appearance were observed briefly by the three beholders and rather as accessories to the head and face of the man, which—especially the latter—were the real sources of the spell cast in common on all who stood looking at him.

The head was open to the cloudless light, except as it was draped with long slightly waved hair, parted in the middle, an auburn tint, with a tendency to reddish golden where most strongly touched by the sun. Under a broad, low forehead and black well-arched brows beamed dark-blue and large eyes, softened to exceeding tenderness by lashes of the great length sometimes seen on children but seldom, if ever, on men.

As to the other features, it would have been difficult to decide whether they were Greek or Jewish. The delicacy of the nostrils and mouth was unusual for the latter type. And when the gentleness of the eyes was taken into account, the pallor of the complexion, the fine feature of the hair, and the softness of the beard, which fell in waves over his throat to his breast, every soldier would have laughed at him, every woman would have confided in him, every child would have with quick instinct given him its hand and whole trust.

The features, it should be further said, were governed by a certain expression that, as the viewer chose, might have been called the effect of intelligence, love, pity or sorrow, though it was a blending of them all—a look easy to fancy as the mark of a soul doomed to the sight and understanding of the utter sinfulness of those among whom it lived. Yet no one could have observed the face with a thought of weakness in the man, at least not those who know that the qualities mentioned—love, sorrow, and pity—are the results of strength to bear suffering. Such was the character of this man.

Slowly he drew nearer to the three.

Now Ben Hur, mounted with his spear in his hand, was an object to claim the glance of a king. Yet the eyes of the man approaching were all the time raised above him—and not to Iras, whose loveliness had been so often remarked, but to Balthasar, the old and feeble.

The hush was profound.

Then the Nazirite, still pointing with his staff cried, in a loud voice, "Behold the Lamb of God, who takes away the sin of the world!"

The many still standing, attentive to the action of the speaker and listening for what might follow, were struck with awe by strange words beyond their understanding. Upon Balthasar they were overpowering. He was there to once more see the Redeemer of men. The faith that had brought him the special privileges of the time long gone yet remained in his heart, and it now gave him a power of vision above that of his fellows—a power to see and know the one he was looking for, the fitting reward of a life in that age so without examples of holiness, a life itself a miracle. The ideal of his faith was before him, perfect in face, form, dress, action, and age. He was in its view, and the view was recognizable. Now if something should happen to identify the stranger beyond all doubt!

And that was what did happen. Exactly at the proper moment, as if to assure the trembling Egyptian, the Nazirite repeated the outcry, "Behold, the Lamb of God, who takes away the sin of the world!"

Balthasar fell upon his knees. For him there was no need of explanation.

And as if the Nazirite knew it, he turned to those more immediately about him who were staring in wonder and continued. "This is he of whom I said, after me comes a man who is preferred before me, for he was before me. And I did not know him, except that he should be made manifest to Israel. Therefore I have come baptizing with water. I saw the Spirit descending from heaven like a dove, and it rested upon him. And I did not know him, but He that sent me to baptize with water, the same said to me, 'Upon whom you shall see the Spirit descending and remaining on him, the same is he who baptizes with the Holy Spirit.' And I saw and bore record, that this—" he paused, his staff still pointing at the stranger in the white garments, as if to give a more absolute certainty to both his words and the conclusions intended "—I bear record, that this is the Son of God!"

"It is he, it is he!" Balthasar cried, with upraised, tearful eyes. The next moment he sank down and was insensible.

In this time it should be remembered, Ben Hur was studying the face of the stranger, though with an interest entirely different. He was not unaware of its purity of feature and its thoughtfulness, tenderness, humility, and holiness, but just then there was room in his mind for only one thought—Who is this man? And what is he? Messiah or king? Never was an apparition more unroyal. No, looking at that calm, benign countenance, the very idea of war, conquest, and lust for dominion smote him like profanity. He said, as if speaking to his own heart, *Balthasar must be right and Simonides wrong. This man has not come to rebuild the throne of Solomon. He has neither the nature nor the genius of Herod. King he may be, but not of another and greater than Rome.*

This was not a conclusion with Ben Hur but merely an impression. And while it was forming, while he yet gazed at the wonderful countenance, his memory began to struggle. *Surely,* he said to himself, *I have seen the man, but where and when?* That the look, so calm, so pitiful, so loving, had somewhere in a past time beamed upon him as that moment it was beaming upon Balthasar became an assurance. Faintly at first, at last clear, a burst of sunshine: the scene by the well at Nazareth that time the Roman guard was dragging him to the galleys returned, and all his being thrilled to the thought. Those hands had helped him when he was perishing. The face was one of the pictures he had carried in his mind ever since. In the rush of feeling excited, the explanation of the preacher was lost by him, all but the last words—words so marvelous that the world yet rings with them—"This is the Son of God!"

Ben Hur leaped from his horse to render homage to his benefactor, but Iras cried to him, "Help, son of Hur, help, or my father will die!"

He stopped, looked back, then hurried to her assistance. She gave him a cup, and leaving the slave to bring the camel to its knees, he ran back to the river for water. The stranger was gone when he came back.

At last Balthasar was restored to consciousness. Stretching forth his hands, he asked, feebly, "Where is he?"

"Who?" asked Iras.

An instant interest shone upon the good man's face, as if a last wish had been gratified, and he answered, "He—the Redeemer—the Son of God, whom I have seen again."

"Do you believe?" Iras asked in a low voice of Ben Hur.

"The time is full of wonders. Let us wait," was all he said.

The next day, while the three were listening to him, the Nazirite broke off in midspeech, saying reverently, "Behold the Lamb of God!"

Looking to where he pointed, they beheld the stranger again. As Ben Hur surveyed the slender figure and his holy, beautiful, and compassionate countenance, a new idea occurred to him.

"Balthasar is right—so is Simonides. Could the Redeemer be a king also?"

And he asked one at his side, "Who is the man walking over there?"

The other laughed mockingly and replied, "He is the son of a carpenter in Nazareth."

72

Guests in the House of Hur

"Esther! Speak to the servant below that he may bring me a cup of water."

"Would you not rather have wine, Father?"

"Let him bring both."

This was in the summerhouse upon the roof of the old palace of the Hurs in Jerusalem. From the parapet overlooking the courtyard Esther called to a man in waiting there. At the same moment another manservant came up the steps and saluted respectfully.

"A package for the master," he said, giving her a letter enclosed in linen cloth, tied and sealed.

It was the twenty-first day of March, nearly three years after the annunciation of the Christ at Bethabara.

Meanwhile, Malluch, acting for Ben Hur, who could no longer endure the emptiness and decay of his father's house, had bought it from Pontius Pilate and, in the process of repair, gates, courts, stairways, terraces, rooms, and roof had been cleaned and thoroughly restored. Not only was there no reminder left of the tragic circumstances so ruinous to the family, but the refurbishment was in a style richer than before. At every point, indeed, a visitor was met by evidences of the higher tastes acquired by the young proprietor during his years of residence in the villa by Misenum and in the Roman capital.

Now it should not be inferred from this explanation that Ben Hur had publicly assumed ownership of the property. In his opinion, the hour for that had not yet come. Neither had he yet taken his proper name. Passing the time in the labors of preparation in Galilee, he waited patiently for the action of the Nazarene, who daily became more and more of a mystery to him and by miracles performed, often before his eyes, kept him in a state of anxious doubt both as to his character and mission. Occasionally he came up to the Holy City, stopping at the paternal house—always, however, as a stranger and a guest.

The visits of Ben Hur, it should also be observed, were for more than mere rest from labor. Balthasar and Iras made their home in the palace, and the charm of the daughter was still working upon him with all its original freshness, while the father, though feebler in body, kept him an unflagging listener to speeches of astonishing power, arguing for the divinity of the wandering miracle worker of whom they were all so expectant.

As to Simonides and Esther, they had arrived from Antioch only a few days before this reappearance—a wearisome journey to the merchant, carried as he had been in a seat swung between two camels, which did not always keep the same step. But now that he had come, the good man, it seemed, could not see enough of his native land. He delighted in the perch upon the roof and spent most of his day hours there seated in an armchair, the duplicate of the one kept for him in the cabinet over the storehouse by the Orontes. In the shade of the summerhouse he could drink fully of the inspiring air hanging over the familiar hills. He could better watch the sun rise, run its course, and set as it used to in the old days. And with Esther by him it was so much easier, up there close to the sky, to bring back the other Esther, his love in youth, his wife, dearer growing with the passage of years. And yet he was not unmindful of business. Every day a messenger brought him a dispatch from Sanballat, in charge of the big commerce back there, and every day a dispatch left him for Sanballat with directions of such minuteness of detail as to exclude all judgment except his own and all chances except those the Almighty has refused to submit to the most mindful of men.

As Esther started to return to the summerhouse, the sunlight fell softly upon the dustless roof, showing that she was a woman now—small, graceful in form, of regular features, rosy with youth and health, bright with intelligence, beautiful with the luster of a devoted nature—a woman to be loved because loving was a habit of life second nature to her.

She looked at the package as she turned, paused, looked at it a second time more closely than at first, and the blood rose reddening her cheeks—the seal was Ben Hur's. With quickened steps she hastened on.

Simonides held the package a moment while he also inspected the seal. Breaking it open, he gave her the roll it contained.

"Read it, please," he said.

His eyes were upon her as he spoke, and instantly a troubled expression fell upon his own face. "You know who it is from, I see, Esther."

"Yes—from—our master."

Though the manner was halting, she met his gaze with modest sincerity.

Slowly his chin sank into the roll of flesh puffed out under it like a cushion. "You love him, Esther?" he said quietly.

"Yes," she answered.

"Have you thought well of what you do?"

"I have tried not to think of him, father, except as the master to whom I am dutifully bound. The effort has not helped me to obtain strength."

"A good girl, a good girl, even as your mother was," he said, dropping into daydreams, from which she roused him by unrolling the paper.

"The Lord forgive me, but—but your love might not have been vainly given had I kept hold of all I had, as I might have done—such power is there in money!"

"It would have been worse for me had you done so, Father, for then I would have been unworthy of a look from him and without pride in you. Shall I not read now?"

"In a moment," he said. "Let me, for your sake, my child, show you the worst situation. Hearing it from me may make it less terrible to you. His love, Esther, is given to someone else."

"I know it," she said calmly.

"The Egyptian has him in her net," he continued. "She has the cunning deception of her race, with much beauty to help her, but, like her race again, she has no heart. The daughter who despises her father will bring her husband to grief."

"Does she do that?"

Simonides went on. "Balthasar is a wise man who has been wonderfully favored, considering he is a Gentile, and his faith suits him well. Yet she makes a joke of his faith. I heard her say, speaking of him yesterday, 'The follies of youth are excusable. Nothing is admirable in the aged except wisdom, and when that leaves them, they should die.' A cruel speech, fit more for a Roman than an Egyptian. I applied it to myself, knowing that eventually the feebleness of her father will come to me also—no, this state is not far off. But you, Esther, would never say of me—no, never—'It were better he were dead.' No, your mother was a daughter of Judah."

With tears beginning in her eyes she kissed him and said, "I am my mother's child."

"Yes, and my daughter—my daughter, who is to me all that the Temple was to Solomon."

After a period of silence, he laid his hand upon her shoulder and resumed. "When he has taken the Egyptian to be his wife, Esther, he will think of you with remorse and much agony of spirit. For at last he will awake to find himself only the instrument of her evil ambition. Rome is the center of all her dreams. To her he is the son of Arrius, the captain, not the son of Hur, Prince of Jerusalem."

Esther made no attempt to conceal the effect of these words. "Save him, Father! It is not too late!" she said entreatingly.

He answered, with a dubious smile, "A man drowning may be saved, but not a man in love."

"But you have influence with him. He is alone in the world. Show him this danger. Tell him what kind of a woman she is."

"That might save him from her. Would it give him to you, Esther? No." His brows fell darkly over his eyes. "I am a servant, as my fathers were for generations, yet I could not say to him, 'Master, my daughter! She is fairer than the Egyptian and loves you better.' I have learned too much from years of liberty and direction. The words would blister my tongue. The stones upon the old hills above us would turn in their beds for shame when I go out to them. No, by the patriarchs, Esther, I would rather have us both sleep with your mother as she sleeps in her grave!"

A blush burned Esther's whole face. "I do not mean for you to tell him so, Father. I was concerned for him alone—for his happiness, not mine. Because I have dared to love him, I shall keep myself worthy of his respect. So only I can excuse my folly. Let me read his letter now."

"Yes, read it."

She began at once, in haste to conclude this painful subject. The letter reads as follows:

> Nisan 8th day
> On the road from Galilee to Jerusalem
>
> The Nazarene is on the way also. With him, though without his knowledge, I am bringing a full legion of mine. A second legion follows. The Passover will explain the multitude. He said upon setting out, "We will go up to Jerusalem, and all things that were written by the prophets concerning me shall be accomplished."
>
> Our waiting draws to an end.
> In haste.
> Peace to you, Simonides.
>
> Ben Hur

Esther returned the letter to her father, while a choking sensation filled her throat. There was not a word in the letter for her— not even in the salutation did she share—and it would have been so easy to have written "and to yours, peace." For the first time in her life she felt the smarting of a jealous sting.

"The eighth day," said Simonides, "the eighth day. And this, Esther, this is the—"

"The ninth," she replied.

"Ah, then, they may be in Bethany now."

"And we may possibly see him tonight," she added, pleased and in momentary forgetfulness.

"It may be! Tomorrow is the Feast of Unleavened Bread, and he may wish to celebrate it. So may the Nazarene, and we may see him—we may see both of them, Esther."

At this point the servant appeared with the wine and water. Esther helped her father, and in the midst of her service Iras came upon the roof.

To the Jewess the Egyptian never appeared so very, very beautiful as at that moment. Her gauzy garments fluttered about her like a little cloud of mist. Her forehead, neck, and arms glittered with massive jewelry. Her face was filled with pleasure. She moved with self-conscious, buoyant steps, though without affectation. At the sight Esther shrank within herself and nestled closer to her father.

"Peace to you, Simonides, and to the pretty Esther, peace," said Iras, nodding to the latter. "You remind me, good master—if I may say it without offense—of the priests in Persia who climb their temples at the end of day to send prayers toward the departing sun. Is there anything in the worship you do not know, let me call my father. He is Magi-bred."

"Fair Egyptian," the merchant replied, nodding with grave politeness, "your father is a good man who would not be offended if he knew I told you his Persian lore is the least part of his wisdom."

Iras hesitated. "To speak like a philosopher, as you invite me," she said, "the least part always implies a greater. Let me ask what you esteem the greater part of the rare quality you are pleased to attribute to him."

Simonides turned upon her somewhat sternly. "Pure wisdom always directs itself toward God. The purest wisdom is knowledge of God, and no man of my acquaintance has it in higher degree, or makes it more manifest in speech and act, than the good Balthasar." To end the dialogue, he raised the cup and drank.

The Egyptian turned to Esther a little testily. "A man who has millions in store, and fleets of ships at sea, cannot discover what simple women like us find in amusement. Let us leave him. By the wall over there we can talk."

They went to the parapet then and stopped at the place where, years before, Ben Hur accidently loosened the broken tile upon the head of Gratus.

"You have not been to Rome?" Iras began, toying for a while with one of her unclasped bracelets.

"No," said Esther demurely.

"Have you not wished to go?"

"No."

"Ah, how little there has been of your life!"

The sigh that succeeded the exclamation could not have been more piteously expressive had the loss been the Egyptian's own. Next moment her laugh might have been heard in the street below, and she said, "Oh, my pretty, simple girl! The half-fledged birds nested in the ear of the great bust on the Memphian sands know nearly as much as you."

Then, seeing Esther's confusion, she changed her manner and said, in a confiding tone, "You must not take offense. Oh, no! I was playing. Let me kiss the hurt and tell you what I would not tell to any other person—not if Simbel himself asked it of me, offering a lotus cup of the spray of the Nile!"

Another laugh, excellently masking the look she turned sharply upon the Jewess and said, "The King is coming."

Esther gazed at her in innocent surprise.

"The Nazarene," Iras continued, "he whom our fathers have been talking about so much, whom Ben Hur has been serving and toiling for so long"—her voice dropped several tones—"the Nazarene will be here tomorrow, and Ben Hur tonight."

Esther struggled to maintain her composure but failed. Her eyes fell, the telltale blood surged to her cheek and forehead, and she did not see the triumphant smile that passed like a gleam over the face of the Egyptian.

"See, here is his promise." And from her girdle she took a roll. "Rejoice with me, O my friend! He will be here tonight! On the Tiber there is a house, a royal property, which he has pledged to me, and to be its mistress is to be—"

A sound of someone walking swiftly along the street below interrupted the speech, and she leaned over the parapet to see. Then she drew back and cried, with hands clasped above her head, "Now blessed be Isis! It's him—Ben Hur himself! That he should appear while I had such thought of him! There are not gods if it is not a good omen. Put your arms about me, Esther—and a kiss!"

The Jewess looked up. There was a glow upon each cheek. Her eyes sparkled with a light more nearly of anger than her nature ever emitted before this time. Her gentleness had been too roughly overridden. It was not enough for her to be forbidden more than fugitive dreams of the man she loved; a boastful rival must tell her in confidence of her greater success and of the brilliant promises that were its rewards. Of her, the servant of a servant, there had been no hint of remembrance. This other one could show his letter, leaving her to imagine all it implied.

So she said, "Do you love him so much then, or Rome so much better?"

The Egyptian drew back a step, then she bent her haughty head quite near her questioner. "What is he to you, daughter of Simonides?"

Esther, all thrilling, began, "He is my—" a thought blasting as lightning held back the words; she paled, trembled, recovered, and answered "—he is my father's friend." Her tongue had refused to admit her servile condition.

Iras laughed more lightly than before. "Not more than that?" she said. "Ah, by the lover-gods of Egypt, you may keep your kisses—keep them. You have taught me only now that there are others vastly more important waiting for me here in Judea. And"—she turned away, looking back over her shoulder—"I will go get them. Peace to you."

Esther saw her disappear down the steps, then, putting her hands over her face, she burst into tears so that they ran scalding through her fingers—tears of shame and choking passion. And to deepen the distress to her even temper, up with a new meaning of withering force rose her father's words: "Your love might not have been vainly given if I had kept back all I had, as I might have done."

And all the stars were out, burning low above the city and the dark wall of mountains about it, before she recovered enough to go back to the summerhouse and in silence take her accustomed place at her father's side, humbly waiting his pleasure. It seemed her youth, if not her life, must be given to such duty. And, let the truth be said, now that the pang was over, she went willingly back to the duty.

73

Ben Hur Tells of the Nazarene

An hour or thereabouts after the scene on the roof, Balthasar and Simonides, the latter attended by Esther, met in the great chamber of the palace, and while they were talking, Ben Hur and Iras came in together.

The young Jew, advancing in front of his companion, walked first to Balthasar and saluted him and received his reply. Then he turned to Simonides but paused at seeing of Esther.

It is not often we have hearts with room enough for more than one absorbing passion at the same time. In its blaze the others may continue to live, but only as lesser lights. With Ben Hur, much study of possibilities, indulgence of hopes and dreams, influences coming from the condition of his country, or from Iras, for example—had made him in the broadest worldly sense ambitious. And as he had allowed this passion a place, he allowed it to become a ruler and finally an imperious governor. The better resolves and impulses of former days faded imperceptibly out of existence and at last almost out of recollection.

It is at best easy to forget our youth. In his case it was only natural that his own sufferings and the mystery darkening the fate of his family should move him less as, in his hope at least, he approached nearer to the goals that occupied all his visions. Only let us not judge him too harshly.

He paused in surprise at seeing Esther a woman now, and so beautiful. As he stood looking at her a still voice reminded him of broken vows and duties undone. It was almost as if his old self returned.

For an instant he was startled, but, recovering, he went to Esther and said, "Peace to you, sweet Esther, peace, and you, Simonides." He looked to the merchant as he spoke. "The blessing of the Lord be yours, if only because you have been a good father to the fatherless."

Esther heard him with downcast face.

Simonides answered, "I repeat the welcome of the good Balthasar, son of Hur—welcome to your father's house, and sit and tell us of your travels and of your work and of the wonderful Nazarene—who he is and what he is. If you are not at ease here, who shall be? Sit, I pray—there, between us, that we may all hear." Esther stepped out quickly and brought a covered stool and set it for him. "Thanks," he said to her gratefully.

When seated, after some other conversation he addressed himself to the men. "I have come to tell you of the Nazarene."

The two became instantly attentive.

"For many days now I have followed him with such watchfulness as one may give another upon whom he is waiting so anxiously. I have seen him under all circumstances said to be trials and tests of men, and while I am certain he is a man as I am, I am no less certain that he is something more."

"More than what?" asked Simonides.

"I will tell you—"

Someone coming into the room interrupted him. He turned and arose with extended hands. "Amrah! Dear old Amrah!" he cried.

She came forward, and they, seeing the joy in her face, did not think once how wrinkled and tawny she was. She knelt at his feet, clasped his knees, and kissed his hands over and over. And when he could he pulled the lank gray hair from her cheeks and kissed them, saying, "Good Amrah, have you nothing of them—not a word—not one little sign?"

Then she broke into sobbing that made his answer plainer than the spoken word.

"God's will has been done," he next said, solemnly, in a tone to make each listener know he had no more hope of finding his people. In his eyes there were tears that he would not wish them to see, because he was a man.

When he could speak again, he took a seat and said, "Come, sit by me, Amrah—here. No? Then at my feet, for I have much to say to these good friends concerning a wonderful man who has come into the world."

But she went off and, stooping with her back to the wall,

joined her hands under her knees, content, they all thought, with seeing him.

Then Ben Hur, bowing to the old men, began again. "I fear to answer the question asked me about the Nazarene without first telling you some of the things I have seen him do. And I wish to do that more, my friends, because tomorrow he will come to the city and go up into the Temple, which he calls his Father's house, where, still others say, he will proclaim himself to be the Messiah. So whether you are right, Balthasar, or you, Simonides, we and Israel shall know tomorrow."

Balthasar rubbed his hands briskly together and asked, "Where shall I go to see him?"

"The pressure of the crowd will be very great. It is better, I think, for you all to go up on the roof above the courtyard—say upon the Porch of Solomon."

"Can you be with us?"

"No," said Ben Hur, "my friends will require me, perhaps, to be in the procession."

"Procession!" exclaimed Simonides. "Does he travel in state with attendants?"

Ben Hur saw the direction of his question. "He brings twelve men with him, fishermen, tillers of the soil, one a publican, all of the humbler class, and he and they make their journeys on foot. They are careless of the wind, cold, rain, or sun. Seeing them stop by the wayside at nightfall to break bread or lie down to sleep, I have been reminded of a party of shepherds going back to their flocks from the market, rather than of nobles and kings. Only when he lifts the corners of his handkerchief to look at someone or shake the dust from his head, do I know that he is their teacher as well as their companion—their superior no less than their friend."

"You are shrewd men," Ben Hur resumed, after a while. "You know what creatures of various motives we are and that it has become a law of our nature to spend our lives in eager pursuit of certain precious objects. Appealing to that law as a way that we may know ourselves, what would you say of a man who could be rich by making gold out of the stones under his feet, yet remains poor of choice?"

"The Greeks would call him a philosopher," said Iras.

"No, daughter," said Balthasar, "the philosophers never had the power to do such a thing."

"How do you know this man has the power?"

Ben Hur answered quickly, "I saw him turn water into wine."

"Very strange, very strange," said Simonides. "But it is not so strange to me that he should prefer to live a poor life when he could be so rich. Is he that poor?"

"He owns nothing and envies no one concerning their possessions. He pities the rich. But besides that, what would you say if you saw a man multiply five loaves and two fish, all he owned, into enough to feed five thousand people and have a number of full baskets left over? I saw the Nazarene do that."

"You saw it?" exclaimed Simonides.

"Yes, and ate some of the bread and fish. More marvelous still, Ben Hur continued, "what would you say of a man who has such healing virtue that the sick have only to touch the hem of his garment to be cured, or cry to him from afar? That, too, I witnessed, not once, but many times. As we came out of Jericho two blind men by the wayside called to the Nazarene, and he touched their eyes, and they saw. So they brought a man with palsy to him, and he merely said, 'Go into your house,' and the man went away well. What do you say to such things?"

The merchant had no answer.

"Do you now think, as I have heard others argue, that what I have just told you are the mere tricks of a magician? Let me answer by recalling greater things that I have seen him do. Look first to that disease accursed of God—comfortless, as you all know, except when one dies—the disease of leprosy."

At these words Amrah dropped her hands to the floor and in her eagerness to hear him half arose.

"What would you say," said Ben Hur, with increased earnestness, "what would you say if I now tell you this: A leper came to the Nazarene while I was with him down in Galilee and said, 'Lord, if you will, you can make me clean.' He heard the cry and touched the outcast with his hand, saying, 'Be clean,' and immediately the man was himself again, healthful as any of us who witnessed the cure, and we were a large multitude."

Here Amrah arose and with her gaunt fingers pushed the wiry locks from her eyes. The brain of the poor creature had long since gone, and she found it difficult to follow the speech.

"Then again," said Ben Hur, without stopping, "ten lepers came to him one day in a group and, falling at his feet, called out—I saw and heard it all—called out, 'Master, Master, have mercy upon us!' He told them, 'Go show yourselves to the priests, as the law requires, and before you get there you will be healed.'"

"And were they?"

"Yes. Going on the road their infirmity left them, so that there was nothing to remind us of it except their polluted clothes."

"Such a thing has never been heard of before—never in all Israel!" said Simonides under his breath.

And then, while he was speaking, Amrah turned away, walked noiselessly to the door, and went out. None of the company saw her go.

"The thoughts stirred by these deeds done under my own eyes I now leave you to imagine," said Ben Hur, continuing. "But my doubts, my misgivings, my amazement, were not yet full. The people of Galilee are, as you know, impetuous and rash. After years of waiting, their swords burned their hands. Nothing would serve them except action. 'He is slow to declare himself. Let us force him,' they cried to me.

"And I too became impatient. If he is to be king, why not now? The legions are ready. So as he was once teaching by the seaside we would have crowned him whether or not he approved. But he disappeared and was next seen on a ship departing from the shore. Good Simonides, the desires that make other men mad—riches, power, even kingships offered out of great love by a great people—do not move him at all. How do you respond?"

The merchant's chin hung low upon his breast. Raising his head, he replied resolutely, "The Lord lives and so do the words of the prophets. Time is in the green yet. Let tomorrow answer."

"Be it so," said Balthasar, smiling.

And Ben Hur said, "Be it so." Then he went on. "But I am not finished yet. From these things, not too great to be above suspicion by those who did not see them performed as I did, let me take you now to others infinitely greater, acknowledged since the world began. Tell me, has any one to your knowledge ever reached out and taken from death what death has made his own? Who ever gave again the breath of a life lost? Who but—"

"God!" said Balthasar reverently.

Ben Hur bowed. "O wise Egyptian! I may not refuse the name you lend me. What would you—or you, Simonides—what would you either or both have said had you seen as I did, a man with few words and no ceremony, no more effort than a mother's when she speaks to wake her sleeping child, undo the work of death?

"It was down at Nain. We were walking through the gate when a company came out bearing a dead man. The Nazarene stopped to let the train pass. There was a woman among them crying. I saw his face soften with pity. He spoke to her, then went and touched the coffin and said to him who lay upon it, dressed for burial, 'Young man, I say to you, arise!' And instantly the dead sat up and talked."

"God only is so great," said Balthasar to Simonides.

"Mark you," Ben Hur proceeded, "I only tell you things of which I was a witness, together with a cloud of other men. On the way here I saw another act still more mighty. In Bethany there was a man named Lazarus, who died and was buried. And after he had lain four days in a tomb, shut in by a great stone, the Nazarene was shown to the place. Upon rolling the stone away, we saw the man lying inside, bound and rotting. There were many people standing by, and we all heard what the Nazarene said, for he spoke in a loud voice, 'Lazarus, come forth!' I cannot tell you my feelings when in answer, as it were, the man arose and came out to us with all his burial clothes around him. 'Loose him,' said the Nazarene next, 'loose him, and let him go.'

"And when the napkin was taken from the face of the resurrected—lo, my friends, the blood ran once again through the wasted body, and he was exactly as he had been in life before the sickness that took him to his death. He lives still and is seen hourly and spoken to by others. You may go see him tomorrow. And now, as nothing more is needed for the purpose, I ask you what I came to ask, being only a repetition of what you asked me, Simonides. What more than a man is this Nazarene?"

The question was put solemnly, and long after midnight the

company sat and debated it. Simonides was yet unwilling to give up his understanding of the sayings of the prophets, and Ben Hur contended that the elder disputants were both right—that the Nazarene was the Redeemer, as claimed by Balthasar, and also the destined King the merchant would have believed.

"Tomorrow we will see. Peace to you all." So saying, Ben Hur took his leave, intending to return to Bethany.

74

The Lepers Leave Their Tomb

The first person to go out of the city after the opening of the Sheep's Gate next morning was Amrah, with a basket on her arm. No questions were asked by the keepers, since the morning itself was not more regular in coming than she was. They knew her to be somebody's faithful servant, and that was enough for them.

Down the eastern valley she went her way. The side of Olivet was darkly green and spotted with white tents recently put up by people attending the feasts. Still, had it not been so, no one would have troubled her. Past Gethsemane, past the tombs at the meeting of the Bethany roads, past the sleepy village of Siloam she went. Occasionally her decrepit little body staggered. Once she sat down to get her breath. Rising shortly, she struggled on with renewed haste.

The great rocks on either hand, if they had ears, might have heard her mutter to herself. Could they have seen, it would have been to observe how frequently she looked up over the Mount, scolding the dawn for its promptness. If it had been possible for them to gossip, not improbably they would have said to each other, "Our friend is in a hurry this morning. The mouths she goes to feed must be very hungry."

When at last she reached the King's Garden she slackened her pace, for then the grim city of the lepers was in view, extending far round the pitted south hill of Hinnom.

She was going to her mistress, whose tomb, it will be remembered, overlooked the well of En-rogel.

Early as it was, the unhappy woman was up and sitting outside, leaving Tirzah asleep within. The course of the disease had been terribly swift in the three years. Conscious of her appearance, with the refined instincts of her nature, she kept by habit her whole body covered. She seldom as possible permitted even Tirzah to see her.

This morning she was taking in the air without a covered head, knowing there was no one to be shocked by the exposure. The light was not full, but there was enough to show the ravages to which she had been subject. Her hair was snow-white and unmanageably coarse, falling over her back and shoulders like so much silver wire. The eyelids, the lips, the nostrils, the flesh of the cheeks were either gone or reduced to rawness. The neck was a mass of ash-colored scales. One hand lay outside the folds of her habit as rigid as that of a skeleton. The nails had been eaten away. The joints of the fingers, if not bare to the bone, were swollen knots crusted with red secretions. Her head, face, neck, and hands indicated all too plainly the condition of her whole body.

Seeing her in this state, it was easy to understand how the once fair widow of the princely Hur had been able to maintain herself incognito so well through such a period of years.

When the sun would gild the crest of Olivet and the Mount of Offense with light sharper and more brilliant in that old land than in the West, she knew Amrah would come, first to the well, then to a stone midway between the well and the foot of the hill on which she made her home. The good servant would deposit the food she carried in the basket and fill the water jar afresh for the day. Of her former great degree of happiness, that brief visit was all that remained to this unfortunate woman. She could then ask about her son and be told of his welfare, with such bits of news concerning him as the messenger could glean. Usually the information was meager enough, yet comforting. At times she heard he was at home. Then she would emerge from her dreary cell at the break of day and sit till noon, and from noon to the setting of sun, a motionless figure draped in white, statuelike, looking invariably to one point—over the Temple to the spot under the rounded sky where the old house stood, dear in memory, and dearer because he was there. Nothing else was left to her. Tirzah she counted as dead. As for herself, she simply waited for the end, knowing every hour of life was one more hour of dying—yet happily, at least it was painless dying.

The beautiful works of nature around the hill were meager. Beasts and birds avoided the place as if they knew its history and present use. Every green thing perished in its first season. The winds warred upon the shrubs and lush grasses. Those they could not uproot were left to drought.

Whenever she would look, the view was made depressingly miserable by tombs—tombs above her, below, and opposite her own tomb—all now freshly whitened in warning to visiting pilgrims. In the sky—clear, fair, inviting—one would think she might have found some relief for her aching heart and mind. In making everything beautiful elsewhere, the sun was unfriendly to her—it only disclosed her growing hideousness. Except for the sun she would not have been the horror she was to herself, nor would she have been waked so cruelly from dreams of Tirzah as she used to be. The gift of seeing can sometimes be a dreadful curse. Why did she not make an end to her sufferings?

The Law forbade her! A Gentile may smile at the answer, but a son of Israel will not.

While she sat there filling the dusky solitude with cheerless thoughts, suddenly a woman came up the hill staggering and spent with exertion.

The widow arose hastily and, covering her head, cried in a voice unnaturally harsh, "Unclean, unclean!"

In a moment, heedless of the notice, Amrah was at her feet. All the long-pent love of the simple woman burst forth. With tears and passionate cries she kissed her mistress's garments, and for a while the latter tried to escape from her. Then, seeing she could not, she waited till the violence of the gestures were over.

"What have you done, Amrah?" she said. "Is it by such disobedience you prove your love for us? Wicked woman! You are lost, and he—your master—you can never, never go back to him."

Amrah groveled, sobbing in the dust.

"The ban of the Law is upon you too. You cannot return to Jerusalem. What will become of us? Who will bring us bread? O wicked Amrah! We are all undone alike!"

"Mercy, mercy!" Amrah answered from the ground.

"You should have been merciful to yourself and by so doing been most merciful to us. Now where can we fly? There is no one to help us. O false servant! The wrath of the Lord was already too heavy for us."

Here Tirzah, awakened by the noise, appeared at the door of the tomb. The picture she presented was grotesque. In the half-clad apparition, patched with scales, lividly seamed, nearly blind, its limbs and extremities swollen, no familiar eye however sharpened by love could have recognized the creature of grace and purity she had been.

"Is it Amrah, Mother?"

The servant tried to crawl to her also.

"Stay, Amrah!" the widow cried. "I forbid you to touch her. Rise, and go away before anyone at the well sees you here. No, I forgot—it is too late! You must remain now and share our doom. Rise, I say!"

Amrah rose to her knees and said, brokenly and with clasped hands, "O good mistress! I am not false—I am not wicked. I bring you good tidings."

"Of Judah?" And as she spoke the widow half withdrew the cloth from her head.

"There is a wonderful man," Amrah continued, "who has power to cure you. He speaks a word, and the sick are made well, and even the dead come to life. I have come to take you to him."

"Poor Amrah!" said Tirzah compassionately.

"No," cried Amrah, detecting the doubt underlying the words. "No, as the Lord lives, even the Lord of Israel, my God as well as yours, I speak the truth. Go with me, I pray, and lose no time. This morning he will pass by on his way to the city. See! The day is at hand. Take the food here—eat, and let us go."

The mother listened eagerly. It was not unlikely that she had heard of the wonderful man, for by this time his fame had penetrated every nook in the land. "Who is he?" she asked.

"A Nazarene."

"Who told you about him?"

"Judah."

"Judah told you? Is he at home?"

"He came last night."

The widow, trying to still the beating of her heart, was silent awhile. "Did Judah send you to tell us this?" she next asked.

"No. He believes you are dead."

"There was a prophet once who cured a leper," the mother

said thoughtfully to Tirzah. "But he had his power from God." Then addressing Amrah, she asked, "How does my son know this man is so possessed with the same power?"

"He was traveling with him and heard the lepers call and saw them go away well. First there was one man, then there were ten, and they were all made whole."

The elder listener was silent again. The skeleton hand shook. She was struggling to give the story the benefit of faith, which is always absolute in its demand, and it was the same with her as with the men of the day, eyewitnesses of what was done by the Christ, as well as the myriads who have succeeded them. She did not question his performance, for her own son was the witness testifying through the servant. But she strove to comprehend the power by which such astonishing work could be done by a man. However, hesitation was brief. She said to Tirzah, "This must be the Messiah!"

She did not speak coldly, like one reasoning away a doubt, but as a woman of Israel familiar with the promises of God to her race—a woman of understanding, ready to be glad over the least sign of the realization of the promises.

"There was a time when Jerusalem and all Judea were filled with a story that he was born. I remember it. By this time he should be a man. It must be—it is he. Yes," she said to Amrah, "we will go with you. Bring the water that you will find in the tomb in a jar and set the food out for us. We will eat and be gone."

The breakfast, partaken with excitement, was soon finished, and the three women set out on their extraordinary journey. As Tirzah had caught the confident spirit of the others, there was only one fear that troubled the party. Bethany, Amrah said, was the town the man was coming from. Now from there to Jerusalem were three roads, or rather paths—one over the first summit of Olivet, a second at its base, a third between the second summit and the Mount of Offense. The three were not far apart. They were far enough, however, to make it possible for the unfortunates to miss the Nazarene if they failed to be on the one he chose to come by.

A little questioning satisfied the mother that Amrah knew nothing of the country beyond the Cedron and even less of the intentions of the man they were going to see, if they could. She discerned, also, that both Amrah and Tirzah—the one from confirmed habits of servitude, the other from natural dependency—looked to her for guidance. And she accepted the responsibility.

"We will go first to Bethpage," she said to them. "There, if the Lord favors us, we may learn what else to do."

They descended the hill to Tophet and the King's Garden and paused in the deep trail furrowed through them by centuries of wayfaring. "I am afraid of the road," the matron said. "Better that we keep to the country among the rocks and trees. This is a feast day, and on the hillsides yonder I see signs of a great multitude gathering. By going across the Mount of Offense here we may avoid them."

"The mount is steep, Mother! I cannot climb it."

"Remember, we are going to find health and life. See, my child, how the day brightens around us! And over there are women coming this way to the well. They will stone us if we stay here. Come, be strong this once."

Thus the mother, no less disturbed herself, sought to inspire the daughter, and Amrah came to her aid. Up to this time Amrah had not touched the bodies of the afflicted, nor they her. Now, in disregard of consequences as well as of command, the faithful servant went to Tirzah and put her arm over her shoulder and whispered, "Lean on me. I am strong, though I am old, and it is but a little way off. There—now we can go."

The face of the hill they tried to cross was somewhat broken with pits and ruins of old structures, but when at last they stood upon the top to rest and looked at the spectacle presented to them over in the northwest—at the Temple and its courtly terraces, at Zion, at the enduring white towers soaring into the sky beyond—the mother was strengthened with a love of life for its own sake.

"Look, Tirzah," she said, "look at the plates of gold on the Gate Beautiful. How they give back the flames of the sun, brightness for brightness! Do you remember when we used to go up there? Will it not be pleasant to do so again? And think—home is but a little way off. I can almost see it over the roof of the Holy of Holies, and Judah will be there to receive us!"

From the side of the middle summit, garnished in green with

myrtle and olive trees, they saw, after next looking that way, thin columns of smoke rising lightly and straight up into the still morning, each a warning of restless pilgrims astir and of the flight of the pitiless hours and the need for haste.

Though the good servant toiled faithfully to lighten their labor as they descended the hillside, not sparing herself in the least, the girl moaned at every step. Sometimes in an extremity of anguish she cried out. Upon reaching the road—that is, the road between the Mount of Offense and the middle or second summit of Olivet—she fell down exhausted.

"Go on with Amrah, Mother, and leave me here," she said faintly.

"No, no, Tirzah. What would I gain if I were healed and you were not? When Judah asks for you, as he will, what would I have to say to him were I to leave you?"

"Tell him I loved him."

The elder leper arose from bending over the fainting sufferer and gazed about her with the sensation that her hope was perishing, which is more nearly like annihilation of the soul than anything else. The supremest joy of the thought of cure was inseparable from Tirzah, who was not too old to forget, in the happiness of healthful life to come, the years of misery by which she had been so reduced in body and broken in spirit. Even as the brave woman was about to leave the venture they were engaged in to the determination of God, she saw a man on foot coming rapidly up the road from the east.

"Courage, Tirzah! Be of cheer," she said. "Over there I believe is one who will tell us of the Nazarene."

Amrah helped the girl to a sitting posture and supported her while the man advanced.

"In your goodness, Mother, you forget who we are. The stranger will go around us. His best gift to us will be a curse, if not a stone."

"We will see."

There was no other answer to be given, since the mother was too well and sadly acquainted with the treatment of outcasts of the class to which she belonged were accustomed to receive at the hands of her countrymen.

As has been said, the road at the edge of which the group was posted was little more than a worn path or trail, winding crookedly through a great passage of limestone. If the stranger kept the path, he must meet them face to face.

And he did so, until he was near enough to hear the cry she was bound to give. Then, uncovering her head, a further demand of the Law, she shouted shrilly, "Unclean, unclean!"

To her surprise, the man came steadily on. "What would you have me do?" he asked, stopping opposite them not four yards off.

"You see us. Be careful," the mother said, with dignity.

"Woman, I am the courier of him who speaks but once to people like you and they are healed. I am not afraid."

"The Nazarene?"

"The Messiah," he said.

"Is it true that he comes to the city today?"

"He is now at Bethpage."

"On what road, master?"

"This one."

She clasped her hands and looked up thankfully.

"Who do you believe he is?" the man asked, with pity.

"The Son of God," she replied.

"Stay here then, or, as there is a multitude with him, stand over there by the rock—the white one under the tree—and as he goes by do not fail to call to him. Call, and fear not. If your faith is equal to your knowledge, he will hear you though all the heavens thunder. I go to tell Israel, assembled in and about the city, that he is at hand, and to make ready to receive him. Peace to you and yours."

The stranger moved on.

"Did you hear, Tirzah? Did you hear? The Nazarene is on the road, on this one, and he will hear us. Once more, my child—only once! And let us go to the rock. It is only a step."

She was encouraged, and Tirzah took Amrah's hand and arose. But as they were going, Amrah said, "Stay. The man is returning." And they waited for him.

"I ask your grace, woman," he said, upon overtaking them. "Remembering that the sun will be hot before the Nazarene arrives and that the city is near by to give me refreshment should I need it, I thought this water would do you better than it will me. Take it and be of good cheer. Call to him as he passes."

He followed the words by offering her a gourd full of water, such as foot-travelers sometimes carried with them in their journeys across the hills, and instead of placing the gift on the ground for her to take up when he was at a safe distance, he gave it into her hand.

"Are you a Jew?" she asked, surprised.

"I am that—and better, I am a disciple of the Christ who teaches daily by word and example this thing that I have done to you. The world has long known the word *charity* without understanding it. Again I say, peace and good cheer to you and yours."

He went on, and they went slowly to the rock he had pointed out to them, high as their heads and scarcely thirty yards from the road on the right. Standing in front of it, the mother satisfied herself that they could be seen and heard plainly by passersby whose notice they desired to attract. There they placed themselves under the tree in its shade and drank from the gourd and rested refreshed. Before long Tirzah slept, and fearing to disturb her, the others held their peace.

75

The Miracle

During the third hour the road in front of the resting place of the lepers became gradually more and more frequented by people going in the direction of Bethpage and Bethany.

Now, however, about the coming of the fourth hour, a great crowd appeared over the crest of Olivet, and as it filed down the road by the thousands, the two observers noticed with wonder that everyone in it carried a freshly cut palm branch. As they sat absorbed by the spectacle, the noise of another multitude approaching from the east drew their eyes that way. Then the mother woke Tirzah.

"What is the meaning of it all?" the latter asked.

"He is coming," answered the mother. "They are from the city going to meet him. Those we hear in the east are his friends bringing him company, and it will not be strange if the processions meet here before us."

"I fear, if they do, we cannot be heard."

The same thought was in the elder's mind. "Amrah," she asked, "when Judah spoke of the healing of the ten, what words did they use in speaking to the Nazarene?"

"Either they said, 'Lord, have mercy on us,' or, 'Master, have mercy.'"

"Only that?"

"No more that I heard."

"Yet it was enough," the mother added to herself.

"Yes," said Amrah, "Judah said he saw them go away well."

Meantime the people in the east came up slowly. When finally the foremost of them were in sight, the gaze of the lepers was set upon a man riding in the midst of what seemed a chosen company that sang and danced about him in an extravagance of joy. The rider was bareheaded and clad all in white. When he was in a closer distance to be more clearly observed, these people, looking anxiously, saw an olive-hued face shaded by long chestnut hair slightly sunburned and parted in the middle.

He looked neither to the right nor left. In the noisy abandon of his followers he appeared to have no part. Nor did their favor disturb him in the least or raise him out of the profound thought that showed clearly on his face. The sun beat upon the back of his head and lighting up the floating hair gave it the delicate likeness of a golden aura. Behind him the irregular procession, pouring forward with continuous singing and shouting, extended beyond view. There was no need of anyone to tell the lepers that this was he—the wonderful Nazarene!

"He is here, Tirzah," the mother said. "He is here. Come, my child."

As she spoke she glided in front of the white rock and fell upon her knees.

Immediately the daughter and servant were by her side. Then at the sight of the procession in the east, the thousands from the city halted and began to wave their green branches, shouting, or rather chanting (for it was all in one voice), "Blessed is the King of Israel that comes in the name of the Lord!"

And all the thousands who were part of the rider's company, both those near and far, replied so that the air shook with the sound, which was similar to a great wind threshing the side of the hill. Amidst the din, the cries of the poor lepers did not seem to be more than the twittering of dazed sparrows.

The moment of the meeting of the hosts had come and with it the opportunity the sufferers were seeking. If not taken, it would be lost forever, and they would be lost as well.

"Nearer, my child—let us get nearer. He cannot hear us," said the mother.

She arose and staggered forward. Her ghastly hands were up, and she screamed with horrible shrillness. The people saw her—saw her hideous face and stopped awestruck—an effect for which extreme human misery, visible as in this instance, is as powerful as majesty in purple and gold. Tirzah, behind her a little way, fell down too faint and frightened to follow any farther.

"The lepers! The lepers!"

"Stone them!"

"The accursed of God! Kill them!"

These with similar yells broke in upon the hosannas of the part of the multitude too far removed to see and understand the cause of the interruption. Some were there, however, who were near by and familiar with the nature of the man to whom the lepers were appealing—some who by long fellowship with him had caught some of his divine compassion.

They gazed at him and were silent while, in clear view, he rode up and stopped in front of the woman.

She also beheld his face—calm, pitiful, and of exceeding beauty, the large eyes tender with benign purpose.

"O Master! You see our need. You can make us clean. Have mercy upon us—mercy!"

"Do you believe I am able to do this?" he asked.

"You are he of whom the prophets spoke—you are the Messiah!" she replied.

His eyes grew radiant, his manner confident.

"Woman," he said, "great is your faith. Be it unto you even as you wish." He lingered an instant after, apparently unconscious of the presence of the throng—an instant—then he rode away.

To the heart originally divine, yet so human in all the best elements possessed by humanity, going with a sure precision to a death the foulest and most cruel of all the inventions of men, breathing even then in the shadow of the awful event, and still as hungry and thirsty for love and faith as in the beginning, how precious and soothing the farewell of the grateful woman: "To God in the highest, glory! Blessed, three times blessed, the Son whom He has given us!"

Immediately both hosts, that from the city and that from Bethpage, closed around him with joyous demonstrations, with hosannas and waving of palms, and so he went away from the lepers forever. Covering her head, the elder hastened to Tirzah and folded her in her arms, crying, "Daughter, look up! I have his promise. He is indeed the Messiah. We are saved—saved!" And the two remained kneeling while the procession, going slowly, disappeared over the mount. When the noise of its singing afar was a sound scarcely heard, the miracle began.

There was first in the hearts of the lepers a freshening of the blood. Then it flowed faster and stronger, thrilling their wasted bodies with an infinitely sweet sense of painless healing. Each felt the plague going from her. Their strength revived. They were returning to be themselves. Directly, as if to make the purification complete, from body to spirit the quickening ran, exalting them to a great sense of ecstasy.

The power bringing about this good end had a swift and happy effect, unlike all others and superior in that its healing and cleansing were absolute and not merely a restored consciousness in progress. It was the planting, growing, and maturing all at once of a recollection so holy that the simple thought of it should be of itself ever after a formless yet perfect thanksgiving.

To this transformation—for it may be called this as well as a cure—there was a witness besides Amrah. Ben Hur had followed the Nazarene throughout his wanderings, and now, recalling the conversation of the night before, the young Jew was present when the leprous woman appeared in the path of the pilgrims. He heard her prayer and saw her disfigured face. He heard the answer also and was not so accustomed to incidents of the kind, frequent as they had been, as to have lost interest in them. Had such a thing been possible with him, still the bitter disputation among bystanders always elicited by the simplest display of the Master's curative powers would have been enough to keep his curiosity alive.

Besides that, there was a further incentive. His hope to satisfy himself about the mysterious question of the mission of the man was still as strong as in the beginning, perhaps even stronger, because of a belief that now quickly, before the sun went down, the man himself would make everything known by a public proclamation. At the close of the scene, consequently, Ben Hur had withdrawn from the procession and seated himself upon a stone to wait its passage.

From his place he nodded recognition to many of the people—Galileans in his conspiracy, carrying short swords under their long tunics. After a while a swarthy Arab came up leading two horses. At a sign from Ben Hur he also drew out.

"Stay here," the young master said, when all were gone by, even those lagging behind. "I wish to be at the city early, and Aldebaran must do me service."

He stroked the broad forehead of the horse, now in his prime of strength and beauty, then crossed the road toward the two women.

They were to him, it should be kept in mind, strangers in whom he felt an interest only because they were subjects of a superhuman experiment, the result of which might possibly help him to find the solution to the mystery that had so long occupied him. As he proceeded, he glanced casually at the figure of the little woman over by the white rock, standing there, her face hidden in her hands.

As the Lord lives, it is Amrah! he said to himself. He hurried on and, passing by the mother and daughter, still without recognizing them, he stopped before the servant.

"Amrah," he said to her, "Amrah, what are you doing here?"

She rushed forward and fell upon her knees before him, blinded by her tears, almost speechless with conflicting joy and fear. "O master, master! Your God and mine, how good He is!"

The knowledge we gain from much sympathy with others passing through trials is but vaguely understood. Strangely enough, it enables us, among other things, to merge our identity into theirs often so completely that their sorrows and their delights become our own. So poor Amrah, aloof and hiding her face, knew the transformation the lepers were undergoing without a word spoken to her and shared their emotions to the full.

Her countenance, her words, her whole manner, betrayed her condition, and with swift understanding he connected it with the women he had just passed. He felt her presence there at that time was in some way associated with them and turned hastily as they arose to their feet. His heart stood still. He became rooted in his tracks—dumb beyond outcry—awestruck.

The woman he had seen before the Nazarene was standing with her hands clasped and eyes streaming, looking toward heaven. The mere transformation would have been a sufficient surprise, but it was the least of the causes of his emotion.

Could he be mistaken? There was never in life a stranger so like his mother, and like her as she was the day the Roman snatched her from him. There was only one difference to mar the identity—the hair of this person was a little streaked with gray. Yet that was not impossible to reconcile, since the person who had directed the miracle might have taken into consideration the natural effects of the passage of years.

And who was it by her side, if not Tirzah? Fair, beautiful, perfect, more mature, but in all other respects exactly the same in appearance as when she looked with him over the parapet the morning of the accident with Gratus.

He had given them up as dead, and time had accustomed him to bereavement. He had not ceased mourning for them, yet, as something tangible they had simply dropped out of his plans and dreams. Scarcely believing his senses, he laid his hand upon the servant's head and asked, trembling, "Amrah, Amrah—my mother! Tirzah! Tell me if I see correctly."

"Speak to them, O master, speak to them!" she said.

He waited no longer but ran, with outstretched arms, crying, "Mother! Mother! Tirzah! Here I am!"

They heard his call and with a cry as loving started to meet him. Suddenly the mother stopped, drew back, and uttered the old alarm. "Stay, Judah, my son. Do not come nearer. Unclean, unclean!"

The utterance was not from habit, grown since the dread disease struck her, as much as fear, and the fear was but another form of her ever-thoughtful maternal love. Though they were healed in person, the taint of the scourge might be in their garments ready to pass to another.

He had no such thought. They were before him. He had called them, they had answered. Who or what should keep them from him now? The next moment the three, so long separated, were mingling their tears in each others arms.

The first ecstasy over, the mother said, "In this happiness, O my children, let us not be ungrateful. Let us begin life anew by acknowledging Him to whom we are all so indebted."

They fell upon their knees, Amrah with the rest, and the prayer of the elder one who spoke was like a psalm. Tirzah repeated it word for word.

So did Ben Hur but not with the same clear mind and questionless faith, for when they were risen, he asked, "In Nazareth, where the man was born, Mother, they call him the son of a carpenter. What is he?"

Her eyes rested upon him with all their old tenderness, and she answered as she had answered the Nazarene himself. "He is the Messiah."

"And from where does he have his power?"

"We may know by the use he makes of it. Can you tell me any wrong he has done?"

"No."

"By that sign then I answer you. He has his power from God."

It is not an easy thing to shake off in a moment the expectations nurtured through years until they have become essentially a part of us. And though Ben Hur asked himself what the vanities of the world were to such a one as this, his ambition would not subside. He persisted as men do every day in measuring the Christ by himself. How much better if we measured ourselves by the Christ!

Naturally, the mother was the first to think of the cares of life. "What shall we do now, my son? Where shall we go?"

Then Ben Hur, recalled to duty, observed how completely every trace of the plague had disappeared from his restored people. Each had back her perfection. As with Naaman when he came up out of the water, their flesh had come again like the flesh of a little child. He took off his cloak and threw it over Tirzah.

"Take it," he said, smiling. "The eye of the stranger would have shunned you before. Now it shall not offend you." The act exposed a sword belted to his side.

"Is it a time of war?" asked the mother anxiously.

"No."

"Why, then, are you armed?"

"It may be necessary to defend the Nazarene." In this way Ben Hur evaded the whole truth.

"He has enemies? Who are they?"

"Mother, they are not all Romans!"

"Is he not of Israel and a man of peace?"

"There was never one more so, but in the opinion of the rabbis and teachers he is guilty of a great crime."

"What crime?"

"In his eyes the uncircumcised Gentile is as worthy of favor as a Jew of the strictest practice. He preaches a new teaching."

The mother was silent, and they moved to the shade of the

tree by the rock. Calming his impatience to have them home again and hear their story, he showed them the necessity of obedience to the law governing cases such as theirs and in conclusion called the Arab, bidding him take the horses to the gate by Bethesda and await him there.

After that they set out by the way of the Mount of Offense. The return was very different from the coming. They walked rapidly and with ease and in good time reached a newly made tomb near that of Absalom, overlooking the depths of Cedron. Finding it unoccupied, the women took possession, while he went on hastily to make the preparations required for their new condition.

76

Pilgrims to the Passover

Ben Hur pitched two tents out on the Upper Cedron east a short space from the Tombs of the Kings and furnished them with every comfort at his command. And without any loss of time he led his mother and sister there, to remain until the examining priest could certify their perfect cleansing.

In the course of his duty, the young man had exposed himself to such serious defilement as to prevent him from participating in the ceremonies of the great feast, which were then near at hand. He could not enter even the least sacred of the courts of the Temple. Out of necessity, much less than choice, therefore, he stayed at the tents with his beloved people. There was a great deal to hear from them and a great deal to tell them about himself.

Stories such as theirs—sad experiences extending through a period of years, intense suffering in body, worse suffering of mind—are usually long in the telling. The incidents seldom follow each other in a logical connection. He listened to the narrative and all they told him with an outward patience that masked his true inward feelings. In fact, his hatred of Rome and the Romans reached a higher degree than ever. His desire for vengeance became a thirst that only intensified with attempts at reflection on the wrong done.

In the almost savage bitterness of his spirit, many mad impulses took hold of him. The opportunity for robbery on the highways presented itself with a strong force of temptation. He thought seriously of insurrection in Galilee. Even the sea, ordinarily a remembered horror to him, stretched itself like a map before his fancy, laced and interlaced with lines of passages crowded with imperial plunder and imperial travelers. But his better judgment matured in calmer hours and was too firmly fixed to be supplanted by his present passion, however strong. Each mental venture in reach of new options brought him back to the old conclusion—there could be no sound success except in a war involving all of Israel in solid union, and all pondering upon the subject, all inquiry, all hope, ended where they began—in the Nazarene and his purposes.

At odd moments the excited schemer found a pleasure in fashioning a speech for that person. "Hear, O Israel! I am he, the promised of God, born King of the Jews—come to you with the dominion spoken of by the prophets. Rise now, and lay hold of the world!"

If only the Nazarene would but speak these few words, what a tumult would follow! How many youths would take up trumpets and blow them abroad for the gathering of armies! Would he speak them?

Eager to begin the work and answering in the worldly way, Ben Hur lost sight of the dual nature of the man and of the other possibility, that the divine in him might transcend the human. In the miracle of which Tirzah and his mother were the witnesses even more than himself, he saw and dwelt upon a power ample enough to raise and support a Jewish crown over the wrecks of the Roman empire and more than ample to remodel society and convert mankind into one purified happy family.

And when that work was done, could anyone say the peace that might then be obtained without hindrance was not a mission worthy of the Son of God? Could anyone then deny the Redeemer nature of the Christ? And discarding all consideration of political consequences, what unspeakable personal glory would there then be to him as a man? It was not in the nature of any mere mortal to refuse such a career.

Meantime down the Cedron and in toward Bezetha, especially on the roadsides almost up to the Damascus Gate, the country filled rapidly with all kinds of temporary shelters for pilgrims to the Passover.

Ben Hur visited the strangers and talked with them, and returning to his tents, he was each time more and more astonished at the vastness of their numbers. When he further discovered that every part of the world was represented among them—cities upon both shores of the Mediterranean far off as the Pillars of the West, river towns in distant India, provinces in northernmost Europe, though they frequently saluted him with tongues unacquainted with a syllable of the old Hebrew of the fathers—an idea covered mistily with superstitious fancy forced itself upon him. Might he not after all have misunderstood the Nazarene? Might not that person by patiently waiting be making silent preparation and proving his fitness for the glorious task before him? It would be much better now for the movement to arise than that other when, by Gennesaret, the Galileans would have forced him to assume the crown. Then the support would have been limited to a few thousand. Now his proclamation would be responded to by millions—who could say how many? Pursuing this theory to its conclusion, Ben Hur moved amidst brilliant promises and glowed with the thought that the contemplative man, with gentleness and wondrous self-denial, was in fact carrying in disguise the subtlety of a politician and the genius of a soldier.

Several times also, in the meantime, low-set, brawny men, bareheaded and black-bearded, came and asked for Ben Hur at the tent. His interviews with them were always away from the family, and to his mother's questions about who they were he answered, "Some good friends of mine from Galilee."

Through them he was kept informed of the movements of the Nazarene and of the schemes of the Nazarene's enemies, both rabbinical and Roman. He knew that the good man's life was in danger, but that there were any bold enough to attempt to take it at that time he could not believe. He seemed too securely entrenched in great fame and an assured popularity. The very vastness of the attendance in and about the city brought with it a seeming guarantee of safety.

Yet, to tell the truth, Ben Hur's confidence rested most certainly upon the miraculous power of the Christ. Pondering the subject from the purely human view, that the master of such authority over life and death, used so frequently for the good of others, would not exert it to take care of himself was simply as much past belief as it was past understanding.

Nor should it be forgotten that all these incidents occurred between the twenty-first day of March—counting by the modern calendar—and the twenty-fifth. The evening of the latter day Ben Hur yielded to his impatience and rode to the city, leaving behind him a promise to return in the night.

The horse was fresh and, choosing his own gait, sped swiftly. The eyes of the clambering vines winked at the rider from the garden fences on the way. There was nothing else to see him, not child nor woman nor man. Through the rocky float in the hollows of the road the agate hoofs drummed, ringing like cups of steel, but without notice from any stranger. In the houses he passed there were no tenants. The fires by the tent doors were out. The road was deserted, for this was the first Passover eve. This was the hour "between the evenings" when the visiting millions crowded the city, the slaughter of lambs in offering reeked the forecourts of the Temple, and the priests in ordered lines caught the flowing blood and carried it swiftly to the dripping altars—when all was haste and hurry, racing with the stars, which were fast arriving with the signal after which the roasting and the eating and the singing might go on.

Through the great northern gate the rider rode and saw Jerusalem before the fall, in her ripeness of glory, illuminated for the Lord.

77

A Serpent of the Nile

Ben Hur alighted at the gate of the inn from which the three Wise Men more than thirty years before had departed, going down to Bethlehem. There, in keeping with his Arab followers, he left the horse and shortly after was at the wicket of his father's house.

He called for Malluch first and through him sent a greeting to his friends, the merchant and the Egyptian. They were being carried out to see the celebration. The latter, he was informed, was very feeble and in a state of deep dejection.

Ben Hur inquired for the good Balthasar and with grave courtesy desired to know if he would be pleased to see him, yet he really was giving the daughter a notice of his arrival.

While the servant was answering for the elder, the curtain of the doorway was drawn aside, and the younger Egyptian came in and walked—or floated, upborne in a white cloud of the costume she so loved and lived in—to the center of the chamber, where the light cast by lamps from the seven-armed candlestick planted upon the floor was the strongest. With her there was no fear of light.

The servant left the two alone. In the excitement brought about by the events of the past few days Ben Hur had scarcely given a thought to the fair Egyptian. If she came to his mind at all, it was merely as a briefest pleasure, a suggestion of a delight that could wait for him and was waiting.

But now the influence of the woman was revived with all its force the instant Ben Hur saw her. He advanced to her eagerly, but stopped and gazed. He had never seen such a change!

Up to then, she had been an ardent lover trying to win him— in her manner all warmth, each glance an admission of devotion, each action an avowal of loyalty. She had showered him with the incense of flattery. While he was present, she had impressed him with her admiration. Going away, he carried the impression with him to remain a delicious expectancy hastening his return. It was for him the painted eyelids drooped lowest over the lustrous almond eyes. For him the love stories caught from the professionals abounding in the streets of Alexandria were repeated with emphasis and lavish poetry.

For him had been endless exclamations of sympathy and smiles. For him little privileges with hand and hair and cheek and lips, and songs of the Nile, and displays of jewelry, and subtleties of lace in veils and scarfs, and other subtleties not less exquisite in flosses of Indian silk. The idea, old as the oldest of peoples, that beauty is the reward of the hero had never such realism as she contrived for his pleasure, insomuch that he could not doubt he was her hero. She displayed it in a thousand artful ways as natural with her as her beauty—winsome ways reserved, it would seem, by the passionate genius of old Egypt for its daughters.

This is what the Egyptian had been to Ben Hur from the night of the boat ride on the lake in the Orchard of Palms. But now! There are few persons who do not have a dual nature, the real and the acquired. The latter is a kind of addition resulting from education, which in time often perfects it into a part of their being as unquestionable as the first. Now the real nature of the Egyptian made itself clear.

It was not possible for her to have received a stranger with a more definite repulsion. Yet she was apparently as passionless as a statue, only the small head was a little tilted, the nostrils a little drawn, and the sensuous lower lip pushed the upper just the least bit out of its natural curvature. She was the first to speak.

"Your coming is timely, O son of Hur," she said in a voice sharply distinct. "I wish to thank you for your hospitality. After tomorrow I may not have the opportunity to do so."

Ben Hur bowed slightly without taking his eyes from her.

"I have heard of a custom that the dice players observe with good result among themselves," she continued. "When the game is over, they refer to their tablets and cast up their accounts. Then they make offering to the gods and put a crown upon the happy winner. We have had a game—it has lasted through many days and nights. Why, now that it is at an end, shall we not see to whom the crown belongs?"

Still very observant, Ben Hur answered lightly, "A man may not stop a woman bent on having her way."

"Tell me," she continued, inclining her head and permitting the sneer to become positive, "tell me, O prince of Jerusalem, where is he, that son of the carpenter of Nazareth and son not less of God, from whom so lately such mighty things were expected?"

He waved his hand impatiently and replied, "I am not his keeper."

The beautiful head sank forward yet lower. "Has he broken Rome to pieces?"

Again, but with anger, Ben Hur raised his hand in protest.

"Where has he seated his capital?" she proceeded. "May I go see his throne and its lions of bronze? And his palace—he raised the dead, and to one such as this, what is it to raise a golden house? He has but to stamp his foot and say the word and the house is pillared like Karnak and wanting nothing."

There was by this time only slight ground left to believe she was playing. The questions were offensive, and her manner was pointed with unfriendliness. Seeing this, he became more wary and said, with good humor, "Egypt, let us wait another day, even another week, for him, the lions, and the palace."

She went on without noticing the suggestion. "And how is it I see you in that garb? This is not the costume of governors in India or vice-kings elsewhere. I saw the satrap of Teheran once, and he wore a turban of silk and a cloak of gold cloth, and the hilt and scabbard of his sword made me dizzy with their splendor of precious stones. I thought Osiris had lent him a glory from the sun. I fear you have not entered upon your kingdom—the kingdom I was to share with you."

"The daughter of my wise guest is kinder than she imagines herself. She is teaching me that Isis may kiss a heart without making it better."

Ben Hur spoke with cold courtesy, and Iras, after playing with the pendant solitaire of her necklace of coins, replied, "For a Jew, the son of Hur is clever. I saw your dreaming caesar make his entry into Jerusalem. You told us he would that day proclaim himself King of the Jews from the steps of the Temple.

"I viewed the procession as it descended the mountain bringing him. I heard their singing. They were beautiful with their palms in motion. I looked everywhere among them for a figure with a promise of royalty—a horseman in purple, a chariot with a driver in shining brass, a stately warrior behind an orbed shield, rivaling his spear in stature. I looked for his guard. It would have been pleasant to have seen a prince of Jerusalem and a cohort of the legions of Galilee."

She threw her listener a glance of provoking disdain, then laughed heartily, as if the silliness of the picture in her mind was too strong for contempt. "Instead of a caesar returning in triumph, helmeted and sworded, I saw a man with a woman's face and hair, riding an ass's colt and in tears. The King! The Son of God! The Redeemer of the world! Ha, ha!"

Ben Hur winced at her mocking.

"I did not leave my place, O prince of Jerusalem," she said, before he could recover. "I did not laugh. I said to myself, 'Wait. In the Temple he will glorify himself as becomes a hero about to take possession of the world.' I saw him enter the Gate of Shushan and the Court of the Women. I saw him stop and stand before the Gate Beautiful. There were people with me on the porch and in the courts, and on the cloisters and on the steps of the three sides of the Temple were other people—I will say a million people, all waiting breathlessly to hear his proclamation. The pillars were not more still than we were. I fancied I heard the axles of the mighty Roman machine begin to crack. My prince, by the soul of Solomon, your King of the World drew his gown about him and walked away. And—the Roman machine is running still!"

Ben Hur lowered his eyes in simple homage to a hope that was instantly lost—a hope that, as it began to fail he unconsciously followed with a parting look as it disappeared.

At no previous time, whether when Balthasar was challenging him with arguments, or when miracles were being done before his face, had the disputed nature of the Nazarene been so plainly put before him. The best way, after all, to reach an understanding of the divine is by studying human nature. We may always look to find God's role in the things superior to men. The portrayal given by the Egyptian of the scene when the Nazarene turned from the Gate Beautiful had as its central theme an act utterly beyond performance by a man under the control of merely human inspiration. A parable given to a people fond of illustrations, it taught what the Christ had so often asserted—that his mission was not political. There was not much more time for thought about all of this, yet the idea took fast hold of Ben Hur, and in the same instant he followed his continual hope of vengeance without anyone else knowing, and the gentle carpenter came to his thoughts near enough to leave an imprint of his spirit upon Ben Hur.

"Daughter of Balthasar," he said with dignity, "if this is the game of which you spoke, take the crown—I give it to you. Only let us make an end to mere words. I am sure you have a purpose. So get on with it, I pray, and I will answer you. Then let us go our several ways and forget we ever met. Speak and I will listen, but speak no more of what you have just discussed."

She regarded him intently for a moment, as if determining what to do—she might have possibly been measuring his will—then she said, coldly, "You have my leave—go."

"Peace to you," he responded and walked away.

As he was walking out the door, she called to him. "A word." He stopped where he was and looked back.

"Consider all I know about you."

"O most fair Egyptian," he said, returning, "what all do you know about me?"

She looked at him absently. "You are more of a Roman, son of Hur, than any of your Hebrew brethren."

"Am I so unlike my countrymen?"

"The demigods are all Roman now," she rejoined.

"And therefore you will tell me what more you know about me?"

"The likeness is not lost to me. It might induce me to save you."

"Save me!"

Her pink-stained fingers toyed daintily with the lustrous pendant at her throat, and her voice was exceedingly low and soft. Only a tapping on the floor with her silken sandal admonished him to be careful of her motives.

"There was a Jew, an escaped galley slave, who killed a man in the Palace of Idernee," she began slowly.

Ben Hur was startled.

"The same Jew killed a Roman soldier in the marketplace here in Jerusalem. This Jew has three trained legions from Galilee to seize the Roman governor tonight. This Jew has alliances finalized for war upon Rome, and Ilderim the Sheik is one of his partners."

Drawing near him, she almost whispered, "You have lived in Rome. Suppose these things were repeated in the ears of others we know. Ah! You change color."

He drew back from her with somewhat of the look that may be imagined upon the face of a man who, thinking to play with a kitten, has run into a tiger.

She proceeded. "You know the lord Sejanus. Suppose it were explained to him with the proofs in hand, or without the proofs, that the same Jew is the richest man in the East—no, in all the empire. Son of Hur! What splendor there would be on exhibition in the circus! Amusing the Roman people is a fine art—getting the money to keep them amused is a finer art still. And there has never been an artist the equal of the lord Sejanus."

The scene at the spring on the way to the Jordan came to his mind again, and he remembered thinking then that Esther had betrayed him. Now he said, calmly as he could, "To give you pleasure, daughter of Egypt, I acknowledge your cunning, and I confess that I am at your mercy. It may also please you to hear me acknowledge I have no hope of your favor. I could kill you, but you are a woman. The desert is open to receive me, and though Rome is a good hunter of men, she would follow long and far there before she caught me, for in the heart of the desert there are wildernesses of spears as well as wildernesses of sand, and it is safe for the unconquered Parthian. In all my toils—fool that I have been—there is one thing due to me—who told you all you know about me? Whether in flight or captivity, or even death, there will be consolation in leaving the traitor the curse of a man who has lived knowing nothing but wretchedness. Who told you all you know about me?"

It might have been a touch of art or might have been sincere—be that as it may—the expression of the Egyptian's face became sympathetic.

"There are in my country, O son of Hur," she then said, "workmen who make pictures by gathering various colored shells here and there on the seashore after storms and cutting them up and patching the pieces as inlaying on marble slabs. Can you not receive the hint in the practice of those who gather secrets?

"It is enough for you to know that from one person I gathered a handful of details of certain circumstances, and from another person yet another handful, and that after a while I put them together and was happy as a woman can be who has at her disposal the fortune and life of a man whom"—she looked away as if to hide a sudden emotion from him, and with an air of painful resolution she finally finished the sentence—"whom she is at a loss to know what to do with."

"No, it is not enough," Ben Hur said, unmoved by the play. "It is not enough. Tomorrow you will determine what to do with me. I may die."

"True," she answered quickly and with emphasis. "I had some things from Sheik Ilderim as he lay with my father in a grove out in the desert. The night was still, very still, and the walls of the tent, it is plain to see, were a poor guard against ears outside listening to things—birds and beetles flying through the air."

She smiled at the allusion but proceeded. "Some other things —bits of a shell for the picture—I had from—"

"Whom?"

"The son of Hur himself."

"Were there no others who contributed?"

"No, not one."

Ben Hur drew a breath of relief and said lightly. "Thanks. It is not polite to keep the lord Sejanus waiting for you. The desert is not so sensitive. Again, Egypt, peace!"

He had been standing bareheaded. Now he took the handkerchief from his arm where it had been hanging and, adjusting it on his head, turned to depart.

But she stopped him. In her eagerness she even reached a hand to him. "Stay," she said.

He looked back, but without taking her hand, though it was very noticeable with its sparkling jewels. And he knew by her manner that the important part of the visit, which was so surprising to him in the first place, was now to come.

"Stay, and do not distrust me, son of Hur, if I tell you that I know why the noble Arrius made you his heir. And, by Isis, by all the gods of Egypt, I swear I tremble to think of you, so brave and generous, under the hand of the remorseless minister. You have left a portion of your youth in the heart of the great capital. Consider, as I do, what the desert will be to you in contrast to this other life. Oh, I give you pity! And if you only do what I say, I will save you. I swear that also by our holy Isis!"

These words of entreaty and prayer were poured forth volubly and with earnestness and the mighty persuasion of beauty.

"I almost believe you," Ben Hur said, hesitatingly and in a low, indistinct voice, for a doubt remained with him that fought against his tendency to yield—a good sturdy doubt, the type that has saved many a life and fortune.

"The perfect life for a woman is to live in love. The greatest happiness for a man is the conquest of himself. And that, prince, is what I have to ask of you." She spoke rapidly and with animation. Indeed, she had never appeared to him so fascinating.

"You once had a friend," she continued. "It was in your boyhood. There was a quarrel, and you and he became enemies. He did you wrong. After many years you met him again in the circus at Antioch."

"Messala?"

"Yes, Messala. You are his creditor. Forgive the past. Admit him to friendship again. Restore the fortune he lost in the great wager. Rescue him. The six talents are nothing to you, not so much as a bud lost upon a tree already in full leaf. But to him, he must go about with a broken body. Wherever you meet him he must look up to you from the ground. Ben Hur, noble prince! To a Roman descended as he is to be a beggar is the most odious name for death. Save him from being a beggar!"

If her rapid speech was a cunning invention to keep him from thinking, either she never knew or had forgotten that there are convictions that do not come from thoughts but appear without notice. It seemed to him, when at last she paused to await his answer, that he could see Messala himself peering at him over her shoulder, and in its expression the countenance of the Roman was not that of a friend. The sneer was as patrician as ever, and the fine edge of his speech as flawless and irritating.

"The appeal has been decided then, and for once Messala takes nothing. I must go and write it in my diary—a judgment by a Roman against a Roman! But did he—did Messala send you to me with this request, Egypt?"

"He has a noble nature and judged you by it."

Ben Hur took the hand upon his arm. "Since you know him in such a friendly way, fair Egyptian, tell me, would he do for me, if there were a reversal of our situations, what he asks of me? Answer, by Isis! Answer, for the truth's sake!" There was insistence in the touch of his hand and in his look.

"Oh," she began, "he is—"

"A Roman, you were about to say. Meaning that I, a Jew, must not determine dues from me to him by the same measure of dues from him to me. Being a Jew, I must forgive him my winnings because he is a Roman. If you have more to tell me, daughter of Balthasar, speak quickly, for by the Lord God of Israel, when this boiling blood, getting ever hotter, reaches its highest point, I may not be able to to see any longer that you are a woman and a beautiful one! I may see only the spy of a master, even more hateful because the master is a Roman. Tell me more, and quickly."

She threw his hand off and stepped back into the full light, with all the evil of her nature collecting in her eyes and voice. "You drink and feed upon emptiness! To think I could love you, having seen Messala! *Women* such as yourself were born to serve him. He would have been satisfied with the release of the six talents, but I say you shall add twenty to the six—twenty, do you hear? The kissing of my little finger that you have taken from him, though with my consent, shall be paid for. The fact that I have followed you with affectation of sympathy, and endured you so long, will not enter into the account less because I was serving him.

"The merchant here is your banker. If by tomorrow at noon he does not have your order carried out in favor of my Messala for twenty-six talents—mark the sum!—you shall settle with the lord Sejanus. Be wise and—farewell."

As she was going to the door, he put himself in her way. "The old Egypt lives in you," he said. "Whether you see Messala tomorrow or the next day, here or in Rome, give him this message. Tell him I have the money back, even the six talents, he robbed me of by robbing my father's estate. Tell him I survived the galleys to which he had me sent, and in my strength I rejoice in his poverty and dishonor.

"Tell him I think the affliction of body that he has from my hand is the curse of our Lord God of Israel upon him, more fit than death for his crimes against the helpless. Tell him my mother and sister, whom he had sent to a cell in Antonia that they might die of leprosy, are alive and well, thanks to the power of the Nazarene whom you so despise. Tell him that, to fill my measure of happiness, they are restored to me and that I will go to share their love and find more than compensation in it for the impure passions that you leave me to take to him.

"Tell him—this for your comfort, you cunning serpent, as much as his—tell him that when the lord Sejanus comes to pillage me he will find nothing, for the inheritance I had from the duumvir, including the villa by Misenum, has been sold and the money from the sale is out of reach, afloat in the markets of the world as bills of exchange, and that this house and the goods and merchandise, and the ships and caravans with which Simonides plies his commerce with such princely profits, are covered by imperial safeguards.

"Tell him if all this were not so, if the money and property were all mine, still he would not have the least part of it, for when he finds our Jewish bills and devalues them, there is still another option left to me—a gift to Caesar. I found out so much, Egypt, in the atria of the great capital. Tell him that along with my defiance I do not send him a curse in mere words, but, as a better expression of my undying hate, I send him a person who will prove to be the sum of all curses. And when he hears you repeat this message, daughter of Balthasar, his Roman shrewdness will allow him to understand my intentions. Go now—and I will go."

He conducted her to the door and, with ceremonious politeness, held back the curtain while she passed out. "Peace to you," he said, as she disappeared.

78

Ben Hur Returns to Esther

When Ben Hur left the guest chamber, there was much more life and energy in his spirit than when he entered it. His steps were slower, and he walked with his head down. Having made the discovery that a man with a broken back may still have a sound brain, he was reflecting on this discovery.

It is easy after a calamity has struck to look back and see the evidence of its effects along the way. The thought that he had not even suspected that the Egyptian was in Messala's service, but had gone blindly on through many years putting himself and his friends more and more at her mercy, was a sore wound to the young man's vanity.

I remember now, he said to himself, *that she had no word of indignation for the treacherous Roman at the Fountain of Castalia! I remember also that she praised him at the boat ride on the lake in the Orchard of Palms! And*—he stopped and pounded his left hand violently with his right—*that mystery about the appointment she made with me at the Palace of Idernee is no mystery now!*

The wound, it should be observed, was to his vanity. Fortunately it is not often that people die of such hurts or even continue to feel the effects for a long time. In Ben Hur's case, moreover, there was a compensation. He exclaimed aloud, "Praised be the Lord God that the woman did not take a lasting hold of me! I see I did not love her."

Then, as if he had already parted with the heavy burden that was on his mind, he stepped forward more lightly. Coming to the place on the terrace where one stairway led down to the courtyard below and another ascended to the roof, he took the latter and began to climb.

"Can Balthasar have been her partner in the long charade she has been acting out? No. Hypocrisy seldom goes with wrinkled age like that. Balthasar is a good man."

With this decided opinion he stepped upon the roof. There was a full moon overhead, yet the vault of the sky at the moment was lurid with a light cast from the fires burning in the streets and open places of the city, and the chanting and chorusing of the old psalms of Israel filled it with beautiful harmonies with which he was pleased to listen. The countless voices bearing the burden seemed to say, "In this way, Son of Judah, we prove our worship of the Lord God and our loyalty to the land He gave us. Let a Gideon appear, or a David, or a Maccabaeus, and we are ready."

That seemed to be an introduction, for next he saw the man from Nazareth. In certain moods the mind is disposed to mock itself with fancies. The melancholy face of the Christ stayed with him while he crossed the roof to the parapet above the street on the north side of the house, and there was no sign of war in that face, but rather as the heavens on calm evenings project peace upon everything, it provoked the most important question: What kind of man was he?

Ben Hur permitted himself a glance toward the summerhouse. "Let them do their worst," he said, as he went slowly on. "I will not forgive the Roman. I will not divide my fortune with him, nor will I fly from this city of my fathers. I will call on Galilee first and fight here. By brave deeds I will bring the tribes to our side. He who raised up Moses will find us a leader, if I fail. If not the Nazarene, then some one of the many who are ready to die for freedom."

The interior of the summerhouse was murkily lit when Ben Hur came to it. The faintest of shadows lay along the floor, from the pillars on the north and west sides. Looking in, he saw the armchair that was usually occupied by Simonides drawn to a spot from which a view of the city over toward the marketplace could be best given.

"The good man has returned. I will speak with him, unless he is asleep."

He walked in and with a quiet step approached the chair. Peering over the high back, he saw Esther nestled in the seat asleep—a small figure snugged away under her father's lap robe. The disheveled hair fell over her face. Her breathing was low and irregular. Once it was broken by a long sigh, ending in a sob.

470

Something—it might have been the sigh or the loneliness in which he found her—gave him the idea that the sleep was a rest from sorrow rather than fatigue. Nature kindly sends such relief to children, and he was used to thinking of Esther as barely more than a child.

He put his arms upon the back of the chair and thought. *I will not wake her. I have nothing to tell her—nothing unless . . . unless it be my love. She is a daughter of Judah, and beautiful, and so unlike the Egyptian. With the Egyptian it is all vanity, here it is all truth. There ambition, here duty. There selfishness, here self-sacrifice.*

No, the question is not do I love her, but does she love me? She was my friend from the beginning. The night on the terrace at Antioch, in her childlike way she begged me not to make Rome my enemy and had me tell her of the villa by Misenum and of the life there! That she should not see I saw her cunning meaning, I kissed her. Can she have forgotten that kiss? I have not. I love her.

They do not know in the city that I have my people back. I shrank from telling it to the Egyptian, but this little one will rejoice with me over their restoration and welcome them with love and sweet services of hand and heart. She will be to my mother another daughter. In Tirzah she will find her other self.

I would wake her and tell her these things, but—the sorceress of Egypt begone! I cannot speak any longer of that folly. I will go away and wait for another and a better time. I will wait, fair Esther, dutiful child, daughter of Judah!

He retired as silently as he came.

79

Gethsemane—"Whom Do You Seek?"

The streets were full of people coming and going or grouped about the fires roasting meat, feasting, and singing. The odor of scorching flesh mixed with the odor of cedar, and as this was the occasion when every son of Israel was full brother to every other son of Israel, and hospitality was without bounds, Ben Hur was saluted at every step.

The groups by the fires insisted, "Stay and partake with us. We are brethren in the love of the Lord."

But with thanks to them he hurried on, intending to take a horse at the inn and return to the tents on the Cedron.

Looking up the street, he noticed the flames of torches in motion, then he observed that the singing ceased where the torches came. His wonder rose to its highest, however, when he became certain that amidst the smoke and dancing sparks he saw the keener sparkling of burnished speartips, suggesting the presence of Roman soldiers. What were they, the scoffing legionaires, doing in a Jewish religious procession? The circumstance was unheard of, and he stayed to see the meaning of it.

The moon was shining full. Yet, as if the moon and the torches and the fires in the street and the rays streaming from windows and open doors were not enough to make the way clear, some of those in the procession carried lighted lanterns.

Ben Hur stepped into the street, so close to the line of marching as to bring every one of the company visible while passing. The torches and the lanterns were carried by servants, each of whom was armed with a club or a sharpened stave. Their present duty seemed to be to pick out the smoothest paths among the rocks in the street for certain dignitaries among them—elders and priests; rabbis with long beards, heavy brows, and beaked noses; men potentially of the class of Caiaphas and Annas. Where could they be going? Not to the Temple, certainly, for the route to the sacred houses from Zion, where these appeared to be coming, was by the Xystus. And if their business was peaceful, why the soldiers?

As the procession began to go by Ben Hur, his attention was particularly called to three persons walking together. They were well toward the front, and the servants who went before them with lanterns appeared unusually careful in their service. The person moving on the left side of this group he recognized a chief policeman of the Temple. The one on the right was a priest. The middle man was not at first so easily placed, as he walked leaning heavily upon the arms of the others and carried his head so low upon his breast as to hide his face. His appearance was that of a prisoner not yet recovered from fright of arrest or being taken to something dreadful—to torture or death.

The dignitaries helping him on the right and left, and the attention they gave him, made clear that if he were not himself the object moving the party, he was at least in some way connected with the object—a witness or a guide, possibly an informer. So if he could discover who this man was, the business at hand might be guessed.

With great assurance, Ben Hur moved to the right of the priest and walked along with him. Now if the man would only lift his head! Then he did so, letting the light of the lanterns strike him full in his face—pale and dazed, the beard roughed, the eyes clouded, sunken, and in despair.

Following the Nazarene, Ben Hur had come to know his disciples as well as the Master, and now at the sight of the dismal countenance he cried out, "The 'Scariot!"

Slowly the head of the man turned until his eyes settled upon Ben Hur, and his lips moved as if he were about to speak, but the priest interfered. "Who are you? Begone!" he said to Ben Hur, pushing him out of the way.

The young man took the push good-naturedly and, waiting for an opportunity, joined the procession again. He was carried passively along down the street, through the crowded lowlands between the hill Bezetha and the Castle of Antonia and on by the Bethesda reservoir to the Sheep Gate. There were people everywhere engaged in sacred observances. It was Passover night, and

the latches of the Gate stood open. The keepers were off somewhere feasting.

In front of the procession as it passed out unchallenged was
the deep gorge of the Cedron, with Olivet beyond, its dressing of
cedar and olive trees darker than the moonlight silvering all the
heavens. Two roads met and merged into the street at the gate—
one from the northeast, the other from Bethany. Before Ben Hur
could finish wondering if he would go farther—and, if so, which
road was to be taken—he was led off down into the gorge. And
still there was no hint of the purpose of the midnight march.

Down they went into the gorge and over the bridge at the
bottom of it. There was a great clatter as the crowd, now a straggling rabble, passed over, beating and pounding with their clubs
and staves. A little farther and they turned off to the left in the
direction of an olive orchard enclosed by a stone wall in view
from the road.

Ben Hur knew there was nothing in the place but old gnarled
trees, grass, and a trough hewn out of a rock for the treading of
oil. While even more wonder-struck, he was thinking what could
bring such a company at such an hour to an area so lonesome,
they were all brought to a standstill. Voices called out excitedly in
front. A chilling sensation seemed to run from man to man. Men
fell over rapidly, blindly stumbling over each other. The soldiers
alone kept their order.

It took Ben Hur only a moment to disengage himself from the
mob and run forward. There he found a gateway without a gate,
opening to the orchard, and he halted to take in the scene.

A man in white clothes and bareheaded was standing outside the entrance, his hands crossed before him—a slender figure
with long hair and a thin face—in an attitude of resignation and
waiting.

It was the Nazarene!

Behind him, next to the gateway, were the disciples in a
group. They were excited, but no man was ever calmer than he.
The torchlight shone redly upon him, giving his hair a tint ruddier
than was natural to it. Yet the expression of his countenance was,
as usual, all gentleness and pity.

Opposite this figure stood the rabble, gaping, silent, awed, cowering—ready at a sign of anger from him to break and run. Ben Hur looked from him to them—then at Judas, conspicuous in their midst—one quick glance and the purpose of the visit lay open to his understanding. Here was the betrayer, and there was the betrayed. The ones with clubs and staves and the legionaires were brought to take him away.

This was the emergency for which Ben Hur had been preparing for years. The man to whose security he had devoted himself, and upon whose life he had been so largely building, was in personal peril. Yet he stood still. Such contradictions there are in human nature! He was not entirely recovered from the picture of Christ before the Gate Beautiful as it had been given by the Egyptian. Besides that, the very calmness with which the mysterious person confronted the mob held him in restraint by suggesting the possession of a power in reserve more than sufficient for the peril.

Peace and goodwill, love and nonresistance, had been the burden of the Nazarene's teaching. Would he put his preaching into practice? He was the master of life; he could restore it when lost; he could take it at pleasure. What use would he make of the power now? Defend himself? And how? A word—a breath—a thought were sufficient. That there would be some clear exhibition of astonishing force, beyond the natural, Ben Hur believed, and in that faith he waited. Yet in all this he was still comparing the Nazarene to himself—by a human standard.

Then the clear voice of the Christ arose. "Whom do you seek?"

"Jesus of Nazareth," the priest replied.

"I am he."

At these simplest of words, spoken without passion or alarm, the assailants fell back several steps, the timid among them cowering to the ground. They might have let him alone and gone away had not Judas walked over to him.

"Hail, master!" With this friendly speech, he kissed him.

"Judas," said the Nazarene mildly, "do you betray the Son of Man with a kiss?"

Receiving no reply, the Master spoke to the crowd again.

"Whom do you seek?"

"Jesus of Nazareth."

"I have told you that I am he. If, therefore, you seek me, let these others go their way."

At these words of entreaty the rabbis advanced upon him. Seeing their intent, some of the disciples for whom he interceded drew nearer. With his sword, one of them cut off a man's ear, but without preventing the master from being taken.

And yet Ben Hur stood still.

Now, while the officers were making ready with their ropes, the Nazarene was performing his greatest work—not the greatest in deed but the greatest in order to illustrate his forbearance, surpassing that of humans.

"Permit this much," he said to the wounded man and healed him with a touch.

Both friends and enemies were confounded—one side that he could do such a thing, the other that he would do it under the circumstances.

Surely he will not allow them to bind him! thought Ben Hur.

"Put your sword into its sheath. The cup that my Father has given me, shall I not drink it?" From the offending disciple, the Nazarene now turned to his captors. "Have you come out against me as a thief, with swords and staves to take me? I was daily with you in the Temple, and you did not take me. But this is your hour and the power of darkness."

The group plucked up their courage then and closed in on him, and when Ben Hur looked for the faithful they were gone—not one remained.

The crowd about the deserted man seemed very busy in movement and conversation. Over their heads, between the torchsticks, through the smoke, sometimes in openings between the restless men, Ben Hur caught momentary glimpses of the prisoner. Never had anyone struck him as so piteous and so forsaken! *Yet,* he thought, *the man could have defended himself—he could have slain his enemies with a breath, but he would not do it. What was the cup his father had given him to drink? And who was the father to be obeyed in this way?* Mystery upon mystery confronted him.

Then the mob started to return to the city, with the soldiers in the lead.

Ben Hur became anxious. He was not satisfied with himself. He knew the Nazarene was to be found where the torches were in the midst of the rabble. Suddenly he resolved to see him again. He would ask him one question.

Taking off his long outer garment and the handkerchief from his head, he threw them on the orchard wall and started after the leaders, which he boldly joined. Through the stragglers he made way and little by little reached the man who carried the ends of the rope with which the prisoner was bound.

The Nazarene was walking slowly, his head down, his hands bound behind him. The hair fell thickly over his face, and he stooped more than usual. Apparently he was oblivious to all going on around him. A few steps in advance were priests and elders talking and occasionally looking back. When finally they were all near the bridge in the gorge, Ben Hur took the rope from the servant who had it and stepped past him.

"Master, master!" he said, hurriedly, speaking close to the Nazarene's ear. "Do you hear, master? A word—one word. Tell me—"

The fellow from whom he had taken the rope now claimed it.

"Tell me," Ben Hur continued, "do you go with these men of your own accord?"

The people were come up now and asked him angrily, "Who are you, man?"

"Master," Ben Hur made haste to say, his voice sharp with anxiety, "I am your friend and follower. Tell me, I pray you, if I bring rescue, will you accept it?"

The Nazarene never so much as looked up or allowed the slightest sign of recognition. A dozen hands were upon Ben Hur, and from all sides there was shouting. "He is one of them. Bring him along. Club him—kill him!"

With a gust of passion that provided him with many times his ordinary force, Ben Hur raised himself, turned around once with his arms outstretched, shook off the hands, and rushed through the circle that was fast hemming him in. The hands snatched at him as he passed, tore his garments from his back, so he ran off the road naked, and the gorge, which was darker than elsewhere, received him into safety.

Reclaiming his handkerchief and outer garments from the orchard wall, he followed them back to the city gate. From there he went to the inn and on the good horse rode to the tents of his people out by the tombs of the Kings. As he rode, he promised himself to see the Nazarene the next day, not knowing that the unfortunate man was taken straightaway to the house of Annas to be tried that night.

The heart of the young man beat so heavily he could not sleep, for now clearly his renewed Judean kingdom had revealed itself for what it was—only a dream. The spirits that calmly endure great disappointments are made of sterner stuff, and Ben Hur's was not of them.

Through vistas in the future he began to catch glimpses of a life serenely beautiful, with a home instead of a palace and Esther as its mistress. Again and again through the slow hours of the night he saw the villa by Misenum, and with his little country wife he strolled through the garden and rested in the paneled atrium. Overhead was the Neapolitan sky, and at their feet were the sunniest lands and the bluest bays.

80

The Going to Calvary

The next morning, about the second hour, two men rode full speed to the doors of Ben Hur's tents and, dismounting, asked to see him. He had not yet risen but gave directions for their admission.

"Peace to you, brethren," he said, for they were from the Galileans and were trusted officers. "Will you be seated?"

"No," the senior replied bluntly, "to sit and be at ease is to let the Nazarene die. Rise, son of Judah, and go with us. The judgment has been given. The tree of the cross is already at Golgotha."

Ben Hur stared at them. "The cross!" was all he could say for the moment.

"They took him last night and tried him," the man continued. "At dawn they led him before Pilate. Twice the Roman denied his guilt. Twice he refused to hand him over. At last he washed his hands and said, 'Be it upon you then,' and they answered—"

"Who answered?"

"They—the priests and people—'His blood be upon us and our children.'"

"Holy father Abraham!" cried Ben Hur. "A Roman kinder to an Israelite than his own kin! And if he should indeed be the Son of God, what shall ever wash his blood from their children? It must not be—it's time to fight!"

His face brightened with resolution, and he clapped his hands. "The horses—and quickly!" he said to the Arab who answered the signal. "And ask Amrah to send me fresh garments, and bring my sword! It is time to die for Israel, my friends. Wait outside until I come."

He ate a crust of bread, drank a cup of wine, and was soon upon the road.

"Where do you go first?" asked the Galilean.

"To collect the legions."

"Alas!" the man replied, throwing up his hands.

"Why?"

"Master," the man spoke with shame, "Master, I and my friend here are all that are faithful. The rest do follow the priests."

"Seeking what?" Ben Hur drew rein.

"To kill him."

"Not the Nazarene!"

"You have said it."

Ben Hur looked slowly from one man to the other. He was hearing once again the question of the night before: "The cup my Father has given me, shall I not drink it?" In the ear of the Nazarene he was placing his own question, "If I rescue you, will you accept it?" Then he was saying to himself, *This death may not be averted. The man has been traveling toward it with full knowledge from the day he began his mission. It is imposed by a will higher than his. Whose but the Lord's! If he is consenting, if he goes to it voluntarily, what shall anyone do?*

Nor less did Ben Hur see the failure of the scheme he had built upon the faithfulness of the Galileans. Their desertion, in fact, left nothing more to it. But how peculiar that it should happen that morning of all others! A dread seized him. It was possible his scheming and labor and expending of treasure might have been only a blasphemous contention with God. When he picked up the reins and said, "Let us go, brethren," all before him was uncertain. The ability to decide quickly, without which one cannot be a hero in the midst of important events, was numb within him.

"Let us go, brethren. Let us to go Golgotha."

They passed through excited crowds of people going south, like themselves. All the country north of the city seemed aroused and in motion.

Hearing that the procession with the condemned one might be joined somewhere near the great white towers of Herod, the three friends rode there, passing southeast of Akra. In the valley below the Pool of Hezekiah, passage against the multitude became impossible, and they were compelled to dismount and take shelter behind the corner of a house and wait. It appeared as if they were on a riverbank, watching a flood go by, there were so many.

Half an hour—an hour—the flood surged by Ben Hur and his companions, within arm's reach, incessant, undiminished. At the end of that time he could have said, "I have seen all the classes of Jerusalem, all the sects of Judea, all the tribes of Israel, and all the nationalities of the earth represented by them."

The Libyan Jew went by and the Jew of Egypt and the Jew from the Rhine—in short, Jews from all East countries and all West countries. They went by on foot, on horseback, on camels, in litters and chariots, and with an infinite variety of costumes, yet with the same marvelous similarity of features that today characterizes the children of Israel, modified as they have been by climates and modes of life. They went by speaking every known tongue, for by that way only were the groups distinguishable. They went by in haste—eager, anxious, crowding—all to behold one poor Nazarene die, a criminal between criminals.

Borne along with the stream were thousands who were not Jews—thousands hating and despising them—Greeks, Romans, Arabs, Syrians, Africans, and Egyptians. So that, studying the crowds, it seemed the whole world was to be represented and, in that sense, present at the crucifixion.

Their going was very quiet. A hoofstroke upon a rock, the glide and rattle of revolving wheels, voices in conversation were all the sounds to be heard above the rustle of the mighty movement. Yet there was on every face the look with which men make haste to see some dreadful sight, some sudden wreck, or ruin, or calamity of war. And by such signs Ben Hur judged that these were the strangers in the city who had come up to the Passover, who had had no part in the trial of the Nazarene and might be his friends.

Finally, from the direction of the great towers, Ben Hur heard, at first faint in the distance, the shouting of many men.

"Listen! They are coming now," said one of his friends.

The people in the street halted to hear. But as the cry rang on over their heads, they looked at each other and in shuddering silence moved along. The shouting drew nearer each moment, and the trembling air was already full of it when Ben Hur saw the servants of Simonides coming with their master in his chair and Esther walking by his side. A covered litter was behind them.

"Peace to you, O Simonides—and to you, Esther," said Ben Hur, meeting them. "If you are going to Golgotha, stay until the procession passes. I will then go with you. There is room to turn in by the house here."

The merchant's large head rested heavily upon his breast. Rousing himself, he answered, "Speak to Balthasar. His pleasure will be mine. He is in the litter."

Ben Hur hastened to draw aside the curtain. The Egyptian was lying within, his wan face was so pinched as to appear like a dead man's. The proposal was submitted to him. "Can we see him?" he inquired faintly.

"The Nazarene? Yes. He must pass within a few feet of us."

"Dear Lord!" the old man cried, fervently. "Once more, once more! Oh, it is a dreadful day for the world!"

Shortly the whole party was in waiting under the shelter of the house. They said little, afraid probably to trust their thoughts to each other. Everything was uncertain and nothing so much so as their opinions. Balthasar drew himself feebly from the litter and stood supported by a servant. Esther and Ben Hur kept Simonides company.

Meantime the flood poured along, if anything more densely than before. The shouting came nearer, shrill in the air, hoarse along the earth, and cruel. At last the procession had passed.

"See!" said Ben Hur bitterly. "That which comes now is from Jerusalem."

The advance was in possession of an army of boys, hooting and screaming, "The King of the Jews! Room for the King of the Jews!"

Simonides watched them as they whirled and danced along, like a cloud of summer insects, and said gravely, "When these come to their inheritance, son of Hur, alas for the city of Solomon!"

A band of legionaires fully armed followed next, marching in sturdy indifference. Then came the Nazarene.

He was nearly dead. Every few steps he staggered as if he would fall. A badly torn, stained gown hung from his shoulders over a seamless under tunic. His bare feet left red splotches upon the stones. An inscription on a board was tied to his neck. A crown of thorns had been crushed hard down upon his head, making cruel wounds from which streams of blood, dry and blackened, had run over his face and neck. The long hair, tangled in the thorns, was thickly clotted. The skin, where it could be seen, was ghastly white. His hands were tied before him.

Back somewhere in the city he had fallen exhausted under the transverse beam of his cross, which, as a condemned person, custom required him to bear to the place of execution. Now a countryman carried the burden in his stead. Four soldiers went with him as a guard against the mob, who sometimes broke through and struck him with sticks and spit upon him. Yet no sound escaped him, neither a rebuke nor a groan. Nor did he look up until he was nearly in front of the house sheltering Ben Hur and his friends.

All of them were moved with compassion. Esther clung to her father, and he, strong willed as he was, trembled. Balthasar fell down speechless. Even Ben Hur cried out, "My God!" then, as if he understood their feelings or heard the exclamation, the Nazarene turned his pale face toward the party and looked at each one, so that they carried that look in their memory for the rest of their lives. They could see he was thinking of them, not himself, and the dying eyes gave them the blessing he was not permitted to speak.

"Where are your legions, son of Hur?" asked Simonides, aroused.

"Annas can tell you better than I can."

"What are they, faithless?"

"All but these two."

"Then all is lost, and this good man must die!"

The face of the merchant contracted convulsively as he spoke, and his head sank. He had borne his part in Ben Hur's labors well, and he had been inspired by the same hopes, but now they were blown out, never to be rekindled.

Two other men followed the Nazarene, bearing crossbeams.

"Who are these?" Ben Hur asked of the Galileans.

"Thieves appointed to die with the Nazarene," they replied.

Next in the procession stalked a turbaned figure clad all in the golden vestments of the high priest. Guards from the Temple curtained him round, and after him, in order, strode the Sanhedrin and a long array of priests, the latter in plain white garments overwrapped by cloaks of many folds and beautiful colors.

"The son-in-law of Annas," said Ben Hur in a low voice.

"Caiaphas! I have seen him," Simonides replied, adding, after a pause during which he thoughtfully watched the haughty priest, "and now I am convinced. With absolute assurance, I now know that the Nazerene who has carried the cross with the inscription around his neck is what the inscription proclaims him—King of the Jews. A common man, an imposter, a felon, was never attended like this. For look! Here are the nations—Jerusalem, Israel. Here is the ephod, the blue robe with its fringe and purple pomegranates and golden bells, not seen in the street since the day Jaddua went out to meet the Macedonian—all proofs that this Nazarene is King. I wish I could rise and go after him!"

Ben Hur listened, surprised.

Immediately, as if he himself were awakening to his unusual display of feeling, Simonides said impatiently, "Speak to Balthasar, I pray you, and let us go. The vomit of Jerusalem is coming."

Then Esther spoke. "I see some women there, and they are weeping. Who are they?"

Following her pointing hand, the party gazed at four women in tears. One of them leaned upon the arm of a man whose manner was not unlike the Nazarene's.

Then Ben Hur answered. "The man is the disciple whom the Nazarene loves the best of all. She who leans upon his arm is Mary, the master's mother. The others are friendly women of Galilee."

Esther pursued the mourners with glistening eyes until they were out of sight.

The large crowd was a forerunner of those crowds by which, only thirty years later, under rule of various factions, the Holy City was torn to pieces. It was quite as great in numbers, as fanatical and bloodthirsty, and had the same elements—servants, camel drivers, businessmen, gate keepers, gardeners, dealers in fruits and wines, proselytes and foreigners, watchmen and servants from the Temple, thieves and robbers, and others who appeared from nowhere, hungry and smelling of caves and old tombs—bareheaded wretches with naked arms and legs, their hair and beard in uncombed mats. Some of them had swords. A greater number flourished spears and javelins, though the weapons of the majority were staves, knotted clubs, and slings with selected stones stored in pouches.

Among the mass also appeared persons of high standing—scribes, elders, rabbis, Pharisees with broad fringing, Sadducees in fine cloaks—serving as prompters and directors of the rabble. If a throat tired of one cry, they invented another. If strong lungs showed signs of collapse, they got them going again. And yet the clamor, loud and continuous as it was, could have been reduced to a few syllables—"King of the Jews!—Room for the King of the Jews!—Defiler of the Temple!—Blasphemer of God!—Crucify him, crucify him!" And of these cries the last was shouted with the greatest fervor, because beyond doubt it was more directly expressive of the wish of the mob and helped to better articulate their hatred of the Nazarene.

"Come," said Simonides, when Balthasar was ready to proceed. "Come, let us go forward."

Ben Hur did not hear the call. The appearance of the part of the procession then passing, its brutality and hunger for life, were reminding him of the Nazarene—his gentleness and the many charities he had seen him do for suffering people. He remembered suddenly his own great indebtedness to the man—the time he himself was in the hands of a Roman guard going, as was supposed, to a death as certain and almost as terrible as this one on a cross. He remembered the cooling drink he had at the well by Nazareth and the divine expression on the face of him who gave it; and the later goodness, the miracle of his mother's and Tirzah's healing.

With these recollections came the thought of his present powerlessness to give back help for help received or make a return in kind. This stung him keenly, and he accused himself. He had not done all he might. He could have prepared better with the Galileans and kept them true and ready. And this—this was the moment to strike! A blow well given now would not merely disperse the mob and set the Nazarene free, but it would be a trumpet call to Israel and precipitate the long-dreamed-of war for freedom. The opportunity was passing. The minutes were carrying it away, and if lost—God of Abraham! Was there nothing to be done? Nothing?

That instant a party of Galileans caught his eye. He rushed through the crowd and overtook them. "Follow me," he said. "I would like to talk with you."

The men obeyed, and when they were under the shelter of the house he spoke again. "You are of those who took my swords and agreed with me to strike for freedom and the King who was coming. You have the swords now, and now is the time to strike with them. Go, look everywhere and find our brethren and tell them to meet me at the cross being made ready for the Nazarene. Hurry all of you! No, do not stand around! The Nazarene is the King, and freedom dies with him."

They looked at him respectfully but did not move.

"Do you hear?" he asked.

Then one of them replied, "Son of Judah"—by that name they knew him—"son of Judah, it is you who are deceived, not we or our brethren who have your swords. The Nazarene is not the King, nor does he have the spirit of a king. We were with him when he came into Jerusalem. We saw him in the Temple. He failed himself and us and Israel. At the Gate Beautiful he turned his back upon God and refused the throne of David. He is not King, and Galilee is not with him. He shall die this cruel death. But hear this, son of Judah. We have your swords, and we are ready now to draw them and strike for freedom, and so is Galilee. Be it for freedom, O son of Judah, for freedom! And we will meet you at the cross."

The supreme moment of his life was now upon Ben Hur. If he could have taken the offer and said the word, history might have been different. But then it would have been a history ordered by men—not God—something that never was and never will be.

A confusion fell upon him. He knew not how, though afterwards he attributed it to the Nazarene. For when the Nazarene was risen, he understood the death was necessary to allow faith in the resurrection, without which Christianity would be an empty husk. The confusion left him without the faculty of a decision. He stood, helpless—wordless even. Covering his face with his hand, he shook with the conflict between his wish and the power that was upon him.

"Come. We are waiting for you," said Simonides, the fourth time.

He walked mechanically after the chair and the litter. Esther walked with him. Like Balthasar and his friends, the Wise Men, the day they went to the meeting in the desert, he was being led along the way.

81

The Crucifixion

When the party—Balthasar, Simonides, Ben Hur, Esther, and the two faithful Galileans—reached the place of crucifixion, Ben Hur was leading them. He never knew how they had been able to make way through the great press of excited people, nor did he know the road by which they came or the time it took them to come. He had walked in total unconsciousness, neither hearing nor seeing anybody or anything and without a thought of where he was going or the slightest semblance of a purpose in his mind. In such condition a little child could have done as much as he to prevent the awful crime he was about to witness. The intentions of God are always strange to us, but not more so than the means by which they are brought about and at last made plain to our belief. Ben Hur came to a stop. Those following him also stopped. As a curtain rises before an audience, the spell holding him in its sleep-awake rose, and he saw with a clear understanding.

There was a space upon the top of a low knoll rounded like a skull, dry, dusty, and without vegetation, except some scrubby hyssop. The boundary of the space contained a living wall of people. Others behind were struggling, some to look over, others to look through it. An inner wall of Roman soldiery held the dense outer wall rigidly in place. A centurion kept an eye upon the soldiers.

Ben Hur had been led up to the very line so vigilantly guarded. At this line he now stood, his face to the northwest. The knoll was the old Aramaic Golgotha—in Latin, Calvaria; in English, Calvary; also translated as The Skull.

On its slopes, in the low places, on the swells and higher hills, the earth sparkled with a strange glitter. No matter where he looked outside the walled space, he saw no patch of brown soil, no rock, no green thing. He saw only thousands of eyes in ruddy faces. This was a gathering of thousands—thousands of hearts throbbing with passionate interest in what was taking place upon the knoll, indifferent as to the thieves, caring only for the Nazarene, only because he was an object of hate or fear or curiosity—he who loved them all and was about to die for them.

In the spectacle of a great assembly of people there are always the bewilderment and fascination one feels while looking over a stretch of a sea in agitation, and never had this one been exceeded. Yet Ben Hur gave it only a passing glance, for that which was going on in the space described would not allow a division of his interest.

Up on the knoll so high as to be above the living wall, and visible over the heads of an attending company of notable people, conspicuous because of his turban and vestments and his haughty air, stood the high priest. Up the knoll still higher, up almost to the round summit, so as to be seen far and near, was the Nazarene, stooped and suffering but silent. The wit among the guards had added to the crown upon his head by putting a reed in his hand for a scepter. Clamors blew upon him like blasts—laughter and derision—sometimes both together indistinguishably.

All eyes were fixed upon the Nazarene.

It may have been pity with which he was moved. Whatever the cause, Ben Hur was conscious of a change in his feelings. A conception of something better than the best of this life began to dawn clearly upon his mind—something so much better that it could serve a weak man with strength to endure agonies of spirit as well as of body; something to make death welcome; perhaps another life purer than this one; perhaps the spirit life that Balthasar held to so fast—bringing him to the conclusion that, after all, the mission of the Nazarene was that of a guide across the boundary for those who loved him, across the boundary to where his kingdom was set up and waiting for him. Then, as something carried through the air out of an almost forgotten realm, Ben Hur heard again, or seemed to hear, the saying of the Nazarene:

"I am the resurrection and the life."

The words repeated themselves over and over and took form, and the dawn touched them with its light and filled them with a new meaning. And as men repeat a question to grasp and hold the meaning, he asked, gazing at the figure on the hill fainting under its crown, *Who is the resurrection? And who the life?*

"I am,"

the figure seemed to say—and say it for him. For instantly he was aware of a peace such as he had never known—the peace that is the end of doubt and mystery and the beginning of faith and love and clear understanding.

From this dreamy state Ben Hur was aroused by the sound of hammering. On the summit of the knoll he observed then what had escaped him before—some soldiers and workmen preparing the crosses. The holes for planting the trees were ready, and now the transverse beams were being fitted to their places.

"Tell the men to hurry," said the high priest to the centurion. "These"—he pointed to the Nazarene—"must be dead by sundown and buried, that the land may not be defiled. For this is the Law."

As a kind gesture, a soldier went to the Nazarene and offered him something to drink, but he refused the cup. Then another went to him and took from his neck the board with the inscription upon it, which he nailed to the tree of the cross—and the preparation was complete.

"The crosses are ready," said the centurion to the priest, who received the report with a wave of the hand and the reply, "Let the blasphemer go first. The Son of God should be able to save himself. We will see."

The people to whom the preparation in its several stages was visible, and who to this time had assailed the hill with incessant cries of impatience, permitted a lull that then became a universal hush. The part of the infliction that was most shocking occurred—the men were to be nailed to their crosses. When for that purpose the soldiers laid their hands upon the Nazarene first, a shudder passed though the great concourse. The most brutalized shrank with dread. Afterwards there were those who said the air suddenly chilled and made them shiver.

"How very still it is!" Esther said, as she put her arm about her father's neck.

And remembering the torture he himself had suffered, he drew her face down upon his breast and sat trembling.

"Avoid it, Esther, avoid it!" he said "I wonder if all who stand and see it—the innocent as well as the guilty—may not be cursed from this hour."

Balthasar sank upon his knees.

"Son of Hur," said Simonides with increasing excitement, "son of Hur, if Jehovah does not stretch forth his hand, and quickly, Israel is lost—and we are lost."

Ben Hur answered calmly, "I have been in a dream, Simonides, and heard in it why all this should be and why it should go on. It is the will of the Nazarene—it is God's will. Let us do as the Egyptian here—let us hold our peace and pray."

As he looked up on the knoll again, the words were wafted to him through the awful stillness:

"I am the resurrection and the life."

He bowed reverently as to a person speaking.

Up on the summit meantime the work went on. The guard took the Nazarene's clothes from him, so that he stood before the thousands naked. The stripes of the scourging he had received in the early morning were still bloody upon his back, yet he was laid pitilessly down and stretched upon the cross—first, the arms upon the transverse beam. The spikes were sharp—a few blows, and they were driven through the tender palms. Next they drew up his knees until the soles of the feet rested flat upon the tree. Then they placed one foot upon the other, and one spike held both of them fast.

The dulled sound of the hammering was heard outside the guarded space, and those who could not hear, yet saw the hammer as it fell, shivered with fear. And without a groan, or cry, or word of retort from the sufferer—nothing at which an enemy could laugh; nothing a lover could regret.

"Which way will you have him faced?" asked a soldier bluntly.

"Toward the Temple," the priest replied. "In dying I would have him see that the holy house has not suffered at his hand."

The workmen put their hands to the cross and carried it, burden and all, to the place of planting. At a word they dropped the tree into the hole, and the body of the Nazarene also dropped heavily and hung by the bleeding hands. Still there was no cry of pain—only a divine exclamation: "Father, forgive them, for they know not what they do."

The cross, reared now above all other objects and standing singly out against the sky, was greeted with a burst of delight. All who could see and read the writing upon the board over the Nazarene's head tried to decipher it. As soon as it was read, the legend was adopted by them and communicated, and presently the whole throng was ringing the salutation from side to side and repeated it with laughter and groans. "King of the Jews! Hail, King of the Jews!"

The priest, with a clearer idea of the importance of the inscription, protested against it, but in vain. So the titled King, looking from the knoll with dying eyes, must have had the city of his fathers at rest below him—she who had so infamously cast him out.

The sun was rising rapidly to noon. The hills bared their brown breasts lovingly to it. The more distant mountains rejoiced in the purple with which it so regally dressed them. In the city, the Temple, palaces, towers, pinnacles, and all points of beauty and prominence seemed to lift themselves into the unrivaled brilliance, as if they knew the pride they were giving the many who from time to time turned to look at them.

Suddenly a dimness began to fill the sky and cover the earth— at first no more than a scarce perceptible fading of the day, a twilight out of time, an evening gliding in upon the splendors of noon.

But it deepened and immediately drew attention so that the noise of the shouting and laughter trailed off, and men, doubting their senses, gazed at each other curiously. They looked to the sun again, then at the mountains, at the sky and the near landscape, sinking in shadow. At the hill upon which the tragedy was taking place. And from all these they gazed at each other again and turned pale and held their peace.

"It is only a mist or passing cloud," Simonides said soothingly to Esther, who was alarmed. "It will brighten soon."

Ben Hur did not think so. "It is not a mist or a cloud," he said. "The prophets and saints find fulfillment in this event within nature. I say to you, O Simonides, truly as God lives, he who hangs on that cross is the Son of God."

And leaving Simonides lost in wonder at such a speech from him, he went to where Balthasar was kneeling nearby and laid his hand upon the good man's shoulder. "O wise Egyptian, listen! You alone were right—the Nazarene is indeed the Son of God."

Balthasar drew him down to him and replied feebly, "I saw him as a child in a manger where he was first laid. It is not strange that I knew him sooner than you, but oh that I should live to see this day! Would I had died with my brethren! Happy Melchior! Happy Gaspar!"

The dimness went on deepening into obscurity and then into positive darkness but without deterring the bolder spirits upon the knoll. One after the other the thieves were raised on their crosses and the crosses planted. The guard was then withdrawn, and the people set free closed in upon the height and surged upon it like a converging wave. A person might take a look, then a newcomer would push him and take his place, to be in turn pushed on—and there was laughter and revilement, all for the Nazarene.

"Ha, ha! If you are the King of the Jews, save yourself," a soldier shouted.

"Yes," said a priest, "if he will come down to us now, we will believe in him."

Others wagged their heads, saying wisely, "He would destroy the Temple and rebuild it in three days but cannot save himself."

Others still, "He called himself the Son of God. Let us see if God will save him."

The Nazarene had never harmed people. The far greater part of them had never seen him except in this his hour of calamity. Yet—how contradictory! They loaded him with their curses and gave their sympathy to the thieves.

The supernatural night, dropping from the heavens, affected Esther as it began to affect thousands of others braver and stronger.

"Let us go home," she asked—even three times—saying, "It is the frown of God, Father. What other dreadful things may happen, who can tell? I am afraid."

Simonides was obstinate. He said little but was plainly filled with great excitement. Observing, about the end of the first hour, that the violence of the crowding up on the knoll was somewhat abated, at his suggestion the party advanced to take positions nearer the crosses.

Ben Hur gave his arm to Balthasar for assistance, yet the Egyptian made the ascent with difficulty. From their new stand the Nazarene was imperfectly visible, appearing to them only as a dark, suspended figure. They could hear him, however—hear his sighing, which showed an endurance or exhaustion greater than those of his fellow sufferers, for they filled every lull in the noise with their groans and entreaties.

The second hour after the suspension passed like the first one. To the Nazarene these were hours of insult, provocation, and slow death. He spoke only once in that time. Some women came and knelt at the foot of his cross. He recognized among them his mother with the beloved disciple.

"Woman," he said, raising his voice, "behold your son!" And to the disciple, "Behold your mother!"

The third hour came, and still the people surged around the hill, held to it by some strange attraction, with which, in probability, the seeming night in midday had much to do. They were quieter than in the preceding hour, yet at times they could be heard off in the darkness shouting to each other, multitude calling to multitude.

It was noticeable also that now as they approached his cross, they approached in silence, received his look in silence, and then departed. This change extended even to the guard, who so shortly before had cast lots for the clothes of the crucified. They stood with their officer a little apart, more watchful of the one convict than of the throngs coming and going. If he merely breathed heavily, or tossed his head in a paroxysm of pain, they were instantly on the alert.

Most marvelous of all, however, was the altered behavior of the high priest and his following, the wise men who had assisted him in the trial in the night and kept in place by him with zealous approval. When the darkness began to fall, they began to lose their confidence. There were among them many learned in astronomy and familiar with the apparitions so terrible in those days to the masses. Much of the knowledge was given to them from their forefathers. Some of it had been brought away at the end of the

Captivity, and the necessities of the Temple service kept it in use. They drew together when the sun began to fade before their eyes and the mountains and hills to recede. They drew together in a group around their priest and debated what they saw.

"The moon is at its full," they said in truth, "and this cannot be an eclipse." Then, as no one could answer the question common to them all—as no one could account for the darkness, or for its occurrence at that particular time—in their secret hearts they associated it with the Nazarene and became alarmed when the long continuance of the phenomenon steadily increased. In their place behind the soldiers they noted every word and motion of the Nazarene and hung with fear upon his sighs and talked in whispers. The man might be the Messiah and then—but they would wait and see!

In the meantime Ben Hur was not once visited by the old spirit of restlessness. A perfect peace was within him. He prayed simply that the end might be hastened. He knew the condition of Simonides' mind—that he was hesitating on the verge of belief. He could see the massive face weighted down by solemn reflection. He noticed him casting inquiring glances at the sun, seeking the cause of the darkness. Nor did he fail to notice the care with which Esther clung to him, smothering her fears to accommodate his wishes.

"Be not afraid," he heard him say to her, "but stay and watch with me. You may live twice the span of my life and see nothing of human interest equal to this, and there may be more revelations. Let us stay to the close of the event."

When the third hour was about half gone, some men of the lowest class—wretches from the tombs about the city—came and stopped in front of the center cross.

"This is he, the new King of the Jews," said one of them.

The others cried, with laughter, "Hail, all hail, King of the Jews!"

Receiving no reply, they went closer. "If you are the King of the Jews, or the Son of God, come down," they said loudly.

At this, one of the thieves quit groaning and called to the Nazarene, "Yes, if you are Christ, save yourself and us."

The people laughed and applauded. Then, while they were

listening for a reply, the other felon was heard to say to the first one, "Do you not fear God? We receive the due rewards of our deeds, but this man has done nothing wrong."

The bystanders were astonished. In the midst of the hush that ensued, the second felon spoke again, but this time to the Nazarene. "Lord," he said, "remember me when you come into your kingdom."

Simonides was startled. "When you come into your kingdom!" It was the very point of doubt in his mind, the point he had so often debated with Balthasar.

"Did you hear?" said Ben Hur to him. "The kingdom cannot be of this world. Yon witness said the King is only going to his kingdom, and, in effect, I heard the same in my dream."

"Hush!" said Simonides, more imperiously than ever before in his speech to Ben Hur. "Hush, I pray you. If the Nazarene should answer—"

And as he spoke the Nazarene did answer, in a clear voice, full of confidence. "Truly I say to you, today you shall be with me in Paradise!"

Simonides waited to hear if that were all. Then he folded his hands and said, "No more, no more, Lord! The darkness is going. I see with other eyes—even as Balthasar, I see with the eyes of perfect faith."

The faithful servant had at last his fitting reward. His broken body might never be restored, nor was there a loss of the recollection of his sufferings, or a recall of the years embittered by them. But suddenly a new life was shown to him, with assurance that it was for him—a new life lying just beyond this one—and its name was Paradise. There he would find the Kingdom of which he had been dreaming, and the King. A perfect peace fell upon him.

Over where the crowd was, in front of the cross, however, there were surprise and consternation. The cunning priests there put the assumption underlying the question and the admission underlying the answer together. For his saying through the land that he was the Messiah, they had brought the Nazarene to the cross. And on the cross, more confidently than ever, he had not only reasserted himself but promised enjoyment of his Paradise to a criminal. They trembled at what they were doing. The high priest, with all his pride, was afraid. Where did the man get his confidence, except from Truth? And what should the Truth be but God? Very little now would put them all to flight.

The breathing of the Nazarene grew harder. His sighs became great gasps. Only three hours upon the cross, and he was dying!

The information was carried from man to man, until every one knew it, and then everything was hushed. The breeze faltered and died. A stifling vapor loaded the air. Heat was added to darkness, nor might anyone not knowing the fact have thought that off the hill, out under the overhanging pall, there were three million people waiting awestruck concerning what should happen next.

There went out through the gloom, over the heads of those who were on the hill within hearing of the dying man, a cry of despair, if not reproach. "My God! My God! Why have you forsaken me?"

The voice startled all who heard it. It touched one uncontrollably.

The soldiers had brought with them a vessel of wine and water and set it down a little way from Ben Hur. Now with a sponge dipped into the wine and put on the end of a stick, they could moisten the tongue of a sufferer at their pleasure.

Ben Hur thought of the draught he had at the well near Nazareth, and impulse seized him. Taking up the sponge, he dipped it into the vessel and started for the cross.

"Let him be!" the people in the way shouted, angrily. "Let him be!"

Without minding them, he ran on and put the sponge to the Nazarene's lips. Too late!

The face then plainly seen by Ben Hur, bruised and black with blood and dust as it was, lighted nevertheless with a sudden glow. The eyes opened wide and concentrated upon someone visible to them alone in the far heavens, and there were peace and relief, even triumph, in the shout the victim gave.

"It is finished! It is finished!"

So would a hero, dying in the doing of a great deed, celebrate his success with a last cheer. The light in the eyes went out. Slowly the crowned head sank upon the laboring breast. Ben Hur thought the struggle was over, but the fainting soul roused itself so that he and those around him caught the other, and last, words, spoken in a low voice, as if for someone listening close by.

"Father, into your hands I commend my spirit."

A tremor shook the tortured body. There was a scream of the fiercest anguish, and the mission and the earthly life were over at once. The heart, with all its love, was broken. For of love the man died!

Ben Hur went back to his friends, saying, simply, "It is over. He is dead."

In a space incredibly short the multitude was informed of the circumstance. No one repeated it aloud. A murmur spread from the knoll in every direction, a murmur that was little more than a whispering. "He is dead! He is dead!" and that was all.

The people had their wish. The Nazarene was dead, yet they stared at each other aghast. His blood was upon them! And while they stood staring at each other, the ground began to shake. Each man took hold of his neighbor to support himself.

In a twinkling the darkness disappeared, the sun came out, and everybody, as with the same glance, saw the crosses upon the hill all reeling drunkenlike in the earthquake. They saw all three of them, but the one in the center was prominent. It alone would be seen, and it seemed to extend itself upwards and lift its burden and swing to and fro higher and higher in the blue of the sky.

Every man among them who had jeered at the Nazarene, every one who had struck him, every one who had voted to crucify him, every one who had marched in the procession from the city, every one who had in his heart wished him dead, felt that he was in some way individually singled out from the many and that if he would live he must get away as quickly as possible from that menace in the sky. They started to run, and they ran with all their might. On horseback and on camels and in chariots as well as on foot they fled.

But then, as if the earthquake were angry at them for what they had done and had taken up the cause of the unoffending and friendless dead, it pursued them and tossed them around and flung them down and terrified them even more by the horrible noise of great rocks grinding and rending beneath them. They beat their breasts and shrieked with fear. His blood was upon them!

Native and foreigner, priest and layman, beggar, Sadducee, Pharisee, were overtaken in the race and tumbled around indiscriminately. If they called on the Lord, the outraged earth answered for Him in fury and dealt with them all the same. It did not even know that the high priest was better than his guilty brethren. Overtaking him, it tripped him up also and besmirched the fringing of his robe, filling the golden bells with sand and his mouth with dust. He and his people were alike in at least one thing—the blood of the Nazarene was upon them all!

When the sunlight broke upon the crucifixion, the mother of the Nazarene, the disciple, and the faithful women of Galilee, the centurion and his soldiers, and Ben Hur and his party were all who remained on the hill. These did not have time to observe the flight of the multitude. They were too loudly called upon to take care of themselves.

"Sit here," said Ben Hur to Esther, making a place for her at her father's feet. "Now cover your eyes and do not look up, but put your trust in God and the spirit of the just man so foully slain."

"No," said Simonides reverently, "let us from now on speak of him as the Christ."

"Let it be so," said Ben Hur.

Then a wave of the earthquake struck the hill. The shrieks of the thieves upon the reeling crosses were terrible to hear. Though giddy from the movements of the ground, Ben Hur had time to look at Balthasar and saw him prostrate and still. He ran to him and called—there was no reply. The good man was dead!

Then Ben Hur remembered to have heard a cry in answer to the scream of the Nazarene in his last moment, but he had not looked to see from whom it came. And from then on he believed the spirit of the Egyptian accompanied his Master over the boundary into the kingdom of Paradise. If faith were a worthy reward in the person of Gaspar and love in that of Melchior, surely he should have some special reward who through a long life had so excellently illustrated the three virtues combined—faith, love, and good works.

The servants of Balthasar had deserted their master, but when it was all over the two Galileans carried the old man in his litter back to the city. It was a sorrowful procession that entered the south gate of the palace of the Hurs at the setting of sun that memorable day. About the same hour the body of the Christ was taken down from the cross.

The remains of Balthasar were carried to the guest chamber. All the servants hastened, weeping, to see him, for he had the love of every living thing with which he had contact. But when they saw his face and the smile upon it, they dried their tears, saying, "It is well. He is happier this evening than when he went out in the morning."

Ben Hur would not trust a servant to inform Iras what had happened to her father. He went himself to see her and bring her to the body. He imagined her grief. She would now be alone in the world. It was a time to forgive and pity her. He remembered he had not asked why she was not of the party in the morning, or where she was. He remembered he had not thought of her, and, from shame, he was ready to make any amends, even more so as he was about to plunge her into such painful grief.

He shook the curtains of her door, but though he heard the ringing of the little bells echoing within, he heard no response. He called her name again—still no answer. He drew the curtain aside and went into the room. She was not there. He walked hastily up to the roof in search of her, but she was not there. He questioned the servants. None of them had seen her during the day.

After a long quest everywhere through the house, Ben Hur returned to the guest chamber and took the place by the dead that should have been hers. He thought how merciful the Christ had been to his aged servant. At the gate of the kingdom of Paradise the afflictions of this life, even its desertions, are left behind and forgotten by those who go in and rest.

When the gloom of the burial was nearly gone, on the ninth day after the healing, the law being fulfilled Ben Hur brought his mother and Tirzah home, and from that day in that house the most sacred names uttered by humankind were always coupled worshipfully together: "The Father and Christ the Son."

About five years after the crucifixion, Esther the wife of Ben Hur sat in her room in the beautiful villa by Misenum. It was noon, with a warm Italian sun making summer for the roses and vines outside. Everything in the apartment was Roman, except that Esther wore the garments of a Jewish woman. Tirzah and two children at play upon a lion's skin on the floor were her companions, and one had only to observe how carefully she watched them to know that the little ones were hers.

Time had treated her generously. She was more beautiful than ever, and in becoming mistress of the villa she had realized one of her cherished dreams.

In the midst of this simple, homelike scene, a servant appeared in the doorway and spoke to her. "A woman in the atrium wishes to speak with the mistress."

"Let her come. I will receive her here."

The stranger entered. At the sight of her the Jewess arose and was about to speak. Then she hesitated, changed color, and finally drew back, saying, "I have known you, good woman. You are—"

"I was Iras, the daughter of Balthasar."

Esther overcame her surprise and bade the servant to bring the Egyptian a seat.

"No," said Iras coldly. "I will leave shortly."

The two gazed at each other. Esther presented herself as a beautiful woman, a happy mother, a contented wife. On the other side, it was plain that fortune had not dealt so gently with her former rival. The tall figure remained, with some of its grace, but an evil life had tainted the whole person. The face was coarse, the large eyes were red and pursed beneath the lower lids, there was no color in her cheeks. The lips were cynical and hard, and general neglect was leading rapidly to premature old age. Her attire was ill chosen and bedraggled. The mud of the road clung to her sandals.

Iras broke the painful silence. "These are your children?"

"Yes. Will you not speak to them?"

"I would scare them," Iras replied. Then she drew closer to Esther and, seeing her shrink, said, "Be not afraid. Give your husband a message for me. Tell him his enemy is dead and that for the great misery he brought me I slew him."

"His enemy!"

"Messala. Further, tell your husband that for the harm I sought to do him, I have been punished until even he would pity me."

Tears arose in Esther's eyes, and she was about to speak.

"No," said Iras, "I do not want pity or tears. Tell him, finally, I have found that to be a Roman is to be a brute. Farewell."

She moved to go.

Esther followed her. "Stay and see my husband. He has no ill feeling against you. He sought for you everywhere. He will be your friend. I will be your friend. We are Christians."

The other was firm. "No, I am what I am of choice. It will be over shortly."

"But"—Esther hesitated—"have we nothing you would wish? Nothing to—"

The countenance of the Egyptian softened. Something like a smile played around her lips. She looked at the children upon the floor.

"There is something," she said.

Esther followed her eyes and with quick perception answered, "It is yours."

Iras went to them and knelt on the lion's skin and kissed them both. Rising slowly, she looked at them, then went to the door and out of it without a parting word. She walked rapidly and was gone before Esther could decide what to do.

Ben Hur, when he was told of the visit, knew certainly what he had long guessed—that on the day of the crucifixion Iras had deserted her father for Messala. Nevertheless, he set out immediately and hunted for her vainly. They never saw her anymore or heard of her. The blue bay, with all its laughing under the sun, still had its dark secrets. If it had a tongue, it might tell us of the Egyptian.

Simonides lived to be a very old man. In the tenth year of Nero's reign he gave up the business so long centered in the warehouse at Antioch. To the last he kept a clear head and a good heart and was successful.

One evening, he sat in his armchair on the terrace of the warehouse. Ben Hur and Esther and their three children were with him.

The last of the ships swung at their moorings in the current of the river. All the rest had been sold. In the long period between this and the day of the crucifixion only one sorrow had befallen them —that was when the mother of Ben Hur died. And then and now their grief would have been greater except for their Christian faith.

The ship spoken of had arrived only the day before, bringing news of the persecution of Christians begun by Nero in Rome, and the party on the terrace were talking of the news when Malluch, who was still in their service, approached and delivered a package to Ben Hur.

"Who brings this?" the latter asked after reading.

"An Arab."

"Where is he?"

"He left immediately."

"Listen," said Ben Hur to Simonides. He read then the following letter:

> I, Ilderim, the son of Ilderim the Generous and sheik of the tribe of Ilderim, to Judah, son of Hur.
>
> Know, O friend of my father's, how my father loved you. Read what is herein sent, and you will know. His will is my will; therefore what he gave is yours.
>
> I have retaken all the Parthians took from him in the great battle in which they slew him—this writing, with other things, and vengeance, and all the brood of that Mira who in his time was mother of so many stars.
>
> Peace be to you and all yours.
>
> This voice out of the desert is the voice of
>
> Ilderim, Sheik

Ben Hur next unrolled a scrap of papyrus yellow as the withered mulberry leaf. It required the most careful handling. Proceeding, he read:

> Ilderim, surnamed the Generous, sheik of the tribe of Ilderim, to the son who succeeds me.
>
> All I have, O son, shall be yours in the day of your succession, except that property by Antioch known as the Orchard of Palms; and it shall be to the son of Hur who brought us such glory in the circus—to him and his forever.
>
> Ilderim the Generous, Sheik

"What do you say?" asked Ben Hur of Simonides.

Esther took the papers, pleased, and read them to herself.

Simonides remained silent. His eyes were on the ship, but he was thinking. At length he spoke.

"Son of Hur," he said gravely, "the Lord has been good to you in these later years. You have much to be thankful for. Is it not time to decide finally the meaning of the gift of great fortune now in your hand, which is growing?"

"I decided that long ago. The fortune was meant for the service of the giver. Not a part, Simonides, but all of it. The question with me has been, How can I make it most useful in his cause? And of that tell me, I ask you."

Simonides answered, "The great sums you have given to the church here in Antioch, I am witness to. Now, instantly almost with this gift of the generous sheik's, comes the news of the persecution of the brethren in Rome. It is the opening of a new field. The light must not go out in the capital."

"Tell me how I can keep it alive."

"I will tell you. The Romans, even this Nero, hold two things sacred—I know of no others they hold in this way—they are the ashes of the dead and all the places of burial. If you cannot build them for the worship of the Lord above ground, then build them below the ground. And to keep them from being profaned, carry to them the bodies of all who die in the faith."

Ben Hur arose excitedly. "It is a great idea," he said. "I will not wait to begin it. Time forbids waiting. The ship that brought the news of the suffering of our brethren shall take me to Rome. I will sail tomorrow."

He turned to Malluch. "Get the ship ready, Malluch, and be ready to go with me."

"It is well," said Simonides.

"And you, Esther, what do you say?" asked Ben Hur.

Esther came to his side and put her hand on his arm and answered, "You will best serve the Christ in this manner. O my husband, let me not hinder you but go with you and help."

If anyone visiting Rome will make the short journey to the Catacomb of San Calixto, which is more ancient than that of San Sebastiano, he will see what became of the fortune of Ben Hur and give him thanks. Out of that vast tomb Christianity issued to supersede the caesars.

Moody Press, a ministry of the Moody Bible Institute,
is designed for education, evangelization, and edification.
If we may assist you in knowing more about Christ
and the Christian life, please write us without obligation:
Moody Press, c/o MLM, Chicago, Illinois 60610.